"If somebody succeeds in identifying the Unknown's body," Walt said slowly, "and if a name is pinned to that corpse, they can't bury him. They'll have to—"

"Oh, come on Walt, that's impossible."

"They'll have to call off the ceremony," he went on. "It might take months, even years, before they get another unidentified body. So they'll have to go on searching."

"But . . ." she started.

"I have the Unknown's file," Walt said. "I can try."

THE UNKNOWN SOLDIER

"Complex, well-written . . . an absorbing suspense thriller."
The Kirkus Reviews

THE
UNKNOWN
SOLDIER

Michael Hastings

FAWCETT GOLD MEDAL • NEW YORK

About him we may well wonder, as others have, as a child, did he play on some street in a great American city? Did he work beside his father on a farm in America's heartland? Did he marry? Did he have children? Did he look expectantly to return to a bride? Thank you, dear son, and may God cradle you in his loving arms.

—*President Reagan at the Tomb of the Unknown Vietnam Soldier, Arlington National Cemetery, May 28, 1984*

❋ PROLOGUE ❋

In the spring of 1984 the White House and the Department of Defense made public their decision to entomb the Unknown Soldier of the Vietnam War. His body was to be interred at the Arlington National Cemetery beside the tombs of the unknown soldiers of the two world wars and the Korean War. The state funeral was scheduled for May 28, 1984.

The American soldier, to be entombed that day in a solemn ceremony, had been designated "the Unknown Soldier" after the Central Identification Laboratory in Honolulu had failed to identify his body. In the entire history of the Vietnam War he had been the only fatality out of 58,000 American dead to remain unknown. And unknown he was to stay forever, according to a decree signed by the President.

Following that decision the Secretary of Defense had issued the order to destroy all identification records related to the Unknown. All blood and tissue analyses, dental records, fingerprint slides, and anatomical charts were to be shredded and incinerated at once. These measures were intended to prevent disclosure of any clues about the identity of the man chosen to become a symbol of all who had died in Vietnam.

The order to destroy all existing records had been signed exactly a month before the Arlington ceremony. A senior Pentagon official, Walt Meredith, was ordered to communicate the decision to the director of the Central Identification Laboratory in Honolulu.

PART 1
⭐
THE BODY

● 1 ●

Cold, still darkness engulfed him as the sliding doors soundlessly met behind his back. Large tall doors they were, sheets of tinted glass; and their rubber edges smoothly fused together, sealing off the scorching sun, the blue skies, the vivid colors of Honolulu. In the obscure hall, with its dull green walls and black floor tiles, the vacation paradise of Waikiki seemed light-years away.

The hall was deserted except for a huge black Marine. He was seated behind a desk, barring access to the double doors at his back. His large hands lay on the desk, on both sides of a thick manila file. On his left stood an old-fashioned telephone made of Bakelite.

As Walt Meredith approached the Marine looked up at him. His eyes were very bright, dominating an angular, impassive face. Meredith thought of Cerberus guarding the gate to the underworld. Over the doors an ancient sign bore the inscription U.S. ARMY—CENTRAL IDENTIFICATION LABORATORY—ENTRANCE RESTRICTED. He flashed his Pentagon pass. The Marine nodded in recognition. "That's all right, Mr. Meredith." His voice was hoarse, but he kept it low, almost a whisper.

Meredith walked through the double doors and took the sloping corridor to the underground level. There were neither windows nor doors along the narrow passageway, only a long succession of neon tubes hanging from the low ceiling. As he approached the lower landing he smelled the pungent odor of formaldehyde, and beneath it the faint, yet sickeningly sweet, foulness of death. The echo of his steps, reverberating against the bare walls, had a metallic edge. The sound was familiar, but today it carried, for him, a ring of finality. It was the last time he walked down this corridor, the last time he descended to the gruesome chambers on the underground level.

The lower landing was empty and spotlessly clean. The corridor leading to the morgue, at the far end, was dark and hostile, like the entrance to a cave. On the right, strong white light filtered under the swinging doors of the main forensic laboratory.

The first time he had descended down here half the space of the landing had been occupied by regulation aluminum coffins in which the Army had been flying the charred, mutilated bodies home from Saigon. He had been seized by a spasm of nausea, but much worse, by helpless, desperate rage. All those boys, he had thought, all those dreams and hopes ending in an aluminum box. The coffins were empty, he was to learn later, but that didn't make any difference, not really. The bodies lay inside the lab, dismembered and tortured even in their death by the awful tools of the forensic specialists.

No corpse could leave its underground realm before it had had a name tag strapped to its toe, or what was left of it. For without the plastic-coated name tag, eternal rest was eternally refused. Without a name, no corpse could be sent on its last voyage to a still undug grave somewhere on the mainland. Without a name, it deserved no flowers, no tears, and no remembrance.

Some of the dead had spent months in the forensic lab morgue waiting for their names and pictures—young and smart and smiling in their freshly ironed uniforms—to be formally restituted to their faceless bodies. Today the long wait was over. All the bodies had finally recovered their identities. All but four, and last week's breakthrough had solved their problem as well. The crisp letter from the Secretary of Defense was in Meredith's pocket. He had read it over and over again in the car on the way from the hotel. Even the last unidentified body would soon set on its final journey.

He suddenly thought of all those live bodies, half naked, oiled, and tanned, luxuriously stretched under the Hawaiian sun beside limpid pools and on powdery beaches barely a couple of miles away. What an ironic whim of fate, he thought, that this enchanted island, for so many Americans the gate of paradise, was for so many others the gate of death. Since the Asian wars had started, and swept the Philippines and the Marshalls and the Solomons, Japan and Korea and Indochina, the dead of America had been returning home by way of Hawaii.

Conveniently tucked behind Oahu's black mountains, safe from the curious looks and the nosy cameras of vacationers, the huge Wheeler Air Base had been for years discreetly servicing the heavy cargo planes thundering down from the western sky with their grisly loads. Here, in this lush, sunny decor painted with exotic colors, swaying to soft music, in this land of black lagoons and flaming craters, America welcomed her dead. And here every unknown dead would be impounded till his decaying flesh yielded his last secret—a name—to a thickset, dark-skinned Hawaiian, Dr. John Natua.

The swinging doors smoothly swung on their hinges and he entered the large, brightly illuminated laboratory. In here the sickening smell was stronger, almost palpable. He walked quickly between the gleaming steel-topped tables, each equipped with its tray of hideous instruments. Macmanus, a tall, hollow-chested man with a mop of silvery hair, dressed in a green surgeon's outfit, was bent over one of the tables dissecting a lump of pale-yellow matter. He absently nodded at Meredith and returned to his occupation, pursing his narrow lips in concentration. His half-moon glasses, perched on the tip of his nose, made him look like a benign schoolteacher. A strange rumor had wafted about the lab for years claiming that Macmanus was writing poetry in secret and publishing it under an assumed name in a West Coast review.

In the far corner a slim blond girl in a white smock was softly whispering into the phone. She merrily waved at Meredith with her free hand. Her gesture seemed rather profane on the background of the glass jars lined behind her, their ghastly contents shockingly displayed.

The opposite wall had always made him think of a game room—a battery of computers, laser scanners, television monitors incongruously projecting a perfect range of vivid colors. Gene Bielski, the enormous, flabby Pole from Milwaukee, was at his usual place behind the electronic microscope, eyes glued to the sights, plump hands lovingly caressing the magnifying knobs. Gene's massive jaws were in a state of perpetual motion, laboriously munching their daily ration of chewing gum. He didn't even look up when Meredith passed by, his shoes sharply squeaking on the crisp linoleum.

Dr. John Natua was lurking, as always, in his inner alcove. Here the lights were several shades softer, and the oblong room was immersed in relative darkness. Meredith shivered slightly. Perhaps it was the whiff of cold air that hit him as he walked in. Or the sight of the four long shapes lying on their steel slabs under large sheets of dull black plastic. Those were the last four bodies left out of the hundreds that had passed through the central laboratory, the last four unidentified soldiers waiting for their names under their plastic shrouds.

Actually the fourth slab was only partly covered, and Natua was bent over it, his large face protected by a surgical mask. A spotlight fastened to his forehead by a metallic ring, like an Inca's bejeweled crown, bathed a black oval object with a dazzling beam. Engrossed in his work, he didn't notice Meredith before his shadow invaded the bright circle of light in front of him. He straightened up, and the white ray of his spotlight wildly swayed about, touching Meredith's face for a brief moment.

"Walt!" Natua exclaimed. His deep voice was slightly muffled by the mask. He was a squat, thick Hawaiian in his late forties, and the long rubber apron he was wearing over his green outfit made him look even more obese. He turned off his spotlight and made a few steps forward, removing his mask and his thin latex gloves. "You son of a gun, popping out of my corpses like Dracula!" He laughed softly, apparently

9

pleased with his humor. "When did you arrive? I didn't expect you before next week."

"Last night," Meredith said. He took a long stride toward Natua and spontaneously hugged him. "Congratulations, John, I thought you'd never make it," he said warmly.

Natua chuckled. His white, perfect teeth flashed in the dark face. He looked quite sloppy, Meredith thought, a pudgy little man with chubby hands, unkempt, tousled hair, wearing clothes that seemed a couple of sizes too large for him. And still this affable Hawaiian, the director of the Central Identification Laboratory, was the best forensic specialist in the United States and probably one of the best in the world.

"Why didn't you let me know you were coming?" Natua asked, mildly reproachful.

Meredith didn't answer. He followed Natua to his small glass cubicle and squeezed into a chair facing the director's desk. "Coffee?" Natua inquired cheerfully. He was a coffee addict and had a half-full pot brewing on a hot plate on his desk.

"No, thanks," Meredith managed. By the glass partition behind Natua's back he could see the four slabs. The uncovered body was the nearest. The round object Natua had been working on was the upper half of a scorched skull.

"How was your flight? You're at the Hilton? How long are you staying?" Natua was firing his trite questions like an overzealous tourist guide. He was a brilliant specialist and a good friend, Meredith thought, but an incurable chatterer.

He took a deep breath. "Come on, John," he said tensely, "tell me how you did it."

Natua had removed his rubber apron and was pouring coffee into a huge brown mug. "Sheer luck," he said. "You know we already had a tentative identification for one of the bodies." He vaguely gestured toward the farthest slab. "An ARVN soldier who had been wounded at the same battle—"

"At Dakto, I know," Meredith said impatiently.

Natua cast him a long look. "Yes. The Vietnamese maintained that the dead man was an American named Bad-lee."

Meredith nodded. "Bradlee. Sergeant Vernon Bradlee." They had gone over those details so many times in the past.

"That's right. We ran the routine checks and it seemed to figure. The site of death, the age, the height, the blood type—everything matched. The dead man was probably Bradlee. But we had no prints and no dental records. His skull had been shattered by a mortar shell."

Meredith didn't comment. The years they had spent probing unidentified corpses had metamorphosed the most appalling sights into matter-of-fact definitions.

"Now, Bradlee was from Wichita, Kansas," Natua went on, taking a sip from his mug, "an orphan, as you might remember, with no living relatives."

"Wasn't there a girl friend?" He knew Bradlee's file almost by heart.

Natua shrugged. "It was rather a weekend fling. The only valuable information she had was that Vernon had spent a few years in Boulder, Colorado. He had worked in a garage before he enlisted."

Meredith nodded. "We knew all that before, didn't we?" Natua was quickly going through a stack of X-ray radiographs. "We didn't know this, though," he said, and raised one of the slides against the overhead light. The X ray represented the upper part of a femur bone.

"What?" Meredith squinted, tilting his head.

"I had the body X-rayed again, bone after bone," Natua explained, "and look what I found." With his left forefinger he pointed at a barely noticeable white line running across the bone, quite close to the femur shaft. "Hip fracture," he said. "The dead man had broken his hip in his youth." He placed the radiograph back on the desk and took another sip of coffee. "In his late teens, to be exact."

"How can you tell?"

Natua smiled shyly, as if apologizing for knowing more than his curious friend. "If it had happened earlier, there would have been no scar," he said gently. "At a very young age there is a remodeling of bone tissue that practically wipes out the fracture."

"I see." Meredith looked at Natua with new interest. "So you started pestering all the Boulder hospitals to find if Bradlee had—"

"There were not so many of them," Natua interrupted. "We found his record at the Veterans Memorial Hospital. It was Vernon Bradlee, all right. He had been treated for a femur fracture." Suddenly, like a child performing a trick of magic, he pulled another radiograph from a stack on his left, and waved it in front of Meredith. "This arrived last week," he announced triumphantly. "From Boulder."

Meredith picked up both radiographs. They were almost identical. The only difference was that in the Boulder radiograph the fracture line was larger and whiter. He nodded, running his hands along his chin. "Yes, that wraps it up," he agreed, leaning back. "Sergeant Vernon Bradlee."

"There's no next of kin," Natua reminded him, suddenly serious.

"I'll speak to the mayor of Wichita, and we'll arrange a city funeral." He put the radiographs on the desk. "Bradlee was last week," he reminded Natua. "You still had three bodies left."

Natua pushed back his chair. "Come," he said briskly, picking up his mug. "Let me show you something."

Meredith followed him back to the outer lab. Macmanus was still busy with his pale-colored lump, softly muttering to himself. The blond girl, who he knew as Pauline, was sitting on a desk, her long legs crossed, and leafing through a bulky yellow file. The collar of her unbuttoned smock was daintily raised and its sleeves rolled up to her elbows. She was wearing it like a Dior negligee, Meredith thought. Pauline looked at them and smiled uncertainly.

"As you might remember," Natua was saying, "two of the bodies were found together."

"Of course I remember," Meredith said, irritated. "I was in this business from the start. They found them north of Khe Sanh, in the demilitarized zone."

"And nobody knew who the hell those two guys were." Natua gently touched Gene Bielski's shoulder. "Gene, will you please get us the fabric samples? I want to show Walt."

"Fabric samples?" Meredith frowned, puzzled.

Natua didn't answer, watching Gene Bielski deftly place a glass plate under one of the microscopes. The skin of his hands, even his fingers, was covered with a thick reddish fuzz.

"Now take a look," Natua said. Bielski moved back, still munching his chewing gum, but there was a glint of triumph in his placid blue eyes. "It was Gene who found it," Natua added unnecessarily.

Meredith bent over the microscope. The two small pieces of fabric looked huge under the magnifying lenses. The woven threads reminded him of hand-tressed ropes. The texture of the piece of fabric on the left, though, was much more delicate, and the threads were thinner. He looked at Natua over his shoulder.

"We found some rags on one of the bodies," Natua explained. "Most of them were pieces of Army fatigues. But one fragment of cloth seemed to belong to the man's underwear." He beckoned with his mug toward Bielski. "When all the other tests failed Gene decided to compare that fragment with a sample of regulation Army underwear." He looked invitingly at Bielski and took another gulp of coffee.

The giant pointed a chunky finger at the glass plate under the microscope. "Both samples are made of cotton fibers," he said. He had a surprisingly thin, high-pitched voice. "The one on the right is taken from standard Army underwear. The one on the left was found on the body. It's a different fabric altogether. We did some checking and found out, finally, that this kind of fiber is rarely used in the U. S. It's European-made. French, to be exact."

"What?" Meredith straightened abruptly, and Bielski smiled. "Exactly," he quipped. "Who's the creep who'd go to battle wearing French-made briefs?" He paused a second for effect. "Nobody, except a Frenchman, of course."

"A Frenchman," Meredith repeated after him, his eyes shifting from Bielski to Natua and back.

Natua nodded. "No wonder we couldn't identify the

guy. We were trying to match our findings about him with our records of the missing Americans. But there were also some non-Americans who disappeared in Vietnam. A couple of Australian commandos, some English observers, two French press photographers..."

"And he was one of the French photographers," Meredith said.

Bielski had picked up a sheaf of papers and photographs held together with a paper clip. "Patrick Mercier," he solemnly revealed. The pink lump of chewing gum flashed between his moist lips as he struggled with the French pronunciation. "*Agence photographique Omega*, 16, Avenue de l'Opéra, Paris." He handed Meredith a photograph of a narrow-shouldered, balding man laden with cameras. He was wearing a loose U. S. Army uniform and a large yellow press tag.

"I never saw such a tag before," Meredith remarked.

"They used them for a while at the beginning of the war," Natua explained. "Mercier disappeared in '67." He regretfully put his empty mug on a nearby table and took the batch of papers from Bielski. "The French sent us his record. As a matter of fact we already had a copy of his file, but it was buried somewhere in Washington." He looked up at Meredith. "Everything matches. That's Mercier." He grinned. "American uniform, French briefs."

"And once you identified him," Meredith said pensively, suppressing a sudden need for a cigarette, "it was easy to pin a name on the other one." He settled in the swivel chair vacated by Bielski and veered around to face him.

"Not easy, but easier," Natua corrected.

"First, you found out in what circumstances Mercier disappeared."

Natua nodded. "That was simple. According to his file, he was last seen leaving Lang Vei on his way to Khe Sanh. He was in a jeep, together with an Army driver and a public relations officer from division headquarters."

"I bet they were missing as well," Meredith suggested, and Natua nodded again.

It suddenly seemed so obvious. "You asked for the records of the two missing soldiers and compared them with the second body."

"Gene used Pacman," Natua said. Pacman, Meredith knew, was their irreverent nickname for Natua's latest invention. It was based on a technique Natua had conceived, which was called "cranio-facial superimposition." It was a mirrors-and-light device by which a skilled technician could match photographs and skulls. Natua had first used his contraption the year before when he had been asked to identify eighteen crates of bones from the crash of a B-24 in 1943. He had identified all of the twenty-one bodies.

Lately he had perfected his invention by feeding it into a computer and superimposing the projection over a video-tape image. The result was Pacman, of which Natua was very proud.

"Do you want to see for yourself?" Natua asked, and without waiting for the answer settled in front of a computer keyboard commanding an eighteen-inch monitor. He selected a couple of magnetic disks and carefully slipped them into the computer drives. Gene fed a large cassette into a video recorder beside him, then Natua punched a few keys.

A dull yellow skull, filmed in profile, appeared on

the screen. "That's the skull of the other body we found beside Mercier," Natua explained without turning back.

Meredith bent over and watched the screen over Natua's shoulder. High heels clicked behind his back, then stopped. Pauline stood by him, intently watching the screen. Her perfume was musky, exotic. Even at this moment he couldn't disregard her sensuality. He stole a look at her and caught a glimpse of tanned skin, partly veiled by soft blond hair, and full dark-red lips.

"Watch it now," Bielski quipped, and moved aside as a blurred blue line appeared at the bottom of the screen and slowly started rolling upward. As it reached the skull's chin something extraordinary happened— the part of the chin emerging beneath the blue line went through a sudden metamorphosis. It wasn't a piece of yellow bone anymore. It was covered with flesh and skin now, a normal lower part of a human face.

Beside Meredith, Pauline gasped in a sharp intake of breath and lowered her eyes. She must have seen that happen scores of times before, he thought, and still couldn't face it. Even Macmanus stopped his ghoulish travail and raised his eyes from his slicing board. They watched the blue line creep upward on the screen, wiping the hideous smile off the naked skull, encasing its teeth in a tight-lipped mouth, enveloping the short nose bone in tissue and dermis, filling the hollow black sockets with slightly drooping eyes, adding ears and eyebrows, topping the head with a shock of dark hair. And there it was all of a sudden, the profile of a young man filling the screen, extraordinarily alive, slightly wavering as the video image failed to stabilize completely.

Pauline stirred. "Like in the old horror movies," she said, trying to sound droll and miserably failing. "*The Curse of Frankenstein.*"

Back from the dead, Meredith thought. It was much more than a horror movie. It was as if some extraordinary power had reached beyond death and brought back a human likeness, a forbidden spark of life from where there was none. He was impressed, and still felt a strange uneasiness, as if he had witnessed the desecration of a holy sepulcher.

"Let's see the full face now," Natua said in a low voice, and Meredith sensed that he, too, was troubled by his own craft. On the screen the head turned halfway to face them. It didn't look alive after all, Meredith realized with relief, watching the dull, expressionless eyes.

Natua was diligently punching his keys. "Let's try a thinner face," he said. The blurred line climbed up the screen again, hollowing the cheeks and bestowing a gaunt look on the oblong visage. "Some facial hair," Natua went on. A thin, elegant mustache materialized on the upper lip. "Regulation Army haircut." The wavy hair was replaced by a crew cut. Natua turned back. "Gene, will you please show Walt the photographs?"

Bielski must have been waiting for that moment, delighting in advance in the forthcoming effect. He picked two glossy photographs from a file on his desk and displayed them before Meredith's eyes. They were both grainy enlargements of two young faces. The one on the left was a broad, square-jawed face with a jutting chin, a full mouth, wide-spaced eyes. It had nothing in common with the features wavering on the screen. The second photograph represented a meager face with salient cheekbones, close-cropped hair, thin lips, receding chin, a dandyish mustache. There could be no doubt. The only difference was a couple of moles on the face in the photograph.

"It's the driver," Natua said. "Private First Class Raphael B. Gianelli of Sheboygan, Wisconsin."

Meredith was slowly emerging from his stupor. "That's amazing, John," he admitted. "Simply amazing."

Bielski took back the photographs and placed them in his file. "It was not as easy as it may look," he chewed. "It took us three months to rebuild the face." He turned to Natua. "John, did you know the Japanese have their own Pacman? They've got a formula calculating the distances between the ear capsule and the extremities of the skull. That way they can make a computerized projection of a face in seconds."

"Yes, I know." Natua was nodding, unimpressed, then he resumed his conversation with Meredith. "That's how we got three out of four." He pointed matter-of-factly. "I sent you the telex the morning we achieved Gianelli's picture."

Meredith nodded. "And now you're working on the last one."

Natua gestured toward the inner room. "The one they found in Na-san, you know. On him we have already a forty percent identification. We can't use dental records, as his mouth has been blown away. But his thigh joints gave us his height and age, and we already have his blood type. You know, the bone-crushing technique. The blood belongs to a quite rare group. I guess that in a couple of months—"

"I'm afraid not, John," Meredith said very gently. "It's all over."

19

A sudden silence fell over the lab. Pauline looked up at them, nervously brushing a few strands of hair off her face. Even Bielski stopped chewing.

"What do you mean, over?" Natua asked, frowning.

Meredith hesitated. "I'm sorry," he said, casting a look at Natua's assistants. "But I'd rather talk to you in private."

Natua threw an oblique look at him, shrugged, and led the way back to his glass cage. Meredith waited for him to refill his mug, then reached into his inside pocket and took the Defense Secretary's letter. He handed it to Natua. "That's why I came, John," he said.

Natua unfolded the letter. "From the Secretary of Defense?" he said in wonder, without raising his eyes. He started to read aloud, omitting the redundant parts. "'. . . to inform you that the unidentified body has been designated as the Unknown Soldier of the Vietnam . . .' What?" He raised his eyes and stared at Meredith, who returned his stare without speaking. He let out a deep breath, then resumed reading. "'. . . and will be entombed in the Arlington National Cemetery beside the tombs of the . . .' yes . . . yes. . . . 'This decision was confirmed by President Reagan in a decree signed this morning. . . . All further efforts to identify the body should therefore cease immediately and all identification records related to it should be destroyed. I'd like to extend to you, on behalf of the President and myself, our warmest thanks for the devoted efforts you and your staff . . .' et cetera, et cetera."

Natua leaned back and carefully placed his mug on the desk. His face was devoid of expression. "The Unknown," he said slowly. "They selected him as the Unknown." He looked closely at Meredith and a deep furrow appeared between his eyebrows. "And you don't like that, Walt," he said, establishing a fact. He placed the Secretary's letter in front of him, smoothing it with both hands.

"No, I don't," Meredith said. An awkward silence settled between them.

"Any particular reason?"

Meredith ignored the question. "And you?" he asked.

Natua shook his head. "I don't know," he admitted. "I don't know. It's too . . . too sudden. I didn't expect that." He picked up a few paper clips from the desk and started linking them into a chain, avoiding Meredith's eyes. "That's the end of the war for me, I guess, the real end. For years this work was all that mattered." Natua paused, idly pulling the frail silver chain. "It was a real challenge, Walt." He shrugged. "But it was bound to end, sooner or later. For the last eighteen months they haven't found a single body in Vietnam." He looked up. "That's also the end of our cooperation, I gather. How long have we been working together? Eight years?"

"Nine," Meredith said.

"I'll miss you," Natua said simply, lowering his eyes again. "We were a good team. I guess you'll be transferred to some other job now."

"I guess so," Meredith agreed, ill at ease. "John, you're more than a friend to me. I can't tell you how much . . ." He stopped abruptly and brought down his hands on the desk. "All right," he said with forced alacrity. "Back to business. I came to carry out the Secretary's orders. First of all, you have to stop all work on the body of the Unknown as of now. It should be placed in a sealed compartment in the morgue till instructions are sent for its transport to Washington."

Natua was nodding calmly, sipping his coffee. He seemed amused by Meredith's formal discourse. "I have been charged with the destruction of all records related to the Unknown, so I must ask you for his file and any other relevant papers."

Natua nodded. "Of course," he said. "You can have the file." He started sifting the stack of envelopes and dossiers piled on his desk. "I have everything here except for one report that hasn't arrived yet. Ballistics. We sent the slugs recovered from the body to the FBI ballistics laboratory in Washington. I called them yesterday. The report is ready but they haven't mailed it yet."

"Why don't you ask them to deliver the report to my office? I'll have it shredded with the other records."

"Fine," Natua said, scribbling a note on a large yellow pad. "We'll call them right away." His voice became warmer. "Walt, will you have dinner with Nancy and me tonight? This is the end of a chapter in our lives. It deserves a . . ."

". . . a celebration?" Meredith asked coldly.

"No, that's not the word," Natua said, embarrassed.

Meredith got up. "I'm sorry, John, I can't make it. I'm leaving this afternoon. I must be in Washington tomorrow morning."

Natua was watching him thoughtfully. "I've never seen you so high-strung, Walt. You must be very upset."

"Get those records for me, will you?" Meredith asked. He hesitated, then impulsively reached across the desk and squeezed Natua's arm. "I'm sorry, John, I

22

didn't mean to be rude. It's just this goddamn decision. . . . " He pushed back his chair without completing his phrase.

On his way out he walked into the inner lab and pulled the black plastic sheet over the charred bones of the Unknown. Natua stood behind him, very still, subdued.

The thin blue file of the Unknown Soldier safely locked in his attaché case, he stretched his legs and tried in vain to get some sleep. The eastbound Boeing 767 was crammed with noisy, suntanned vacationers in Hawaiian shirts and sweet-smelling, withering leis. He had grown to like those gregarious, easygoing people with whom he had shared so many flights in the last nine years. They were always relaxed, mellowed by their fun-and-sun packages in vacationland, while he was the eternal outsider, carrying in his memory the macabre sights from Natua's death chambers.

Still, he had always regarded his work with Natua as a formidable challenge. Never before, either in Korea or in Indochina or Lebanon, and certainly not in his shadow years with the CIA, had he devoted himself with such intensity, such deep intensity, such deep conviction, to a goal or a cause. Yet, his fervor had all but shattered his relationship with Barbara. In their endless arguments she stubbornly maintained that his dedication to the missing had turned into an obsession, a morbid addiction. It was Benjamin's disappearance, she insisted, that had made him abandon everything and plunge into this fanatical search for corpses. How could she be so cocksure, for Christ's sake? She didn't even know him when it had happened.

It was in January 1972, a very cold, very still winter

night. He had a few guests in the Chevy Chase cottage, the woman he was dating at the time and another couple, and they were drinking by the fireside and discussing a trip to Barbados, or was it St. Thomas? The Green Berets captain knocked on his door shortly before midnight. He had a sharp, ferretlike face and apparently had cut himself shaving; he remembered well the hairline nick on his chin. When he saw his guests the officer asked him to step outside. The snow was deep and the air dry. With every breath he took he felt his chest freezing solid. The captain asked if he was the father of Sergeant Benjamin Meredith. When he said yes the captain told him in a formal voice that his son had been reported missing in Vietnam.

He listened to him in silence, his chest aching, watching the captain's words turn into puffs of white mist that instantly dissolved in the night air. He asked when it had happened and where and if they had informed Benjamin's mother. Virginia was living in San Francisco. Years ago, after their divorce, she had moved to California. The captain said no, they thought perhaps Mr. Meredith would prefer to tell her himself, and he agreed that would be better, he would fly to the West Coast the next morning.

No, the captain didn't know Benjamin personally, but he had seen his record, he was a fine boy it seemed, and if he was alive he would certainly find his way back to our lines. He was a Green Beret, after all, the captain said, a tough one. And he knew, he added, that Mr. Meredith himself had been a Marine officer, that was a fine family tradition. And he nodded without speaking, for he had nothing to say.

Then the captain shook his hand and left, his boots crisping on the fresh snow, and Meredith noticed he was rather short and skinny. There was a car waiting for him at the curb, and somebody sitting in the back. Meredith wondered if it was a doctor, just in case. Inside the house he told his friends Benjamin was missing. They tried to cheer him up and he got drunk and threw them out.

But only three years later Meredith decided to leave the Company and apply for the Pentagon job. By that time he had already resigned himself to the thought that Benjamin was dead. Only once in a while, in those short, fitful dreams he dreaded, would he see Benjamin coming home, a frail, serious little boy with big almond-shaped eyes and long black eyelashes. He never dreamed of him grown up and in a uniform. He would awake in cold sweat, and for a second there would be a glimmer of hope, till the dream faded away and the hope died with it.

His application for the Pentagon position had raised a few eyebrows in Langley Woods. That would be a demotion for him, his colleagues at the CIA said. He had excellent chances of becoming deputy director of Intelligence, considering his impressive experience with defectors. But he had shrugged them off and finally gotten what he wanted.

He was appointed Director of the Bureau of MIA Affairs. His job consisted mainly of maintaining liaisons with the families of soldiers missing in action in Vietnam. In no time his Washington office became the unofficial headquarters of the League of MIA Families. He investigated every rumor about the secret detention camps in North Vietnam where American prisoners were allegedly held. He led delegations of embittered relatives to Capitol Hill, inundating senators with petitions for further inquiries.

He handled the families, gathering from them all available data about their sons and husbands. He dispatched or personally took the files to John Natua, whose team was painstakingly building anatomical profiles of the missing soldiers and comparing them to the bodies flown from Vietnam. In the last nine years that grisly task had resulted in the identification of 347 soldiers. In every single identification Meredith saw a personal triumph, as if Benjamin himself had been identified.

Barbara had moved in with him shortly before he got his Pentagon job. At the beginning she approved of what he was doing, but after a couple of years she had started drifting away, and today she didn't spare him her criticism. He was living in the past, she used to throw at him. He was haunted by a guilt complex for Benjamin's death. She couldn't understand, of course, that it was mainly the plight of the families, not Benjamin, or not only Benjamin, that inspired him. A fine woman, Barbara, but she had read too much pseudo-psychological nonsense.

He drained his vodka and ordered another one from the middle-aged hostess, who minced about in a colorful Hawaiian dress. He skipped dinner and nursed his fresh drink, leaning against the porthole window while darkness settled over the ocean. A couple of times he almost drifted into sleep, but this morning's experience kept jolting him back to consciousness. He couldn't get off his mind that wavering face staring at him from Natua's monitor. He visualized the mother or the wife of Gianelli watching Natua's infernal contraption and seeing the hideous skull turn into the image of their beloved. Such horror could haunt them all their lives, them or anybody else.

What if it were not Gianelli's but Benjamin's face emerging from a scorched death's-head before his eyes on a full-color television screen? He gulped down the rest of his glass, crushing the ice cubes with his teeth, and the chill spread in his mouth and his entire body. What would they do next? he wondered. Once Natua had found the way to reproduce a dead face, nothing could prevent some smart kid making it live on the screen, move, smile, and talk. Like raising spirits from the dead.

His plane landed in Washington at dawn, in a drizzling rain. A car from the Pentagon pool was waiting for him. The driver was a heavy, sour-faced man in a plastic raincoat. He didn't bother to help him with his luggage. Once inside the car, Meredith hesitated. He didn't want to go home. He didn't want to see Barbara, not yet. "To the office, please," he told the driver, and saw his puzzled frown in the mirror.

The vast corridors of the Pentagon were deserted at this hour. The cleaning women were chattering inside the office next to his, and their easy, fresh laughter sounded oddly reassuring. He sank into his chair and turned on his desk lamp. His secretary had left him a small, tidy pile of letters.

The one on top was from the Assistant Secretary of Defense. It started with the usual formulas of congratulation for a job well done, then went on to praise the symbolic meaning of the designation of the Unknown Soldier. He perused quickly the pompous, superfluous paragraphs till he reached the last part of the letter, which contained its real purpose. After the entombment of the Unknown, the Assistant Secretary wrote, the liaison with the League of MIA Families wouldn't require a full-time job anymore. Therefore, he urged Meredith to apply for a new job in the department. It was time for him to move up the ladder, while the care for the missing could henceforth be entrusted into the hands of a junior employee.

He pushed the letter aside. It confirmed his worst fears. Nobody seemed to care about the MIA's anymore. Nobody minded that there still were 2,489 Americans somewhere in Vietnam, dead or alive or both. The forthcoming burial of the Unknown was about to seal the Vietnamese chapter in the nation's history.

The cleaning women, their work in the nearby office completed, carried their buckets and their laughter elsewhere, and a strange, gloomy silence descended upon his room. Only the rain kept monotonously drumming on the window panes. He idly sorted the little pile of letters, spreading them in disorder over the desk. The bottom letter attracted his attention. It was a large manila envelope sent by the ballistics laboratory of the FBI. It had been delivered by a messenger.

He tore the flap open. The envelope contained about a dozen enlarged photographs of bullets and hand-grenade fragments. A slip was attached to each photograph describing in professional lingo the compostion, caliber, and characteristics of the slug. The typewritten report was accompanied by a short letter addressed to him. It specified that the report was dispatched to his office on the demand of Dr. John Natua.

He lit a cigarette, but it had an unpleasant, papery taste and he dropped it in the ashtray, watching the trembling wisp of smoke rise toward the ceiling. That was the last piece in the file of the Unknown, he thought, the ballistics report on the bullets found in the unidentified body. He absently arranged the photographs in a neat stack and put the accompanying letter on top. The report itself was a three-page document full of numbers and formulas. He turned the pages without reading till he came to the last, laconic paragraph.

He glanced at it, then, wide-eyed, read it again. The amazing meaning of the concluding sentence slowly soaked into his mind, and he felt his blood run cold. He read it again and again, refusing to believe, refusing to accept its terrible meaning. But there it was, a single sentence based on three pages of scientific analysis, supported by twelve big, glossy photographs.

And he suddenly realized that the report in his hands could trigger one of the ugliest scandals in American history.

⭐ 2 ⭐

His reading lamp off, he sat stiff in his chair, chain-smoking, while the darkness faded away and a timid morning light crept into the room. A couple of times he felt the urge to share his discovery with somebody. He reached for the phone and dialed the numbers of John Natua and the Assistant Secretary. Both times he replaced the receiver before the phone started ringing. It was so easy, after all, to defuse the time bomb he held in his hands. All he had to do was shred the ballistics report together with the Unknown's file, as he had been instructed. Nobody else understood what the report implied. The FBI experts ignored the real meaning of their findings. They hadn't even been told that the body in question had been found in Vietnam. And nobody would ever know.

His secretary's cheerful arrival turned into a panicky retreat when she saw him emerge, unshaven, out of a cloud of stale cigarette smoke, yelling at her not to disturb him. Somewhere around noon she made a mousy incursion into his office with a tray of sandwiches and vanished for the rest of the day. His only decision, finally, was to disregard the Defense Secretary's instructions. Instead of destroying the Unknown's file and the ballistics report, he shoved them in his briefcase before leaving the office. And he had them at hand's reach now, on the imitation leather bench beside him, as he waited for Barbara at Archibald's.

He still hadn't decided whether he should tell her about the ballistics report when she walked in, her silhouette briefly outline against the stained-glass door. She saw him at once and waved. He leaned back and watched her move through the crowd. A bearded man in an expensive beige blazer, all golden buttons aglow, raised his beer glass as she passed. But Barbara breezed by, leaving him with his mug in the air and his smile frozen in his beard.

They had been together for nine years now, and he was still excited by the way she carried her slender figure. She had that indefinable touch of class that made most men hesitate before accosting her. He wondered if he would have tried to talk to her had he seen her in a bar or some other public place. Probably not, he concluded. He had simply been lucky that faraway winter morning at the University of Georgetown.

That first encounter, so strange it sometimes seemed to him predestined, vividly surfaced in his mind. For it was one of those few chosen memories about Barbara he would often summon from the far provinces of his past, eager to release again the fierce passions they treasured, secretly hoping they would rekindle a dying fire.

His plane had landed in Washington, chased by the bleak January winds, during a short break in the blizzard that had kept the city paralyzed for almost a week. Tommy Pritchard, of U.S.S.R./Satellites 2, was waiting for him at the gate, profusely sweating in his sheepskin coat. His brown hairpiece had slipped over his right ear, exposing a grizzled sideburn and bestowing a comical, rather impish air upon his plump, smooth face.

"You look ghastly," Tommy had chirped cheerfully. "Are you dying or what?"

Meredith had shrugged vaguely and followed him through the NO ENTRY door and down the stairs to the Company car. In the rearview mirror of the vintage Impala he had caught a glimpse of a bleary, furrowed face invaded by a blond stubble, that painted it an unhealthy ashen hue, of weary, red-rimmed eyes, and a grimly drawn mouth, which he recognized as his own. He hadn't slept for thirty-six hours, throughout the intensive debriefing of Razumov in the Innsbruck safe house, and later, during the long flight home, when a vague malaise had surreptitiously crept into his mind and a persistent—although obviously unfounded—suspicion had undermined his initial exhilaration. There was nothing to worry about, he kept repeating to himself. Razumov's stuff was prime grade. The papers he had brought with him to Innsbruck had plunged the Company experts into an ecstatic nirvana.

They had landed their best catch in years. Razumov was a high-ranking Soviet diplomat, former ambassador to Warsaw, and a former protégé of Yevgeni Karpin, the influential deputy director of the KGB. Meredith had been working on his defection for a few months, since the first rumors of his falling from grace had alerted the Company station in Moscow. He had made a satisfactory contact with Razumov at the annual session of Unesco in Paris, and they met again at the Peace Movement Congress in Stockholm. Cold, humorless, beady-eyed, Razumov didn't attempt to conceal his greediness. He wanted money, lots of money, a new identity and a new life in Canada, which Meredith readily promised. They agreed on January and Vienna, where Razumov was to assist at the European Broadcasting Union Conference.

That January night Razumov walked into the Hotel Imperial in Vienna and came out by the side entance, straight into a waiting taxi that was a Company vehicle. At daybreak, after switching cars and escorts a dozen times, zigzagging across the Austrian countryside, even donning for a while a black wig and a false mustache, he finally stepped into the overheated living room of the Innsbruck safe house, where the reception committee had kept a tense all-night vigil.

The debriefing had entered its second stage now. But the importance of Razumov's revelations was such that Meredith decided to fly to Washington and report to the deputy director of Intelligence. And it was during the flight, when he was finally alone, dwelling upon the hectic events of the last few days, recalling the droning, monotonous voice of Razumov as he condescendingly spurted his amazing disclosures, that a nebulous doubt had slowly shaped in his mind. It was nothing but a gut feeling, probably the rotten fruit of his disillusioned, distrustful imagination.

Still, he had been in this game for too long to disregard the warning flashes of his instincts. Razumov was too goddamn confident, an inner voice kept whispering; he was too relaxed throughout their night journey to Innsbruck. Later, in the safe house, he was the coolest person present. That was rather strange. Meredith had been enrolling Soviet defectors for the last ten years. He had been watching them in hotel rooms, back streets, escape cars, and shabby safe houses.

Even the brave were badly frightened. In the slight tremor of their hands, the film of sticky sweat on their brows, the liquid glint in their eyes, he always discerned the uncontrollable, poorly suppressed symptoms of their fear.

Could it be that Razumov didn't show any fear simply because he had nothing to fear? Because he knew that no KGB security squads would be chasing him, and no KGB murder squads would ever take revenge on him? Because his astounding information was utterly false, cunningly concocted in the disinformation directorate of Moscow Center?

And so it was that the haughtiness of a Soviet defector in a graceless Alpine chalet brought Meredith face to face with Barbara Stuart. For even before they reached Langley Woods he had made up his mind. He interrupted Tommy Pritchard, who was blabbering something about the bloody Arabs and their bloody oil embargo. "Tommy," he said, "before going back to the office I must talk to a Kremlin-watcher."

Tommy's hand froze on the steering wheel and he shot him a startled glance from beneath the perfect cowlick of his hairpiece. "A Kremlin-watcher? They're all in Innsbruck, aren't they?"

"No," he said, irritated. "I don't mean a Company expert. I need a second opinion from somebody independent, an outsider. You've got a few consultants you use once in a while."

Yes, Tommy conceded, there were a couple of Sovietologists at the George Kennan Institute and the Acheson Foundation, but their clearance was limited, operational details were strictly taboo, and on top of all that they were unsupportable prima donnas. One had to make an appointment weeks in advance and then they were doing you a big favor, the bloody left-wingers. Under his persistent questions, however, Tommy finally admitted that the best were Lutwak and Stuart and agreed to try and set up an urgent meeting with one of them while Meredith got a shave at the Sheraton barbershop.

An hour later they walked into Barbara Stuart's office at Georgetown University. He had intended to meet her alone, but the moment he saw her he felt grateful for Tommy's presence. Her unusual, poignant beauty dazzled him and left him strangely troubled. Her handshake, however, was cold, formal, and so was her voice.

"I agreed to meet you," she said, "because Mr. Pritchard insisted it was a matter of national security. But I want you to know that I disagree with the foreign policy of this country and I disapprove of the organization to which you belong."

The telephone was ringing. As she picked up the receiver Tommy whispered to him, "Another bloody liberal." He didn't answer. He could not stop looking at her.

Her huge, intense eyes were the most striking feature in her face. Black, burning with an inner fire, and still conveying a mute hint of sadness, they dominated her oval face, attracting attention like two vibrating magnets. Years ago, in Spain, he had seen a painting by Hollander of an Andalusian woman framed by an open window. The artist had created the passionate face by spare, suggestive strokes, using only white, black, and gray. The slightly salient cheekbones were a mere hint in the chalk-white visage; the half-parted lips were barely outlined, the nose unachieved, as if the painter didn't care about such trivial details. But the eyes were enormous, deep, two irregular stains of black, haunted by secret pain and dark, disillusioned wisdom.

Her initial hostility gradually melted during the conversation that followed. His inner turmoil didn't, however, and he desperately strove to concentrate on his questions. He needed her comments on certain information he had obtained lately, he said. He didn't tell her where the information came from and she didn't ask. She was very knowledgeable, he discovered as he quoted the main points of Razumov's debriefing and listened to her reactions.

Yes, she said, there had been indications of a power struggle in the Kremlin during the last few months, but Brezhnev had won with the support of KGB Director Yuri Andropov. Yes, the secret meeting of a Soviet envoy with Mao had been a failure, and the rapprochement between Peking and Washington was a source of growing worry in Moscow. She had no information about a military confrontation between Russian and Chinese troops on the Ussuri River, but it seemed to figure, as did the item about a transfer of seven armored divisions from the Ukraine to the Chinese border. Yes, there could be a purge in the Red Army if the cruise missile tests in the Caucasus had failed, as he said.

Item by item, she confirmed, agreed, admitted the credibility of Razumov's report. And he started feeling like a fool for having succumbed to an instinctive, totally groundless suspicion.

Till he quoted Razumov's startling disclosure about the transfer of nuclear warheads to the Middle East following the 1973 war. For the first time she afforded a wry smile and leaned back. "That's a lie," she said. "That's what the Kremlin wants us to believe."

Tommy Pritchard turned to him, puzzled, as if seeking help. "But I was given the full details," Meredith said. "Dates, numbers, names of the carrier ships, destinations—"

"That's a lie," she firmly repeated. "Brezhnev didn't allow a single warhead to leave the Warsaw Pact territory. As long as he is in power he'll avoid any nuclear confrontation." She paused, casting a quick look at the window. It had started snowing again. "Mr. Meredith, all the former items seem genuine. I knew some of them, I believe in the authenticity of the others. But I know how the Russians work. They'll feed you all that material—even deliberately sacrificing some state secrets—in order to make you swallow the bait."

"And the bait is what—the warheads?" Tommy grunted, perplexed.

The telephone rang again. "Not now," she said dryly into the receiver and turned back to them. "They want to force our hand in the Geneva conference on the Middle East. That's why they'll go to any length to make us believe they have deployed atomic weapons in the Mediterranean." She got up. "If your questions are based on a document, it's a fake. And if it's a defector, he's a KGB agent."

Back out in the cold, Tommy Pritchard raised his fur collar. "What a looker," he breathed wistfully.

"Let's go," Meredith said.

Two weeks later he knocked on her office door. She was leaning on the windowsill, frowning at a voluminous file. Its faded blue cover was stamped with Cyril-

lic characters. "Mr. Meredith," she said, surprised.
She didn't look displeased.

"I just dropped in to tell you that you were right,"
he said. "The man is a KGB agent."

She nodded gravely, then looked up at him in puzzlement. "When you were here the other day I thought
I disappointed you, but you left smiling. You still are."

"You didn't disappoint me at all," he said. "You
told me what I wanted to hear."

She returned his smile. "You had guessed," she
concluded. "You knew it all along, didn't you?"

Yes, he knew it, and he had been right, after all.
Perhaps it was this surge of self-confidence that made
him turn back to her. He felt absurdly young, light-
headed. "Will you have lunch with me?" he heard
himself saying.

All that seemed ages away, he thought now as he
absently returned her kiss. Her lips were moist and
cool. "Something's wrong," she said immediately,
sinking into the armchair across from the table and
looking at him closely. He watched her unbutton her
tan raincoat with quick, deft gestures. Her Lanvin
scarf matched to perfection her elegant brown suit and
beige silk blouse. "You look terrible," she said in her
breathless way, pausing a second before throwing in
her diagnosis. "It's the Unknown, right?"

"Right," he echoed, secretly relieved for not being
the one to raise the subject. He had told her about the
President's decision before he took off for Hawaii.

She laid her hand on his, gently caressing his skin.
Her hand was like her body, narrow, lithe, with long
delicate fingers. "Let it be, Walt. You'll hate me for

38

saying it, but this is the best thing that could have happened to you."

His anger surged at once, and he pulled his hand away. "You're right," he muttered.

She eyed him guardedly. "Right about what? That—"

"That I'll hate you for this," he said, hating himself for saying it. "You don't understand," he resumed quickly, "you really don't understand what that decision means."

She shook her head, bitter lines emerging at the corners of her mouth. "How many times do we have to go through that, Walt? Does it always have to turn into a fight between us?"

Peace was saved, at least temporarily, by the appearance of a rosy-cheeked English lass by their table. Archibald's claimed to be the most authentic English pub on this side of the Atlantic. The owners, a couple of Canadian businessmen, had at great expense decorated it like the real London thing, including mirrors, dart boards, and drawings of hunting scenes. Two cockney bartenders, complete with East End slang, checkered waistcoats, waxed mustaches, and mutton chops, reigned behind a square bar. Beside the ales and the Guinness, the place featured typical pub dishes like pickled eggs, London sausages, and other inedible monstrosities. The last imports from the old country were several waitresses whose milky complexions and alluring accents made the patrons easily forget that a real pub employed no waiters at all.

"Chivas, no ice, please," Barbara quickly said, nervously fumbling in her bag. Her long auburn hair shimmered in the artificial light. He ordered a double brandy. The waitress smiled at him and left.

"She likes you," Barbara said with a hint of irony. "They all fall for the combination of blue eyes and blond hair turning white. And this rugged, tanned face. They find it irresistible." She lightly touched his cheek with her fingertips.

He shrugged. "Oh, for God's sake, Barbara." He was tense and angry. He lit the cigarette she had taken out of a crumpled pack, then retreated into a grim silence.

Barbara gave up first. "We can talk about it if you wish," she said, avoiding his eyes.

"About what?" he asked gruffly. "My obsession?"

She drew on her cigarette, still looking away. "About what that decision means."

He took a deep breath. "Okay. Fine." She looked oddly vulnerable, her head slightly bowed, and he suddenly felt a strong urge to convince her, win her to his side. "You know there are still two thousand four hundred and eighty-nine men missing in Vietnam."

He waited for her to nod, then resumed. "You might find it strange, but all that the relatives of those boys want is to give them a decent burial, have a grave to visit, a stone to cover with flowers. You may call it an obsession, I don't."

She seemed about to say something, but changed her mind. "The families of the missing are convinced that if a real effort were made, many of the bodies could be recovered. And if the government really cared, a mission could be sent to Vietnam to find out if Americans are still being held in concentration camps."

"The Vietnamese will object," she said, frowning.

"Perhaps they will," he agreed. "So we'll have to use other means. Anyway"—he leaned toward her—"what matters is not to give in but keep searching, make the Vietnamese understand we're determined to bring those boys back home at all costs. Dead or alive," he added, immediately regretting the bombastic formula.

The waitress brought their drinks and a bowl of salted nuts. "Here you are, sir," she chirped with a dazzling smile.

"Here you are, sir," Barbara mimicked with sarcasm when the girl was gone. Her imitation of the distinctive English accent was perfect. "Did anybody tell you, sir, that you look like Paul Newman?" She paused. "Do you like her?"

He was about to say something unpleasant, and then it occurred to him that Barbara was trying, rather awkwardly, to dispel the tension between them. He raised his glass. "To young English maidens." He smiled wanly. The brandy was strong, but not warm enough to release its aroma, and he cupped the bell-shaped glass, rubbing it with his palms.

Barbara's voice was low, cautious. "I don't see what all this has to do with the Unknown." She was aimlessly turning the whiskey glass with her fingers. Behind her back he could see more people, mostly men, come in by the glass doors. A tall man with a florid face was shaking his glistening umbrella. It had started raining again.

"We feel that the Unknown means the end to the search," he stated, and sensing her puzzlement, hastened to explain. "The funeral of the Unknown Soldier has a symbolic meaning. It's the formal end of the Vietnam War. A symbolic burial of the war and its memories, a sort of finishing touch. Once the Unknown is buried, the government will abandon the search for the missing."

"What makes you so sure?" she asked, looking at her glass.

"People live by symbols," he said. "For years the establishment has been trying to forget Vietnam, but the families of the missing wouldn't let them. The Unknown is going to change everything, though." He took the Assistant Secretary's letter from his pocket. "I got this today. I wasn't surprised, I expected it."

She read it quickly, slightly frowning, then looked at him. "This organization of families . . ."

"The League of MIA Families," he said.

"Whatever. Why didn't they object to the Unknown project if they thought it was so bad?"

"But they did," he said. "Why do you think it took so long to designate an Unknown Soldier?"

She shrugged. "I don't know. Perhaps they had no body to bury?"

He took a sip of his brandy. A couple of executives in pin-striped suits squeezed by him, laughing loudly. One of them brushed against him and he spilled some of his drink on the Assistant Secretary's letter.

"Oh, hell," she breathed, "this place is getting too crowded."

He tried to wipe the liquid away with the back of his hand. "No," he said, "it wasn't a matter of the body." She handed him a crumpled tissue and he daubed the amber drops from the letter. The pale brown stains refused to go away. "The White House has been trying to bury the Unknown Soldier for eight years now. Gerald Ford even ordered a crypt built at Arlington, but had it dismantled a few months later."

"Why? What happened?"

"The League of Families, that's what happened. They objected, claiming that the entombment of the Unknown would inhibit any further efforts to find MIA's."

"They're so powerful?"

"They've got a lot of clout. Some very good connections on Capitol Hill."

"And you at the Pentagon, of course."

"Of course," he said.

She sipped her drink, watching him over the rim of her glass. "So Jerry Ford gave in."

"He gave in, and after him Jimmy Carter gave in. He had promised the congressional leaders to build the tomb, but he, too, yielded to pressure."

She chuckled dryly. "Jimmy Carter was never the man to say no to pressure."

"Well, as far as I know, Reagan himself hesitated for quite a while before he signed the decree."

She put her unfinished glass on the table and crushed her cigarette in the ashtray, then leaned over. "Okay, he hesitated. But he did sign the decree at the end, didn't he? And he designated the body. So there's nothing to be done now."

His throat was oddly contracted. "Yes, there is one thing."

"What?" There was a hint of mockery in her voice. "What thing?" A game of darts was going full blast behind them, and the players welcomed each hit with loud cheers and catcalls.

"If somebody succeeds in identifying the Unknown's body," he slowly said, watching her, "and if a name if pinned to that corpse, they can't bury him. They'll have to—"

"Oh, come on, Walt, that's impossible!"

"They'll have to call off the ceremony," he went on. "It might take months, even years, before they get another unidentified body. So they'll have to go on searching."

"But . . ." She started. A ripple of shrill laughter set out from the bar.

"I have the Unknown's file," he said softly. "I can try."

She stared at him, perplexed, then sparks of sudden fury exploded in the big black eyes. "You must be out of your mind," she murmured, pulling back. Then she was on her feet, collecting her things. "Let's get out of here," she said. Her hand, clutching her small brown bag, was trembling. She started for the door without waiting for him.

He threw some bills on the table and followed her. A roll of applause erupted in the back as the darts' champion of the day hit the bull's-eye.

Their embittered confrontation continued in the rain-swept streets of Washington, then in the tiny Italian restaurant where they had a quick, morose dinner. And throughout the long, agonizing night in their large bed, while a storm thundered outside and sporadic flashes of lightning painted their distant bodies in a deathly white pallor.

Later, when he recalled those endless, tormented hours, he would fail to distinguish between the blunt accusations she threw at him and the distorted *cauchemars* he had during a short spell of exhausted sleep. For after their minds had turned away from each other, they had let their bodies vainly try a reconciliation in their own way. He could vaguely recall how they clung together in a desperate effort of lovemaking before he drifted into sleep, still captive in her body. And how he whispered to her how much he loved her while his inner voice told him how impossible that love had become.

But he couldn't recall the moment when Benjamin's name had surfaced in their harsh duel, and Benjamin's ghost had settled between them, beloved yet unwanted, lost forever yet stubbornly present. Perhaps he was there all the time, haunting their thoughts, waiting for his name to be called.

It's Benjamin he was after, Barbara whispered to him in the dark; it's because of him he wanted to set out on that insane quest for the Unknown. And the plight of the families of the missing was nothing but a pretext, although he wouldn't admit it, even to himself. His son was his Unknown, she went on, a boy who had grown up far from his eyes, far from his mind, while he was playing his cloak-and-dagger games in Europe, talking Communist master spies and killers into betraying their countries.

"He should have grown up hating you for deserting him," she said, "but the opposite happened. And you can't cope with the guilt, Walt."

The opposite had happened, indeed. Benjamin was eight years old when he had divorced Virginia. He didn't know how she had raised the boy. She hadn't remarried for many years. He saw them very rarely, on his brief, irregular visits to the West Coast.

And he hadn't noticed how he had gradually, almost secretly, become the hero of his little son. How the gentle, delicate boy had grown up admiring his father, the daring Marine officer who had fought in Korea, braved death with the Flying Tigers in French Indochina, landed in Lebanon at the head of his men; how the same Benjamin who was afraid of the dark, who preferred books to softball, who would rather run than fight the neighborhood bully, had developed a fervent ambition to emulate his father, to be worthy of Major Walt Meredith. An ambition that had driven him to volunteer for the Green Berets, and to die in a Vietnam jungle.

"You feel responsible for his death," Barbara bluntly said, "that's why you've gotten hooked to that senseless search for bodies. It's time you faced the truth, Walt. He's dead and nobody can bring him back."

He didn't remember afterward what he had answered, or if he had answered at all. Not that it really mattered. What mattered was that during the night the fantastic idea he had spontaneously blurted at Archibald's matured into a firm decision. And between the spells of sleep and wakefulness, of tense silence and angry conflict, he grew determined to set out on his search for the Unknown.

"I owe it to those families," he whispered as Barbara lay immobile, her back turned to him. "I can't let them down now, after nine years."

And later, when morning came and they faced each other over untouched mugs of black coffee: "I know it sounds crazy, but it isn't. I'll find that name, Barbara. They'll have to call off the Arlington ceremony."

She didn't comment. Her face was distraught, shadows of exhaustion and misery nesting under her eyes. She watched him sullenly over the kitchen table, holding her nightgown against her chest.

He knew well this stubborn silence of hers at the end of an argument. When she felt that everything had been said she would raise her drawbridge and retreat into herself, refusing any further contact. But he couldn't admit defeat, not yet. As she didn't say a word, he brought over his briefcase and took out the file of the Unknown. He leafed through several pages of notes, on the stationery of the Central Identification Laboratory.

"They have already determined his age, height, and blood type," he said, pretending to ignore the blank look of Barbara's and her surly silence. "That's something to start with."

He wished he were as sure as he pretended. He had read the file several times, the day before, and there was practically nothing to start with. The Unknown had been shot several times in the chest, and a bullet had exploded in his mouth, shattering his teeth. His groin and belly had received the full impact of a hand grenade. His corpse had been badly scorched by fire. It seemed as if the soldier had gone several times through death. Such horrid deaths did actually occur in some Vietnam battles.

But the charred remains of the Unknown made identification practically impossible. A handwritten note, attached to the file, described the discovery of the corpse. It had been found in a burned hut, in the village of Na-san, about twelve miles east of Bienhoa. The village itself had been partly destroyed in 1969 during the fierce combats of the Tet offensive.

As she watched him, her weary face devoid of expression, he was for a moment tempted to show her the ballistics report. Its startling conclusions might tear her from her apathy. Perhaps she would even approve of his intentions. But at the last moment he changed his mind. He couldn't share his findings with her yet, not as long as she was so hostile. He couldn't reveal to her the conclusions of the report, stated in a short paragraph that had turned his last twenty-four hours into a nightmare.

He had read it so many times he could quote it by heart. "The bullets and hand-grenade fragments extracted from the body went through a series of optical and chemical analyses in our laboratory," the report said in its dry, factual language. "The analyses were intended to determine the caliber and the alloys of the bullets and fragments. The consecutive tests, described above, established that they all are of American manufacture and correspond to the standards of the U. S. Army."

American manufacture.

The bullets and the hand grenade were of American manufacture.

He knew, of course, that it was quite a common practice among the Vietcong to use captured American weapons and ammunition.

He knew, of course, that fatal mistakes occurred in combat, and American troops had been fired at and hit by other U. S. units.

Still, he couldn't rule out the horrible possibility that the Unknown Soldier of the Vietnam War hadn't died in battle but had been murdered by his fellow Americans.

⭐3⭐

Laura Lewis kept staring at the last page of the ballistics report long after she had finished reading it. Then, with deliberate slowness, she collected the papers and the photographs and slipped the sheaf back into its envelope. The Unknown file lay at her feet, beside the reclining armchair. Meredith watched her bend to pick up the file, some gray strands escaping from her old-fashioned chignon. She was a tall, robust woman with broad shoulders, a big chest, and strong arms. She looked up at him. She wore no makeup and the straight, unplucked eyebrows, the big nose, and stubborn chin still conveyed a lot of strength. But old age had already veiled her shrewd eyes with an opaque coat that made the pupils blend with her dark-brown irises.

She motioned toward the glowing fireplace. "I feel tempted to make three steps and throw this into the fire." She had a raucous, deep voice that could have belonged to a man.

"And condone a murder?" Meredith suggested, watching her thoughtfully. He felt strange, using the word *murder* for the first time.

"Oh, rubbish," she muttered. "First of all, my boy, you don't know yet if it was murder." Although he was fifty-two, she had been calling him that since they started working together nine years ago. Perhaps she was right, after all, as her boy, her only son, was about Walt's age when he was reported missing. Colonel Harold Lewis was the highest-ranking American pilot to be shot down, during a bombing mission over Haiphong.

"And then," the old lady was saying, "that wouldn't be the first murder in Vietnam to go unpunished, would it?" She paused a second, watching him sternly. "Do I have to tell you how many officers have been murdered in firefights because they messed up their soldiers?"

He sustained her stare without answering. She was right, of course, although every effort had been made by Army authorities to conceal that ugly truth from the families of the fallen. During the last years of the war the murders of officers or NCO's by their own men, in combat, had reached alarming figures. An officer who roughed his soldiers too much, searched them for drugs, or applied disciplinary regulations to the letter risked being killed in the next firefight with the Vietcong.

In some cases vengeful soldiers shot the officers they loathed while under enemy fire. But mostly they blew them up with fragmentation grenades. In Vietnamese slang that practice was dubbed "fragging." Meredith had never mentioned the word in his conversations with the families of fallen soldiers. He could well imagine the unbearable agony of a mother learning that her son had been blown to bits by one of his own men because he had dared to cancel his furlough. But Laura Lewis knew. There were very few secrets about Vietnam that the keen president of the League of MIA Families didn't know.

She was looking closely at him, divining his thoughts. "Come on, my boy," she said in a softer voice, "we both need a drink." She got up and walked to the Sheraton chest by the far wall where a tray with two decanters and several glasses had been prepared. A painting of the London fire hung over the chest. He watched her pour generous measures of brandy into two glasses. Her blue ankle-length dress was plain, but she didn't seem to care. Laura Lewis obviously nourished a sublime indifference for her outward looks.

"You must be thinking that the old hag is getting cynical," she said, handing him his glass. "And you're wrong. I can't bear the idea that we might bury as the Unknown somebody murdered by American soldiers. That makes me sick. It's worse than a sacrilege." She took a long sip of her drink. "But it is not of my concern. Do you understand?"

Raising her voice, she caught him by the arm. Her grip was firm, insistent. "Do you understand? What matters for me and for the League is not how this boy died, but how to continue the search for the other boys. If we let them go ahead with the funeral on May . . . twenty-ninth?"

"May twenty-eighth," he said.

She let his arm go and her hand slipped down, touching his fingers. "May twenty-eighth. If they bury the Unknown they'll bury with him all the plans for any further search. Vietnam is bothering them too much, they want it out of the way."

A hint of bitterness slipped into her voice. "They built us this wall in Washington and now they'll build us that tomb in Arlington, and that will be it. Then

we'll make up with Vietnam, we'll call it a historic reconciliation, and, who knows, perhaps we'll even start
selling them weapons, as we did with China. While so
many boys are still rotting in their damn jungles, and
maybe some are rotting alive in their camps."

He took his glass and drifted toward the window.
Night had fallen and the Virginia countryside was a
host of blurred shadows, frozen in the dark. The night
in the Vietnam jungle was never still, he recalled. It
was a breathing, lethal presence, feverishly weaving its
web around the living and the dead. Benjamin had
disappeared in the jungle of Chaudoc, close to the
Cambodian border.

The brandy flowed inside his body like liquid fire.
The room seemed overheated all of a sudden. He
leaned forward and the cold glass felt good against his
burning forehead. We should keep searching, he
thought, we can't give in. "So?" he uttered loudly,
turning back.

"So we should prevent the burial of the Unknown,"
Laura Lewis said firmly. "We did it in '74 and in '76."
She turned away from him, staring at the fire. "I'll
never forget that meeting we had with Gerald Ford.
Were you there?"

"No," he said, "I joined the department in '75."

She nodded. "We had quite an argument with Ford
in the Oval Office. You should have seen the late Sen-
ator Palmer. He got so hyped up, I was afraid he'd get
a heart attack. He was all red in the face, and he was
brandishing a roll of papers like a club—I think it was
the list of the missing—and shouting at the President,
'History will never forgive you! The American people
will never forgive you.' And Ford, pounding on his
desk, yelling back at him, 'There's no way back. The

crypt is ready and I'll keep my word.' Well, we went home heartbroken, but two weeks later, very quietly, they started dismantling the crypt. We'd done it. We'll do it again."

"This time it's different," Meredith said. "The press release is scheduled for tomorrow morning."

She nodded, letting out a deep breath. "That's why I'll back you. I've no other choice. Your plan is the only way to prevent the burial of the Unknown." She looked at her watch. "They'll be here any moment now."

"And they'll go along?"

"Leave that to me," she said.

He leaned back on the windowsill. Laura Lewis always had her way, be it with the press, Congress, the White House, or, as was now the case, with her vice presidents in the League. One of them, Waldmann, had nicknamed her "the Iron Lady." Her husband, a prominent Washington banker, hadn't survived the calamities that had befallen his family, with the disappearance of his son and, a year later, the death of his two grandchildren in a car accident in Wisconsin.

But Laura had been cast in a different mold. At the age of seventy she had pulled herself together, liquidated the family business, and focused all her energy in the one and only direction where she could still perceive a flicker of hope—the search for the missing. Six months later she had been elected president of the League of MIA Families. Her rough voice had a ring of authority as she handed him the Unknown file.

"I'll back you," she repeated. "But I warn you. Not a word about that ballistics report. It will scare them off." She hesitated. "Armstrong is all right, you see, but Waldmann . . ."

"What about Waldmann?" he asked, but she wasn't listening.

"Anyway," she went on, "as I told you before, it's irrelevant. We're not private detectives, and we are not trying to crack a real or imaginary murder. We're the League of MIA Families, and we'll help you find out who the Unknown is for one, and only one, reason—to keep the search going. Are you with me?"

"But Laura..." he started, and then the doorbell rang. And Laura Lewis went to the front door to greet her two vice-presidents.

She was the Iron Lady indeed, he had to admit as he drove back along the deserted Washington avenues. As soon as Waldmann and Armstrong had been served drinks and seated in her living room, she had gone straight to the core of the matter. "I won't waste your time by describing how disastrous the burial of the Unknown will be to our cause," she had started.

Both men had nodded their assent and she had carried on, explaining that there was practically no way to prevent the Arlington ceremony. Except one, of course, if the body was officially identified before the funeral.

"And how will you do that?" Martin Armstrong had asked in his booming baritone. A huge black man of about sixty, Armstrong seemed very much at ease in his armchair by the fireplace, dressed in a charcoal-gray suit and a dazzling white shirt. His big, calloused hands and broken nose, however, bore witness that he had come a long way before becoming the successful construction entrepreneur he now was.

"Walt has got the complete file of the Unknown," Laura said. "I asked him, in the name of the League, to try and discover the real identity of that soldier." By assuming the initiative and placing them before an accomplished fact, Meredith thought, she was leaving them no other way out.

Or almost none. For Herbert Waldmann was on his feet, his triangular face crimson. "That . . . that's illegal!" he stammered. His falsetto voice was trembling, and his eyes were wide with disbelief. He turned his balding head with quick, birdlike movements toward Armstrong and Meredith, as if seeking their help. "Oh, I'm sorry," he mumbled incongruously, noticing that he had spilled a few drops of his Diet Coke on the carpet. He had refused an alcoholic drink.

"It's not illegal," Laura Lewis said in rectification. "It's merely irregular."

"What difference does it make?" Waldmann shot back, but he seemed surprised by his own outburst. A slight, gentle school principal, he had adhered to the cause of the MIA with an all but religious zeal since the disappearance of his younger son, but he couldn't defy the system he served and revered.

"We can't disobey a presidential decision," he uttered, almost desperately.

His upper lip, adorned with a square mustache, quivered slightly. A white residue had formed at the edges of his small mouth. Faced with the mute stare of Laura Lewis, he finally sat back on the edge of his chair. His forehead glistened with sweat. He drained his Diet Coke and carefully placed the glass on the small table beside him.

"There is no law against trying to identify a body," Laura Lewis said coldly.

"Oh, come on, Laura," Martin Armstrong said conversationally. "You're rather on thin ice there. Even if there is no law against it, it's against the law, see?" He chuckled softly. "The least that could happen is that Walt would lose his job."

"He's willing to take the risk," Laura Lewis said.

Walt nodded. "I'm going on leave as of tomorrow."

A brief smile touched Armstrong's lips, and Meredith realized that the black man was his ally. "Fine, so let's forget about the League asking him to do it, okay?" he said to Laura Lewis, and without waiting for her answer, turned back to Meredith. "You're going to do it anyway, on your own, right?"

"Just a moment," Laura said, but Meredith understood where Armstrong was leading. "Yes," he said. "I'll do it anyway."

"So there's no problem," Armstrong said, spreading his arms. The man should be a diplomat, Meredith thought. He had natural authority, and his easy manners concealed a clever, intuitive mind. "If Walt's ready to assume the responsibility, I don't see how we can stop him." He winked at Waldmann, who was stubbornly shaking his head.

"Wait," Laura Lewis said. "If Walt needs any information from us we'll help him. And if he has any expenses in the course of his research, we'll cover them, of course."

"Of course," Armstrong said.

"I don't want any money from the League," Meredith said, irritated.

"You don't want it, but you'll need it," Laura Lewis stated staunchly. That was her way of making the League a partner in his quest, he realized, and didn't pursue the argument.

"I demand a meeting of the board," Waldmann exclaimed nervously, wringing his soft, feminine hands.

"There's going to be no such thing," Laura started, but Armstrong interrupted her. He seemed to perceive better the weaknesses in Waldmann's character.

"Now, now, Herb," Armstrong said in a soothing tone. "A meeting of the board is worse than a press conference. I'm sure you don't want that matter publicized." He leaned forward in his chair and looked insistently at Waldmann. "You won, don't you see? Walt isn't going to do his thing in the name of the League. He'll do it on his own, right?" Meredith nodded. "We're not involved. We'll just help him with the financing. Let's say that he came over to us and said he was privately working on some identification project of his, so we decided to help him with his expenses."

"But the Unknown..." Waldmann protested, yet his voice was less aggressive.

"The Unknown hasn't even been mentioned tonight, all right? So what else do you want? We're not concerned. If Walt succeeds—fine, we won. If not, there's no harm done. But remember that the League and your own conscience will never forgive you if you blow our last chance to continue the search. Now take it easy, okay?"

And that sealed the argument. Waldmann understood Armstrong's hint. He didn't want to be the one to blame for the sabotage of any future search. He didn't speak anymore and sought refuge in a sullen silence. Uneasily perched on his seat, he shot angry glances at his friends while they discussed the practical arrangements with Meredith. And he morosely watched Armstrong hug Meredith on Laura Lewis's doorstep.

"God be with you, Walt," Armstrong said. "Anything you need—just call me, okay?"

Laura Lewis walked with him to his car. "How are you going to proceed?" she asked. "Do you have any starting point?"

He shrugged. "The body was found in a Vietnamese village a few months after the Tet offensive of '69. I'll try to find out which units took part in the fighting over there, then I'll go over their missing lists."

Her voice was dubious. "And nobody thought of that before? Nobody checked those lists in fifteen years?"

"They did," he admitted. "They ran routine checks of all the missing lists, unit by unit. They got no results. I'll have to dig deeper and review all those lists again. At least I know exactly what I'm looking for."

She didn't seem convinced. "It seems too simple, Walt, too obvious."

"I know," he conceded, "but that's all I have for the moment." He watched her go back up the driveway, an old, bereaved mother walking into an empty house. A bitter wind was softly whispering in the black treetops.

Shortly before midnight Meredith crossed the Fourteenth Street Bridge. The heavy mass of the Potomac dully glowed in the faint moonlight. He left his car in the empty parking lot and walked into the dark maze of the Pentagon.

In the underground Data Center the first night shift was idling about the situation desk, killing the last hour before its relief. A beefy Army sergeant, his shirt collar unbuttoned, was viciously torturing an ancient coffee maker that refused to yield one more drop into his cup. In the far corner a couple of men watched an old horror movie on the television set, bellowing in laughter every time another actor grew a pair of crooked fangs.

The night supervisor, a stocky man with a drooping mouth and small, weary eyes, looked up from his dog-eared Ludlum paperback and raised his hand in mock salute. "Hi, Walt, what's cookin'?" He didn't wait for an answer and returned with a yawn to his literary occupations.

Two other men sitting beside the situation desk interrupted their discussion about Walter Mondale's chances to win the presidential race and smiled at him. They were used to Meredith's forays into their entrenchments at the most ungodly hours. On quiet nights his unusual requests often injected some excitement into their boredom.

He found Bobby Dole behind his computer, a half-consumed plastic cup of Coke by his side. Spare, skinny, a mop of sandy hair hovering over his glasses, Bobby played the keyboard like a piano virtuoso attacking the finale of a Rachmaninoff concerto.

"Playing at war games again, Bobby?" Meredith inquired severely.

Bobby smiled, his drawn upper lip revealing a pair of rabbit teeth. "Quiet," he whispered connivingly. "I just launched a couple of MIRV's on the Kremlin."

In his jeans and sneakers, his sparkling eyes magnified by the thick lenses, Bobby looked indeed like a whiz kid who had broken into the nation's secrets. He punched a few more keys, then cleared the screen and veered around on his swivel chair.

"I grant you one wish, stranger," he announced solemnly.

Meredith had his notes ready. "Vietnam," he said, pulling up a chair and settling beside Bobby.

"You don't say," the young man quipped and reached for the keyboard. Since the military archives of the Vietnam War had been computerized, detailed information could be obtained in seconds.

"Na-san. That's a village twelve miles east of Bienhoa."

"Year?" Bobby asked.

"Sixty-nine."

Strings of letters and figures were flashing on the screen, projecting a green incandescence on Bobby's pale face. "Na-san, Bienhoa District," he said. "Two hundred and thirty inhabitants . . . '67, '68. . . . Here we are . . . '69. A firefight in February '69, shortly after the Tet offensive. . . . Well"—he turned to face Meredith —"what exactly do you want to know?"

"American casualties." It suddenly struck him that as of this moment he was actually acting against his superiors' instructions. He was making the first move in his attempt to identify the Unknown.

"In '69?" Bobby was looking at him.

Meredith nodded, striving to sound casual. "We are trying to identify the body of an American soldier that was found in Na-san in '69."

"In February?"

"They found him in November, but I believe he was killed in February. We know nothing about him. I need to find out if any American unit suffered casualties in Na-san in February or March. He might have belonged to the same unit."

Bobby was nodding repeatedly, punching his keys. "That would be Na-san, cross-reference casualties," he said without looking up.

"Hey, Bobby!" somebody called, and the operator's hand slipped on the keyboard. He swore under his breath. "Damn, I messed it up. I have to redo it from start." He turned back, irritated. "What?"

The sergeant had apparently succeeded in imposing his will on the reluctant coffee maker, for he now held a steaming cup in his hand as he leaned against the opposite wall. "Do you want a ride? I'll be leaving in five minutes."

"Well . . ." Bobby started, and Meredith intervened quickly. "That's no problem. I'll take you home after we're through."

"What are you doing anyway?" the sergeant asked, and stepped forward to take a look at the monitor.

"Look, why don't we finish this thing tomorrow?" Bobby said. "I live on the other side of town. It's quite far, really."

"I don't mind," Meredith assured him. He couldn't tell Bobby that the next morning his request for urgent leave of absence would be on the Assistant Secretary's desk and he would have no more right to cross the threshold of the Data Center. "I'd rather like that wrapped up tonight, if it's okay with you."

Bobby shrugged. "Okay." He took a gulp of his Coke and deliberately replaced the plastic cup on the wet brown circle that the soft drink had left on the desk.

"I'll stay around for a while," he said to the sergeant, who raised his coffee cup and turned away. "Thanks, Al." And leaning back over his machine: "Now where were we? Oh yes, Na-san, casualties." He conversed with the computer for a few minutes, peering closely at the ever-changing green patterns on the monitor.

"What do you know," he said at last. "That village of yours was quite popular, I'd say. Look . . . '67, four skirmishes, three dead, eight wounded . . . '68, an ambush south of the village, one wounded, one missing. . . . No, no, the missing was taken prisoner and exchanged in '72. Same year, two exchanges of fire with the VC two miles south of the village, no casualties, and in November a full-scale firefight. Six wounded, two dead." He turned to Meredith. "Are you interested in that?"

Meredith hesitated, then shook his head. "No, later perhaps. Let's see what we've got in '69." He felt tense and lit a cigarette.

"In '69," Bobby said. "Here we are. February '69, two dead."

"February?" He felt a surge of excitement. "That might be the battle I'm looking for. Can we have the full details?"

"He wants the full details," Bobby said to his keyboard. "Let's give them to the gentleman, pal." He paused. "Here it is. February the nineteenth. The dead men are Private Jeff Lippmann and Corporal Edward Bellamy, both of them Marines."

"Officially identified?" he asked, without much hope.

"Sure," Bobby droned indifferently. "If they weren't identified and buried, they wouldn't be on my computer."

Meredith nodded. "What's their unit? How were they killed?"

"You heard the man," Bobby said to the computer, and punched a few keys. He waited a moment and frowned. "What the hell is that?"

"What the hell is what?" Meredith asked, leaning forward.

"Wait. Let's ask him again. Na-san, February the

nineteenth, '69, casualties, Private Jeff Lippmann, Corporal Edward Bellamy, USMC " He gulped the rest of his Coke and reached for the keyboard again. "What do we want to know? Unit, period, combat report, period. Well?" A single line flashed on the screen and he leaned forward. "I'll be damned," he said. "Look at that."

The text on the screen repeated the instructions: Na-san, 02.19.69, cas. 2 dead, Pvt. Jeff Lippmann, USMC, Cpl. Edward Bellamy, USMC, RQ: Unit ID, RQ: Combat report. And the answer: "Classified. No further information available."

"Classified?" Meredith echoed, leaning toward the monitor.

"I've never seen anything like that before," Bobby murmured.

At the end of the line the cursor was blinking like a live, pulsating question mark.

The bedroom was warm and the covers had slipped down, revealing Barbara's nude back. Pale moonlight filtered through the curtains, drawing milky arabesques on her skin. She slept noiselessly, her head framed by the graceful bend of an elbow, the contours of her long legs etched against the folded sheet. The easy abandon of her body made her look trusting, serene, still oddly vulnerable.

He felt a surge of tenderness. A strange tremor rippled his chest as he bent over and hesitantly caressed her cool skin. She stirred, and he caught the scent of her hair, the warm, gentle breath of her parted lips. On their first night together, ten years before, he had been too elated to sleep, and had spent long hours lying beside her contemplating her blissful repose.

And yet she had been so tense, so confused, when she had first walked into his apartment that night. At first she had surprised him by her hungry, febrile response to his touch. Then she had retreated into desperate hostility, fighting his aroused body, twisting in panic in his arms. Dark fear had exploded in her eyes and distorted her quivering mouth.

"Don't, don't..." she had rasped, "we'll do that tomorrow, Walt, okay? Tomorrow, I promise, stay away, please, Walt."

But then her voice had changed, and she was not fighting him anymore, only pleading, her own instincts taking over, and finally they had made love, half undressed, and she had clung to him, in sharp conflict with herself, her nails wildly digging into his flesh but her body stiff, restrained.

She had softly cried afterward, her head shyly buried in his chest, and he hadn't asked why, and she hadn't told him until much later that he was the first man she had let inside her body and inside her scarred emotions since that cruel night in Moscow. But he had been grateful to her for falling asleep in his arms, her confident tranquility more eloquent than words. And he knew then that she was offering him more, much more, than the depths of her lithe body.

Was all this going to end? he now asked himself as he slipped into his side of the bed, gently removing Barbara's outstretched hand from his pillow. Had their discord reached the point of no return? Were they drifting apart because of his obsession? For obsession it was, he had to concede, an obsession that had changed their roles, gradually turning her into the cool, poised character while he had grown tense and restless.

But he could not go back now, not after the meeting at Laura Lewis's house, and certainly not after he had seen the cryptic phrase flash on Bobby's screen. Classified. No further information available. What could be classified, for Christ's sake, about a forgotten battle in Vietnam fifteen years ago? What was the dark secret they were trying to conceal? The key to the enigma of the Unknown? An ugly demon they had locked in their Pandora's box for fear it might shatter another American myth?

He lay there for hours, tortured by fragmented ideas and hypotheses. And in his brief, restless fits of sleep he would see Bobby Dole punching his keyboard and the face of a little boy filling the screen, watching him with almond-shaped, reproachful eyes.

⚬4⚬

"Good God, Meredith, do you know what time it is?" The voice on the other end of the line was irritated, interspersed with the dry, rasping cough of a tobacco addict.

He took another sip of the black, bitter coffee and pulled aside the voile curtain. The street was deserted except for some figures in nylon parkas at the far corner that were throwing garbage bags into a dirty yellow truck. "It's morning, isn't it, Phil?" he suggested into the mouthpiece.

"You call that morning? It's a quarter past six, man, and you call that morning?" Phil seemed to choke in another coughing fit. His lungs were a mess since that winter in Korea, but at that very moment he was probably fumbling for his cigars on the night table even before reaching for the lamp switch.

"I need your help, Phil, it's rather urgent," Meredith said soothingly.

"What's so urgent that couldn't wait a couple of hours?"

"And besides, you're a night owl. You never sleep." Phil Conway also looked like an owl, with that fixed, puzzled stare of his unblinking round eyes and his thin beaked nose drooping over his grizzled beard. A restless, lonely man, he haunted—rather than inhabited—his dark apartment, reading, drinking, compulsively switching television channels and mainly smoking his pestilent cigars till the wee hours.

"I just fell asleep a half hour ago," he bitterly complained. "Shit, Meredith, I knew you were bad news since I laid my eyes on you in Seoul."

"Pusan," Meredith corrected, "the Yankee Doodle Bar in Pusan." A few years older than Meredith, Conway had retired from active duty after freezing almost to death in Korea. "They had to use ice picks to take me out of that bloody mountain," he recounted later. "For months afterward I kept shitting ice cubes, yes, sir, that's what I did." He had stayed in the Marine Corps as a civilian employee. For the last six years he had been assistant director of the Marine Corps Archives. "I need your help," Meredith repeated. "We're trying to identify a body."

"A Marine?"

"Possibly a Marine. He was killed in '69."

"He got killed in '69 and you call that urgent," Phil groaned with indignation. "Damn, Meredith, the guy waited for fifteen years without complaining, he could wait till sunrise." The trouble with Phil was his predictability, Meredith thought. He would make his cynical cracks, he would grunt and grumble and bark, and finally, of course, he would do his best to help.

"He can wait but I can't, Phil. I'm going on leave this morning, I might even change jobs, and this is one of the last cases I'm trying to solve before I'm out."

Phil's rasping cackle dryly popped into the receiver. "So she finally talked you out of it, did she?"

"Who?"

"Your professor, that's who. She never wanted you in that office, did she?"

"No, she didn't," he confirmed reluctantly. Conway was a sworn misogynist, and Barbara seemed to be one of his all-time favorite targets. "Now, will you write down the details?"

Phil sighed, conceding defeat. "Go ahead, I've got a good memory."

He told him about the unidentified body found in Na-san, but didn't reveal it had been chosen as the Unknown. He didn't breathe a word about the ballistics report either. He quoted the puzzling answer to Bobby Dole's computer inquiry. "What do you make of it, Phil? What could still be classified after all those years?"

"Well . . ." Phil paused, probably using his cigar butt to light a fresh one. "There still are a few cases, you know. Special operations, use of new weapons and techniques, contacts with agents who might still be active . . ."

"After fifteen years? Come on, Phil."

"Okay, I'll check that. Where are you?"

"Home."

"Fine, I'll call you from the office." Phil rattled a last hack into the receiver and hung up.

He called back three hours later. The apartment was peaceful, strangely quiet. Barbara had left early, after a quick breakfast gulped down in uneasy silence. She hadn't asked him where he had been last night or what he intended to do. They were both avoiding the subject of the Unknown as people refrain from speaking about an incurable malady. Only at the door she had suddenly turned back and hugged him. For a second she had stood close to him, her face snuggling in the hollow of his neck. Her hair was soft, delicately scented. Then she had rushed to the elevator, and the spell was gone.

"*Errare humanum est*," Phil's voice now croaked in the receiver.

"What?"

"Erring is human," the voice explained. "Didn't the professor teach you any Latin? I thought she was—"

"God, Phil, give me a break," he groaned. "I'm not in the mood for this, believe me."

"It was classified, and still is." One had to get used to the abrupt leaps of Phil Conway's interest from one subject to another. "But I guess it was a mistake."

He was falling in pace with Phil's line of thought. "You mean there's a file about Na-san and it was classified by mistake?"

"That's how it seems to me," Phil said. "I can see no reason to keep it classified."

"You read it then?"

A hint of strain seemed to slip into Phil's voice. "Sure, of course I read it."

"Look, Phil, can we meet?" He didn't care about precautions anymore. "Could I come to your office? I can get to Bethesda in forty-five minutes. Phil?"

There was a short silence on the other end of the line. "No," Phil said rather cautiously. "Not here, not in the office."

"All right," Meredith said in mock surrender. "I'll buy you lunch. Twelve-thirty at Wheeler's?"

"No," Phil said. "My apartment, tonight. Any time after eleven will do." He chortled. "And don't tell the professor. Let her guess where her handsome beau is spending his nights."

* * *

Phil preceded him like a shadow, soundlessly leading the way through the maze of his obscure abode. And a maze it was indeed, a succession of small irregular rooms and poorly lit corridors. By the open doors, Meredith could discern heaps of books, newspapers, and magazines stacked all over the place, which was permeated by the stench of Phil's cigars. He was puffing on one now, and the murky cloud of smoke stubbornly stuck to his skeletal, stooping figure, which cantered purposefully forward with quick birdlike steps.

This singular trot and the foul fat cigars seemed to be all that remained on the young sinewy officer who had once been a fairly legendary figure in the lore of the Marine Corps. Meredith had joined the Marines at the age of seventeen, thrilled by the halo of heroism that surrounded their exploits in the South Pacific, dreaming of emulating their feats of bravery on the beaches of Korea. And "Wild Phil" Conway, the lean, fierce-looking, foul-mouthed captain who had shed some of his blood on Tarawa and Iwo Jima, had earned the admiration of Second Lieutenant Walt Meredith while he waited for his baptism of fire in the glum port of Pusan. Then Phil had disappeared, to cross his path again years later when Walt no more believed in wars and Phil no longer won them.

In his den, tucked away on the far end of the apartment, Phil busied himself pouring whiskey into two unmatching glasses, then curled into an ancient armchair between puffs of yellow upholstery protruding from cracks in the old leather. On the wall above his head hung war photographs from Korea and the Solomons, in cheap black frames. Marine badges and medals, a belt, a holstered pistol, and a rusty Japanese bayonet were displayed in a brown, glass-paneled cupboard. A crack in the glass had been fixed with Scotch Tape.

"First the facts, then the assumptions," Phil said without preamble. His prominent Adam's apple throbbed under the frayed collar of his turtleneck pullover as if it had a life of its own.

Meredith settled on the couch, shoving away a blanket, some magazines, and a couple of books on the Lebanese war. The room was cold, unheated, and the sting of the whiskey in his throat carried a pleasant warmth. "Did you bring the file?" he asked.

Phil's face was blank. "No, sir, I didn't. The file is still classified, and mistake or no mistake, you won't expect me to smuggle classified material out of the archives." He paused for effect. "But I took some notes, which are all you need."

From the top of the television set he picked up a sheaf of yellow leaflets covered with a spidery handwriting in bright green ink. He turned on a standing lamp, crowned by a dull brass shade, and a circle of timid light descended on his papers.

"So, as I said, the facts. On February 11, '69, after the enemy assault on Bienhoa had been repelled, several patrols were sent after the retreating VC. It was a search-and-destroy operation. Most of the patrols were teams of Marines from the Thirty-seventh Marine regiment. Regiment's commander"—he raised his eyes, severely watching Meredith like an exacting schoolteacher—"Colonel William J. Briggs. Rings a bell?"

"Yes." Meredith had talked to Briggs over the phone several times during the last few years. Briggs was retired now, but knew his former regiment better than any other living man. He had willingly helped Meredith and the League in their inquiries about missing Marines. "He was with us in Korea, right?"

"He was the best Marine officer in Korea, yes, sir, that's what he was." Phil gulped down his drink, smacking his lips, and resumed his narrative. "One of the teams was commanded by Captain Steve Rainey of Bravo Company. It numbered seven men and was sent to the sector of Na-san. In the outskirts of the village they encountered a large VC unit. Two soldiers were killed—"

"Lippmann and Bellamy?"

"Yes. Two others were captured by the Vietcong, and three returned to Bienhoa, including Captain Rainey. Another drink?"

Meredith nodded and held out his glass. A sudden fit of dry cough convulsed Phil's meager chest. "Rainey, by the way, was wounded at Na-san. Got the Purple Heart."

"And the two POW's?"

"I'm coming to that," Phil said reproachfully. "A later report specifies that one of them, Private Ray Walton, died in captivity. The other broke down. Completely. He was repatriated at the end of the war and committed to the Alma Viva Sanatorium in Mesa, Colorado."

"Name?" Meredith took out his notebook.

"You don't have to take notes, I'll give you mine. The guy who went nuts is Frank Wyatt, Corporal Frank Wyatt." Phil fell silent, fixedly staring at Meredith with his owlish eyes.

"That's it?"

Phil nodded, and neatly bit off the tip of a new cigar.

Meredith frowned. "It sounds pretty routine to me. Why the hell would this file be classified?"

"Ah," Conway breathed. "Those were the facts, now the assumptions." He struck a match, then spoke in a whiff of smoke. "Assumption number one. Like all operational records at the time, this file was stamped secret. That was routine procedure, you know. Standing orders. Later, by sheer negligence, it wasn't declassified."

Meredith shook his head skeptically.

"Second assumption," Conway continued. "The Na-san operation was based on intelligence from an undercover agent we had in the Vietcong, and all material connected to his activity was automatically classified."

He looked up at Meredith, but getting no reaction, went on. "Third assumption. Here's something you didn't know. Ray Walton, one of the prisoners taken by the Vietcong, was the son of Ambassador Walton."

"Ambassador Walton? Never heard of him."

"You should have," Phil Conway said. "Your learned professor certainly has."

"Well . . ." Meredith started, containing his annoyance. He was fed up with Phil's jabs at Barbara.

"Walton was the head of one of our delegations to the SALT talks in Geneva. Knew quite a lot of secrets."

"And you think we didn't want the Vietcong to know they held his son. What could they do, blackmail him?"

Conway shrugged. "Maybe. Anyway, after the boy died we should have declassified the file, but we didn't. Ray Walton's name is on the Wall, of course."

"So you think your people just . . ."

"I think they just overlooked the file." Conway collected his notes and handed them to Meredith. "Anyway, I filed today a request for declassification. If there's any other reason, we'll know it pretty soon."

Meredith leaned back on the couch, watching Conway. "You know all that is a lot of bull, don't you, Phil?"

Phil didn't answer immediately, and it seemed to Meredith it took him too long to stub out his cigar in the overflowing ashtray. "What are you talking about?" he finally inquired, his Adam's apple twitching.

"I'm talking about the fact that a burned body was found at the same place where this patrol was attacked. That nobody knows who the dead man is. And that just by the sheerest hazard, this most innocent file describing the incident was stamped classified and kept out of reach for fifteen years. So, if you don't mind, I'll add another assumption to those you thought of."

"Oh really?" Conway said sourly. "And what's your assumption?"

"Foul play," Meredith said, and got up. "You thought of it, too, didn't you?"

Phil saw Meredith to the door. His bony hand was cold and hard. "Go ahead, what do you want to say?" he finally blurted, irritated. He was staring over his visitor's shoulder.

Meredith shrugged. "Do me a favor, Phil, okay?"

"I thought I just did."

"Check with your sources." He sought Phil's eyes. "Find out if there was an eighth Marine on that patrol to Na-san."

He stepped into the decrepit elevator, which whined and moaned in the dark all the way down to the ground floor. Outside, sudden gusts of wind shrieked in the empty street.

Conway called him early the next morning. Meredith was in the kitchen, immersed in the editorial of the *Washington Post* praising the upcoming entombment of the Unknown.

"Just wanted to tell you there wasn't any other Marine on that patrol," Conway rasped. "No, sir, no eighth Marine."

The man who opened the heavy oak door was bald, stocky, with a heavy jaw and short, thick arms. His stiff posture and shining thick-soled shoes made Meredith think of a Marine sergeant major. Even the dark blue suit looked like a uniform on his upright, bulky torso. He bowed slightly, rather ceremoniously. "The colonel is expecting you, sir." His voice was sharp, with a trace of Southern accent. "This way, please."

The sprawling, massive house was nicely furnished without being opulent. By the open doors, Meredith caught a glimpse of a large sitting room and a library. But it was unmistakably a man's house. The wood-paneled walls, the paintings of hunts, battles, and sailing ships, the leather upholstery covering the sofas and armchairs, the dark shades of the carpets, and finally the collection of ancient firearms displayed on an entire wall in the room he entered now, eloquently described the master of the house, who had just risen from behind a large mahogany desk and stepped toward him, extending his hand. A tall, lean man he was, a mane of iron-gray hair crowning his leathery face, which seemed chiseled in stone by strong, sharp strokes that had carved a salient forehead, a blunt nose, a strong, somewhat brutal mouth, a jutting, stubborn chin. But the most fascinating of his features were his gray, piercing eyes, glowing with a metallic glint under the bushy eyebrows.

He was sixty-five today, Meredith reflected, a retired officer in a sober tweed suit surrounded by the serene greenery of the Maryland countryside. But fifteen years ago, in combat gear, a gun dangling from his belt and the ruthless fire burning in his eyes, Colonel William Briggs must have been an awesome warrior, a charismatic leader of men.

"Mr. Meredith, it's a pleasure." The voice was deep, confident, exuding strength. "I know what you're doing, and after all those phone conversations over the last few years, I'm delighted to meet you in person."

He was the kind of man who would never grope for words, Meredith thought. He knew exactly what he wanted to say and his ideas came out already shaped and molded, like neat, compact capsules.

"I'm grateful you could find some time for me at such short notice," Meredith said.

"Nonsense," Briggs said. "First, it's my duty to assist you in your operation. Second, I'm not so busy." He let out a short, dry laugh. "I have a nice office in Washington with a couple of secretaries and the chairmanship of two investment companies, which are the most boring thing ever invented. But I have strictly nothing to do there and could as well stay home and wait."

"Wait?" Meredith asked. "Wait for what?"

The short laugh again. "Remember what they used to say about old soldiers? They don't die, they just fade away. Well, I'm very busy fading away."

Meredith looked at him in wonder. The despair was in the colonel's words, not in his tone of voice.

Briggs gestured to a seat and returned to his straight-backed chair. "Would you like a cup of coffee or perhaps a drink, Mr. Meredith?" He sat very upright, placing his hands on the desk.

"Coffee will be fine." The desk was bare except for a telephone, a digital clock, and a miniature replica of the Iwo Jima monument cast in bronze. The statuette was embedded in a hunk of uncouth black rock adorned with a tiny plaque. He couldn't make out the lettering.

"How do you take your coffee, sir?" the man who had let Meredith in asked behind his back. He had almost forgotten him.

"Black, please, no sugar."

"For me, too, Henry," Briggs said. And turning to Meredith while Henry's heavy steps faded out: "He was with me in Korea, and later in Vietnam. Followed me here, for the last time." The bitterness was out in the open again, unmistakable.

"You were at Iwo Jima?" Meredith nodded toward the statuette.

"No. I fought in Europe. Landed in Normandy with the Rangers and joined the Marines only after the war. You are a Marine, too, I understand."

"Yes," Meredith said. "I was in Korea with the Twenty-ninth Regiment."

"With Dave Sawyer?"

"He was my commanding officer," Meredith confirmed, and accepted a sturdy mug of black coffee from Henry's hands.

"Thank you, Henry," Briggs said. "I knew Dave.

He was a brave officer. A war-horse. Didn't deserve to die of cancer."

"What did he deserve, Colonel?" Meredith ventured.

A brief, lopsided grin flashed on Briggs's face. "Would I sound ridiculous if I said that there are people who deserve a soldier's death?"

A soldier's death. Meredith recalled the sleepless nights of his youth when he drank with bated breath the fiery verses of Lord Byron and dreamt, like him, of dying a hero in the battlefield. He looked up at the rugged soldier across the desk in his executive swivel armchair.

"No," he said thoughtfully, "you wouldn't sound ridiculous." You, too, crave a soldier's death, Colonel, he wanted to add, and you, too, are going to die from cancer or a heart attack or a stroke in your bed and you know it. And fear it.

Briggs was watching him steadily over the rim of his cup. He put it down and leaned forward. The bay windows behind him offered a view of a gently sloping lawn strewn with low bushes. Dusk was already tinging the grass with a dull gray and elongated shadows crept around the shrubs. "Were you ever in Vietnam, Mr. Meredith?" he suddenly asked.

Meredith hesitated. "I was there a couple of times after the peace treaty was signed to negotiate the search for MIA's. But my real experience in Vietnam" —he smiled—"dates from the time when it wasn't called Vietnam but French Indochina."

Briggs stared at him in astonishment. "You were in French Indochina? When was that?"

"Between December '53 and May '54," Meredith said, "at the time when the French were losing their own war in Vietnam. Almost twenty years before we lost ours."

"Yes, 1954," Briggs repeated, still puzzled. "What in heaven were you doing there?"

Meredith chuckled. "Heaven is the right word. I was an air conveyer in a Packet C-119 that had been leased to the French by the U. S. Air Force."

"I still don't understand," Briggs said. "I didn't know any American military personnel had fought with the French."

"We weren't in uniform, actually," Meredith said. "You see, after the armistice in Korea I was approached by a couple of officers from Intelligence. They told me that the French were in trouble in Indochina and the American Government had decided to lease them sixteen C-119 aircraft for dropping supplies to their troops. As they didn't want to involve military personnel . . ."

". . . that would have been considered a direct American intervention," Briggs offered.

"Exactly. So they thought of forming civilian crews that would fly and service the planes."

Briggs tilted his head, frowning. "But you were a Marine, not an airman."

Meredith left his cup of coffee on the table. "They offered me a job as an air conveyer. I didn't need a pilot license for that. I had just to drop the supplies from the aircraft to the French units in the field."

"And why did you accept?"

"The pay was good," Meredith stated, "seven hundred dollars a month. In '54 that was a lot of money. I was already married, I had a family to support. They also promised me that after my contract was over they would reinstate me as an officer in the

Marines and promote me to captain. Which they did."
He grew serious. "No, it wasn't that, really. The truth
is that I was young, I was adventurous, I wanted to
taste new experiences, see action . . ."

"And you saw some?"

He nodded his head, a flow of memories surging in
his mind. "For six months we flew supplies to the
French base in Dien Bien Phu, before it was finally
overrun by the Viets. My plane was hit three times. It
was hell, believe me. Every time we took off, we
thought it was the last. The Viets had brought over all
the American antiaircraft guns captured in Korea, and
their fire was murderous. Once we were badly hit, and
crashed. Our pilot was killed. Captain James Mac-
Govern—we had nicknamed him 'Earthquake Mac-
Goon'—became the only American who died for Dien
Bien Phu. As you know, the fall of Dien Bien Phu
sealed the defeat of the French in Indochina."

Briggs was repeatedly nodding. "And then it was
our turn." He leaned back, pondering. "Fascinating,
Mr. Meredith, your story is absolutely fascinating."

"So you see," Meredith pointed out quietly, "when
we got involved in Vietnam, I had no illusions that we
might win."

A bitter smile touched the colonel's mouth. "Of
course. You were there before. You knew." He suddenly looked up, his voice changing. "Well, you didn't
come to tell me your war memoirs, and I don't want to
abuse your time." He propped his face on his clasped
hands, his elbows leaning on the desk. "What can I do
for you, Mr. Meredith?"

The commonplace question jolted him back to the
present, and to his forbidden quest. For a short moment he had been reliving another tragedy, in another

time. "I am trying to identify the body of a soldier we found in Vietnam," he said cautiously. "I believe you can help me."

"Certainly," Briggs nodded. "I'll be glad to give you a hand."

Without any further comments, Meredith took the FBI ballistics report out of his briefcase and handed it to Briggs. The colonel frowned at the sight of the photographs of the bullets, then swept them aside and picked up the report. He held it at arm's length to adjust it to the focus of his eyes. He needed glasses, Meredith thought, but wouldn't use them for fear he might look like what he really was—a man on the threshold of old age.

"A ballistics report?" Briggs said with wonder. Meredith leaned back in his chair, watching him. He had given a lot of thought to the tactics he would use with the colonel. He couldn't just inquire about the Na-san incident, as he had with Bobby Dole and Phil Conway. Briggs might not remember it or refer him to a subordinate officer. Neither could he tell Briggs that the body was the Unknown Soldier's. Briggs was the kind of man who could pick up the phone in his presence and ask to be connected to the Secretary of Defense.

Still, there was a lever Meredith could use. Briggs, he assumed, was a man of honor, identified with his regiment and very keen to preserve its glory intact. To get his full, wholehearted assistance, Meredith had to impress upon him that something had happened in Vietnam that might tarnish the image of the regiment. Therefore, he shouldn't spare any effort to get to the core of the matter.

Briggs's frown deepened as he progressed in his

reading. Darkness was slowly filling the room. Briggs switched on a copper reading lamp, shaped as a half globe, which cast a cone of bright light on the papers before him. His left hand casually slipped along the rim of the desk and closed on the Iwo Jima replica. As he watched the colonel's fingers inadvertently caress the small statue, lovingly touching that sculptured symbol of the Marines' dedication, Meredith realized that his assumption had been correct. Briggs would tolerate no stain on the reputation of his Marines.

"You suspect that this soldier has been murdered." Briggs's resonant voice tore him from his reverie.

"Yes," Meredith said firmly. It was no use speculating about friendly fire or the VC using captured American weapons.

"And you assume that the man might be a Marine or his murderers might be Marines from my regiment."

He nodded.

"Where was the body found?" Briggs asked. A mean, angry fire glowed in his eyes.

"Na-san." Meredith told him about the incident and the classified file.

"I remember Na-san," Briggs said slowly. "Rather vaguely, I'm afraid. It was at the end of the Tet offensive, and we were still licking our wounds. We had been hit badly. But that!" He furiously slapped the report on the desk, then leaned toward Meredith. "You said the file was classified?" He seemed perplexed.

Meredith nodded. "It still is."

Briggs looked away, an angry scowl distorting his features, then stuck his chin forward, his mind made up. "How can I help, Mr. Meredith?"

"The same way you did in the past," Meredith said.

"Every time we turned to you for help, you obliged. I know you keep detailed records of your operations in Vietnam and a full roster of the soldiers in your regiment. I must know how many soldiers participated in the Na-san patrol. And I need their names and addresses."

"What for?"

"I want to meet them and talk to them," Meredith said. "I must know what happened at Na-san."

Briggs stared at him for a long moment, his features drawn, somber. Finally he let out a deep breath, bringing down his hands on the desk with a thud. "Will you excuse me?" he said, getting up.

Briggs walked out of the room and Meredith heard him call Henry. Somewhere inside the house a woman's voice also spoke, and he wondered if there was a Mrs. Briggs. He got up and approached the opposite wall, where several documents and commendations were displayed in discreet frames. He found the ceiling light switch by the far door. A few photographs represented a younger Briggs, in combat fatigues, posing with his soldiers. In one of them he was wearing a blood-stained bandage on his head. There wasn't even one photograph of the colonel shaking hands with a political dignitary or his Army superiors.

"Mr. Meredith," Briggs said. He hadn't heard him coming back. The colonel was standing at the door. Henry appeared behind him, carrying a couple of files and two black cardboard boxes. They returned to the desk and Henry neatly placed his load under the light, then opened one of the boxes and started thumbing through the cards it contained. Briggs didn't sit down.

"Quite frankly, Mr. Meredith," he said, and his voice was stiff, formal, "your theory seems rather farfetched. There is a very slight chance that it might even approach the real events of Na-san."

Meredith was about to object, but Briggs raised his hand. "Nevertheless, I fully agree that you should thoroughly investigate this matter. I must compliment you for your devotion. As far as I'm concerned, I'll do all that I can to help you expose the truth about Na-san. We must make sure that the honor of the regiment and of the Marine Corps is kept intact."

"Thank you," Meredith said. "Thank you indeed."

Briggs seemed ill at ease. "Don't," he said. On his right, Henry was jotting a few lines on a sheet of the colonel's personal stationery.

"Is that your own operation, Mr. Meredith?" Briggs inquired, his head slightly tilted.

Meredith hesitated. "No, of course not. I've got my bureau staff." Briggs was watching him sternly. "And we work hand in hand with the League of MIA Families."

"The League," Briggs nodded. "And how's the Iron Lady? Still kicking?"

Meredith chuckled. "Oh, so you know Laura." He must know her well, he thought, to be familiar with her nickname.

"You bet," Briggs said. A brief, amused smile lighted his face. "What a woman! I'm a sworn admirer of Laura. She's been fighting for the MIA's as if each of them was her own son. Whenever she needed help at Army headquarters or on Capitol Hill, I was the first to jump to attention. Give her my best regards when you see her."

"I sure will," Meredith said. "Now about those names."

"Yes, of course," Briggs said. "The names. According to my records"—he vaguely gestured toward the files on his desk—"there were seven Marines on that patrol to Na-san. Two were killed and one died in captivity." He took the sheet from Henry and handed it to Meredith. "You have here the addresses of the four surviving men. One of them, unfortunately, is in a mental institution."

"Wyatt," Meredith said.

Briggs nodded, coming around the desk. "Perhaps they've got the answer to your terrible question." He paused. "I can only wish you luck." His handshake was firm, encouraging.

He escorted Meredith to the door and stepped outside after him. They stood silent for a moment. The night was mild but very dark. "Damn that bloody war," Briggs suddenly blurted, his voice heavy with bitterness. "Damn Vietnam, and the politicians who dragged us in and those who pulled us out."

Meredith looked at him. Briggs's face was in shadow. "They made Kennedy a symbol," he said angrily, "and gave Kissinger the Nobel Peace Prize. And what did they give all those fine boys who died for their country? Hatred, contempt, and a few inches of stone wall with their names on it. And they call it the home of the brave."

The oak door closed with a thud and Meredith was alone, in the night.

★5★

"**H**e sailed early this morning," the old man in the checkered shirt said. He pulled his frayed baseball cap over his eyes, then ran the back of a gnarled hand over his white bristle. In his other hand he held a tin of white paint with a brush stuck in it. "Took a couple of Canadians over to the back country. You wanna charter his boat, mister?"

A graceless, stooping girl in dirty sneakers and a T-shirt praising "Enchanted Islamorada" came toward them from the far side of the marina and tilted her head, sourly staring at Meredith. She was carrying a plastic bucket full of bait shrimp. "He's asking after Steve," the old man said. A sea gull clumsily circled over his head before landing on a blackened mooring pole.

"Steve Rainey?" The girl hesitated, apparently reluctant to divulge information to a stranger in a suit and tie. "Sailed to the back country this morning." She pointed vaguely to the north. "Said he was going to Shell Key with those Canadians. Went after bonefish." She nodded her head toward a rectangle of murky water across the pier. "That's his slip." It seemed to be the only vacant slip in the small marina. Most of the

86

boats were sailboats and modest yachts, probably used only on weekends.

"He wanna charter his boat," the old man said knowingly. "She's a fine boat, and Steve's a hell of an angler, ain't he, Marge? Last December he brought back the biggest tarpon I'd ever seen. A real monster, that one." The Florida sun lay low in the sky, mercilessly breathing fire over the still, turquoise ocean.

"Why don't you go to the office?" Marge hopefully suggested. The shrimp in her bucket looked like a yellow-gray mass, its thousand feelers idly twitching.

"It's closed," Meredith said. "Is Rainey coming back tonight?"

"Sure," Marge said indifferently. "The Canadians' wives are waiting at the motel."

"I ain't sure it's their wives." The old man went into a fit of soundless laughter, his meager body shaking. His left hand shot up to his face to conceal his bad teeth. "I'd say they left them wives in Canada and flew over with those cute little secretaries." He noiselessly guffawed again.

"If I were you, I'd wait at the motel," Marge said. Her limp hair had a faded, lusterless shade. "See the trees over there?" She pointed at a clump of ailing palmettos across the marina. He looked up, squinting in the dazzling afternoon glare. "From the pool deck you'll see him coming." She languidly sauntered away, swaying her bucket.

"She's right, you know," the old man said, falling in step with Meredith, who followed her. "You'll see Steve's boat coming, you can't miss it. A big white cruiser, fifty feet long. The *Fidelis*, that's her name. You'll see those Canadians on the deck. They sure'll be loaded by then."

"Why, they don't fish?" Meredith asked. The marina office was still closed. He stopped by the rented Camaro, fumbling with his keys.

"They ain't fishin'," the old man explained, plunging again into his convulsive giggle. "Steve is doin' the fishin', they're doin' the drinkin'. You should've seen the crates of beer and ice they took along on the *Fidelis*. Why don't you go 'n' get yourself a nice cold beer at the motel? I'll tell Steve you wanna charter his boat. I'll be here, don't worry. My name's Chuck, they all know me."

"Okay, Chuck, you, too, go get yourself a beer." Meredith smiled and gave him a couple of dollar bills. The old man accepted the tip with unexpected shyness. "Thank you kindly," he said, holding his arms along his body and bowing his head. The tin of paint left another white streak on his soiled pants. "Thank you very much, sir. Much obliged, indeed."

He checked in at the Fisherman's Haven motel and carried his overnight bag to his room. The kidney-shaped pool was scarred and patched; still its light-green water sparkled temptingly in the sun. A South American family with two kids splashed at the shallow end. The father had a trim black mustache and a large, inflated belly that spilled over his swimming trunks. On the near side two girls in bikinis and mirror sunglasses chattered merrily, massacring the French language with their Canadian accents. One of them turned as Meredith approached, took off her sunglasses, and gave him a long appraising look, studiously fluttering her eyelids. The other was too busy painting her face with thick white cream.

Only when he lay down on the bed in the dark

room, listened to the roar of the ancient air conditioner, did he realize how exhausted he was. He had spent most of the evening checking addresses and placing phone calls all over the country. Briggs's list was at least ten years old. The only valid address was the Alma Viva institution in Mesa, Colorado, where Frankie Wyatt was confined, probably for the rest of his life.

Of the three other surviving Marines, both Steve Rainey and Lyndon Hughes had left with the colonel their parents' addresses. He followed the trail of the Rainey family across the country. Originally from Ohio, they had moved to Nebraska and then to Florida. The last number he dialed was in Flagstaff, Arizona. The Raineys were both dead, an old woman's voice had sadly whispered in the phone.

She was Stella Borden, and she had taken over the apartment. She was a widow, Stella said, originally from New York, and he visualized the old woman sitting alone in her apartment, happy to talk to anybody, even a stranger on the phone who didn't care a damn bit about her. After a long introduction describing her sorry life and her late husband—God bless his soul, he was a man with a golden heart, they don't come like that anymore—she had reluctantly come to the point.

Yes, she had moved into the Raineys' apartment a year ago, soon after Betty's funeral. Betty had been her friend, the old woman explained, they had been going to the same doctor for their arthritis. Buck had died first. They said it was because of the toxic fumes he had inhaled when he worked in a zinc factory back in Ohio. And then Betty had passed away. Such a tragedy. They had hoped to spend their last years in peace close to their daughter, in Flagstaff.

Yes, sure, they had a son, too, Steve. He had come a couple of times to pick up some old trunks, he was living in the Florida keys now, managing a boat-charter company. He had been wounded in Vietnam, a real hero, and poor Betty, may she rest in peace, she was so proud of him, she always showed her his picture in a Marine officer's uniform.

It took him another hour to locate Rainey in Islamorada. But all he got was a recording of a hoarse male voice assuring him how important his call was and urging him to leave a name and number after the beep, which he did not.

He found Lyndon Hughes's father in Chicago. The cold, irascible voice on the other end of the line was overtly suspicious. What the hell did the Department of Defense want with his son, the voice wanted to know, what the hell did they do for him after all he had done for his country, and why the hell didn't they leave him in peace?

Hughes gave in only after Meredith had warned him that keeping information from a senior Pentagon official was a federal offense. Lyndon was married, his father grunted, and living with his family in Montana. Yes, he said, defeated, he had his address and phone number.

The third Marine, Eddie Paris, had left a Baltimore phone number. But the phone had been disconnected and the Paris name wasn't listed in the city directory. Meredith had called Patty, his secretary, and she promised him she would try and locate Paris from the office, first thing in the morning.

He decided to start his investigation with Steve Rainey. Rainey had been a captain, he had been the commander of the patrol. If anything unusual had happened in Na-san, Rainey was bound to know. He got up before dawn and quietly packed his bag.

Barbara was asleep, having spent the evening nervously smoking on the couch, watching him in surly silence while he was on the phone. When they had gone to bed she had retreated to her side, turning her back toward him, refusing him her nudity. She was slipping away from him, becoming a stranger again, and the long lonely nights were formally sealing their disunion.

Before he went into the shower he scribbled a note, which he left on the kitchen table: "I am sorry, but I must do it."

While shaving he thought he heard Barbara's light steps on the carpet, but when he came out the bedroom was dark and Barbara immobile on the bed, her silken hair fanned on the pillow. The note in the kitchen didn't seem to have been touched. He hesitated a second before taking out his pen and adding "Love" to the laconic message. Then he furtively sneaked out and hailed a cab to the airport.

The interior of the cab was damp, unheated, and he shivered in his thin raincoat as the driver sped across the empty Washington streets. The black shadows of the fading night still lay low over the city, sneaking into doorways and alleys, clinging to tree trunks as opaque sheets of morning mist seemed to chase them over deserted lawns. A bleak mood had pervaded his mind. He felt like a coward, running away from Barbara under the dark cover of night. He had to leave early, he kept foolishly repeating to himself. He had to be on the 8:05 A.M. flight to Miami if he wanted to reach Islamorada in the afternoon. Still, he hadn't dared to wake Barbara and risk another confrontation but had stealthily tiptoed out of her bed and perhaps out of her life.

But Barbara's image stubbornly remained in his mind, refusing to dissolve and fade away as he tried to concentrate on the purpose of his voyage. She was vividly present as he shifted in his seat in the Miami-bound plane. She troubled his thoughts hours later as he gunned his rented car up the tall bridges that chained the Florida keys. And she kept haunting him now as he turned and tossed on the squeaking bed in the dark Islamorada motel room. He was the second man who was turning his back to her, he thought, after the one she had lost that fiendish night in Moscow.

She had told him about Moscow several months after they met, as the first vacation they spent together was drawing near its end. They had lazed it away in Cozumel, off the Mexican coast, exploring the unspoiled Caribbean beaches and the ruins of Tulum, but mostly exploring and observing each other, their initial wariness slowly fading away. At dinner that night he vaguely suggested that she move in with him when they returned to Washington. Back in their room, they made love slowly, tenderly, then lay side by side, easy and spent, caressed by the cool night breeze. "I had forgotten love could be so good," she said.

He propped up on his elbows. "You told me once you were very much in love with your husband."

"When I married him." Her voice was unsteady. Her hold on his arm suddenly became intense, urgent, conveying a resolution which he failed to decipher. She pulled herself to a sitting position, her back leaning against the wall, her arms clasping her knees. When she spoke again her voice had dropped to an irregular, broken murmur and she groped for words. "I married

John when I was fresh out of college," she said. "He comes from a well-known Boston family. They're mainly in banking. I loved him very much." There was a long pause again. She was struggling with ancient shadows, he guessed, willing to open herself and yet reluctant to let him into the nightmares of her past.

"Let's go out," she said nervously, reaching for her beach robe. He followed her down the cracked bungalow steps. The sand was soft and cool beneath his bare feet. The deserted cay stretched in the moonlight like a giant yellow horseshoe. She walked slightly ahead of him, her head bent as the wind blew into her hair. Her story finally came out, interspersed with spells of uneasy silence.

When they had married, Barbara's story went, John ws already a junior diplomat. "I was determined to be more than just a pretty face in his shadow," she said fervently. Therefore, she had gone back to school, first in Washington, then in Paris—his first assignment abroad—where she studied political science and Russian at the Ecole des Langues Orientales. She was already fascinated by the devious, secretive nature of the Soviet political system. "For the first five years John was rather amused by my zeal," she recalled. "Afterward, I started getting on his nerves."

She bent to pick up a rotten coconut shell and furiously broke it into jagged, fibrous pieces that she tossed on the wet sand. John's change of mood, she said, coincided with a slowdown in his career. After eight years in the service, he still was a second secretary. But only after he was posted to Moscow did he realize that another change had imperceptibly taken place—his wife had outgrown him. Recently awarded her Ph.D., she was quickly becoming an authority on Soviet foreign policy.

"I published a few articles in some American magazines, and the reaction was good. I got some very encouraging letters from the editors, and they also printed a couple of readers' letters. Abrams wrote... Do you know Leonard Abrams?"

"No," he said, looking up. A bank of clouds was drifting low over the oddly opaque ocean. A dark shadow sneaked across the yellow tropical moon and the waves turned black, suddenly sinister.

"He's one of the leading experts on Soviet affairs." A note of restrained pride slipped into her voice as she quoted, "'Mrs. Barbara Stuart has a keen flair for the subtleties of the Soviet political ritual and her analysis of the undercurrents in the party leadership is outstanding.' That's what he said, word for word. 'Outstanding.'"

After a piece she wrote about the Politburo was printed in *Foreign Affairs*, Barbara went on, she was invited to visit the ambassador. She was the wife of a diplomat, he reminded her, therefore she should refrain from publishing articles. But she would be very helpful to him, the ambassador added, if she agreed to join an "informal" group of advisers who met at his office regularly to discuss recent developments in the Kremlin.

"And you were immensely flattered," Meredith concluded. He tossed his cigarette into the sand, where it kept glowing like a firefly.

Yes, she said, it was flattering indeed. But when she went to the group meeting the following afternoon, she was surprised to find out that her husband wasn't invited. "That same night," she said, "he got drunk for the first time."

She stood for a moment at the edge of the surf, the froth swirling around her bare ankles. Then she was swiftly walking again, her body rigid, her head bowed. He watched the tiny waves erasing her footsteps in the wet sand. For quite a while, she admitted, she failed to perceive the connection between her success and his drinking.

"You must have been quite dazzled by your achievements," he offered.

She shrugged. "Maybe. Anyway, I overlooked the warning signs. I blamed his bouts of drinking upon the stress in the embassy work. I didn't understand that John was going through hell, realizing that he was condemned to remain a junior diplomat while I was on my way up. All he could expect in the future was the grim status of being Barbara Stuart's husband. I kept unconsciously fanning the fire by describing my conversations with the ambassador and showing him letters from universities back home that offered me senior positions."

Before Barbara's unseeing eyes her husband's acute feeling of inferiority gradually turned his love for her into bitter resentment. Till the argument they had the day she left for a Sovietologists' convention in London and he slapped her face, vehemently.

"I should have left him then and there," she said. "But he seemed more shaken than me. He started crying, he was distraught, he begged forgiveness." She paused again. The churning surf had become louder, impatient, he noticed. Or maybe it was his imagination. "He had never done that before. We made up, and he was the most loving husband when he drove me to the airport."

When she returned, ten days later, John wasn't at the airport. The apartment was dark and neglected. By midnight he still hadn't returned, so she phoned the duty officer at the embassy. He promised he would try to locate John Stuart at once. She hung up, puzzled. There was something awkward, artificial in the young man's voice, and even more in his silences.

John showed up about an hour later. By his unsteady steps on the landing and the hesitant rattle of the keys in the lock, she understood he was drunk again. But she wasn't prepared for the look of hatred and savage triumph that glowed in his blood-injected eyes. "He told me he'd come to pick up his things. He was leaving me for a woman who loved him, respected him, and didn't humiliate him in front of the entire diplomatic community."

"He told you who she was?"

"No, not then. I was to discover later she was the cultural attaché at the embassy." Her voice suddenly filled with spite. "A plain, foolish woman."

Meredith sought her eyes. Her face was in deep shadow. He reached for her, but she shook his hand away. The wind was stronger now, blowing a humid chill upon them, and she wrapped herself tightly in her robe. She was shivering, and Meredith wondered if it was only the cold.

Her confrontation with her husband had taken a nasty turn, she said in a low voice. At first, John kept yelling at her. But her silence soon drove him crazy. He hit her once, she said, then once again; as she stepped back, he suddenly hurled himself upon her, and she fled in panic before him. Her voice exploded with distress. "But I had nowhere to run to, Walt. I was trapped!"

John had cornered her in the bedroom, knocked her down and beaten her, with savage satisfaction. All his bitterness had exploded in a perverse catharsis.

"I was afraid to scream, to call for help." She was desperately fighting her tears now, as forgotten horrors surfaced from the past. "We were in Moscow. We were American diplomats. Our apartment was under surveillance. The slightest disturbance would bring the police and the KGB running." She could do nothing but double up on the floor and try to protect her face from the hail of savage blows.

"I was desperate. I didn't know what to do." She took a couple of steps into the water. The waves growled around her, soaking her robe up to her thighs. The first drops of the tropical rain splashed on his face and he took her by the shoulders. "Let's go, Barbara."

She turned to him. "I didn't scream," she kept repeating, her fingers clutching his arms. "I didn't scream." Not even when John ripped her clothes, a wild grin distorting his face. He kicked and punched her till he managed to part her legs.

No, Meredith thought, his throat suddenly dry, no, it couldn't be.

"He raped me!" she cried out. "Walt, he raped me!" She couldn't control herself anymore. Bitter sobs shook her chest as the rain came down in a sudden outburst, streaming over her face, which distant lightning colored a sickly pallor. Her hands were locked on his wrists and she was shaking him as if possessed. "He raped me, his own wife! He was panting, and gurgling and laughing like a madman. Oh God, I wanted to kill him."

She let him go, took a few disjointed steps, and collapsed on her knees on the wet sand. "I would have killed him," she rasped. "I would have killed him if only I could."

He hugged her closely and pulled her up, bending over her to protect her from the rain. "Why did he do that to me, Walt?" She was moaning now. "Why did I deserve that?"

"Revenge," he muttered, but she didn't seem to hear. "The sonofabitch wanted you to pay for his humiliation."

They scurried back in the sand, chased by the rain. He pulled her into a cluster of palms and made her sit on a fallen trunk, pointlessly wiping her face. She gradually regained control of herself. Two days later, she said, determined to bring her story to its end, they were separately whisked out of the country by a badly scared ambassador. The scandal was hushed up, although it turned out that the entire embassy staff knew of the affair John Stuart was having with the cultural attaché. John was fired from the State Department, and after their divorce married his adoring mistress and returned to his father's bank in Boston.

"Let's go," she said, and stepped into the rain, then stopped and looked back at him. The raindrops savagely whipped her exposed face. "I heard he is very successful and very happy."

"And you?" he asked. Through the wavering sheets of rain he made out the blurred contours of their bungalow.

There was a long pause. She removed a lock of hair plastered over her forehead. "I found you," she breathed, and ran up the steps into the black doorway.

They had never been so close as that night in Cozumel, Meredith now thought. And they had never been so far apart as last night, when they had gone to sleep like strangers, already resigned to their parting.

He glanced at his watch. It was barely 3:20 P.M., and Rainey wouldn't be back before another couple of hours at least. He was too tense to sleep, too numb to read. He got up and switched on the television set. On the screen, a handsome blond fellow had just won back his lovely sweetheart because he started using Dentyne.

The *Fidelis* sailed into port shortly after sunset. It was a forty-six-foot Bertram Sportfish, its sturdy white bulk topped with a flying bridge and a marlin tower. She was at least four or five years old, but in fine condition and virtually loaded with fishing equipment. Two middle-aged men, whose martial poses couldn't conceal their impressive girth, stood on the yacht's deck. The taller one was dressed in a blue polo shirt, long tan slacks, and brand-new sneakers. His baseball cap was adorned with the blue, white, and red colors of the French flag and the slogan "Quebec Libre." His friend wore shorts. His pink fat thighs were badly sunburned. They proudly held up a medium-sized bonefish and a smaller silvery tarpon, its armor-plated gill covers dully gleaming. The two Canadian girls, in sexy tops and tight white jeans, scurried on their high heels down the pier toward the boat, cheering and waving.

From his observation point beside the marina office, Meredith could see the two men turn and speak to somebody in the yacht, then depart in an effusion of thanks, good-byes, and unexpected eruptions of booming laughter. They went down onto the pier without the fish and passed by Meredith, closely holding their girls. They were slightly swaying, and Meredith could tell by their flushed faces and glazed eyes that old Chuck was right. Those two had been too busy uncapping beer bottles all day to waste energy on fighting the big fish.

At the moment Chuck was on the pier, busy mooring the *Fidelis*. He heard Meredith's footsteps and cast a look at him over his shoulder. "Hi," he panted. "I was just going to tell Steve—"

"It's okay," Meredith said. "I'll talk to him myself." As he stepped toward the yacht Chuck called after him, "You'd better take off your shoes, mister. Steve might get upset." Steve Rainey was obviously a respected man in Islamorada.

He bent down and removed his shoes. He had left his jacket and tie in his room. He rolled up his sleeves. As he straightened up he saw a man watching him. He was standing on the *Fidelis* deck, his arms crossed. Dusk was quickly falling, and all he could see at first was a mop of long sandy hair bleached to a dirty white shade. "Good evening," Meredith said, "may I talk to you?"

The man silently nodded, and Meredith climbed aboard. Rainey was lean, of medium height, in a sleeveless t-shirt and crumpled khaki shorts. He had powerful shoulders and bulging arms. A thin golden chain glowed on his throat. "My name is Walt Meredith," he said. "You must be Steve Rainey."

"That's right," Rainey said. His voice was hoarse, reserved. The dead fish lay at his feet.

"I am with the Defense Department," Meredith said. "I am the director of the Bureau of MIA Affairs. Came down from Washington this morning. Could we go somewhere and talk?"

"Talk about what?" Rainey asked flatly. The tropical night was settling down, and a dark mass was creeping low over the ocean, chased by sudden gusts of wind. The lights in the marina came on, and the nearest globe shed a faint illumination on Rainey's features. He was about forty, in excellent shape. His pale blue eyes made a sharp contrast with his deeply tanned skin. A long scar ran across the right side of his face between the bridge of the nose and the clear-cut angle of the jaw. The streak of discolored tissue didn't disfigure him, though. It bestowed upon the swarthy face a challenging, faintly cruel expression that gave Rainey a rugged, daredevil look.

"You were a captain in the Thirty-seventh Marine regiment in Vietnam," Meredith said. Rainey sucked his teeth. His pale eyes had a cold blank expression. "I want to talk to you about the patrol you led to Na-san."

For a long moment Rainey observed him without speaking. Far away to the west a succession of streaks of lightning snaked in the clouds and distant thunder rolled over the waves.

"I led several patrols to Na-san," Rainey said finally. "Which one are you talking about?"

"The last," Meredith said. "February '69, after the Tet offensive." There was a sudden spell of silence between two gusts of wind.

"What about the patrol?" Rainey asked, sucking his teeth again.

"I'd like to check some details with you."

"Check with me," Rainey repeated, tilting his head back. His eyes narrowed, and angry furrows emerged in the skin around them.

"Yes." Meredith nodded. "I'd like to know how

many soldiers took part in that patrol, what exactly happened, when—"

"What's that got to do with the MIA bureau or whatever?" Rainey was overtly hostile.

"We found the body of an American soldier at Nasan." Meredith picked his words carefully. "We haven't identified it yet. We believe it might be the body of one of the missing soldiers of your patrol."

"No way," Rainey said. "The missing soldiers of my patrol were accounted for. Now will you excuse me and leave me alone? I don't want to talk about Vietnam, okay?" He crouched beside the dead fish. "Excuse me," he repeated, his voice rude, impatient. "I have some work to do, and it's going to be quite messy."

Meredith shook his head. "Look, I need that information very badly. Can't we go somewhere and talk?" On the pier, Chuck had finished tying up the boat and was watching them, his mouth slightly open.

"This is as good a place as any," Rainey said. "Besides, there's nothing to talk about. Will you please go away?"

"Now, listen . . ." Meredith started.

A killer gaff and a long-bladed knife lay beside the fish. Rainey grasped the ugly head of the tarpon with his left hand, took the knife in his right, and looked up at Meredith. Then he stuck the knife in the tarpon's belly and with a swift, violent move ripped it open. Blood and guts spurted out and spilled on the deck. Rainey threw the knife down and stood up. Blood had spattered on his bare feet. "Will you go now?" he repeated.

"I saw Colonel Briggs yesterday," Meredith said. "He told me—"

"I don't give a shit about what he told you," Rainey rasped. "I don't want to talk to you."

"Look, Captain, this is an official inquiry," Meredith lied. "You are required by law to cooperate."

Rainey took a step toward him. "Cut the crap, Meredith," he muttered. "I wrote a report about Na-san and it's in my file. It's been there for fifteen years. I ain't required to do nothing else. Now get off my ship or else..."

"Or else what?" Meredith said, unruffled.

Rainey defiantly placed his hand on his waist. Meredith noticed a tiny Marine eagle tattooed on his right arm "Or else," he growled, his face suddenly hateful, distorted, "I'll throw you overboard. Got it, Mr. Defense Department?"

He shrugged. "It's your ship."

The first heavy drops of rain splashed on his face as he stepped down onto the pier. Chuck was gaping at him in alarm, his face haggard.

He spent more than an hour in his car, lights off, the tropical torrent furiously pounding on the windshield. He was dead sure now that something sinister had happened in Na-san and that Rainey was personally involved in it. But he could bet Rainey wouldn't talk, and he would have to try his luck elsewhere. He had nothing to do here anymore. Still he waited, lighting one cigarette after another. Finally he saw Rainey jump off the yacht and run along the pier holding an oilskin over his head. He hurriedly stubbed his cigarette in the ashtray. The former captain stepped into the phone booth beside the marina office and fed some coins into the slot. He dialed a number and spoke into the mouthpiece, turning about so that he stared straight at Meredith's car. Meredith could swear that Rainey knew he was there and didn't care.

But he couldn't hear Rainey's gruff voice as he spoke into the phone. "I called to warn you," Rainey was saying to his party, hundreds of miles away, "that a man called Walt Meredith is prying into the Minerva affair."

PART II

★

THE QUEST

✪ 6 ✪

White and thick and armored, the doors opened before him in a dry snapping of locks and closed behind his back with dull metallic thuds that reverberated along the endless corridors. White and starched and anonymous were the uniforms of the two men who walked slightly ahead of him, a tall, scrawny black holding a bunch of keys and a squat Mexican, his salient cheekbones and jet-black hair attesting to his Indian origins. From the tiny portholes in the doors along the corridors eyes were watching him, some of them wide open, focused in space, some dull and brooding, others narrow and hateful, but all of them tainted with hopeless, infinite madness. And from behind the padded doors screams and moans and whispers sounded at his approach, muffled sobs and monotonous groans or desperate appeals from cracked and maimed minds.

And as he followed his two escorts he thought that his secret quest might well end here, in the closed wing of a Colorado madhouse. Here, in the Alma Viva Sanatorium, lay his last hope. For all his efforts till now had miserably failed and the solution was as distant, as inaccessible, as it had been on the day he set out on his search.

After the disastrous meeting with Steve Rainey he had spent two days in vain efforts to reach the second former Marine, Lyndon Hughes, in Montana. He kept calling his home but he couldn't get past his neurotic, high-strung wife. Lyndon wasn't home, she would stubbornly repeat, although a couple of times he distinctly heard a male voice in the background. Who was he, Mrs. Hughes asked, and what did he want, he could tell her everything, Lyndon kept no secrets from her, and why didn't he leave his name and phone number and Lyndon would call him back. Which Lyndon never did. And his initial suspicions quickly grew into certainty. Hughs didn't want to talk to him. Hughes had been warned, probably by Rainey, and had willingly joined him in a conspiracy of silence.

But if conspiracy there was, it was bound to shield a secret linked to the enigmatic death of the Unknown Soldier. Were Rainey and Hughes involved in the murder of an American soldier? And was Eddie Paris, the third ex-Marine, a member of the conspiracy? Meredith had called Patty Hurwitz, his secretary, to find out if she had succeeded in locating Paris. A petite, dark, and lonely girl, Patty was ridded with complexes because of her plain looks and her two broken marriages. But she was smart, stubborn, and devoted to her job. By her conspiratorial tone he deduced that the shrewd little woman had sensed there was something secret and not quite regular in his request, although she couldn't guess what it was.

No, she said, she hadn't been able to find any Paris in Baltimore, therefore she had turned to the Marine Corps Veterans' Association. But Paris didn't figure on their lists either. And if a former Marine didn't figure on their lists, it would be for one of two reasons. One reason could be that he had left the country for good.

"And the second?" he asked.

"That he is dead," she replied.

And that had left him with no other choice but to dial Colorado information and ask for the number of Alma Viva.

The director of the hospital, a Dr. Hardie, was rather sympathetic on the phone. Yes, he said after hearing his request, Frank Wyatt was a patient of the hospital, but he was a hopeless case, didn't Mr. Meredith know? He strongly doubted that Frank Wyatt could ever give any coherent answer to Mr. Meredith's questions. Anyway, Dr. Hardie added, he would willingly cooperate with the Defense Department, but in order to visit the patient Mr. Meredith needed the consent of the ward administrator, the patient's doctor, and his next of kin. The request should be done in writing, naturally, we never do that by telephone.

"Well, if you insist, Mr. Meredith, you can try. Hang on, I'll connect you," the amiable Dr. Hardie said. And Meredith's call plunged down into the intricate labyrinth of the hospital's hierarchy. He negotiated his way from switchboard to switchboard and from one official to another, charming some with deference and easy humor, bullying others with imaginary warnings against impeding a national security operation, by turns threatening, explaining, cajoling, inventing. Finally he let out a deep sigh of satisfaction when Dr. Leahy, Frank Wyatt's personal psychiatrist, gave his agreement.

"Under normal conditions I would have objected," Leahy said, "but in this case I shall not stand in your way. Frank Wyatt is incurable, and there's nothing that can make his situation worse. I doubt you could get anything from him. On the other hand, you might trigger a reaction. . . . Who knows?"

When he asked about the next of kin, Frank Wyatt's wife, he was surprised to hear that she was at the hospital. "She'll be with you in a moment," Dr. Leahy said.

But he was twice as surprised when the warm, melodious voice of a young woman, so incongruous in the grim context of a mental hospital, filled the receiver. "Jane Wyatt," the voice said. He identified himself and concisely outlined his request, hesitating a moment before clumsily uttering the words "your husband." Good God, he thought, the man has been mad for twelve years, could she really think of him as her husband?

When she spoke again her voice was reserved, oddly strained. She couldn't give him an answer right away. She said she preferred to talk to him face-to-face and then make up her mind. He started arguing, but she cut him short. "There's no use, Mr. Meredith." Her voice was gentle but firm. "I'll meet you here, and we'll discuss the matter. You can come whenever you wish. I'll be with Frankie."

She was with Frankie indeed, down on her knees in the padded cell, speaking softly, soothingly, feeding with infinite tenderness the miserable wretch that squatted in the corner. From the slit in the door, which he had approached on the mute invitation of the stubby Mexican nurse, he saw her from the back: a honey-blond woman in a cream-colored blouse and a jean skirt, holding a white bowl and pouring into the gaping mouth spoonfuls of some dark-brown mush. But Meredith's look hardly dwelt upon her.

His eyes were riveted to the pitiful creature that once had been Frank Wyatt. He had been preparing for the shock; still he felt a sharp pang of revulsion at the sight of the skeletal figure in the gray pajamas and woolen socks that tightly huddled against the walls, as if seeking refuge from an unspeakable horror. The body had shrunk to the size of a small, starved child. The chest was inwardly sunk. The arms and legs protruding from the loose gray garments were nothing but mere lengths of fleshless bone enveloped in waxen skin. The skull-like head, topped with sparse tufts of hair, was rammed deep between the upraised shoulders. And between the sallow forehead and the gaunt hollow cheeks, two black, enormous eyes were frozen in a lifeless, unseeing stare. Some of the substance that his wife was feeding him trickled down from the corners of his mouth, mixed with saliva.

A mélange of contrasting emotions, disgust and compassion and pity, enveloped Meredith. Then a wave of despair surged into his heart. Could the solution to the ghastly mystery that haunted him lurk somewhere in the diseased mind of Frank Wyatt? Was there any force on earth that could extract that secret, any secret, from its impregnable armor of sheer madness? How could he expect that this demented manikin might ever understand his questions, and even if he did, be able to answer them? He was fighting a battle he could not win. The answer he was after would be buried with the Unknown at the end of the month, when the flags at Arlington would plunge to half-mast to the sad call of a bugle.

"Excuse me," the nurse said, and Meredith moved

aside. "Mrs. Wyatt," the Mexican softly called, looking into the cell. "Mrs. Wyatt, there's somebody to see you." He waited a moment, then opened the door, and Meredith found himself facing Jane Wyatt.

After hearing her voice on the phone the previous day, he expected to meet a young, maybe even attractive, woman. But he was totally unprepared for the vivid radiance exuding from her open smile and her sparkling green eyes. Jane Wyatt was in her mid-thirties, a tall, voluptuous woman with a slim waist and a lovely, passionate face. She had a direct, confident look and a firm handshake. "Mr. Meredith? I've been expecting you." It was her large, slightly protruding mouth, he decided, that imprinted on her face its sensual appeal. Her full dark lips looked as though carved on the smooth ivory skin.

She was speaking to the Mexican, handing him the white bowl. "Will you please finish feeding him, José? He's quiet today." And turning back to him: "Is anything wrong, Mr. Meredith?"

Her words jolted him back to reality. Good God, he realized with a start, he certainly had picked the right time and place to stare at a woman like that. In an insane asylum, in front of her mad husband. He couldn't help smiling, amused by the absurdity of the situation. "It's okay," he managed. "Can we go somewhere and talk?"

She smiled back, slightly puzzled. The tiny dimples on her cheeks bestowed a youthful, mischievous air on her face. "Let's go to my office," she said.

"Your office?"

She nodded lightly. "Didn't they tell you? I work here. It's been more than ten years now."

She led the way through some more doors, which

she unlocked with her passkey. The black nurse had stayed with the Mexican in Frank Wyatt's cell. He walked closely behind her, troubled by her appeal, casting oblique looks at her long, strong legs. As she locked behind her the main door to the ward, their eyes met. "You saw Frankie," she said. There was a flash of pain in the green eyes.

He nodded.

"Today is a good day," she said, and he discerned the slight quiver of her lips as she smiled again. "He might get quite disturbed, you know." She stopped, spontaneously reaching for his arm. "But not violent." She seemed very keen to impress that upon him. "He never gets violent. He's never hurt anybody."

Her office was a mere cubicle at the end of a cold, dark corridor. "Reuben Leahy's office is across the hall," she said as they squeezed in. Her ramshackle desk was laden with files and typewritten documents. Several fat volumes on psychology stood on a rack on the wall. But most of the wall was covered with weird, disturbing drawings, probably the work of some Alma Viva inmates. On the opposite wall hung a framed diploma from the University of Colorado testifying that Jane Wyatt had obtained a master's degree in psychology in 1977.

Meredith raised his eyebrows. "Impressive," he said.

She had settled in her chair, across the desk. "I always wanted to study psychology," she explained. "When Frankie came back, in '72, I joined the hospital as a volunteer nurse, just to be close to him. I took evening courses in psychology for five years, and now I'm fully employed here."

"As a psychologist?"

She shrugged. "Psychologist, nurse, assistant to Reuben Leahy, anything they let me do."

"I thought you spent all your time with your husband," he said, sitting down in the only other chair.

She shook her head. "I couldn't even if I wanted to, that's against hospital regulations. I've got a lot of other patients."

He pointed at the leather-framed photograph of a handsome young man in Marine uniform that stood at the corner of the desk. "That him?"

"Was," she corrected. "That was him." She paused, then she spoke again in a very quiet, very tired voice, as if she was repeating a formula learned by heart. "Six foot two, a hundred and seventy pounds, the best athlete at the University of Colorado and a brilliant student of artificial intelligence. Computers, that is."

A tense silence suddenly pervaded the room.

"Now, Mrs. Wyatt—" he started, but she interrupted him.

"I expected your call," she said.

He frowned. "I don't understand."

She nodded. "The evening before you spoke to me, I got a phone call from Steve Rainey."

"You know him?" he asked, nervously lighting a cigarette. She pushed toward him a massive pewter ashtray.

"Sure. I met him quite a few times after Frankie came back." She didn't seem too eager to talk about her relationship with Rainey. "Anyway, he called and said that a certain Walt Meredith . . ."—she cast him a long, level look—"was harassing former Marines, asking questions about Na-san."

"Did he say—harassing?" Meredith asked, annoyed.

114

"Steve said that you were a Pentagon official, but he made some inquiries and found out that you were acting on your own initiative, without official authorization." The level, inquisitive look again. "He expects you to be recalled as soon as your superiors find out what you're doing."

He shook his head, clenching his teeth in anger. Rainey was smarter than he thought. He wondered who he had called at the Pentagon. He had to expect that kind of reaction, but it came too soon. They could throw him out of the hospital any moment now if they learned he had bluffed his way in.

She watched him closely, but there was no hostility in her eyes. "Steve insisted that I should refuse to talk to you or let you see Frankie. He said you were bad news. You could only stir up painful memories that we are all trying to forget."

"What did you answer?" he asked.

She ignored the question. "He was very persuasive," she said. "He almost convinced me."

"Almost?"

She nodded. "I also made a few phone calls and learned what you've been doing for the families of the missing boys." She smiled dryly. "I also was an MIA family once."

"That's why you didn't refuse to see me outright?"

She nodded again. "And that's why I didn't tell Reuben Leahy that you had misled him." She was idly drawing small sad faces on a yellow pad with a chewed-out pencil. "May I have one of your cigarettes?"

"Sure." He lit it for her and leaned back, watching her. A heavy lock of hair fell on her forehead and she impatiently tossed it back.

"I'd like to forget Steve's phone call if you give me a good reason," she said slowly. "And when I say good reason, I mean your real motives, not the cover story you told everybody else. I want to know why a Pentagon official would leave his office and fly all over the country, spending his money and lying to people, to investigate a rather banal incident that occurred fifteen years ago."

He took a deep breath and stubbed out his cigarette. "If you insist," he said.

In the turbulent days that followed, that odd, dark afternoon kept surfacing in his memory. And he couldn't help wondering what had made him overcome his natural reticence and reveal his most precious secrets to a person he had just met. Was it the feeling that he had reached the end of the road and if he failed now his endeavor was doomed? Had the burden of his secret become too heavy for him, and he needed to share it with somebody who had undergone an affliction similar to his own? Or perhaps it was Jane Wyatt's sincere compassion as she listened to him, her face distraught, her eyes locked into his own. Jane Wyatt was a total stranger after all, a woman he didn't know. Still, he revealed everything to her, including the grisly details about the scorched, bullet-ridden body, the conclusions of the ballistics report, and the terrible suspicions that haunted his thoughts.

Once this secret was off his chest, he briefly hesitated. He had just dealt Jane Wyatt a terrible blow. He had implicitly insinuated that her husband might have taken part in a murder. She had the right to know why he was stirring up the shadows of the past now, why he had set on his grim crusade fifteen years after Na-san.

Nothing but the whole truth, he felt, could convince Jane Wyatt of the honesty of his motives. The formal arguments about the MIA families' struggle and the honor of the American Army suddenly seemed to him hollow, oddly trite. And in his eagerness to win her support, he laid himself bare before her. Unlocking for the first time the most intimate, the most private chambers of his soul, he described his own hell, his excruciating longing for the little boy who was gone, for Benjamin.

He couldn't tell how long he spoke, but when he fell silent dusk had already descended upon the tiny room and they were sitting in the thickening obscurity. Jane Wyatt was immobile in her chair, very rigid, her eyes two fading sparks in the invading darkness. For a while she seemed stunned, unable to utter a word. Then, slowly, she emerged from her stupor. "You say," she cleared her throat, "you say the Unknown might have been murdered. And Frankie might be one of the killers."

He didn't answer.

"That's a horrible accusation." Her voice, in contrast to her words, was low, muffled. "Horrible."

"I know," he admitted.

"If it's true, then . . ." She suddenly buried her face in her hands and a desperate sob shook her body.

A lump contracted his throat as he watched her fight to regain control over herself. He wanted to touch her, comfort her, but he couldn't budge.

She was breathing deeply. "Steve, too . . ." she started, then paused. "What does Steve know of the . . . the ballistics report?"

"Nobody knows a thing," he said, "nobody but you and Laura Lewis. She's the president of the League of

117

MIA Families. I had to tell her." Laura Lewis suddenly seemed to him very far, very irrelevant.

She nodded. "And you set out on this investigation," her voice sank to a murmur, "because of your son." If Barbara had said that to him, he would have indignantly denied it, but now he just sat still. She suddenly reached across the desk and gently touched his hand. "You must have loved him very much," she whispered, and he nodded in the dark, answering to himself, yes, he did love him very much, and he did feel responsible for his death. And he felt grateful to her for showing concern for him, for his distress, instead of jumping at him for accusing her husband of taking part in a murder back in Vietnam.

"Will you help me?" he asked.

She didn't answer for a long moment, and he thought that she hadn't heard his question. "Yes," she finally said, "yes, I'll help you."

He broke three matches trying to light another cigarette.

"Not because of you or the MIA League," she admitted. She had calmed down and her voice was controlled, reflective. "But I must find out if Frankie took part in a murder that night at Na-san. And if that was what caused his madness."

"Thank you," he said. "Thank you very much." He clumsily got up as she switched on her desk lamp. Her eyes were dry. "Well, I guess I should be on my way. I'll be back tomorrow."

His hand was on the doorknob when she spoke, her voice uncertain. "Don't go, please. I'm afraid I can't face all this alone." He turned back. She was bravely trying to smile. "Why don't you stay and have dinner with me?"

"Well . . ." he started, surprised. "Sure, I'd like that. I guess that . . ." He stopped abruptly, in a sudden need of a cigarette. "You certainly know the restaurants—"

"No," she said, "I don't feel like people tonight. We'll have dinner at my house, all right?"

The raucous, desperate voice of Bruce Springsteen on the stereo followed them as they took their drinks out to the back porch. The spacious deck overlooked a gently sloping valley whose outlines were softened by the faint moonlight. Jane Wyatt's cottage was in the hilly outskirts of Mesa, barely a few miles from the hospital. He had liked the house for its pleasant simplicity whose only exception was the multitude of paintings hanging all over the place, bright-colored, vaguely Impressionist tableaux that suited her vivacious character.

The dinner, too, had been quite simple—steaks, salad, and a bottle of St. Émilion. By an unspoken agreement, they didn't mention the Unknown anymore and avoided any allusion to Meredith's search. At the beginning their conversation was forced, rather artificial. But as the hours went by, and a second bottle of wine made its appearance, the awkward tension slowly faded away. By the end of the meal, flattered by her questions, charmed by her spontaneity, he had told her quite a lot about himself, his past in the Marines and with the Company, his life with Barbara.

"I have a right to one question too," he said as they settled into two comfortable wicker chairs on the dark porch. "How come you're such a happy person? You spend most of your time in a madhouse, your husband is in bad shape, and still you seem so pleased with everything."

She let out a short laugh. "That was why you stared at me like that when you first saw me." Her spontaneous, uninhibited behavior only intensified her charm.

He sighed. "You noticed."

The silvery laugh again. "Of course. You're not the first who is surprised. Well, you see, I like what I'm doing. I am fascinated by working with those people. Frankie is in bad shape, as you say. I had to learn to live with that, even if it was quite a nightmare at first. But other patients are making amazing progress. Some of them really get cured. I think there's nothing as fascinating as the human mind. And there's nothing as fulfilling as the taste of success when one of your patients makes a step forward, even if it's only one little step."

He took a sip of his wine. "When did you realize that you wanted to work with those people? When your husband came back?"

"No," she said, "it was years before, I guess." She got up and leaned on the banister, looking down at the valley. Her figure was clearly outlined on the clear night sky. "I can't really pinpoint the moment I made up my mind. But I believe it was something that I saw when I was a teenager, in Switzerland."

"Switzerland? You lived over there?"

"For a couple of years." She turned back to face him, leaning on the railing. "My father was an importer of watches, clocks, timing mechanisms. Did you see the grandfather's clock in the living room?"

"It looks very old," he remarked.

"That's what they call a museum piece. It's from my father's private collection. Anyway, we spent two years with him at La Chaux de Fonds, one of the centers of the watchmaking industry, in the mountains near Neuchâtel. A very boring place." She paused. "You really want to hear about this?"

"Yes," he said, "please."

"Okay. Once, in the first year I was there, I had to take a train, a local. It was early morning, and pitch dark. It was cold on the track, but there was this glass booth in the middle of the platform. It was full of people and seemed heated. There was white mist on the inside of the windows. The faces of the people inside were blurred. I rushed in and sat down at the edge of a wooden bench."

She paused. "The first thing that struck me were the voices. Shrill, high-pitched, some of them slurred. I looked up. There were eleven or twelve people in the booth, three boys and eight or nine girls of different ages. And they all had something monstrous in their faces. There were a couple of Mongoloids, two squat women with tousled hair and short arms, big round faces and small round eyes. One of the boys had a sparse beard, another's mouth was open, his lower lip dangling. A blond-haired girl and a boy with glasses were eating sweets and giggling foolishly, like idiots."

"They were idiots, weren't they?"

"It took me a while to realize they were. Another girl looked almost normal, but when she opened her mouth she kept stuttering for a full minute. But she seemed very proud of her red jacket, red slacks, red socks, and red sneakers."

"Little Red Riding Hood," he offered.

"I panicked," she admitted. "I suddenly realized I was in the middle of a tribe of retarded . . . of idiots. I had no idea what they were doing there. Some of them looked strangely at me. That was weird. I retreated into my corner, afraid to move. The only reassuring sight was a little boy who sat beside me. He was dark-skinned, probably Greek or Italian, the child of an immigrant worker. He looked normal, although on the skinny side. He was totally indifferent to the idiots, and very busy stuffing into his knapsack boxes of chewing gum, chocolates, and mints. At the same time he was gulping quantities of sweets. His mouth never stopped working. Still, I waited for the train in terror. Here I was, a sixteen-year-old American girl, sharing a glass cage with a family of Swiss nuts."

He chuckled, amused by the way she compressed the absurd situation into a single phrase.

"What scared me most"—she was looking at her glass—"was that an entire family—brothers, sisters, children—had turned into idiots. I couldn't understand how it had happened. Some rotten genes, perhaps? And then the girl in red—Little Red Riding Hood—asked the bearded boy, '*Co . . . comment est ta maman?*' How is your mother? And I breathed more easily. His mother wasn't hers, therefore they weren't brother and sister. They were just a group of retarded going somewhere together."

"All the village idiots," he said.

"The little boy had finished stuffing his goodies into his bag and now was stuffing bubble gum into his mouth. Then he stood in front of one of the Mongoloid girls, blowing huge pink bubbles and exploding them in her face. She started screaming and crying, panicked. I suddenly grasped that they were more scared than I.

"The train came and they all ran toward a car where some other retarded youngsters were sitting." She seemed to smile in the dark. "I ran to the last car, in the opposite direction. At Les Hauts Geneveys I saw all of them getting off. There were a lot of people at the station, and the idiots huddled in a corner. They looked alarmed, insecure. Two nuns in black robes were checking their plastic bags."

"It must have been an outing of some church school for retarded kids," he said.

"Probably. The blond girl with the thin legs and the boy with the glasses were holding hands. Little Red Riding Hood was foolishly swirling around beside a small puddle left from the last night's rain. A teenager in blue coveralls passed by, and when he saw the idiot he jumped on purpose into the puddle. Muddy water splashed all over her, and her clothes were drenched. The poor idiot stood still, helpless, staring at her soiled outfit, then at the boy who had done this to her. Scream at him, I wanted to shout, hit him, kick the bastard for what he did to you. But she kept staring at the boy, her arms dangling at her sides. The train moved away, and I suddenly started to cry. I felt for her and for her wretched friends." She fell silent.

"And that's why you went to study psychology," he concluded.

She shrugged. "I was quite shaken by that experience, you know. I guess that . . . yes, that might have been the main reason."

"I thought it had to do with your husband," he said carefully.

She put her glass down and rubbed her bare arms. It was getting cold. "Before Frankie came back," she said, "I was planning to study psychology, but never did anything about it. After I saw him, though, I felt I couldn't waste time anymore." She suddenly became aware of the silence inside. "Will you excuse me a moment? I'd like to turn the record over."

"Sure," he said. She went in, and a moment later he heard Springsteen again. "I ain't nothing but tired," the hoarse voice sang. "Man, I'm just tired and bored with myself; hey there, baby, I could use just a little help."

I could use a little help, too, Meredith thought, and the quiet, cool night, the blurred sky, the unfamiliar surroundings, and the woman moving inside stirred in him a sharp pang of loneliness. What am I doing here, he said to himself, shouldn't I be back home where I belong? Why can't I, as Barbara said, let things be?

Jane Wyatt was back on the porch. She had put on a white, loose sweater. "I brought the bottle," she said. "Would you like some more?"

He gratefully drank the smooth red wine. She had returned to her place by the railing. "Tell me," he suddenly said, emboldened by the alcohol. "You're young, you're attractive, and . . . you're human. How could you stay married to your husband for all those years?"

She raised her glass: "I expected that question." She took a few steps to the far corner of the deck and back. "As a matter of fact, it started as a challenge." Her voice became one shade softer. "You see, I was very close to Frankie."

"You loved him very much, I guess."

"Yes." The answer was tinged with impatience, as if she didn't wish to dwell upon the subject. "My parents didn't love him though, not at all. His family was very poor, he was lower class, he went to college on a football scholarship—in short, he was not good enough for the only daughter of Albert Sondheimer. My father. I didn't care. I was infatuated with him, he was the first real man in my life. We got married against my parents' will. That's why we got married so young, by the way. We had to do it before he went to Vietnam. Otherwise..." She let the phrase hang in the air, unfinished. "Anyway, after he came back from North Vietnam, my parents arrived. They came to this house for the first time in their lives."

She let out a bitter laugh. "Actually, we had our conversation here, on the deck. Frankie was in Alma Viva already. For my parents it was clear that I was going to divorce him, immediately, on grounds of insanity. 'You were married only a couple of years,' my father said, 'you'll make a new life for yourself.' They had it all planned, you see? Like they had it all planned for me before, till I met Frankie. The little fine girl from the little fine family. What I thought or felt didn't really matter."

She took a sip of her drink. "So I said no. We were here, on the porch, and my father and mother were sitting in those two chairs. I said I was going to take care of Frankie, and go back to school, and live my own life. They were stunned. And that's how it started."

He frowned. "And you never had second thoughts afterward? You didn't feel you were making a mistake?"

"Of course I did," she said. "I had some rough times. And as you said, I'm human. I had a few affairs, one of which was very intense." She sighed. "It was hard getting over that one, when it ended."

He preferred to keep quiet.

"But I had my work, my studies, and I took care of Frankie. I live a full life now."

"And your parents?"

She shook her head. "My father's dead. But my

125

mother still expects me to come back to my senses." A cloud slowly crept over the moon and the darkness thickened. He heard her making a few steps, then settling in the chair beside him. "What do the French say?" she asked. *"C'est la vie.* That's life."

"And at times you get very lonesome," he said softly.

She didn't answer.

They sat silent for a long time. Bruce Springsteen's voice had also faded away, but his poignant, disturbing outcry still hung in the air. When she spoke again he suddenly realized that tonight, for a very short time, he had forgotten his own ordeal.

"I don't understand," she said. "Why did you wait three whole years before deciding to do something about Benjamin? What made you suddenly resign from the . . . the Company, as you call it, and apply for the Pentagon job? The end of the war?"

He shook his head. "No, not the end of the war. It had nothing to—"

"So why didn't you do that earlier?" she interrupted. "Didn't you care for Benjamin before?"

Oh yes, he wanted to say, I did care about Benjamin. I thought of him, and remembered him. He haunted my sleepless nights and rose in my nightmares. But I had been trained to despise my emotions, to be ashamed of my weaknesses, to be a man. And he suddenly wanted to describe his childhood in the austere New England community of Brenton, Vermont, to engrave into her mind the gaunt, ascetic features of his despotic father, the high school principal Joshua Meredith, and make her hear his dry, humorless voice, his long sermons about being strong, and manly, and unyielding, his solemn quoting of the British concept about keeping a stiff upper lip. Emotions and crying and hurting is for girls, his father used to say, and his servile, self-effacing mother and sisters never dared to contradict him.

That's how he was raised—molded and trained and indoctrinated to be a man. And a man he had been, a tough Marine officer, a daredevil mercenary in Vietnam, a cold, cynical CIA agent, hunting his defectors all over Europe, ready to yank his prey from the lion's mouth. His father would have been proud of him, of his big boy who never cried and never succumbed to emotional weakness. And when the news about Benjamin missing in action had reached him, he had acted like his father would have expected him to. Grind your teeth, keep a stiff upper lip, carry on, boy, be a man!

He didn't tell her all that, but she must have guessed some of it with her sharp instincts, for she was with him, understanding, very close, when he spoke. "There was this Israeli general I met in Washington..." he started, and paused in a sudden surge of panic, for he realized he was about to tell her things he hadn't admitted even to himself, never before. "It was in '74, in the winter. He was a member of a military intelligence delegation that came for talks on the Soviet buildup in the Middle East. His name was David Sturmann, and he was one of the most legendary fighters of Israel, a real hero. He had fought in the war for independence and led commando raids into Egypt and Jordan. He had been wounded in the Six Day War and was awarded the highest military medal."

"You knew about him beforehand?"

He lit a cigarette, the sudden flicker of light blinding him momentarily. Then his eyes got accustomed to the darkness again and her visage emerged from the black, the clear eyes faintly glowing, the full lips parted. "I had heard quite a lot about him," he said.

His mind wandered back to that bitterly cold day in Langley Woods. There were four American representatives in the conference room: himself and Bob Dudley from the CIA, a general from the Pentagon, and one of Kissinger's assistants. The Israelis had arrived, looking rather uncomfortable and ill at ease in their suits and ties. He had eagerly scanned their faces in earnest anticipation of meeting the Israeli hero.

Bob Dudley had introduced the visitors. "David Sturmann," Bob had said, and he had offered his hand to the tall, lanky Israeli with the silver hair and the slack, dark pouches under the eyes. After the meeting was over he had invited him for a drink. And had found himself facing a broken man.

"His son had been reported missing in the Golan Heights during the Yom Kippur War," he said. "He wasn't in the lists of prisoners submitted to the Red Cross. He wasn't in any hospital in Israel. The army authorities were convinced he was alive, as well as fifteen other soldiers missing at the northern front. The army assumed they were held by the Syrians as a secret trump card to use at the forthcoming negotiations. The Syrians are known to be the most ruthless people in the Middle East.

"But Sturmann didn't believe that. He left the division he was commanding in the Sinai to his deputy and flew to the Golan Heights. The boy had been among the soldiers manning an electronic warfare station on top of Mount Hermon. The Syrians had overrun it at the very outbreak of the war, and the Israelis had reconquered it only a few hours before the cease-fire.

Sturmann decided to search for his son's body in the battlefield outside the station. His army friends told him he was out of his mind, the area had been thoroughly combed several times. But he was stubborn as a bulldog."

The cigarette suddenly tasted bitter in his mouth and he dropped it into the ashtray, where it kept glowing, an evil red eye watching them. "It was late winter by then. The land was frozen, some of it covered with snow. Sturmann, all alone, started his search, yard after yard. He was sure that the boy had never left Mount Hermon, but had been killed and buried on the spot, for some reason."

"The Syrians used to bury the enemy dead?" she asked quickly.

"No, never. But this man had . . . what shall I call it, animal instincts? For three weeks he turned up around the station carrying a shovel. A rumor started that he had gone nuts. And finally he found his boy."

He felt she was very close, leaning toward him, holding her breath.

"He found him with another twelve bodies," he said. "They all had their hands tied behind their backs with pieces of wire. They had been murdered, shot at close range. Probably a few hours after they were captured."

"That's why the Syrians buried them," she whispered.

"He dug out all of the thirteen bodies. There wasn't much left of their faces. He recognized his boy by the woolen pullover he was wearing under his uniform. His mother had knitted it for him."

She shivered. "A father finding his own son. My God!"

"They say Sturmann was never the same afterward," he added dryly.

She thought a long moment before speaking again. "And how long after meeting him did you apply for the MIA job?"

"Two weeks," he said, and got up to leave.

✪ 7 ✪

I won't torture you with professional mumbo jumbo," Dr. Leahy said and flashed him a quick, unsteady smile. "I'll try to avoid formulas like morbid depression, negativism, or dementia praecox, even if that might tarnish my learned image." The fleeting, insecure smile again. "I'd just like you to get some basic notions about Frank Wyatt's illness." He waited for Meredith to nod, repeatedly blinking his soft brown eyes.

Meredith smiled vaguely and rubbed the bridge of his nose with his fingertips. He couldn't take his mind off Barbara's hysterical phone call, which had wakened him at dawn. Since leaving Washington he had called her twice, and both times she had been very reserved, very remote, answering his questions with icy monosyllables. But this morning he hardly recognized her distressed voice when the persistent ringing of the phone tore him from an eerie black dream.

As he reached for the phone, painfully surfacing into the bleak dawn, some of his nightmare instantly dissolved, like the blurred shapes on a roll of film fading away at the touch of light. But he still remembered the dream was about the entombment of the Unknown. He still recalled the image of the deserted Ar-

lington cemetery and six grim, black-garbed pallbearers lowering the Unknown's coffin into a bottom-
less grave. The cemetery was swept by torrential rain,
and the muddy water was gushing into the freshly dug
hole. At first he was one of the pallbearers, and everybody was staring at him. And then he wasn't with them
anymore but running across the immense cemetery,
screaming at the pallbearers to stop and remove the
coffin's lid, for he knew with absolute certainty that it
was all a monstrous mistake, and inside the coffin lay a
sad-eyed little boy.

And then the shrill rings had summoned him back
from his dream, and he had awakened, his skin sticky,
his mouth foul. For a long moment he didn't respond
to the voice echoing in the receiver, the image of the
black coffin still etched in his memory. But Barbara
kept calling his name, and the sound of her urgent appeals finally tore the shroud of horror that enveloped
his mind. And her troubled voice pulled him back to
reality.

Somebody had been phoning, Barbara was saying,
all night long, every hour on the hour. He wouldn't
speak, he wouldn't threaten, just hold the phone and
listen till she slammed it down. She was scared, she
didn't know what to do, she was all alone. Perhaps it
was just a freak, he suggested without much conviction, one of those heavy breathers who gets a kick out
of listening to a woman's voice in the middle of their
sexual fantasies.

But even before she answered he saw before him
the roguish, sunburned face of a blond man, a small
Marine eagle tattooed on his forearm, and the guts of
a dead fish spilled on the deck of a smart fishing yacht.
And he could feel, with absolute certainty, that Steve

Rainey had made those calls, that Rainey was stalking him now, doggedly following his trail, set upon preventing him from meeting Lyndon Hughes and gaining access to Frankie Wyatt's cell.

He had soothed Barbara with some trite speculation about obscene calls, which she pretended to accept, apparently from choice, and hung up. Before leaving he called his secretary in Washington to inquire if she had gotten any unusual calls as well. There had been no freak calls, Patty said, giggling, but on the other hand she had gotten two "very very important" calls, one from the Assistant Secretary, she eagerly chirped, and one from Dr. John Natua in Honolulu. They wanted to inform him that the Vietnamese Government had unexpectedly delivered to the military attaché in Hanoi seventeen bodies of Americans killed in the war. That was the first time in eighteen months that the Vietnamese were showing some goodwill in the search for MIA's. The bodies were already being flown to the Central Identification Laboratory in Honolulu. The Assistant Secretary was very excited, Patty said, and asked her to make sure Meredith got the good news at once. Then she fell silent, waiting for Meredith's enthusiastic effusions. Great, Meredith blurted right on cue, terrific, really. He suddenly realized that such news, a couple of weeks ago, would have overjoyed him, but today it left him cold. The one thing that really mattered was the Unknown. He skipped breakfast, drove recklessly to Alma Viva, and was only a few minutes late for his meeting with Jane Wyatt and Dr. Reuben Leahy.

Dr. Leahy was staring at him strangely now, and Meredith realized that his thoughts were still haunted by his obsessive dream. He stared back at the psychiatrist, trying to focus his attention on what he was saying. Dr. Leahy was in his early forties, a lanky, narrow-shouldered man with a small torso and disproportionately long arms and legs. The upper part of his head was quite handsome, Meredith noticed—a shock of graying wavy hair, a clear forehead, and a delicate nose. But the mouth was tiny and feeble, and the short, well-tended beard failed to conceal the receding chin. In his right hand he clenched a briar pipe and punctuated his narrative by swift, precise motions of its crooked stem, as if conducting an invisible orchestra. The pipe, the wood-paneled office, the leather-covered armchair, the framed diplomas on the wall, all seemed to fuse into a conscious effort by Dr. Leahy to project the reassuring image of an old-school psychiatrist.

"Frank Wyatt has been affected by a traumatic shock," Reuben Leahy was saying, "or by a succession of shocks." He blinked at Meredith. "I mean several disruptive experiences. They've plunged him in a state of perpetual horror, coupled with a sense of total helplessness. He couldn't cope with the trauma, therefore he has found refuge in madness."

He cast a quick, uneasy look at Jane Wyatt, who stood by the window, very still. The torrential rain that had started with dawn was furiously lashing the square glass panes, and the branches of the nearby trees, yielding to the wind, swayed before the window.

"Frank knows—unconsciously, of course—that he can't resist or fight the cause of the shock. Therefore he is not violent, and wouldn't react violently to other people. But"—the pipe stem froze in the air, stressing a point—"he might become terribly agitated, searching for an escape from the fears that haunt him. Therefore he would throw himself about, knock his head and body on the walls, and hurt himself seriously."

"That's why he is in a padded cell," Jane offered, still looking out of the window. Her back was ramrod-stiff.

Dr. Leahy paused a second, sucking the unlit pipe. "He has suffered a total blackout. He doesn't remember anything, or anybody." Jane turned, about to speak, and Leahy quickly added, "Jane thinks that he remembers her." He spread his hands. "Perhaps there is a very dim memory, and perhaps he just shows signs of recognizing her because she's been taking care of him for eleven, no, twelve years now."

"Does he ever speak?" Meredith inquired.

"I was coming to that," Leahy said severely, obviously resenting being interrupted. "He can't really speak, in the proper sense of the word. But he utters certain words, or sounds. We are able to understand quite a few of those." He leafed through the yellow file lying on the desk before him. "Here. He very often repeats the word *fire*. He uses it when he reaches the peak of agitation. We don't know if he means fire as in flames, something burning, or fire as in shooting, fighting, you see what I mean?" He was blinking again, staring at Meredith. "You see?"

"Yes," Meredith said. The Unknown's body was found scorched, in a burned hut, he thought.

"He also uses the words *food, mother, dead,* and *cage. Mother* is a very common cry in this sort of case. That's the instinctive appeal for help and protection. *Cage* must be an allusion to the cages in which the Vietcong were keeping their prisoners, sometimes parading the civilians before them to jeer at and insult their American enemies. That practice, exposing the prisoners to the population like animals in a zoo, had a terrible effect upon our boys, as you might know. They did it mostly with pilots."

"Yes, I know."

"Frank often uses two words that seem to be *VC* and *shoot,* but we aren't sure of that. Now"—Leahy pointed the glistening stem of his pipe at Meredith— "we believe he might be able to articulate more words, perhaps even phrases, if we succeed in triggering a short chain of feelings, or reflexes, in his mind. Till now we've totally failed."

Meredith stirred in his seat. "Could it be possible," he slowly started, feeling Jane's eyes boring into his back, "that Frank Wyatt was already insane when he was captured?" Leahy frowned impatiently, the edges of his mouth dropping downward. "I mean, that traumatic shock you mentioned"—Leahy nodded, still frowning—"could it have occurred before the VC got hold of him?"

Leahy took his time before answering. "It's possible, of course, theoretically speaking," he said without much conviction. "But highly improbable, in my opinion. In all the cases we've had of POW's becoming mentally deranged, it was as a direct result of their life in captivity." He opened an ornate brown box and started filling his pipe. "Why do you ask?"

Meredith hesitated. "I think you should explain what you're after, Walt," Jane Wyatt said softly, and Meredith noticed the quick look of surprise—and displeasure?—that flashed in Leahy's eyes when he heard her addressing him by his first name.

"Of course," he said, and turned to Leahy again. "I couldn't think of asking for your help without giving you the full details of the case. As you'll see, it's a very sensitive investigation, Dr. Leahy. Therefore I count on your discretion."

Leahy coldly nodded while unsuccessfully trying to light his pipe. "It goes without saying. Even if it weren't a classified investigation, I'd be bound by professional secrecy. You must be aware of that." The last phrase rang as a reprimand.

"I'm sorry," Meredith said. He waited for Leahy to nod back, acknowledging the apology, before resuming. He described the discovery of the unidentified body at Na-san, the ballistics report, and the circumstances in which Rainey's patrol had been attacked by the Vietcong close to the hut where the body was found. He'd gotten used to telling the story, and the sentences flowed out easily, almost automatically. He didn't mention the Unknown.

His narrative was followed by a long silence. When Leahy finally raised his eyes, in a cloud of smoke, he was watching Jane Wyatt. "It's terrible, Jane," he said in an unsteady voice, blinking more than before, a tiny nerve pulsating under his left eye. "You must be going through hell. Hearing all this, I mean."

"I'll be okay," she murmured, but her cracked voice betrayed her. She was going through hell indeed, all over again. "I'll be back in a moment," she blurted, and quickly walked out of the room. Leahy looked sternly at Meredith, who shrugged helplessly.

"I guess you had no choice," Leahy said. "You had to tell her." He got up and went to the window where Jane had stood before. "How did she take it when you first told her?"

"Bad," Meredith said. A new surge of rain splashed on the windowpanes.

Leahy took a few aimless steps across the office. He

was nervously running his fingers through his hair. He sighed as he sank back into his chair. "Poor Jane." His voice was distraught, compassionate. "She really didn't deserve that after all her suffering. Life is so unfair." He added, after a short pause, "It doesn't figure, you know. I've read Frank Wyatt's file hundreds of times. I feel I know him better than his own mother." He laid both his hands, palms down, on Wyatt's open file. "He was a fine guy before he lost his mind, certainly not the kind to take part in a murder."

Meredith looked back at him. "I'm afraid there's nothing we can do," he said quietly.

"That's right," Jane Wyatt echoed. She was standing at the door, composed, her navy-blue dress enhancing her pallor. "There's nothing you or I can do, so why don't we go ahead with the planning?" Her voice had a hard edge.

Leahy slowly nodded toward the ashtray in front of him. "Okay," he said. "I didn't mean . . ." His phrase faded away. He closed and reopened Frank Wyatt's file, picked up a pencil and put it back, finally took a silver pipe tool and viciously stuck it into his briar. "I think the best way is, like I said, to try and initiate a chain reaction in Frank's mind by an external influence. I don't believe he would react to sights, or pictures, therefore we should use words. You must spend some time with him," he said to Meredith, "and do your best to shock him. You have to tear him from his present state by forcing him to listen to a sequence of words that might revive in his mind the memory of that night at Na-san."

"Wait," Meredith said, suddenly feeling uncertain. "Why me? I'm an outsider, I have no experience." He glanced sideways at Jane, who was standing by the door, her arms tightly clasping her shoulders as if she were cold. He then turned back to Leahy. "Why not Jane, or you?"

Leahy shook his head. "He is familiar with Jane and me. We've spoken to him many times, and he is used to our voices and our presence. It must be you, Mr. Meredith. A stranger who he's never seen before and who should become identified with those key words we're about to use."

"Where shall we do it?" Jane asked quickly. She wasn't looking at them. Her eyes had a vague, vacuous look. "In the VTR room?"

"Of course." Leahy turned back to Meredith. "We have a special room equipped with video-recording instruments. We use it to record experiments or new methods of treatment. We'll record the session you'll have with Frank and analyze it later."

"I'll be in the recording booth," Jane Wyatt said.

Leahy blinked at her in embarrassment. "Jane, I wouldn't advise—"

"I'll be there," she repeated stubbornly.

Leahy shrugged. "If you wish . . . I still think you're making a mistake."

She didn't answer. Leahy threw a mute look upward, conceding defeat. "Now, the words you're going to use," he said to Meredith. "You will sit very close to him, facing him. You'll call him Frankie. You should also address him as Corporal Wyatt or Marine Wyatt. You'll use his serial number. You'll ask him over and over again about that night at Na-san. Like that."

Leahy suddenly underwent a startling metamorphosis. In two quick strides he was away from his desk, pulling a chair to the middle of the room, bending over an imaginary Frank Wyatt. He wasn't anymore the shy, insecure man Meredith had encountered, but the confident, experienced psychiatrist, moving around the empty chair, shouting his questions in a loud, maddening voice. His spidery body hovered over the chair.

"Na-san, Corporal Wyatt, what happened at Na-san? The fire, who lit the fire? Who is dead? Marine Wyatt, who is dead? Who else is dead? Where are the Vietcong? Where are the VC? Who's shooting? Where is Captain Rainey? Where's Eddie Paris? Marine Wyatt, where's Eddie Paris . . . et cetera, et cetera. Remember"—he turned back to Meredith—"use their names repeatedly, and the following words—*Na-san, patrol, VC, fire, shooting, body, dead man, battle, hand grenades*—"

"I suggest," Jane Wyatt flatly interrupted, "using one more word. *Murder.*"

"Murder," Meredith roared, "was there a murder at Na-san, Corporal Wyatt? Wyatt, I'm talking to you, goddammit!" He felt simultaneously ridiculous and cruel, watching the poor wretch cowering in his corner, emaciated arms hugging the bony knees, haunted eyes riveted to faraway horrors. "Who was murdered at Na-san? Who is the dead man? Dead, Marine Wyatt, who's dead?"

Behind the partition of thick dark glass, across the room, he could sense, more than see, the presence of Jane. The room was roughly the same size as Wyatt's usual cell and as thickly padded. The glass panel of the recording room was set in the upper part of the opposite wall, out of reach of the patients inside to prevent them from hurting themselves. The VTR cameras were fixed on the ceiling, pointing down at a sharp angle.

When Meredith entered Frank Wyatt was already inside, squatting in his corner, pressing his meager body against the spongy padding. "Go ahead," Jane's voice had impersonally cracked in the concealed loudspeakers, and he had awkwardly stepped toward her mad husband.

That's how the session had started about an hour ago, and now he felt he couldn't carry on much longer. Everything seemed to him, right now, totally useless. All his efforts to tear Frank away from his horrified torpor had failed. That was where his search had brought him, he sourly thought—into a padded cell, screaming at a poor madman who had lost his mind in a Vietnam jungle.

"The fire!" he yelled at Wyatt. "Who lit the fire? Marine Wyatt, why did you light the fire? You lit the fire, Corporal! You lit the fire!" For a split second he thought he discerned a slight tremor in Wyatt's jaw, as if he was about to move his lips. But nothing happened and the mouth remained slack, oozing saliva on the sallow chin.

"The fire!" he tried again. "Frankie, the fire!"

But Frankie didn't budge, didn't hear, didn't turn. A pungent stench suddenly hit him, and he noticed a trickle of fluid snaking on the rubber matting between Wyatt's legs. The poor man had defecated in his pants.

He turned helplessly toward the central camera. "I'm afraid we have to stop here," he said. "Frank needs to be cleaned."

There was a moment of silence, then Jane's voice came on the loudspeaker. "I'll take care of it," she said calmly. "You can go out now, Walt."

"I'm sorry," he said, suddenly feeling guilty, as if by

141

seeing her husband squatting in his waste he was humiliating both of them. "I'm really sorry."

"That's okay," the loudspeaker said. He passed Jane as he was getting out of the room, but she looked sullen, her face sealed, and he didn't know what to say.

They got together only much later, for a cup of coffee at the employees' cafeteria. They had to wait for Dr. Leahy to complete rounds before viewing the videotapes together. She was her usual self again, lively and smiling, and he wondered where she found the force to cope with all the pressure. She had refused the assistance of a nurse and had insisted on cleaning and changing her husband herself.

"You did fine, Walt," she said, and her voice carried a ring of compassion that wasn't there the previous evening.

"Come on, now," he said. "I was a complete failure."

She took a sip of her coffee. "I'm not so sure," she said. "Let's wait for the viewing."

He furiously ripped the wrapping of a new package of cigarettes. "How's Frankie?" he asked, spending a few matches before managing to light his cigarette.

She smiled wanly. "He'll be fine." She fell silent for a moment, then leaned toward him. "There's something you should know." Her voice was a shade lower and a concerned look slipped into her eyes. "I wanted to tell you earlier, but I was never alone with you. Steve Rainey called this morning."

He frowned. "Did he?"

"He wanted to know if you'd gotten in touch with me."

"Clever," Meredith conceded. The former Marine captain was much more cunning than he looked. Since their brief confrontation aboard the *Fidelis,* Rainey was after him, smartly guessing his next moves, systematically trying to thwart his endeavors. He looked up. "What did you tell him?"

She was nervously fidgeting with her spoon, stirring the residue of her coffee. A nurse with dyed hair and a mud wrestler's body encased in a rather short skirt playfully waved at her, casting a long look at Walt. Jane waved back, rather coldly, and the nurse, who was on her way to their table with her food tray, hesitated, then retreated to the opposite end of the room, her stiff back exuding wounded pride.

"I told him," Jane Wyatt said, "that you called but I refused to let you see Frankie. And you said to me that you were going back to Washington to get an official government request to visit his cell."

"Good," he nodded. "I appreciate that."

She wasn't looking at him. "Still," she said, "I'd advise you to change hotels. Where are you staying now?"

"The Sheraton Inn. Why?" he said, puzzled, then added ironically, "Is my life in danger?"

She shrugged. "Steve can get pretty violent. You'd better register in some motel, under another name."

He chuckled. The last time he had used an assumed name was in the early seventies, when he still was with the Company. "Don't you think you're getting too dramatic about Steve Rainey?"

She suddenly flared. "No, I don't. And don't you get too condescending with me. You're investigating a probable murder in which Steve might be implicated. I know Steve, believe me. And if he has taken part in a murder, he won't sit still while you build the case against him. Somebody else might, but not Steve."

"You seem to know him pretty well," he said sarcastically, convinced now that she had been involved with Rainey but not daring to ask. "And what about you, why don't you take any precautions?"

"He won't hurt me," she said curtly, answering both his questions.

He felt an unexpected pang of jealousy, then spread his hands in mock defeat. "Okay. You win." He stubbed out his cigarette and pushed away his empty cup. "But after I change my name and my hotel," he said in a lighter tone, bending over the table and peering at her with a grin, "and after I promise to behave, will you have dinner with me?"

She returned his stare, obviously still upset, then tiny sparkles sneaked into her eyes and she gave a breezy laugh. "We'll see about that, cowboy."

Reuben Leahy materialized beside them, chewing his pipe. "I'm all yours," he announced briskly.

But the viewing of the tapes, back in the windowless VTR room, was another frustrating experience. He disgustedly watched himself scurry across the television monitor, yelling his rehearsed questions at the terrified psychopath who quailed in his corner. Jane Wyatt, who sat beside him, didn't speak throughout the screening. She looked grim, miserable, and he caught a quick glance of her clenched fists and liquid eyes.

Reuben Leahy wouldn't admit defeat, though he made a big fuss over the rare instances when a faint convulsion had puckered Wyatt's face and the bloodless mouth had soundlessly trembled. He ran the tape back and forth, slowed its speed, froze a couple of frames on the screen, and plunged into learned inter-

pretations of the "slow awakening of the patient's suppressed memory." In the next sessions, he predicted,
this phenomenon was bound to develop and a breakthrough might be achieved. But his voice lacked conviction, and Meredith knew there had been no
progress and that the cocoon isolating Wyatt's mind
from the outside world was as thick and impervious as
ever.

"What did you think?" Jane mildly rebuked him
later as they made their way across the windswept
parking lot. "That you'd declaim your magic formula
and the toad would turn into a prince?"

"Of course not," he retorted. Dusk was falling and
the lights of the building projected dull yellow patterns
on the wavering puddles left from the morning rain.
"But I hoped for a reaction. A word, a gesture, anything."

She turned to him, holding the door handle of her
aging Sunbird. Her voice was unsteady. "I understand
your frustration, Walt. But in my profession, despair is
a luxury I can't afford. It takes a lot of patience, a lot
of perseverance..." She pulled the car door open.
"And yet, you never know if at the end you won't
bump against a blank wall."

He had been running into blank walls ever since he
set out on this venture, he bitterly mused as he drove
back to his hotel. First the classified file in the Pentagon archives, then Rainey's obstruction, Lyndon
Hughes's reluctance, Frank Wyatt's hopeless malady.
Those sessions in the asylum could go on for months,
and the blank wall looming behind Wyatt's haunted
look might remain as solid, as impregnable, as ever.

Yet another blank wall was in store for him that
night. A message from his secretary was waiting for

him at the Sheraton Inn. Eddie Paris, the fourth survivor of the Na-san patrol, was dead.

It had started as a stroke of luck, Patty breathlessly narrated into the phone. Marilyn Wilcox, the girl who worked in the office next door, had popped in while she was phoning around inquiring about Eddie Paris. Did he remember Marilyn, Patty asked. He had a fleeting memory of a tall, awkward black woman with a neat Afro hairdo and a large, generous mouth. When Marilyn heard the name Paris, Patty resumed, she had asked if they were looking for the Reverend Paris. The Reverend seemed to be a well-known public figure and one of the leaders of the American black community. Till last November he had been president of the Confederation of Southern Churches. He lived, as far as Marilyn remembered, in Birmingham, Alabama.

On the spur of the moment, Patty had decided to call the Reverend's office. Long-distance information had supplied her with the number, and a couple of minutes later she was talking to the clergyman's secretary. The Reverend was out of town, the woman had announced, he wouldn't be back before next week. Pushing her luck, Patty had asked if by any chance he was a relation of Eddie Paris.

"There was a long silence on the phone," Patty now breathed dramatically, "then the woman said, 'Why do you ask?' Her voice was weird, Walt, she seemed in a state of shock."

"Go ahead," he grunted impatiently, loosening the knot of his tie. He was sitting on his bed, still in his raincoat. He hadn't even bothered to switch on the lamps when he walked into the dark hotel room and saw the red message light urgently pulsating on the telephone console.

"I told her I was calling from the Pentagon and we were updating the list of the Marine Corps veterans. I said we were planning a national rally of Vietnam veterans in Washington."

Patty paused, probably expecting his reaction, but as there was none, she resumed her story, which was approaching its dramatic peak. "Eddie ain't going to no rally," the woman said. "Eddie's been dead more than ten years now."

"Ten years!" Meredith echoed, baffled.

Eddie was Reverend Paris's nephew, his secretary had revealed to Patty. He was the son of the Reverend's older brother, who was a clergyman too. Eddie's father had moved with his wife to Baltimore soon after his marriage, but after Eddie's tragic death, ten years ago, and the death of his wife, which had ensued, he had returned to Alabama and settled in Huntsville to be close to his brother.

"A tragic death?" Meredith asked quickly. "Did she say a tragic death?"

"There had been an accident," Patty said slowly, obviously delighted by his response. "He had gone deer hunting with some friends in Pennsylvania, and there had been an accident."

His mouth was dry. "What friends?"

"Army buddies," Patty disclosed, and paused for effect. "How come they didn't teach them to shoot straight in the Marines, the woman asked."

"They killed him, Jane, don't you see?" he said fervently, raising his voice. At the nearby table an elderly couple suddenly became very still. The man abruptly turned to face him, his rimless spectacles glinting over the oblong, meager face. The woman, her hair dyed in an outrageous purple, stared at him in fear, her laden fork freezing halfway to her open mouth.

Jane smiled nervously. "We don't know that for sure, do we?" She beckoned to a middle-aged waiter. "May we have some more fried rice, please?"

"One fried rice coming," the slight Chinese chanted and sauntered away. The old couple beside them hesitantly came back to life and returned to their chop suey.

Meredith grinned uneasily. "I scared them stiff," he admitted. "I am sorry, I'll keep my voice down." He grew serious again. "As I was saying, I'm sure it was no accident. I bet that you'll find Rainey's name among the Army buddies who went hunting with Eddie Paris."

For a while she kept silent, idly toying with a red ashtray inscribed in mock Chinese characters "Honorably stolen from the Golden Dragon Restaurant, Mesa, Colorado." Then she looked up, her forehead puckered in thought. "It doesn't figure, Walt. I'm sure Rainey, or whoever did it, had plenty of opportunities to kill Paris in Vietnam. If he was dangerous, I mean. Why would they kill him back home, two years after the war ended?"

He shrugged. "Perhaps something happened. Perhaps he threatened to reveal the truth about Na-san."

She tilted her head back, pressing her lips in a skeptical moue. "And they lured him to Pennsylvania and shot him dead?"

The waiter was back, ceremoniously placing their steaming plates on the table. "One chicken Thailand, one beef Cantonese."

"We asked for some fried rice," Jane reminded him.

The Chinese flashed her his ready smile. "One fried rice coming!" he happily announced.

Meredith picked up his chopsticks. On the lacquered wood tiny green dragons were breathing curly puffs of red fire. "I think I should catch the first flight to Huntsville and have a talk with his father," he said. "He might remember something that Eddie told him before his death. Perhaps he even left a diary or some letters."

"And I think," Jane said quietly but forcefully, "that you should stay here, and return to Alma Viva tomorrow, and after tomorrow, as long as is needed, and keep trying to make Frankie talk." She reached for her wineglass. "That's your goal now, and you'd better stick to it."

He leaned back, watching her with a half-smile. "Do you know that you've been running my life since we met? You took me to dinner last night, made me speak about myself as I never had before, talked me into this project with Frankie, ordered me to leave my fine Sheraton accommodation for a shabby motel room, and register under a phony name. And now you're ordering me to stay."

"Dinner tonight was your idea," she protested, the mischievous dimples flourishing in her cheeks.

"But if I stay"—he fell in step with her, watching the sparks of laughter scintillate in the limpid green eyes—"I might try to monopolize all your dinners." Good God, he suddenly realized, it was not small talk, he really was after this woman.

She was watching him with an odd expression, her smile rather insecure. "I'll take that risk," she said.

"Fine," he announced with contrived gaiety. "I'll postpone the trip to Huntsville for next week then."

They started eating, but after a few minutes she broke the silence. "You'll complain again that I'm ordering you around," she said, thoughtful, "but frankly I don't think it's a good idea that you should go to Huntsville."

"Oh really? And why, if I may ask?"

She pushed her plate aside. "You're a Pentagon official, Walt. For ten years nobody in the establishment showed any interest in the family of Eddie Paris. Nobody even knew he was dead. And now you're going to pop out of the blue with a strange story about something that happened in Vietnam fifteen years ago, and you think anybody will talk to you? Those black people have their pride, you know. They'll all clam up and you'll get nowhere with your Pentagon credentials."

She made sense, he conceded. "So what do you suggest?" he asked, less belligerently. The old couple beside them was leaving, and the woman shot a curious look at him over her shoulder.

"Don't you have any friends who could go to Huntsville instead of you? Somebody to whom Reverend Paris could relate? A priest or . . . a bereaved father perhaps?"

"I am a bereaved father," he uttered grimly.

She reached across the table and laid her hand over his. Her skin was warm and soft. "No, Walt. You are, first of all, a government employee, a representative of the white Washington establishment, which doesn't give a damn about the death of Eddie Paris. And only afterward are you a bereaved father."

He let out a deep breath. "Okay." He nodded. "I'll ask a friend of mine to go."

"Good," she said, and wiped her mouth with the wine-red napkin. "Did you enjoy your dinner?"

The Chinese waiter was beside her, beaming. "One fried rice, madam!" he cheerfully proclaimed, and presented her the bowl with a flourish.

It was only after midnight that he succeeded in reaching Martin Armstrong, the black vice president of the League of MIA Families, in his Washington home. "Walt!" the deep baritone resounded in the receiver. "Where are you? What's up?"

He decided to skip the etiquette. "Remember what you told me at Laura Lewis's house, Martin?" he said. "That if I ever need you . . ."

". . . just whistle and I'll be there," Armstrong laughed softly.

"Well, here is what I want you to do . . ." Meredith started.

He spoke for ten minutes without interruption.

And the next morning he was back in the VTR room, tense, feverish, loathing his repulsive role, feeling the green eyes boring into his back from behind the dark glass, and still assailing with savage determination the trembling figure crouching in the corner.

"Answer when I talk to you, Marine Wyatt!" he hoarsely yelled. "Why did you light that bloody fire? Whose body did you burn? Who did you murder? Answer the fuckin' questions, Corporal. Who the hell did you murder?"

✪ 8 ✪

At the near corner of the dusty square a portable music box was braying a strident beat. Martin Armstrong paid the cab driver and unhurriedly stepped toward the small group of people clustered in the shade of two moribund oaks. From a glossy poster, freshly plastered to one of the trees, the Reverend Jesse Jackson smiled challengingly under the heading "Jackson for President." The crowd was mostly black, except for two middle-aged men—apparently shopkeepers from across the street—and a big blond girl whose tight mini-skirt desperately struggled against her plump thighs. They were watching a couple of kids, a tall, long-limbed teenager and a small, skinny child, breakdance on the sidewalk.

The older boy moved with the mechanical, disjointed jerks of a robot, head and arms twitching, rigid feet smoothly gliding in their dirty, thick-soled sneakers. The small child didn't seem to have a single solid bone in his body and effortlessly twirled and rolled in insolent defiance—or perhaps ignorance—of the law of gravity. A minuscule, agile elf he was, dancing on air, responding to the frenzied rhythm with fluid motions and easy grace.

The crowd accompanied the performance with

cheers, whistles, and catcalls. On Armstrong's right stood a matronly woman with heavily oxidized hair and a smart business outfit who kept clapping her hands. Farther to the right, on a peeling wooden bench, sat an old man in a shabby black suit and a collarless shirt, his bare feet encased in cracked, shapeless shoes. He was apparently oblivious to the commotion, his toothless mouth slightly agape, his extinct eyes vaguely staring ahead. But the gnarled hands forcefully gripped an ancient walking stick as if it were a lifeline. His hunched back made a blurry outline against the low, smoke-gray sky. A sour smell hung in the humid air.

The music abruptly came to an end, a ripple of applause rolled across the square, and the nimble waif whirled between the bystanders collecting their contributions in a blue baseball cap. The woman beside Armstrong donned her pink-rimmed sunglasses, which were hanging on a golden chain on her bosom, and discreetly slipped away. As he took some coins from his pocket Armstrong stared for an instant at the child's face. And taking in the big anxious eyes, the matted hair, the full, mutely pleading mouth, he suddenly felt catapulted back in time to the hungry, bitter days he had tried to bury in the darkest recesses of his memory. In Memphis, too, they used to dance on street corners, then stretch a trembling hand toward a stranger.

"Where's Elm Street, kid?" he asked hoarsely. The coins clanged in the baseball cap. The child pointed across the square and plunged into the crowd. Armstrong purposefully strode by the old oaks and stepped on the patch of dry yellow grass. Quick, guarded looks converged upon him and he knew he was being expertly appraised and classified—a stranger in Huntsville, apparently well-off by the cut of his three-piece suit, sixtyish but still strong, mean-looking, the big black hands and the broken nose betraying a boxing or wrestling past. Nobody spoke to him except for an elderly woman who gravely nodded and said, "Good afternoon." He returned her greeting and walked past a couple of slim girls who swilled their Cokes while giggling softly. Behind him the shrill music reverberated again, and a couple of cheers heralded another performance of the break dancers.

The house on Elm Street was modest but neat. The walls were immaculately white, the lawn well-tended, the porch tidy and freshly swept. The door was opened by a small, trim man wearing a dark blue suit and a sober old-fashioned tie over a crisp white shirt. His snow-white hair crowned a wizened face ravaged by a web of deep, tortuous wrinkles. In the intelligent eyes Armstrong detected the singular expression haunting the look of bereaved people. It was a regard of remote, detached calm, mistaken by so many for indifference or passivity. But he recognized it, with the clarity of a man deeply afflicted, as the ultimate resignation that creeps into one's eyes only after the last spark of hope has died.

"Reverend Paris?" Armstrong said deferentially.

The short man nodded. "I am Abner Paris," he said. He had a clear, firm voice.

"My name is Martin Armstrong. I am vice president of the League of MIA Families. I believe my secretary called your office this morning."

"Come right in, Mr. Armstrong," Paris said, moving aside. Armstrong awkwardly squeezed into the narrow vestibule, hovering above the small, frail man.

"We expected you at the church," Paris added in the same placid tone.

"My plane was late," Armstrong said apologetically and followed the minister into a small sitting room. The brown carpet was old but spotless. Starched lace doilies lay on the headrests of the armchairs and the old-fashioned sofa. Two symmetrical photographs, framed in black, hung over the austere walnut chest. On the left a middle-aged woman wearing a flowery hat was shyly smiling at the camera. The portrait on the right represented a young black man in smart Marine uniform. He had his father's almond-shaped eyes. "This is Eddie?" Armstrong asked.

"Yes," Abner Paris said. And pointing to the second photograph: "This is my late wife, Helen Paris. She died shortly after him." He marked a pause. "Will you sit down? I understand you want to talk to me about Eddie."

Armstrong carefully eased his bulk into one of the armchairs. It was hard and uncomfortable. "You live alone, Reverend?"

"Yes. I have another son but"—for the first time Paris hesitated—"he'd rather live by himself. He doesn't exactly agree with me."

Armstrong nodded, puzzled by the unusual formula.

"I was just preparing my afternoon coffee," Abner Paris said rather formally. "Will you join me?"

"Thank you, Reverend," Armstrong said. He wondered if he should call Paris "father." He had broken all his ties with religion years ago when he had left Memphis. Abner Paris was a Methodist minister, as far as he knew.

Paris soundlessly left the room and was back almost

155

immediately, carefully carrying a large tray. He put it on the low table that stood between the armchairs and the sofa. The tray was covered with a white napkin on which had been placed a jug of coffee, two china cups in their saucers, a bowl of sugar, some milk, and biscuits. With the same neatness and calm that characterized all his gestures, the minister poured the coffee, gravely inquiring about the measures of milk and sugar, helpfully offering tablets of artificial sweetener from a tiny silver box. He waited for his guest to take a sip of his coffee and nod his agreement before reaching for his cup. Then he raised his head, and his eyes were suddenly very intense, holding Armstrong's face in keen focus. "You came all the way from Washington to talk about my dead son," he said softly.

Armstrong nodded, ill at ease. "We need your help, Reverend." He described the plight of the MIA families and the decision of the League to back Meredith's efforts to identify a body found in Vietnam. Just one more body. Don't mention the Unknown, Meredith had warned him. He should never suspect that your mission has any connection to the Unknown Soldier. Paris is a minister of religion, he had added, a law-abiding man. He would never willingly cooperate in an effort to thwart a presidential decision.

Armstrong's narrative, rather erratic and hesitant at first, grew more fluent as he recounted his telephone conversation with Meredith the previous night. "Walt Meredith claims that the unidentified soldier was killed at Na-san while several Marines, including your son, were nearby. It seems that there are very few details available about the patrol in which Eddie participated. Meredith thought that Eddie might have told you about the Na-san operation after he returned from Vietnam."

Easy, Meredith had told him, don't rush the man, don't ask him about Eddie's death, let him get to it on his own steam, at his own pace.

Paris, who had sat in silence throughout Armstrong's discourse, looked up at him with a faint smile. "And as Mr. Meredith was determined to take no chances, he preferred to send a black man to meet me instead of coming himself."

Reverend Paris was nobody's fool, Armstrong decided, picking up his cup of coffee. The only way to keep up with him was by being honest. "Wouldn't you do the same if you were him?" he asked. The brew was strong, bitter.

Paris stared at him thoughtfully. "Yes, I guess I would," he admitted. He got up and approached the portrait of his dead son, then turned back. "You lost a son in the war, didn't you, Mr. Armstrong?" His voice was very soft, almost apologetic.

"My boy is missing since '68," he said.

"Your only son?"

"I have two older daughters, twins." He was answering mechanically, trying not to think. "Michael was my youngest child."

"And you loved him very dearly," Paris said quietly, with a singular undertone of finality. He wasn't asking a question, he was discreetly, almost shyly, calling a painful truth to his attention.

"I was hoping he'd take over my business," Armstrong said awkwardly.

"What kind of business you're in?"

"I'm a building contractor in Washington."

The minister nodded and returned to his chair, retreating again into a long, ambiguous silence. His eyes didn't leave Armstrong's face. "Mr. Armstrong," he finally said, "we both have been struck by a terrible tragedy. We both have learned to live with pain, and that pain is going to be our intimate and faithful companion till the day we die." Armstrong noticed that Paris's fingers were digging deep into the armrests. "Don't you think we should be frank with each other?"

Armstrong nodded uncertainly.

"I believe," the minister said, his voice firm and severe again, "that there is more in your mission than just inquiring about a routine patrol in which my son participated. You didn't fly all the way from Washington just to ask me a couple of innocuous questions."

"I don't understand," Armstrong said, placing his cup on the table, then picking it up again.

"Don't you indeed?" He discerned a faint note of irony in the Reverend's voice. "Maybe you don't. Maybe Mr. Meredith didn't tell you. Or maybe he did. Well . . ." He waved his right hand deprecatingly, and even this impulsive gesture seemed neat and stiff coming from him. "It doesn't really matter. What matters, Mr. Armstrong . . ." He paused, letting his phrase fade away. When he resumed his voice was choked, oddly tense. "What matters is that Eddie came back from Vietnam a haunted man. A terrible burden was weighing on his shoulders. A secret, perhaps, or a memory he couldn't lock away. And he carried it like a cross till his dying day."

"Didn't he—" Armstrong started.

"No," Paris said forcefully. "You wanted to ask if he didn't tell me what it was, if it had anything to do with Na-san. No, he didn't. I never heard about that patrol until today. But Mr. Meredith, or your president, and

158

you, too, perhaps, seem to attach a special importance to the Na-san patrol. Eddie didn't just happen to be around when that poor soldier was killed, did he?"

Armstrong kept quiet, his head bowed.

"Maybe he knew something about that soldier's death. And maybe this was the secret that haunted him." His voice was suddenly poignant, almost desperate. "Eddie was my son, Mr. Armstrong. I raised him in my beliefs, in my principles. I educated him to be a God-fearing man, just, and honest, and faithful to his country." He paused again. "He couldn't cope with that . . . that murky secret of his. During the last years of his life, after he returned from the war, he was a very miserable young man."

"Till his death, you say."

Abner Paris hesitated. "Yes. Well, a few months before his accident something happened that made things worse. He became a bundle of nerves."

"What—" Armstrong began, but Paris raised his hand.

"Don't ask me what it was, because I don't know. He wouldn't talk to me and his mother. There were some long-distance phone calls. He would hang up the moment I walked into the room." He suddenly got up. Tiny beads of perspiration glistened on his forehead. "Would you mind if we went out to the yard? Some fresh air would do us good."

Armstrong rose, somewhat puzzled, and followed Abner Paris through a dark corridor and a small, gleaming kitchen into the backyard. He paused on the threshold, taken aback by the unexpected sight. The small lot had been transformed into a lush garden. Magnificent patterns of bright-colored flowers formed graceful arabesques between clumps of shrubs, resplendent rose bushes, and a variety of young trees. Reverend Paris knelt by a cluster of blood-red tulips and plucked some weeds with his agile, expert hands. He apprehensively looked up at the sprawling boughs of a cypress, apparently foreseeing the death that their dense shade held in store for the flowers.

"So this is your secret hideaway, Reverend," Armstrong said, trying to adopt a lighter tone.

Abner Paris seemed not to hear. "We had a beautiful garden in Baltimore," he said. "It was Eddie's garden. He spent a lot of time with his flowers. The garden survived him by a couple of months, no more."

And you planted a new one here in his memory, Armstrong thought glumly. He knew well this pathetic urge of bereaved parents to keep their dead sons alive and present by picking up their hobbies where they had left them and thus trying to reach beyond death and create a spiritual bond with their deceased children. Didn't he, too, spend long evenings in Michael's room working on his stamp collection? Before the boy died, he hated the bloody stamps.

Paris got up, needlessly dusting his knees, and turned back to Armstrong. "One day he suddenly told us he was going hunting with his Army buddies," he said without transition. "I was rather surprised, he had never hunted before, you see. But he was very excited. I felt that trip meant a lot to him. He said he was going to Pennsylvania for five days. And they brought him back in a wooden box." He was looking away, his bloodless lips slightly trembling.

"You think"—Armstrong looked away, unable to sustain the clergyman's direct stare— "you think this hunting trip had anything to do with his trouble?"

Paris winced. "You want to know if they killed him,

do you?" His voice was suddenly fierce, strangled with contained wrath. He took a step forward, unaware of the flowers he was trampling, his body struck with the rigidity of the blind. "Do you?" he repeated. His stiff arm was raised halfway across his chest, the clenched fist trembling.

Armstrong watched him in silence tearing a leaf of a nearby bush and nervously crushing it in his hand. A sharp, pungent odor briefly spread in the air.

Abner Paris let out a deep breath and spread his arms in despair, a small overwhelmed man in a secret garden that had become his private hell. "I don't know," he said in a cracked voice, answering his own question. "I don't know, and I don't care. It won't bring him back, and Helen neither, so what difference does it make?"

Armstrong took a step toward him and spontaneously reached for his arm. It was stiff, unyielding to his touch. "I am sorry, Reverend," he said.

Paris slowly shook his head. "I can't help you, Mr. Armstrong," he said. "I don't know what happened to Eddie or why. And I don't want to know. The coroner's report said his death was due to an accident, and that's all that matters."

"You don't want to dig deeper for fear you might find something horrible, don't you, Reverend?" Armstrong said very gently.

Paris's visage was blank, ungiving. "I have my faith in the Lord, and I've learned to accept the inevitable." His voice lacked confidence. He was about to speak again but hesitated, and Armstrong felt he was torn by contradictory feelings.

"Perhaps you should see Eddie's brother," Paris finally blurted, quickly averting his eyes. "He worships a different god, a cruel god who doesn't know how to forgive." He threw a quick glance at Armstrong's baffled face. "Eddie and Adam were very close, you know." He reached for his pen in the inner pocket of his jacket and scribbled a few lines on a blue leaf he tore from a small notebook.

Armstrong folded the paper and put it in his pocket. "Can I go out this way?" He pointed at a narrow path snaking around the house.

"Yes," Paris said. He was standing closer to the trees now, with his back to him. "You know," he said without turning back, "there is an oriental saying I often recall. It says, 'The trees die standing.' Good day, Mr. Armstrong."

And that was how Armstrong remembered him—a small, lonely man, cruelly torn from his beloved, from the dead and from the living, vainly seeking refuge in the green shrine erected to a lost boy, and himself a dead tree still standing in an illusory Garden of Eden.

The name scribbled on the blue leaf was Adam Paris. But the tiny plaque under the doorbell, in the dilapidated apartment building, read Salah Ad'din. A name undoubtedly suiting the young black man in the hand-knitted cap and embroidered Arab shirt who appeared at the door staring at him in open hostility. Deep, permanent scorn oozed from each furrow in his forehead, from the small, burning eyes, from the tightly clamped mouth surrounded by a drooping mustache and a short stringy beard. Only now did Armstrong understand what Reverend Paris meant by saying that his son worshiped another god. Adam Paris had become a Black Muslim.

"Yes?" he said gruffly, tilting his head and narrowing his eyes. Behind him Armstrong made out a dim, bare room, poorly furnished with a few chairs and a large desk. A faded poster with Arabic lettering, probably verses from the Koran, was hanging on the far wall.

"You're the brother of Eddie Paris, aren't you?" Armstrong said.

The young man crossed his arms on his chest, watching him suspiciously. He was in his mid-twenties, Armstrong decided. "And who are you?" he reluctantly inquired.

"Who's there?" a woman's voice called from the inside.

The young man didn't answer, and kept staring malevolently at Armstrong.

"I'm trying to find out who killed your brother," he said bluntly.

The young man winced. "You what?" he managed, staring at him in amazement.

"May I come in?" Armstrong advanced upon Adam Paris without waiting for his answer but the young man barred his way, stretching a skinny arm across the doorway.

"Who's there?" The woman's voice again.

"Your father gave me your address," Armstrong continued. "He said you and Eddie were very close. He said you might know why he died."

"My brother died in an accident," Adam Paris muttered.

"Oh no," Armstrong said, gently pushing him back. "You don't believe that crap, do you?"

Adam Paris diffidently retreated. "Who are you?" he asked again. A skeletal woman, a good ten years older than he, came in through the far door. She was wearing a long, loose African gown and a tall brown turban wrapped around her head. She cast Armstrong the same suspicious look he had received from Paris. "We should be going," she said. Her voice was rough, unpleasant. There was something ascetic about her that made Armstrong dislike her at first sight.

The young man hesitated, gathering his sparse beard in his hand. "You go first," he finally said. "Take the proofs with you. I'll join you later." He turned back and collected a batch of galley proofs from the decrepit desk that stood by the near wall. Armstrong noticed the fat title on the top proof. *The Voice of Islam*, it read.

"No way," the woman spat angrily. "They won't wait for you. We have a deadline, remember?"

With Paris obviously at a loss, Armstrong judged it was high time for him to interfere. "Why don't you go right ahead, sister?" he threw at her casually. "You heard the man, he'll join you shortly."

She stiffened, fury sparkling in her wide-spaced eyes. "The printers won't wait for you," she hissed at Paris, and realizing that he wouldn't move, gathered the proofs and sailed purposefully toward the open door. "Don't be late," she warned him, "we won't wait." And turning to Armstrong: "Don't you 'sister' me, okay, 'brother'?"

As she stormed through the door, slamming it behind her, Armstrong whistled softly. "Wow, this lady is something," he remarked. Getting no comment from Paris, he stepped toward the desk. Its bare, unpolished top was scarred with discolored rings and cigarette burns. A dusty black telephone was perched at the desk's corner but its cord dangled loose, disconnected. Armstrong picked up the topmost of a pile of brochures. "*The Voice of Islam*," he said. "You're the editor?"

"That's none of your business," Adam Paris said belligerently. He was slowly regaining his good old aggressive self, Armstrong decided.

"You're right," he said. "That's none of my business. What should I call you, Mr. Paris or Mr. Ad'din?"

The young man intently scanned his face, apparently trying to detect a hint of mockery. As there was none, he finally shrugged. "Adam Paris doesn't exist anymore," he said solemnly. "I changed my name to Salah Ad'din when I became a Black Muslim. And what's your name?"

"Does the name mean something?" Armstrong asked.

The small suspicious eyes were trained on him, watching his reactions. "Salah Ad'din was the Muslim leader who declared a holy war on Christianity and destroyed the Crusaders' kingdom in Jerusalem. That was eight hundred years ago."

And you, poor kid, also dream of destruction and holy wars, but you can't even pay your telephone bill, Armstrong sadly reflected. But he thought it wiser to keep his judgments to himself. Instead, he said, "I know Muhammad Ali. Was a fighter myself, in the good old days."

"Oh really?" Salah Ad'din took a box of cheap cigars from the desk, chose one, and lit it. He didn't bother to offer one to Armstrong. "You still haven't told me who you are," he said in a cloud of acrid smoke.

Armstrong introduced himself and described the purpose of his visit. His young host listened, avidly puffing on his cigar. When Armstrong narrated his conversation with the Reverend Paris, a surge of fury distorted Ad'din's face. "It's so typical of him," he groaned.

Armstrong looked at him questioningly.

"They killed his son," Ad'din vehemently muttered. "And he didn't revolt, or pound on their desks, or ask for an inquiry. He just kept licking their boots, as he has been doing his whole life. He's still a slave, that's what he is. A white man's slave, keeping the niggers under control for his masters, with his church and his gospels and his promises of paradise."

"Now, Mr. Ad'din," Armstrong started, but the young man had apparently embarked on his favorite subject, and no force on earth could contain the deluge. He feverishly paced about the room, waving his fists, his voice frenzied, slightly hysterical.

"That's what their government needs. People like my father, to keep the blacks in line." He briefly stopped, his blazing eyes boring into Armstrong's face. "Oh boy, do they know how to control us. They buy our jazz, and buy our black voices, and sell us those flashy clothes, and shed alligator tears about the wrongs they did to us. They think that by reading *Roots* and quoting Martin Luther King they've bought themselves eternal absolution. They make us look like monkeys in their TV series and we split our sides watching the Jeffersons and Benson fooling our white masters. Black liberation? Shit. How many white friends do you have? How many? Tell me!" Armstrong helplessly shrugged. "How many blacks are in government, except for a couple of bozos they send to Africa to make the natives feel better?"

166

Armstrong was watching him, trying to figure a way to stop the flood.

"And you know why they succeed?" Salah Ad'din asked rhetorically. "Because they've got people like my father slaving for them, that's why. Keeping the blacks down, making them sing and wriggle their asses every Sunday in church and promising them eternal happiness in paradise. And those fools believe it. This country is worse than South Africa, man, because these poor slobs here think they're free.

"And when they kill us, like they killed my brother, my father keeps kissing their white asses. It was an accident, he says. He doesn't want to know, he says. He's got his religion, he says. They spit in his face, and he says thank you, come again. Shit. That's why I became a Black Muslim. Because I couldn't take it anymore. They killed my brother, blew his head off with buckshot like a bloody hog, and said it was an accident. And I had to say yes, sir, thank you, sir, how kind of you to send over the poor nigger's body, sir, he was such a nuisance anyway, stepping in the way of them flying bullets."

"How do you know they killed him?" Armstrong said, settling in a chair that faintly squeaked in protest.

"How do I know?" Ad'din almost choked with indignation. "They wanted to silence him, that's why. They didn't want him to expose their bloody secrets, that's why."

"Why don't you sit down and tell me what really happened?" Armstrong suggested.

Ad'din seemed not to hear, and continued pacing up and down the room, pulling his beard and waving his fists. Still, amid his fiery diatribes against the whites, and his father, and the black slaves of American imperialism, the story of Eddie Paris's death slowly took shape.

It had all started almost exactly ten years before, Ad'din's story went. They were still living in Baltimore, and Eddie was watching some program on television. Something about the war. No, not the Vietnam War. The World War, or was it Korea? Anyway, he had seen or heard something that had disturbed him deeply. His young brother had never seen him that way. Eddie seemed horrified, as if he had seen a ghost. He had locked himself in his room, and later had virtually run out of the house. He had returned at dawn, shut himself in his father's study, and made a couple of long-distance calls.

"I was awake," Ad'din said. "I heard his voice on the phone." Ad'din had the impression that his brother was crying.

"You didn't ask him what it was all about?" Armstrong inquired.

"I sure did, " the young man said. "But he wouldn't answer. He just looked through me, as if I didn't exist." Other sleepless nights had followed, and other long-distance calls. And then, one day, Eddie had told them that he was going hunting with some buddies from the Marines. They had decided to spend a few days deer hunting in the Poconos, in Pennsylvania. Since that announcement Eddie seemed much better, even his appetite was back.

They brought him back two days after he left, Salah Ad'din concluded. His head had virtually been blown off; he had taken a whole charge of buckshot in the face. The police never established who had fired the fatal shot. It was at the height of the hunting season, and the Poconos were swarming with hunters.

"Did they run a weapon check?" Armstrong asked, frowning.

Ad'din nodded. "'Inconclusive,' that's what they said," he mouthed contemptuously. "They brought him back, his loving friends—a couple of former Marines from Bravo Company, Thirty-seventh regiment. They told us it had been a terrible accident." Eddie Paris's commanding officer had sent a handwritten letter to the family praising his courage and devotion during the Vietnam War and a short obituary had been published in a Baltimore paper.

"And what do you make of it?" Armstrong asked in a conclusive manner.

"It's clear, isn't it? Eddie saw something on television that triggered a memory. He called somebody at the Marines and threatened to reveal what he knew."

"Blackmail?" Armstrong interrupted, but Ad'din was angrily shaking his head. "No bloody way. Eddie was the straightest guy on earth, he wouldn't've dreamed of doing anything immoral. He just warned those bastards, and they decided to get rid of him."

The wild fire was dancing again in Salah Ad'din's eyes. "So they say to him, okay, Eddie, let's meet and discuss the matter, let's go together on a picnic or hunting or whatever. And he says sure, they're his buddies, they've fought together in 'Nam, right? And once they lured him out of his house, they just made a target of that poor, trusting nigger's face and blew his head off."

The sun had set while they were talking. But only after midnight did Martin Armstrong get hold of Walt Meredith in the Rocky Mountains Motel at Mesa and repeat to him Salah Ad'din's story.

"Did he tell you who organized the hunting trip?"

169

Meredith's voice resounded in the receiver with a vibrating echo.

"A guy named Railey," Armstrong said.

"Wouldn't that be instead Rainey, Steve Rainey?" Meredith asked cautiously.

"That's right," Armstrong said. "Rainey. He also brought the body back to Baltimore."

There was a long silence on the other end of the line.

"But the funny thing is," Armstrong resumed, "that Rainey wasn't there when the accident happened. He had been delayed apparently—some urgent business, it seems—and he only reached the hunting camp a day after Eddie had been killed."

When Meredith spoke again his voice sounded weary, resigned, the voice of a man who had known the answer all along. "But of course, Martin," he said. "Steve Rainey is a very busy man indeed."

⭐9⭐

Was it because he had become so infatuated with Jane Wyatt, Meredith later wondered, that he didn't give up when he logically should have and didn't go on his way, a defeated, disillusioned man at the end of his sterile quest? Was it because he so longed to hear her voice again, to contemplate her passionate face, detect the hidden hints in the luminous green eyes? Was it because of her that he kept returning to the asylum day after day and maltreating the miserable wretch who cringed in fear in his padded universe?

And he had to concede that yes, indeed, it was his fascination with Jane Wyatt that had kept him at Mesa. And he thanked fate for placing her in his path. For hadn't he kept returning against all odds and all logic, and hadn't he kept trying even after all hope seemed lost—he would never have pierced the shield of silence of Frank Wyatt and learned the ghastly truth. And never found who the Unknown Soldier of the Vietnam War was.

It was late morning on the sixth day of what he had come to consider an all but routine exercise in futility. Again, the VTR room; again, the cowering, trembling shape of Frankie Wyatt, and again the sordid questions he would yell at the horrified psycho with a sickly feeling of self-disgust. Dr. Leahy was in the room, too, awkwardly leaning against the far wall. Leahy had started coming to the sessions two days before, following a stormy argument with Jane Wyatt. In the middle of a videotape viewing she had suddenly jumped from her seat, switched off the VTR, and turned on the lights. She was nervous, pale, and her voice trembled as she came to face Leahy and tell him bluntly that his approach was totally wrong. "I've given the matter a lot of thought," she managed, her clenched fists bulging in the pockets of her smock. "I believe we are making a grave error."

Leahy was too startled to speak, his round eyes blinking.

"We want to make Frankie talk," she went on, speaking quickly, breathlessly, as if she feared her time would run out. "We use threats and pressure and fear as tools to break his silence and generate a reaction, right?" She shot a glum glance at Meredith. "This will never work, don't you understand? Never. Frankie has withdrawn into himself precisely because of that, and . . ."

Leahy was on his feet. "Now, Jane, listen—"

"No, now you listen!" she retorted vehemently. "Frankie lost his mind because he couldn't cope with the stress and the horror. He escaped in his own way from the pressure and the threats and whatever and found refuge in madness. What we're doing now can only aggravate his situation, don't you see? More threats, more fear, more pressure will only make him withdraw deeper into himself. This method will never trigger a reaction, quite the contrary."

"And what would trigger such a reaction, if I may inquire?" Leahy's voice was cold, sarcastic, but Meredith could tell he was deeply offended. His professional judgment had been openly questioned by his assistant, and in front of an outsider.

"The exact opposite," Jane said fervently. "We should show him tenderness, compassion, some real affection. He should get to feel that the horrors and the stress are over, that he has nothing to fear from us. We're here to help him, not to hurt him."

"Absolute nonsense," Leahy fiercely muttered, with the rare but stubborn rage of a weak man. "We'll be sweet to him and he'll be sweet to us. Where did you learn that Mickey Mouse psychiatry?"

She winced. "In the patients' cells," she slowly articulated, her eyes blazing, challenging his. "Not in a wood-paneled office."

The insult scored. Leahy glowered at her for a moment, his small mouth twitching. "You've been watching too many soap operas on TV lately," he cracked, and angrily strode out, slamming the door.

But the following morning Meredith found him in the VTR room. "I'd better be around when you work with Frankie," Reuben Leahy said, blinking awkwardly. "It's better than watching a tape."

"But you said that your presence..." Meredith started. Behind the dark glass Jane's silhouette was upright, immobile.

"Don't worry, I won't interfere." Leahy was assiduously sucking his unlit pipe and shifting his weight from one foot to the other. "I'll just hang around. Frankie won't even notice me."

He had spent that morning and the next in the VTR room watching Meredith in silence. He had kept out of his way and abstained from any comment. Jane had only briefly brushed by them, her face sullen, and retreated into her glass cage. She had twice refused Meredith's invitations for dinner.

Today Frankie seemed more erratic than usual. He huddled in his corner, at times totally immobile, his head slackly dangling over his caved-in chest. And at times, jolted by short, sporadic convulsions, his eyes wildly wandered about the room. His fragile psychological defenses, or what was left of them, might be wearing down, Meredith thought.

"Corporal Wyatt!" he started, firing his questions almost automatically, pacing before the crouching figure, his eyes striving to pierce the glaze of insanity sealing Frankie's stare. As his voice grew louder, more demanding, Frankie's unrest increased and low, gurgling moans burst from his mouth. Meredith glanced at Leahy, who nodded silently, encouraging him to proceed. And it was at this moment that Frankie started screaming.

More than a scream, it was a high-pitched animal wail. As it erupted from Frankie's mouth, his entire chest contracted, and wildly pulsating veins emerged beneath the ashen skin of his throat. His arms darted to his face in a pitiful defensive gesture, and he flung himself against the wall, repeatedly knocking his head against the spongy padding. Meredith's voice died and he stepped toward Frankie. Leahy also approached, and as they bent toward the wailing man, Meredith thought of two inquisitors standing over their tormented victim.

A sharp sound behind him made him turn around. Jane flung the door open and darted out of the recording booth, her eyes smoldering, two vivid red spots flaming on her cheeks. In a couple of strides she was beside Frankie, kneeling by his convulsed figure, her back becoming a rampart between him and Meredith. She hugged Frankie possessively, almost violently, pressing his head against her breasts, her hands caressing his shivering shoulders and gently slipping along his flanks. He let her do this, instinctively responding to her tenderness, and his emaciated figure nestled against her like the docile body of a frightened child seeking solace and protection at his mother's bosom.

"Jane, please..." Leahy started, but she ignored him, her arm enveloping Frankie's head. She pressed her mouth against his face, wet with tears and saliva, rocking him gently. "It's okay, Frankie," she gently murmured, "it's okay, my darling, don't be afraid, it's okay." She repeated the same words over and over again, crying softly with him, her voice mixing with his rasping moans.

His first words erupted in unintelligible spurts, distorted by his sobs, muffled by her body, and then his back stiffened and he shook his head violently. "Ill . . . ill . . ." Meredith heard. "Ill . . . ill," again, and then he realized that the word was *kill*, and Frankie was repeating it, screaming it, a man possessed offering them the key to his madness. "Kill . . . kill . . ." he cried, tears running down his cheeks, and Jane bitterly wept with him, and Meredith painfully swallowed, feeling the tears well in his own eyes.

"Yes," Jane was whispering soothingly, stroking the sweat-drenched hair of her mad husband, "yes, darling, tell me, what is it, what are you trying to say, don't be afraid, Frankie, speak to me, Frankie, okay? Frankie?"

He pulled away from her, his torso swaying back and forth as if engaged in some secret prayer, eyes burning with a new, savage fire. An increasing tremor agitated his arms, and his hands clenched into hard bony fists. The slack mouth moved and quivered soundlessly, the mouth of a landed fish, frantically gulping. Then, jerking his head forward, he blurted out some hoarse, incoherent strings of sounds. Meredith and Leahy impulsively leaned toward him. And all of a sudden the parched lips tightened, and the voice emerged, forming horror-filled but mercilessly clear words, which he shouted in desperate, uneven outbursts.

"Kill him! Shoot him! Poor Andy! Shoot poor Andy! But, Captain, sir! Shoot him, kill him, shoot him in the mouth!"

He was hoarsely screaming and crying now, his body frenziedly shaking and bolting. Jane squatted on the floor beside him, petrified with terror. "Shoot him in the mouth! No, no, God, no! In the mouth, yes, sir, in the mouth! Light the fire and run away, light the fire, yes, Captain, sir, but poor Andy, where is Andy, shoot him in the mouth!" He flung his arms around his head and collapsed, facedown, his chest torn by hoarse sobs.

Jane raised her tearful face toward Meredith. Her eyes were blurred by raw, profound pain. He reached down and felt the wetness of her cheek on his fingertips.

"So there was an eighth Marine," she murmured.

The rest was only a matter of hours. While harried male nurses, hounded by Dr. Leahy's confused orders, carried away the drugged and sedated Frank Wyatt, Meredith was already dialing his Washington office on the VTR booth phone. Patty answered almost immediately, as if she had been sitting by the phone waiting for his call. "Walt, where are you?" she breathed in her newly acquired conspiratorial whisper. "I called your hotel but they said you'd left without—"

"Not now, Patty." The receiver was slippery in his hand. "I've no time to explain. You must get for me the last name and the file of an MIA, first name Andy, a Marine. Bravo Company, Thirty-seventh Regiment. Did you get that?"

"Yes, but . . ." she started, puzzled.

"Probably reported missing in February or March '69, after the battle of Bienhoa."

"Bienhoa, February '69," she repeated. "But how shall I find his last name, I mean . . ."

He had it all figured out. "You'll run our list of MIA's through the computer and sort out the names of all the MIA's of the Thirty-seventh Marines. Got that?" As he spoke he was nervously doodling on the back of a manila envelope.

"Thirty-seventh Marines, yes," Patty echoed.

"Now, from those names you'll single out the missing Marines whose first names are Andy and make a cross-reference check with the first months of '69."

There was a short silence. "And if . . ."

"Don't worry," he said impatiently, divining her question. "When you reach that stage there won't be many Andys left." Before hanging up he added urgently, "As soon as you get the name I want you to find his file and send it to me by Express Mail. I am at the Rocky Mountains Motel, registered as Walt Benjamin."

"Walt Benjamin," she repeated excitedly. She seemed to enjoy thoroughly her sleuthing adventure.

He replaced the receiver and vaguely stared at the wild scrawl on the envelope. "POOR ANDY," he had scribbled, "KILL POOR ANDY," over and over again, and he thought of a torn country deliberately sacrificing her son in a faraway killing field.

From the VTR room he went to Jane Wyatt's office. He knocked on the door and entered. Jane was on the phone, talking to somebody named Mabel. She was trying to locate the secretary of the 37th Veterans' Association, Jane said. She needed some information about a missing Marine. She raised her eyes and glanced at Meredith, but he only waved and went out.

Shortly after lunch Meredith called Washington again. "I've got some news for you," Patty announced triumphantly. "The Thirty-seventh Marines had twenty-eight soldiers missing in action throughout the year 1969. Out of those, eleven were reported missing in the first three months of the year. There were two Marines by the name of Andy among them. One was a lieutenant whose jeep was destroyed by a land mine north of Bienhoa on February 12."

"And the second?" Meredith asked, his blood throbbing in his temples.

Dusk was settling in when he drove to Jane Wyatt's house. In the fading daylight the sky was an oppressive, smoky mass lying low over the blurred ridges. Only far to the west an eerie blood-red incandescence was rapidly dissolving. She led him in silence to the back porch. The lights were on, and her face looked drawn, exhausted. She wore no makeup and shivered beneath her heavy woolen cardigan. He stood by the railing, his face exposed to the sporadic gusts of wind that glided from the mountaintops, carrying the dank smell of rain. Without speaking she poured him a large scotch and replenished her empty glass.

"I've got the name," he said.

She nodded, looking away. "I got it too," she said. "I called the office of the Thirty-seventh Veterans'. Their secretary just returned my call. He said finding the name was child's play." She pointed at a pad lying on the small table beside the wicker chairs.

He took a folded note from his pocket and laid it down beside the pad. Both carried the same inscription: Private First Class Andy Cunningham, Bravo Company, 37th Marines.

They looked at each other in silence.

Andy Cunningham was the Unknown Soldier.

PART III

★

UNKNOWN SOLDIER

☆ 10 ☆

"Murder," Jane said bitterly. "I thought it was only murder."

Black, thick darkness was furtively sneaking into the valley below and creeping up the wooded slopes.

"Murder is too weak a word for it," she went on, her voice choking with fury. "It was a deliberate slaughter, ordered by an officer. Shoot him, he said, and they did. Yes, sir, yes, Captain, sir. In the mouth, sir." She was striving to catch her breath. "Jesus, Walt, how could they do such a horrible thing?"

He stood stiff by the railing, following the somber, menacing clouds. A thin wisp of smoke rose from the black hills to the north, fluttering in the wind.

She moved closer to him. "What was it, Walt? I must know. Drugs?"

"Why drugs?" He turned back, watching her feverishly light a cigarette. The bare bulb fixed over the door cast a raw light on her haggard face. She sucked the cigarette avidly, as if it were an oxygen tube.

"I heard entire units were on drugs in Vietnam, buying them in the villages and pushing the stuff back in the camps." She inhaled again, almost crushing the cigarette between her fingers. "It seems that a bunch of guys made a fortune this way. Somebody told me there were quite a few murders connected with the drug traffic."

"So?" he asked coldly. He had a strong suspicion who had told Jane about the drug traffic in Vietnam.

"Maybe they had a fight about drugs"—she hesitated—"or Andy threatened to report them, and they shot him."

He shook his head. "This was no drug murder, Jane. Officers don't formally order their men to kill people for drugs. Captain Rainey"—he was watching her closely as she grimly pressed her lips—"ordered his men to shoot Andy Cunningham. Your friend Steve Rainey turned your husband and his buddies into murderers."

She stared back at him. "Steve didn't tell you that, did he?" Meredith said. "He didn't tell you he ordered his soldiers to shoot Andy Cunningham and then destroy the evidence. Frankie, and perhaps some of the others, questioned the order, but he forced them to carry it out. He didn't tell you Frankie went nuts right there, at Na-san, because of what he forced him to do." His hatred for Rainey didn't stem only from the barbaric murder, Meredith realized, but also from his affair with Jane, which kindled his jealousy.

"How can anybody force an American soldier to kill another American?" she threw back.

"That's what I don't understand," he muttered. He took a drink from his glass and picked up the bottle from the low table. He needed more. "Not only did they do it, but they kept the secret. Lyndon Hughes was there and didn't breathe a word. Eddie Paris kept his mouth shut for years, and was murdered when he probably threatened to reveal what he knew." He turned away. "I wonder what threats Rainey used to make those guys clam up."

"They shot him in the mouth," she whispered. The hand holding her cigarette was trembling. "How could they be so vicious?"

"Don't you understand?" he shouted, then lowered his voice, trying to control himself. "After he was dead, they shot him in the mouth. Rainey wanted to destroy his teeth, to make his identification impossible. That's why he also made them burn the body."

He abruptly broke off as she threw her unfinished cigarette away and turned from him. On the inner screen of his imagination he was visualizing the scene in all its grisly details. The Vietnamese hamlet at the jungle's edge, barely visible beyond the tall elephant grass. The small team of Marines in helmets, flak jackets, and combat fatigues, haunted by the sounds and the shadows of the treacherous Asian night. The blond captain repeatedly screaming his orders. The Marines riddling the poor devil with bullets, then emptying their rifles into the slack mouth of their assassinated comrade, dragging the body to a straw hut, and pulling the pins off a couple of grenades. And after the explosions, setting the hut on fire, turning the corpse into a blazing torch.

He involuntarily shuddered. Why did they do it? Why did they obey Rainey's orders? Those were illegal, criminal orders. They should have refused. The answer to that question eluded him. The main piece in the macabre puzzle was still missing.

Jane had buried her face in her hands. "That's horrible," she murmured, as if responding to his thoughts. She didn't look at him. "And this boy they butchered,

185

Andy, will now become a national symbol. The Unknown Soldier."

"They made such a thorough job of destroying the corpse that nobody could identify it," he said softly. "Steve Rainey is the one who made him the Unknown."

She turned back to him. "Jesus, Walt, do you understand what we've found? This country is going to blow its top when they learn who the Unknown Soldier was and how he died. And the Army—" She abruptly fell silent as the telephone in the living room started ringing. She stood still for a second, disconcerted, then took a deep breath and disappeared into the house.

Meredith slumped into one of the chairs, and for the first time the inevitable questions surfaced in his mind. What should I do, he asked himself, where do I go from here? Should I call Laura Lewis? Colonel Briggs? Should I reveal to the press the name of the Unknown? Ask for an urgent meeting with the Assistant Secretary, or perhaps bring the matter to the President himself?

And then it dawned on him that he still had no formal proof that Andy Cunningham was the Unknown. Nobody would accept the hallucinations of a madman as evidence.

Jane was back. Her voice was low, dispirited. "It was the hospital," she said. "Frankie woke up from the sedation. He's"—she averted her eyes in confusion— "he's the same as before the session. No change." He sensed the agony building in her voice, saw her lips tremble, and quickly pulled her toward him as she burst into tears. There was dark despair in her sobs, and the pain of a shattered, secret illusion. She had apparently hoped that the tremendous shock might extricate Frankie from his pitiful state. And now she was told he remained as he was, a mad, horrified wretch, doomed to be hounded by ugly chimeras in a sealed labyrinth till his dying day.

"Perhaps it's better for him this way," he murmured, holding her tightly. "For Frankie to recover means to remember."

She nodded against his shoulder, guessing his unfinished thought. Frank Wyatt was trapped between madness and reality, between the protective stupor of insanity and the maddening memories of the night when he became an assassin.

She pulled back, desperately fighting her tears. She was trying to say something but ended biting her lips and looking away. "Easy," he whispered rather foolishly, gently turning her face toward him, "easy." Her hair brushed against his face, soft and fragrant. All of a sudden she was so close, so accessible, and the dark full mouth slightly quivered, inches from his own, irresistibly tempting.

God, he thought as a tremor of anguish and anticipation shot through his body, this is neither the time nor the place, and he knew it wasn't, indeed, but his impulses had already taken over and he leaned toward her, his mouth very softly, very lightly, touching hers. Had she stiffened at that moment, or recoiled, or opened her eyes, he would have moved back, never to touch her mouth again. He deserved to be rejected for taking advantage of her weakness.

But she didn't wince, and didn't resist, and stayed in his arms, her face docilely upturned, her mouth vulnerable, offering itself. He kissed her again and again, growing bolder, his mouth drinking hers. Her breath was heavy, uneven, and suddenly she moved in his arms, clinging to him. He felt her lips flutter in response, at first timidly, guardedly, then with increasing passion. And her hands locked at the nape of his neck, her fingers digging into his flesh, pulling him toward her.

Afterward he couldn't recall how they had gotten inside the house and into her dark bedroom. He couldn't remember how he had undressed her, and how he had peeled off his own clothes. As he tried to clear his befuddled memory and taste again those feverish moments, he had some vague visions of the blinking red numerals on the clock radio beside her bed, the white of the bedspread, the glitter of a delicate golden chain on her neck.

But what he did remember, sharply, vividly, was the silky touch of her skin, the tautening of her hard, swelling breasts against his mouth and her throbbing body as she wrapped herself around him and pulled him deep inside her. Her mouth was on his throat, kissing and biting his skin, whispering words he didn't grasp, panting in his ear, and he felt sucked down into a whirlpool of liquid fire, sinking into her pulsating depths, till his lips touched her eyes and he felt the salty taste of her tears.

He came back to his senses much later, when the Swiss grandfather clock chimed softly in the living room. She stirred in his arms and reached for the light switch. He squinted in the strong light, seeking her eyes. "Come here," he said.

She bent over him, her long, fine hair gently touching his face, and he noticed a new determination. "I must go," she said quietly, and her lips briefly rested on his mouth. "I have a plane to catch."

"A plane?" He propped up on his elbows, staring at

her in surprise. "You didn't tell me. Where are you going?"

She shook her head. "I must go and . . . see somebody. I have to." She reached over and very tenderly stroked his cheek.

"I can't let you go alone," he said as a vague suspicion started forming in his mind. "I'll come with you, okay?"

"No," she said resolutely and straightened up. "I've got to do something, and do it alone." She threw a quick look at the bedside clock. "Wait for me, Walt, please. You may stay here if you wish. I'll be back tomorrow night at the latest."

"Listen . . ." he began.

She got up and for the first time he saw her body in full light. He felt aroused again, a hard knot building in the pit of his stomach. She gracefully moved about the room, collecting her clothes, then she bent over him. "This wasn't casual," she said with sudden fervor. "Not for me, anyway. This was the real thing."

He held her by the wrist. "Where are you going?" he asked again.

She wanly smiled and tossed her hair, feigning sudden playfulness. "I'm entitled to my little secrets," she quipped, and gently disengaged herself from his grip. "You don't own me yet." Then she leaned forward, her eyes very intense, very serious, cupped his face in her hands, and passionately, possessively, kissed him on the mouth.

Alone, he slowly dressed and went back to the porch. He refilled his glass and leaned on the balustrade, letting the cool wind caress his burning skin. The place was oddly silent, now that she was gone. He thought of the past couple of hours, surprised by the intensity of his own passion. "It's the real thing," she had said.

The plaintive call of a night bird rose from the black ravines, and the sound carried him back to his past, thirty years ago. He suddenly recalled the morose, monotonous song of the Vietminh that would roll from the mountains surrounding Dien Bien Phu before the final onslaught. A barefoot girl from the village, a black-robed elf with small breasts and an anxious cameo face, had translated the song for him in broken, warped French. "Friend," the Vietnamese chanted in their mewing, high-pitched voices, "do you hear the black flight of the raven in the plains? Friend, do you hear the muffled cry of our country in chains?"

The black flight of the raven. He let himself drift into the haunting memories of his youth. Yes, he had heard and seen the black wings of death over that tragic, accursed land of Vietnam. Death, in its most gruesome expressions, seemed to be the foremost contribution of Vietnam to the history of mankind. And Andy Cunningham's atrocious murder was only another link in a long bloody chain.

He still remembered the heaps of corpses in Dien Bien Phu, hacked by the Communist cannon, rotting in the humid heat till the last, bloody assault of the Vietnamese and the humiliating surrender of the French. And he vividly recalled the scorched cadavers lying in the ashes of burned Vietnamese villages, destroyed by the merciless raids of the Foreign Legion and the French-backed local partisans. Bloodshed and senseless death were everywhere, yet surpassing any known record of horror because of the unique mélange of ideological fanaticism, cynical cruelty, and oriental refinement.

In the bleak hills of Ban Cao, close to the Chinese border, he had seen an old man crucified on a tree before his son, who had been tied, unharmed, to a stump. The Vietnamese had cut the jugular vein of the father and stuck a tiny rubber tube into the wound, making the old man slowly bleed to death before his child's eyes, inflicting upon him a terrible mental torture.

South of Ninh-binh, in the Tonkinese jungle, he had watched French soldiers recover a score of headless bodies from a village well. The retreating Vietnamese, determined to sabotage the water supply of their pursuers, had slaughtered the innocent inhabitants of a hamlet and polluted the well with their blood and corpses.

Not far from there he had seen French-backed partisans of the Rhade Mountain tribes eagerly remove the livers of dead Vietminh guerrillas and cook them on campfires. "It's the best food in the world,"· the Rhade Montagnards assured the appalled French officers, smacking their lips and giggling happily, "especially when it's fresh."

Most of all, Meredith remembered the gruesome vendetta waged between the Vietnamese and the mercenaries of the French Foreign Legion. He had been shaken by the grim resolution of the legionnaires not to fall alive into the hands of the Vietminh. In the back-street bars of Saigon, in the seedy brothels of Hanoi, he heard them, drunk, sweating, their basic French distorted by the multitude of their accents, discussing the safest way to die before being captured by the Vietnamese.

One should keep the last bullet for himself, some said. Others maintained that the best way was to blow away your chest with a hand grenade. But many rejected both methods, claiming they were nothing but a waste of good ammunition, which could still serve to kill a couple of Vietnamese bastards.

"One should die like a legionnaire," he heard a huge albino German bellow one night, brandishing his mug of beer. "Bravely and quietly. Bravely and quietly, ja?"

He pushed his mug away, tore his shirt open, and pulled his combat knife from its belt sheath. "You hold your knife like that"—with his left hand he stuck the tip of his dagger between two ribs, at the level of the heart—"and then, one blow!" He mimicked a swift, violent blow with his right fist on the knife's handle. "You're sure to die this way. Guaranteed!" He burst out in hoarse laughter and reached for his mug.

As he buttoned his shirt a red stain quickly spread on the khaki cloth over his heart. In his zeal to make his point, he had wounded himself. He contemplated for a second the crimson stain with the dazed eyes of a drunk, then guffawed again. "You see that? I told you it was guaranteed!" Nobody had laughed. Meredith was to learn later that the Legion doctors willingly instructed the soldiers how to kill themselves with their own knives.

The choice of death over captivity, he assumed, was another macabre tradition of the mercenary tribe that was the Foreign Legion. Only later was he to learn that the legionnaires had sworn to die by their own hands, not by tradition, but by fear. For they knew well what fate awaited them if they fell alive into the hands of the Vietminh.

A Corsican sergeant, his voice slurred, told him once about the seventeen legionnaires from the 3rd Regiment Etranger des Parachutistes who had been captured by the Vietminh barely twelve miles to the southeast of Saigon. They had been crucified in the ruins of a burned-out village. The Vietnamese had used razors to make horizontal incisions in the skin of their backs, between their shoulders. Their skin had been nailed to the transverse bar of each cross, while their hands had been tied behind the vertical pole. Thus, their bodies hung on nothing but a piece of their own skin, nailed to the cross. They had been left like that, sliding downward inch by inch, flaying themselves alive. It had taken them days to die in terrible pain.

"They hate the legionnaires," the Corsican had growled into his beer, "the legionnaires in particular." He went on telling about a patrol captured in the jungles to the north. The Vietnamese had stripped the legionnaires naked, smeared molasses all over their bodies, and left them on top of an anthill. "You know the Indochina red ants, Yankee? Each one as large as a cockroach."

Close to Cao-Mit, he said, another group of captive legionnaires had been impaled on bamboo stalks. The prisoners had been tied, sitting, on rudimentary chairs, a sharpened bamboo stalk piercing through a hole in the seat. Growing slowly, a few inches a day, the bamboo stalks had torn their insides. Their excruciating agony had lasted about a week.

The most horrendous story, though, had been brought back from the Tan-Xuan Pass by Oscar Quint, a Hungarian legionnaire. His platoon had been charged with a routine mission of escorting a small train traveling from Phan-Thiet to Dakao, in south Annam. As the tiny locomotive was painfully crawling on the rails, panting and groaning up the steep slope of Tan-Xuan, hundreds of Vietnamese launched a lightning attack on the train. The surprised legionnaires hadn't even had the time to reach for their weapons before being virtually hacked to pieces by machine-gun fire and a hail of hand grenades. In a few minutes the Vietnamese had won.

They carefully searched its four cars. As the small, emaciated men in the black tunics entered the legionnaires' car, Oscar Quint, who was badly wounded but conscious, feigned death. Lying immobile under the dead bodies of two of his comradesa, he watched the Vietnamese drag out of the car four other legionnaires, who were, besides him, the sole survivors. A few moments later Quint heard bloodchilling screams and a ghastly stench penetrated the car.

The Vietnamese had thrown the legionnaires alive into the furnace of the locomotive.

In spite of the six bullets that had hit him, Quint survived, the Corsican said. He was rescued and reported his gruesome experience to his commanding officer. But while describing the death of the four legionnaires, he cracked. One could visit him at the psychiatric hospital in Saigon. The man had gone mad.

No, the Corsican said, he couldn't imagine a reason why the Vietminh hated the Legion so much. It couldn't be because they were mercenaries. After all, the Vietminh were also mercenaries, Communist mercenaries, weren't they? He didn't know either who had burned the village where the seventeen legionnaires

had been crucified. The Vietminh, probably. Meredith
had agreed and nodded into his beer.

One phrase the drunk Corsican had said engraved
itself in his memory: *"La France se meurt en Indo-
chine,"* the legionnaire had rasped—France is dying in
Indochina.

He had witnessed that agony as he flew daily to the
entrenched camp of Dien Bien Phu, which the French
had built in a lost valley north of Hanoi between the
Black River and the border of Laos. Dien Bien Phu
had been born from the condescending folly of a few
French generals who had dreamed of it as a gigantic
snare for the shadow army of Giap. They had para-
chuted thousands of the finest fighters of France, commandos and legionnaires, into the obscure valley,
hoping to lure the elusive battalions of the Vietminh
into an open battle and crush them against the rocky
flanks of the surrounding mountains. With the help of
American money and American equipment the death
trap was soon ready. Heavy transport planes unloaded
on the freshly built airstrip scores of cannon, tanks,
ammunition.

But while complacent French officers were contentedly rubbing their hands, the Vietnamese were silently,
surreptitiously, tightening an invisible noose around
their necks. Very soon the hunter was to become the
hunted, Dien Bien Phu was surrounded and cut off,
the airstrip was destroyed, Communist cannon myster-
iously appeared on the inacessible cliffs, spreading
death in the exposed valley.

Day after day Meredith and the other Americans
aboard the ramshackle C-119 Packets dropped supplies
to the besieged garrison amid murderous antiaircraft

fire. When the situation grew desperate they were thrown into the battle as well, diving on the mountain peaks and dropping napalm on the Vietnamese positions.

But Dien Bien Phu was doomed. Modern equipment, sophisticated weapons, strategic experience and pretentious, overconfident planning were all swept away by the underfed, underequipped, badly trained Vietnamese, whose deadly offensive turned Dien Bien Phu into a hecatomb. The French had been caught in their own death trap. And with the death of Dien Bien Phu, France, too, died in Indochina. Soon after, the French Government fell, and the new prime minister, Pierre Mendès-France, pulled his army out of Vietnam.

Meredith recalled his flight out of a glum, defeated Saigon, and a verse of Kipling emerged in his mind: "We have had no end of a lesson; it will do us no end of good."

No, America had had no end of a lesson from the French debacle in Vietnam. Less than ten years later she was busy turning Vietnam into her own death trap, feasting on body counts, eagerly dispatching her children, the naive, pampered, confident American boys, to a living hell, to a faraway planet of insatiable horror.

There was a question he tried to chase from his mind, but it always emerged again, mercilessly pursuing him in his thoughts when he was awake, in his nightmares when he closed his eyes. How did Benjamin die? That was, he knew, the maddening question that kept tormenting the MIA parents without respite. And like them, he could only pray and hope that his boy had been spared the cruelty that flourished in that damned land. The Vietnamese horror was contagious, a plague that struck the dead and the living. Those who were lucky enough escaped death, but the hell they encountered contaminated them, too, at times turning them into assassins, as it had that night in Na-san.

He went into the house, latching the back door behind him. Barbara was right, he admitted to himself, he couldn't escape the haunting memories of his dead son. But throughout their endless arguments he had never dared to tell her how much he wanted to be cured of this obsession that had taken total control over his emotions. As he crossed the living room he almost tripped against the low table on which the telephone stood. He picked it up impulsively and dialed his Washington home number. The phone kept ringing for more than a minute, but nobody answered. Barbara wasn't home.

He wondered how she would have reacted to Frank Wyatt's outburst at the asylum this morning. His screams surfaced in his mind again as he turned off the lights and left the house, taking his car keys out of his pocket. Jane must be made of steel, he thought, to cope with the ghastly discovery that her husband was an assassin, and her lover had made him such.

And what did I give her, Meredith reflected, besides pain and suffering? I turned her life into a nightmare, and still she offered me her love. He felt a sudden pang of raw, painful longing. His skin still carried the silken caress of her body, and he could taste the fiery touch of her mouth on his own. Was he in love with her or was it their loneliness and the ghosts of their past that drew them together? Why did she have to go? Where was she?

☆ 11 ☆

Jane Wyatt parked the rented Buick outside the gate and walked up the driveway, her high heels dryly cracking on the gravel. A timid breeze faintly rustled in the bushes but the air was warm, humid, and she took off her woolen jacket. The low house was bathed in darkness except for a bright all-night light over the porch.

The light was always on, even when he was gone for a few days, but tonight he was home. His hefty Chevrolet Blazer was parked by the door behind a smart BMW coupe with Dade County plates. Besides, she had called twice along the way, once from the Miami airport, after she landed, the second time from a gas station in Key Largo. He had answered the phone both times, and she had hung up without speaking, the receiver oddly moist in her grip.

The second time she heard music in the background and his voice was slightly slurred, as if he had been drinking or smoking a joint. She wondered if he had a woman in the house. He had told her once that women, many women, were a physical need for him.

"Honest to God, baby, I need a couple good lays a week to function properly. I can't make it with the same broad all the time, see, I can't help fooling around, and that's what screwed up my marriage." And she had said sure, she understood, but she didn't believe a word of course. In bed he was abrupt, impatient, and didn't seem to derive much pleasure from the act of sex itself. If it had been sex alone that mattered, she wouldn't have gotten so intensely involved with him.

She had been attracted to him by his rugged, handsome looks, his fiercely independent character, and his secret but ardent ambition to become somebody. Disappointment had come much later, when she learned to really know him and found about his odd fixation for women. She suspected that his appetite for women didn't spring from a sexual need but from an altogether different urge. What he really wanted was to raise the number of pubic scalps dangling from his belt. Sex for Steven Rainey was a means of proving something, like everything else he did in his life.

The clumps of bushes and lush tropical plants surrounding the house had grown tall and thick since the last time she had been here. The house, too, had changed—a wing had been added at the northern side, where the toolshed had stood before, and a new coat of elegantly textured paint covered the walls. He was doing well, obviously. She wondered if he had finally dug that swimming pool he used to talk about. As a matter of fact, he had told her about the pool the very first time they met, when he came to Mesa to see Frankie. She had been vaguely amused by his boyish determination to own the largest pool in Islamorada.

She stepped on the illuminated landing by the door and rang the bell. The swarm of bugs whirling under the porch light briefly hesitated, then resumed their suicidal dance around the glowing lamp. A fat lizard raised its monstrous head, watching her with a mean, annoyed eye, and unhurriedly crawled into the shadows. The door lock snapped almost immediately: Steve was a light sleeper. Vietnam, he used to say, always Vietnam. "Those of us who didn't wake up at the first shot, baby, would soon not wake up at all." She disliked him calling her baby, but never told him that.

He appeared on the threshold, naked except for a towel wrapped around his waist. She had guessed right, there was a girl in the house. He squinted in the strong light. "My God, Jane!" he blurted. A hesitant smile slowly spread over his face. But his eyes were suddenly alert, and she knew the tiny wheels of his suspicious mind were already rolling. "What are you doing here?" he asked. His voice was uncertain and she sensed his anguish. Steve Rainey was no fool. He should figure out that by emerging like that from the thickness of night, his one-time lover was bringing an ill omen to his doorstep.

She peered over his shoulder into the dark living room. "Is she a transient or a resident?" she asked.

"Who?" He frowned.

"The girl in the bedroom," she said coldly. She was surprised at her own self-control. Back in Mesa this afternoon, she had felt she could strangle him with her bare hands. "Come on, Steve, you heard me. She's your roommate?"

He angrily crossed his arms on his chest. "What difference does it make to you? We're through, you and I, aren't we?" He stared at her for a moment, then shrugged. "She's a visitor," he conceded.

"Then pack her off and send her home. The BMW is hers, I guess." She walked past him into the house.

"Now wait a minute, he started. "Nobody's telling me who stays here and who's going home. Do you read me?"

She turned back and faced him, her fists tight, her nails painfully digging into her palms. "I read you, Captain," she said. "You'd rather have her stay and hear how you murdered Andy Cunningham, right?"

She turned away, catching a fleeting glimpse of his chalk-white face. After a moment of silence he blurted out a string of curses, then dashed into the bedroom, slamming the door behind him. She pulled the drapes of the large bay windows and fumbled for the light switch. Artfully concealed lamps flooded the seaside lawn with soft white light and shimmered on the still expanse of limpid green water. He had built his dream pool all right.

She heard the shuffle of steps and the angry whispered exchange between Rainey and the girl. But she didn't speak until he had closed the door behind her. "Yes," she said, without turning around, feeling melodramatic to the point of foolishness. The pool and the lawn looked so pleasant, so serene. "They know where I am and with whom, and I wouldn't recommend a hunting accident."

"You must be out of your mind," he said, sucking his teeth.

"Eddie Paris had a hunting accident, didn't he?" she coldly reminded him.

"You're out of your mind," he repeated.

She turned around. He had traded his towel for a pair of white jeans and a purple muscle shirt. "My husband, Frank Wyatt, is the one who is out of his mind," she said. "You drove him mad by forcing him to participate in the murder of Andy Cunningham at

201

Na-san. Then you came to visit him at the asylum in Mesa, and screwed his wife." She was speaking like an automaton, hardly recognizing her own voice. "I guess I was your prize for a job well done."

He was standing very still, his hands hanging at his sides. "Who told you all this crap?" he said hoarsely. His face was taut, uncertain. "Meredith?" She didn't answer and he went on, hatefully, "I knew the mother-fucker was bad news when I first saw him. I should have taken care of him right there, on the boat."

"Like you took care of Andy," she countered.

"You're screwing him now, or what?"

She fell silent and stiffly walked to the far end of the room where a handsome rosewood cabinet housed his electronic equipment. The video recorder was in its place on the lower rack. She unzipped her large shoulder bag and took out the VTR cassette she had smuggled from Alma Viva that morning. On a sudden impulse, she turned around. "I should have brought a gun instead," she said scornfully.

He didn't speak, watching her in mute dismay. She knelt by the recorder, introduced the cassette, and switched on the TV set. She had mentally rehearsed every gesture over and over again during the flight to Miami. For a brief moment, Shirley MacLaine flashed on the screen, revealing to Barbara Walters how her knees wobbled when she got the Oscar for *Terms of Endearment*.

Jane selected the video channel, pressed the PLAY switch, and Frankie's crouching body appeared on the screen, partly concealed by the stooping frame of Walt Meredith. She turned the sound knob to full volume and Meredith's magnified voice suddenly boomed throughout the room. "Who did you murder, Corporal Wyatt? Answer the fucking question, Corporal!"

"Enjoy the show," she muttered. "I can't go through all that again." She flipped the latch of the large glass doors and stepped outside. She felt her head sway and groped for a chair.

In the living room, Steve Rainey stood petrified, his eyes glued to the screen.

Fifteen minutes later, he was still in the same position, his throat caught in an iron vice, his jaws clenched, when the inhuman screams burst from the screen. "Kill him! Shoot him! Shoot poor Andy! But, Captain, sir!..."

When it was all over he blindly walked to the cabinet, stumbling over the furniture, and switched off the video recorder. Then he crossed the room. The glass doors were open. Jane had turned off the outside lights. It took him a while to get accustomed to the darkness and perceive her immobile figure at the lawn's edge, facing the ocean. He stood close behind her.

"You want the truth, don't you?" he said. And he thought of the video cassette she had brought, that reel of magnetic tape that could strip him of everything he had achieved in his life, since the faraway time when he had been branded as white trash.

White trash. He had heard those words for the first time in Toledo, when the landlord had thrown them out of the small, dark apartment by the railroad tracks. The police had arrested his father that morning, and five minutes after they left, the landlord was yelling at his mother to get the hell out of his house. It was a respectable residence. He didn't want no dogs, no bloody niggers, and no white trash in his building.

The landlord was a bald, burly man with bad teeth and a huge belly who wore soiled collarless shirts and always smelled of bourbon and garlic. Steve, who was five at the time, hid behind the broken sofa, listening to his mother's sobs and fantasizing how he would suddenly jump on the landlord and kick him in the balls.

But he didn't dare to budge, and the landlord didn't even know he was there, while his mother pleaded with the man, insisting that they were good people and her husband had been arrested by mistake. The landlord screamed back at her not to give him that shit and said they were two months late with the rent and everybody was complaining about the noise, and her husband was always drunk, and he beat her and the children, and he was a no-good sonofabitch and a criminal type, thank God they caught him before he killed somebody.

Steve didn't remember where they went afterward, but he recalled visiting his mother at the Mayfair Hotel, where she was a cleaning woman, and six months later they released his father and they moved to Cleveland, where he worked in a zinc factory till he was arrested again, but only for drinking, his mother said.

That's how he grew up, migrating from one city to another, from squalid apartments to tumble-down shacks, and when his father wasn't in jail, he was most of the time unemployed. But Buck's real problem, his mother said, was that he couldn't hold his liquor, and once he had a couple under his belt he would grow mean and violent and head for trouble. Every time he went into a bar he ended up fighting with somebody. A couple of times he was arrested for mugging and petty thefts, and once he stole a car and crashed into a trailer while under the influence.

When he came home drunk Steve would escape to the street, at any time of day or night. Buck Rainey was a blond-bearded giant, two hundred pounds of evil, stone-hard muscle, and anyone who crossed his path when he was loaded did so at his own risk. His mother ran away from home once, taking Steve and his sister to her parents' house in Oregon, but after Buck Rainey found them and devastated the house, the old folks wouldn't take them again.

Then, all of a sudden, his father contracted a lung disease, and in a few months lost almost half his weight, quickly deteriorating into a bitter, choleric invalid, a new kind of burden on the wretched family. And Steve, who had grown into a tough, streetwise teenager, swore to God he would do anything to get out of that miserable existence.

Crime was an obvious solution, an obvious temptation, but his father's typical behavior, writhing and swearing as he was repeatedly dragged into police cars, kept him away from it. For a while he thought education was the answer. He worked his way through school with dogged application, studying during the day, working at night in garages, parking lots, scraping boat keels at the marinas. He even had a girlfriend at school, a pretty, cheerful redhead who lived in an affluent beach community in North Miami. In her house he discovered nice furniture, plenty of food, pleasant manners, and a private swimming pool. But the dream was soon to turn sour when his girl's father forbade her to see him anymore. He was white trash, a pariah, and nothing could change that, not even a high school diploma.

At the age of seventeen he joined the Marines. He instinctively sensed that in uniform everybody was equal. And he wanted to get as far away from home as possible. This time he had made the right choice. He was a good soldier, a born fighter, and the Army was good to him. Four years later, he was a second lieutenant, and among the first to be sent to Vietnam. He came back with a scarred body, a Purple Heart, and combat-tested captain's bars.

He was driven by a burning obsession—to climb as high as he could on the social ladder. As soon as he took off his uniform, he plunged with fiery dedication into his new endeavor. The sea had always appealed to him, offering him a formidable physical challenge, an unequaled sense of freedom, and the delightful taste of utter solitude. He started scraping boat keels, as he had in his youth, then became a deckhand on some of the sleek yachts at Bahia Mar. With a friend he mounted a sea retrieval-and-rescue operation, later founding a boat chartering company. He sailed unscathed through a number of shady but lucrative deals, buying and selling boats across the Mexican border but managing to keep on the right side of the law.

It took him more than ten years of hard work, but now he was a success. He owned the *Fidelis* and another fishing yacht, the *Veteran*, which he leased to a chartering company at Siesta Key, on Florida's west coast. He was also the major partner in a fishing company operating off the keys. He had as many women as he wanted. He had a large house in Islamorada and was a respected member of the local community.

No social event took place on the Florida keys without him being invited. He was liked, even admired, as a brave officer and a skilled sailor. An influential local politician had even approached him once to find out if he would consider running for a political office, but he had declined the offer. His only failure during those years had been a disastrous marriage that left him with some ugly memories and twice-a-month visiting rights to a little boy in Hallandale.

And always menacing, always present in his mind, lurked the haunting secret of Na-san.

He had been a fine Marine, Steve Rainey thought, and a good American. He was convinced he had done the right thing at Na-san. He was as certain, however, that if the secret of Andy Cunningham's death ever came to light, he would be crucified by some hare-brained judge and rot in jail for the rest of his life. The hysterical press would have a field day prying into his dark origins, revealing his father's criminal record, evoking his hereditary violent streak. And his little boy would forever be branded as an assassin's son.

That, he had decided long ago, was never going to happen. That was why Eddie Paris had to die in that hunting accident. That was why he had flown to Mesa, pretending he wanted to welcome Frankie Wyatt on his return from captivity but actually intent on finding out if the man was indeed crazy. In Mesa he had met Jane Wyatt, and for the first time in his life had been infatuated with a woman. He would still wake at night longing for her body and her sharp wit.

But even Jane wasn't going to destroy what he had built with such effort for so many years. He had to make a couple of long-distance calls as soon as she was gone. If he kept his head cool and took the necessary steps, he could still solve the crisis. Nobody was going to accuse him of murder. Nobody was going to smear his name. Never.

"You want to know the truth, don't you?" he asked Jane again, stifling the impulse to reach for her.

She turned toward him. Her face was in shadow; her eyes glared with a cold, hostile fire. Behind her the moon cast a broken silvery pattern on the ocean, and the sound of regular, heavy breathing rolled on the waves that languished on the white beach.

"You murdered Andy Cunningham," she said.

He took a deep breath. "Executed is the word." He cleared his throat. "I had to fulfill my duty as an officer, so I shot the bastard dead."

✪12✪

The insistent pounding on his door woke Meredith early in the morning. A faint light filtered through the heavy window drapes. The motel clerk, a heavyset young man with tallow-colored hair and an acne-ravaged face, handed him a large manila envelope. "Just came in by Federal Express from Washington," the room clerk gravely announced, wiping his face with his sleeve. It was raining again. He unhurriedly pocketed the dollar bill that Meredith handed him and waddled away in the rain.

Meredith pulled the curtains and the cold gray light softly settled on the room. A few raindrops had splashed on the envelope, smudging the sender's return address. He recognized Patty's neat, rounded writing. He ripped the envelope open and took out a yellow file stamped with the Department of Defense seal and with the heading "Personnel—MIA Bureau." An old "Restricted" stamp had been crossed off with two vigorous strokes and a couple of more recent "Unclassified" stamps, in vivid purple ink, had been superimposed over it. Another stamp spelled "COPY" in black capitals and beneath it, in smaller print, "Original file in Department of Defense, Central Archives, Washington."

A rectangular label at the upper right corner carried the inscription, in block letters, "Private First Class Andrew B. Cunningham, 10570988, Bravo Company, 37th Marines, Bienhoa." And a date, "February 4, 1969." He frowned. According to that file, Andy Cunningham had been reported missing in Bienhoa a week before Rainey's patrol had set out for Na-san. The date and the place were false, of course. Rainey had spared no effort to cover up his crime. He had even backdated Andy's disappearance by a week to make it coincide with the first, chaotic stage of the Tet offensive. During those days of fire and death nobody could remember who had disappeared, when, or how. Meredith was convinced that Rainey himself had filled out the forms reporting Andy Cunningham missing in action.

He paced up and down the room, leafing through the file. It consisted mostly of the anatomical profile of Andy Cunningham, all those painstakingly assembled reports about his physical characteristics, body measurements, blood tests, fingerprint charts, X-ray slides, medical history, back and front body sketches representing particular characteristics, like moles, scars, and outstanding features.

Later he was going to read the documents, one by one, and compare them with the few fragmentary data that John Natua had succeeded in extracting from the heap of charred bones in his Hawaiian laboratory. That test, he hoped, would produce the formal proof he wanted to submit to the League of MIA Families. But right now his mind was set upon finding out a few more facts about Andy Cunningham. The very name roused a morbid fascination in him. What kind of a man had he been, the Marine so savagely murdered by his buddies? Who was the man America had blindly chosen as the symbol of her lost sons?

He was in for a disappointment, for the one-page document at the end of the file was utterly parsimonious in details. It was a printed form, its rare white spaces barely sufficient to hold some laconic data. Andrew B. Cunningham, the form stated, was from Emerald Lake, Minnesota, the son of Brett Cunningham, a farmer, and his wife, Karen. But besides Cunningham's address, parents' names, and date of birth—born in December 1949, he was barely nineteen when he was reported missing—the document didn't mention anything of importance. Andy Cunningham had enlisted in January 1968, and seven months later had gotten his first stripe. He spoke English, some high school French, and a few words of Swedish that he had learned from his grandparents on his mother's side. He used to play basketball with the Emerald Lake local team and had won a couple of swimming trophies in high school.

Meredith turned the page. Under it, fastened to the back cover of the file with a couple of paper clips, was an enlarged photograph of Andy Cunningham. Meredith suddenly became very still, staring at the solemn young face, then slowly, heavily, sank into an armchair by the window.

No, Andy didn't look at all like Benjamin, of course. He was blond while Benjamin had his mother's raven-black curls. His face was oval, with high cheekbones and a delicate mouth, whereas Benjamin had an angular face and a pointed chin. But under the heavy eyelashes Andy's huge, almond-shaped eyes had the same sad, poignant look he knew only too well.

He sat immobile for a long moment, his eyes glued

to the photograph. It was nothing but a photograph, after all, in fuzzy black and white, badly enlarged, and the melancholy look he read in the boy's eyes was probably the fruit of his imagination. How many bereaved parents he had met who discovered their sons' features, their looks, their smiles, in any blurred, grainy snapshot he handed them, clinging with desperate conviction to the faint glimmer of hope that perhaps, in spite of all, it was their boy, alive, miraculously spared. He knew he was as weak, as vulnerable, as the others, perhaps even more so. Still, why did it have to be Andy Cunningham, why did that horrible death strike the boy who had Benjamin's eyes?

A minute later he was leaning over the phone, feverishly punching a long-distance number. After a few rings a very distant but very clear woman's voice answered, and he hoarsely asked to speak to Brett or Karen Cunningham.

"Karen Cunningham speaking." She had a warm, friendly voice.

He introduced himself with his real name and position. "Oh yes," she said immediately, "we've received several letters and circulars from your office, Mr. Meredith." She sounded slightly puzzled.

"I'm sorry to disturb you like this, but we are working now on a special project," he lied. "We want to commemorate the missing boys, not by a monument, but by the publication of a written testimony about them." It wasn't a total lie, he had submitted the project to the Assistant Secretary a year ago, but it was gathering dust in some forgotten archive for lack of funds.

"We are collecting from the families of our MIA's

anything written by their sons—letters, high school diaries, articles published by them or about them in their community papers. We also collect photographs, of course, and interview their friends and relatives." He paused. "Many boys have secretly written poems, essays, short stories...you know how young boys are."

"Yes," she said, "I have a younger son."

"What we want to do," he went on, "is edit and publish this material in a series of volumes. We feel this is the best memorial we can preserve for the missing, so that any American—"

"Will the families get their own copy?" she interrupted.

"Certainly. As I was saying, everyone would be able to pick up a volume in a library and find who the young men were who disappeared in Vietnam."

"Yes, I see," she said awkwardly. She still wondered, he felt, why he was calling. "It's a fine idea, Mr. Meredith, a very nice idea, indeed."

"I'll be in Minnesota today," he said, "I'm on my way to the West Coast on official business. I wondered if I could come and visit you and your family."

"Oh yes." She seemed pleased. "Of course you may. My husband is away, though, he won't be back for a couple of weeks."

In a couple of weeks," he thought, it will be too late. "I'd rather see you today," he said. "I'm not sure I'll have another opportunity to visit Minnesota in the near future."

"It's fine with me," she assured him. "But we live in the country, it's a long drive. When do you think you'll be arriving?"

"In the late afternoon," he said quickly. "I'll fly to Minneapolis and rent a car there."

"It will take you about two and a half hours to reach us," she said. "Are you sure you want to make the trip?"

"Positive," he said eagerly. "If it's okay with you, I mean."

"It sure is," she concluded pleasantly. "We'll be expecting you then."

He hung up, his forehead covered with sweat. He felt disgusted with himself for having to cheat on Andy Cunningham's mother. But he couldn't fight his strange obsession with the dead boy. Before sharing his secret with anybody in Washington, he had to find out who the boy was.

On his way to the airport, he stopped at Jane's house. The heavy raindrops fell in slanted sheets on the shuttered windows and burst on impact, like tiny silver flames. He kept the engine running and scribbled her a short note. "Have to leave immediately," he wrote. "I'll call you tonight."

It had happened only last night, he thought, and tried to recall the taste of her mouth, the look in her eyes before she left him. But it was Barbara's face that emerged from his memory, Barbara's dark, troubled eyes. He had phoned her office before leaving the motel, but her secretary had told him Professor Stuart had unexpectedly had to leave. Something very urgent had come up, didn't Mr. Meredith know? No, she had no ida when Professor Stuart was due back. Perhaps at the end of the week, but how come Mr. Meredith didn't know? He had slammed down the phone in a surge of anger. His life was in such a turmoil lately, his emotions so bare, so vulnerable.

THE UNKNOWN SOLDIER

Before he slipped the note under Jane's door, he added at the bottom of the page, "You were right. It was the real thing." Hell, he thought, she could have called me this morning.

The men who had built Emerald Lake must have been fervent fans of Sinclair Lewis, he mused as he drove, shortly before dusk, through the main street of the small town. Time had stopped its flow in Emerald Lake, and the low houses, the old-fashioned grocery store, the barbershop, the bank facade, the vintage cars, even the taciturn, vigorous farmers in their floppy wide-rimmed hats, checkered shirts, and ankle-high working shoes—all of which seemed to have been beamed over straight from the twenties by some nostalgic time machine. And here she was, the old, unchanging America, with her somnolent Main Street and her antique movie theater, home-cookin' restaurant, and Millie's last-year fashions. Its quaint harmony was only rarely broken by an incongruous steel and glass high rise, a brightly lit pizza parlor, or a neon sign counting McDonald's billions.

The countryside, too, seemed immutable, with its scattered farms, huge antique barns, and rugged wooden cabins. Although Meredith suspected that the archaic windmills, soundlessly turning against the limpid sky, had been left there just as an endearing vestige of old times, while the water was being discreetly pumped out of the wells by electric power. But the serenity of the landscape was breathtaking, the air smelled of freshly cut grass, and the sun painted the rippling wheat fields in intense gold-green colors.

The Cunningham farm was twenty miles west of the city, the elderly reception clerk at the Town Inn said.

He uttered the Cunningham name with deference, which Meredith found rather intriguing. He left his bag at the inn, a two-story colonial structure with immaculate white walls and a stately entrance surrounded by slender stucco columns. The narrow country road leading to the farm followed for a few miles the elliptical coast of the lake. And watching its clear waters shimmer at the far end between a dense growth of reeds, Meredith recalled a canoe trip with Virginia and Benjamin in an Indian lake years ago when they had watched the Sioux harvest wild rice, the men effortlessly paddling, the women bending the tall stalks and batting the ripe grain into the canoes. Big white birds were circling above them, avidly watching the swelling heaps of rice.

As he drove west he heard a special flash on the car radio about the killer tornadoes raging in Kentucky and Louisiana. At least fourteen dead, a male voice breathlessly announced, then the country music resumed with a sad ballad of Emmylou Harris mourning her lost love. For a while he followed a battered pickup truck that bounced and squeaked on the uneven country road. On its rear window a sticker showed the sun emerge behind a suggestively clefted mountain over the legend, "I'm so horny that even the crack of dawn turns me on."

In the pickup's rearview mirror he could vaguely make out the dark glasses and bushy beard of the sex-starved Minnesotan. At an abandoned railroad crossing the pickup turned sharply to the right and disappeared in a cloud of dust down a dirt road. And in front of him, clearly etched against the evening sky, he saw the Cunningham farm, a cluster of light-brown buildings dominating a vast expanse of wheat fields and grazing lands. As he drove through the open gate and approached the main house, he noticed the lace curtains at the open windows gently floating over resplendent flowerpots, stacked on every sill.

Here he was, at last. At the house where the Unknown Soldier had been born and raised. For he was certain now that Andy Cunningham was the Unknown Soldier. Aboard the plane, during the long flight from Colorado, he had systematically examined the documents in Cunningham's profile, comparing them with Dr. Natua's records on the last unidentified body in his laboratory. Every finding John Natua had deduced from the small pile of scorched bones—blood type, body measurements, skull shape—suited Cunningham's file to perfection. The hideous remains Meredith had seen in John Natua's underground alcove belonged to the blond boy who had grown up in these golden fields, under these tranquil Midwestern skies.

The front door opened as he got out of the car, and a Belgian shepherd darted toward him, wiggling its tail and barking joyfully. It stood on its hind legs before Meredith, its paws leaning against his chest, and sniffed him diligently, offering its handsome black head to his caress. Meredith looked up. A woman of about sixty, wearing a prim blue dress, had come out on the porch, watching him with a smile. Her snow-white hair was pulled back in a tight bun.

"He won't hurt you," she said pleasantly. "That's the trouble with him. Too friendly to be a watchdog. Come here, Ranger, here!" The dog reluctantly retreated and curled up on the porch, its tongue dangling.

"You must be Mr. Meredith," the woman said, ceremoniously shaking his hand. "I am Karen Cunningham." She had a large but surprisingly soft hand. "Will you come in, please? My son will join us for dinner, but in the meantime we can have some coffee. Or perhaps you'd prefer a drink?"

"I'd love some coffee, thank you," he said, following her into the house. Karen Cunningham was a tall, bony woman with the intense blue eyes and smooth rosy complexion of her Swedish forebears. He could discern her Scandinavian heritage in the austere living room, in the ancient glass figurines displayed in a narrow chest, in the stern family portraits hanging on the wall, and in the pure design of the aged dining table and the tall-backed chairs surrounding it.

She noticed his look and smiled, inviting him with a graceful gesture to sit down and settling on a chair across from him. She had a luminous, innocent smile that made her entire face light up. "This table is home-made," she said proudly. "A wedding present from my oldest brother. He was the best carpenter in the country, a real artist. My Brett is a fine farmer, but not very good with his hands." She got up and switched on the lights.

"Your husband isn't home, I understand," he said, turning around and following her with his eyes. A spotlight, brighter than the other lamps in the room, cast a dazzling illumination on a tall portrait of Andy Cunningham in Marine uniform. It hung on the wall behind him, and Meredith had failed to notice it in the evening shadow. A black ribbon was stretched diagonally across the lower right corner of the portrait.

"No," she said. "Brett's out of the country for the first time since the war. He left for France three days ago."

He couldn't take his eyes off the black ribbon. "Pleasure or business?"

"Neither," she said, brushing some specks of dust from the aged television set. "He's going to visit the graves of his buddies." Noticing Meredith's baffled look, she explained, "You see, my Brett was with the U. S. Rangers in the war. When they landed in Normandy—it will be forty years in a couple of weeks—he was with the team that climbed the cliffs at Pointe du Hoe." She stepped closer, needlessly tidying the needlework cloth covering the table. "They're going to have quite a few ceremonies in Normandy this year to commemorate the landing. Brett decided to fly to France with a group of former Rangers. A charter flight. Quite cheap, you know."

Brett Cunningham and his friends, she went on, were to spend a few days touring the old battle sites in Normandy, where a veterans' convention would be held. A week later they would meet with German war veterans who had fought against them and later attend the official ceremonies commemorating D-Day. "Brett is going to lay a wreath at Pointe du Hoe in the name of the U. S. Army."

"Well," Meredith said, "that's quite an honor. You must be very proud, Mrs. Cunningham."

She sounded oddly apologetic. "He was the first to reach the top of the cliff, you see. He was wounded twice, but went on fighting."

Meredith frowned, cocking his head. A vague memory was surfacing in his mind. "Hold it," he said, raising his hand, "just a moment. I knew I'd heard about your husband, but I didn't remember his name. He's a hero, isn't he?"

She shrugged, her face suddenly flushed with embarrassment. "No," she said firmly. "Not a hero. He was fighting for his country, he did what he had to do." The disarming smile again. "They gave him all those medals, though." A note of pride had slipped into her voice. "Here, you see?"

He followed her to the old chest. On the shelf beneath the glass figurines, several medals were displayed, decorated with faded ribbons. "This is the Congressional Medal of Honor," she pointed out. "The British Victoria Cross, the French Croix de Guerre and Legion d'Honneur. And the Purple Heart." He leaned over, trying to read the engraved plaques placed behind the decorations.

Karen Cunningham abruptly struck her forehead with her hand. "Oh, my God, I forgot the coffee. I'm sorry, I'll be right back." She hurried toward a swinging door at the far end of the room.

"Mrs. Cunningham," he called after her on a sudden impulse. "Was your husband on television ten years ago, in June of '74?"

There was a short silence, then she replied from the kitchen, "June of '74? Sure, it was the thirtieth anniversary of the landing. He was interviewed by all the networks. You saw him?"

He hadn't seen him, but her answer solved another mystery. He thought of Martin Armstrong's visit to Eddie Paris's house in Huntsville. Eddie had been watching some television program about the World War, his brother had said, and had heard or seen something that shook him terribly. Immediately afterward he had made those long-distance calls that had, finally, ended with his death.

And all that had happened exactly ten years ago.

There was no doubt in Meredith's mind that Eddie

Paris had seen one of the interviews with Brett Cunningham or a program describing his exploit in Normandy. He knew about him beforehand, of course. Andy had certainly told his buddies about his famous father. The television program had stirred afresh the guilt feelings that haunted Eddie, and he had called some of his former buddies—Hughes perhaps, and Rainey, certainly—and told them he was going to make a clean breast of Andy's murder. Steve Rainey had pretended to go along with him and suggested a hunting expedition, where they could discuss when and how to reveal their secret. Eddie had said yes.

And sealed his own death warrant.

Meredith was torn from his dark reverie by a gentle hand on his shoulder. He turned around. Karen Cunningham was standing behind him, watching him with a puzzled smile. She held a steaming mug in her hand. "Your coffee, Mr. Meredith."

He crossed the room and stood facing Andy's portrait, watching the clear forehead and the deep brown eyes. "He had his father's eyes," Karen Cunningham said, her voice wavering. "Brett was very proud of him. He raised him on his principles, and educated him to serve his country, even at the cost of his life. When he was reported missing, people came to console us. But Brett was the one who consoled them, saying that Andy gave his life for his country."

Meredith nodded. "Why the black ribbon?" he gently asked, pointing at the portrait.

"Because he is dead," she said simply.

He quickly raised the mug to his lips to conceal his confusion. The brew was strong, but too sweet to his taste. "He is missing, officially," he managed.

She shook her head, her face resigned. "No, Mr. Meredith." Her voice had a ring of calm dignity. "We don't play with words. We are country folks, simple people, you know. We don't believe in all those stories about surviving Americans kept somewhere in the jungle by the Vietnamese. We know our Andy's dead. We know nothing will bring him back. But he was a fine, brave boy, and we're sure he didn't die in vain."

Not in vain, Meredith reflected, only gunned down by his buddies. Jesus, he thought, how could I, or anybody, tell her the truth about her boy?

"Did he leave any diary?" he asked.

She shook her head. "He wasn't the kind who kept a diary, I'm afraid." She was suddenly less confident, fidgeting with a small white handkerchief she took from her pocket. "But after he was reported missing, Brett assembled a sort of scrapbook about him. We got letters from his teachers, his friends, his basketball coach, you now, and a couple of cuttings from the Emerald *News*. That's our local paper."

"Can I see that?" he said eagerly.

She nodded. "It's up in his room."

On the wood-paneled wall of the narrow staircase hung two more photographs of Andy Cunningham. In one of them he was in bathing trunks, standing in the middle of a group of teenagers and triumphantly brandishing a swimming cup. His athletic torso was wet and his hair was plastered over his forehead.

In the second photograph he was clad in jacket and bow tie, hugging a pretty dark-haired girl and smiling at the camera. The photograph had apparently been taken at a high school prom. Farther up hung two amateur paintings in watercolor representing a brown dog running in a wheat field and a bleak sunset over a leaden lake. He didn't have to look for the signature to find out who had painted the watercolors. Even before they walked into Andy's room Meredith had acquired the feeling that this entire house had been turned into a private shrine, a memorial to the dead boy.

And if the house was a shrine, Andy's room was the holy of holies. The Cunninghams had preserved the small, frugal room of their dead boy exactly as he had left it when he went to war sixteen years before. The furniture consisted of a ramshackle wardrobe, hand-painted in brown, a hard narrow bed covered with a spread of coarse gray fabric, a small schoolboy desk, and two straightbacked chairs. A threadbare tan rug lay on the waxed wooden floor.

Black-and-white posters hung on the walls: James Dean, staring away from the camera with anguished, troubled eyes; Elvis Presley swaying with a sleek microphone; John Kennedy in short sleeves and sports slacks, a light sweater casually thrown over his shoulder, walking through a vast field under an ominous black sky. An old, battered helmet—Meredith assumed it was Brett's—had been tightly fixed against the wall over a large photograph of the landing at Normandy. A baseball bat, its handle childishly engraved with the name Andy B. Cunningham, leaned on the far wall under a rough shelf laden with sports trophies and colorful pennants.

But what captivated Meredith's attention was the tall bookcase, which seemed about to crumble under the weight of hundreds of books. His disbelieving eyes swept along the stacked volumes, the worn, thumbed tomes, hard covers and paperbacks, frayed by time and use, patched with cardboard and Scotch Tape but lovingly arranged by height and by subjects, like regiments of soldiers in a legendary realm.

There were adventure books, Jules Verne, Robert Louis Stevenson, Conan Doyle, and Jack London. There were the greatest works of literature, ancient and modern, from Homer and Dante and Shakespeare to Sir Walter Scott and Cervantes and Thomas Mann, to Hemingway, James Joyce, and Kafka. Two entire shelves were dedicated to poetry, mostly English, with a prominent place reserved for the romantics like Shelley, Lord Byron, and Keats, flanked by two fat volumes of T. S. Eliot, *Mountain Interval* by Robert Frost, and an all but disintegrating copy of *The Raven and Other Poems* by Edgar Allan Poe.

A title in a foreign language attracted his attention and he picked up an old volume in a moldy cover. It was the *Marionetterna* by the Swedish writer Bo Bergman. The first ten pages had been diligently translated by a teenager's hand, the English words penciled above the Swedish text. But afterward Andy had apparently given up the Sisyphean task of deciphering his distant heritage. The Swedish-English dictionary, though, stood faithfully beside the Bergman book, as if expecting its master to return and resume his journey into the past.

"He loved reading," Karen Cunningham said, peering over his shoulder. "He worked during his summer vacations as a waiter at Emerald Lake, and spent every penny on books. I wish Johnny was like him." And noticing Meredith's questioning look, she explained, "Johnny, my younger boy. You'll meet him at dinner."

She took from the desk a medium-sized scrapbook. A white label pasted on its blue cardboard cover carried the inscription, in large characters, "Andy," and underneath, in smaller block letters, "December 17, 1949—February 4, 1969." He accepted the book from Karen Cunningham's hand and opened it. Its first page consisted of a large photograph of a small barefooted boy in short pants flashing a sunny smile at the camera.

"I'll leave you now, if you'll excuse me," Karen Cunningham said awkwardly, averting her eyes. "I'll go down to prepare dinner." Her pain was still intense, he thought, and time hadn't healed her wounds.

Alone, he sat on the uncomfortable bed and plunged into the life of Andy Cunningham. He read attentively every letter, every document, and was soon engrossed by the personality emerging from the testimonies assembled into the modest volume. Andy Cunningham wasn't impeccable, of course. In the official school reports and between the lines of the laudatory letters, Meredith discerned some of his shortcomings. Andy was brilliant in literature and the humanities. He was rather mediocre in exact sciences, and his marks in mathematics, physics, and chemistry were below average. He was a good swimmer and an agile basketball player. But the school coach doubted if he could ever make the football team. He was too soft, the coach wrote, lacking the tough streak and the burning, aggressive ambition that made a champion.

Still, Andy Cunningham materialized before Meredith's eyes as an honest, idealistic youth, a fine athlete, a loyal comrade. He seemed to be the eternal volunteer, the romantic dreamer always ready to embrace a just cause or join a noble endeavor. An old clipping told how, at fifteen, Andy had organized a fund collection, and later worked as a volunteer, to install a new heating system at the Emerald Lake Orphanage.

A letter, obviously written by a child in large, unsteady characters on a piece of notebook paper, thanked Andy "for saving my very beloved dog Prince when somebody gave him poison and you carried Prince all the way to the hospital and told the doctor what to do, so Prince and I thank you very much sir."

Another newspaper clipping, entitled "Boy Saves Girl From Drowning," described how Andy had jumped into the turbulent Black River during the floods of 1965, and rescued a little girl at the risk of his life. The scores of letters, clippings, and the proud item the Emerald *News* had devoted to his joining the Marines made clear that the small Minnesotan community regarded Andy Cunningham as its fair-haired boy.

He heard hesitant steps on the staircase, and Karen Cunningham entered the room. She was wearing a starched white apron over her dress and held some papers in her right hand. "I've got here something that might interest you," she said uncertainly. "When Andy was reported missing his commanding officers sent us some letters. Very nice letters. Would you like to see them?"

"Oh, yes," he said, "definitely."

She solemnly handed him two letters, one after the other. They had been folded and unfolded endless times, to the point that they were already falling apart at the crease lines. The first letter was from Colonel William J. Briggs, Commander of the 37th Marines. Although addressed to both parents, Briggs's letter was actually directed to Brett Cunningham. It was imbued with deep respect for Cunningham's heroic feats in Normandy and praised Andy as a worthy son of his father who valiantly carried on the family tradition of courage and selfless devotion.

"I was informed by Andy's superior officer that he distinguished himself in combat during the first stage of the Tet offensive, when many of his comrades-in-arms were still confused and bewildered by the violence of the Vietcong onslaught." His superior officer could be none other than Steve Rainey, Meredith thought, and went on reading. "Till the day he was reported missing, Private First Class Andy Cunningham fought with a dedication that honors the U. S. Marines and his distinguished father."

For a moment Briggs's tough, lined face flashed before Meredith's eyes. He, too, had been grossly cheated by Rainey and led to believe that Andy had disappeared at Bienhoa. How would Briggs react when he learned the truth? Meredith wondered. He made a mental note to call the old colonel and break the grim news to him. He owed Briggs the truth, as bitter as it was.

He had guessed beforehand who had written the second letter, which he now unfolded before the eyes of Karen Cunningham. And still he felt a sharp pang of revulsion at the sight of the poised bold writing, the confident signature, and under it the identification: Steve B. Rainey, Captain, U. S. Marine Corps.

He stared at the letter, unable to read it, his eyes picking out individual words like *courage, utmost devotion, comradeship, sacrifice.* You sonofabitch, he thought, the hatred surging in him. You write to his mother about sacrifice, about comradeship, about his buddies who survived thanks to Andy.

A verse from the Old Testament that his father used to quote emerged in his memory, the words of the Lord to Naboth: "Hast thou killed and also taken possession?" Rainey had killed and taken possession of the parents' image of their dead son. The assassin had taken possession of their pride, for it was his phony report that had engendered Briggs's eulogy. It was his perfidious words that had instilled strength in their hearts throughout the long dark years of their bereavement. And it was his deceitful letter that was cherished with awe by the innocent Karen Cunningham, as if it were a holy relic.

Unable to meet her candid gaze, he stared at the letter again and his eyes focused on Rainey's concluding sentence: "We all hope our comrade Andy Cunningham is alive and well, and we look forward to the day when this fine Marine will be back among us."

"A wonderful letter, isn't it?" she asked, and he said yes, an exceptional letter indeed.

Downstairs, Ranger joyfully barked, and Karen Cunningham smiled. "That must be Johnny," she said, and carefully, lovingly, folded the letter from her son's assassin.

☆13☆

He saw him at first from the back, a big fat guy with a spindle-shaped body, drooping shoulders, and a flabby, thick waist. Johnny Cunningham seemed absorbed in his brother's portrait, and Meredith stopped at the foot of the stairs, watching him. There was a large bald spot at the back of Johnny's skull and a fold of fat spilled over the collar of his light-blue shirt. Johnny wore a suit of good quality, but on such an ungainly frame any garment was bound to look graceless and ill-fitting.

Andy's brother veered back and Meredith winced, surprised by the bitter, resentful expression stamped on his burly features. Johnny saw him and his scowl instantly dissolved, but Meredith had noticed the rancor distorting the heavy-jowled visage. For a mere photograph to have such effect, it could only mean that Johnny Cunningham nourished a secret hatred for his dead brother.

"I'm Walt Meredith," he said, and stepped forward into the dining room.

"Johnny Cunningham." His handshake was elusive, and the voice wary, reserved. The light-blue eyes were sunk in layers of fat tissue that made the straight nose and the pursed mouth look even smaller. Johnny had fair skin and his sparse hair was light blond. He wore a neat, trim mustache, several shades darker than his hair, and so thick it didn't seem to belong to his face. It looked as if it had been glued to his upper lip.

"I see you've already met," Karen Cunningham said behind Meredith's back. She had come out of the kitchen carrying a large, steaming casserole. "Why don't we sit down? Johnny, there's a bottle of red wine by the sink. Will you bring it out?"

The table had been laid for three with aged china, heavy cutlery, and crisp, immaculate napkins. "You'll have to take potluck with us, Mr. Meredith," Karen Cunningham apologized, filling his dish with a generous helping of rich, deep-brown stew. "You caught me at short notice, and I go to town only once every two weeks."

He mumbled some banality, Johnny poured the wine, and they started eating without further formalities. After a couple of forkfuls, Meredith complimented Karen Cunningham, but she answered absentmindedly, anxiously watching her son. Johnny's arrival had changed her completely, and a strained, uneasy atmosphere soon settled in the room. Karen Cunningham's efforts to bring up the subject of Andy failed miserably, with Johnny contributing almost nothing to the conversation.

He was slightly more cooperative when Meredith asked him about himself, and he described his work as a computer engineer at Emerald Lake. He had left home at an early age and was living in town. He was now spending a month at his parents' farm while his apartment was being refurbished.

After the pie and the coffee, which they swallowed in silence, Karen Cunningham hurriedly retreated to her kitchen. "Let's go outside," Meredith said to Johnny. "It's a beautiful night."

The young man looked at him in surprise, then shrugged and followed him outside. The black dog, Ranger, bolted from its corner and playfully galloped in widening circles around them. It was a magnificent night indeed, with myriads of stars twinkling in a clear, velvety sky. The air was crisp and chilly, and the monotonous mating song of the cicadas bestowed a sensation of peace and tranquility upon the dormant plain. Meredith offered a cigarette to Johnny and lit one for himself. They smoked in silence for a while, then Meredith said quietly, "You didn't like him, did you?"

To his surprise, Johnny laughed softly. "Does it show that much?" he asked with disarming frankness. Meredith shrugged, and Johnny answered his question himself. "Yes," he said, "I guess it does." He took a few more puffs on his cigarette, then added, "To be precise, I didn't dislike Andy, not at all. But I hate what he represents. To me, I mean."

Johnny apparently didn't need any further encouragement to tell his story. As they strolled toward the north fence of the farm, he spoke in a relaxed, intelligent manner, with the hindsight of a mature man looking detachedly upon his youth. When he was a kid, he said, he had worshiped his older brother. Andy was his hero, and he was the proudest youngster in the country when Andy joined the Marines and went to fight in Vietnam. His troubles started after Andy was reported missing.

"I was fourteen years old, and I suddenly discovered that nothing mattered for my parents but Andy. Andy the bright, brave, golden boy. Andy the athlete, the fighter, the hero. And then they decided to make another Andy out of me."

He threw away his cigarette. Soon, he said, his life became a nightmare. He had to be worthy of Andy, his father would repeat to him, he had to become a good American like him, be ready to give his life for his country. His parents didn't seem to care what he wanted, or liked. He was forced to follow in Andy's footsteps.

"I couldn't stand their sermons about Andy. I started hating his very name. At night, in my prayers, I used to thank God he was dead." He paused. "I wanted to be Johnny Cunningham, not a carbon copy of my dead brother."

The frustrated youngster was gradually driven to open rebellion against his parents. "They wanted me to become an athlete—so I refused to practice. They wanted me to be tough and lean—so I started eating, compulsively, like a maniac."

Meredith thought of the beefy, sagging face and the fleshy belly. Johnny had the bright blue eyes of his mother, and his features could have been quite handsome, actually, if he hadn't kept fattening himself to spite his parents. Were it not for Andy's cult, a different person would have been standing before him tonight.

"They wanted me to read books like Andy," Johnny was saying, "so I went to play electronic games." And the worst, the unpardonable crime: "They wanted me to become a soldier, like Andy—so I went and joined the antiwar movement." He paused, his bulk towering over Meredith, waiting for his reaction.

"That must have been very hard," Meredith pointed out matter-of-factly.

"Hard?" Johnny bitterly echoed. "That was hell, Mr. Meredith."

"Walt," he said softly. The blurred shape of a black bird rose before him, noiselessly circling, then faded away.

"It was hell," Johnny repeated. "This is the heart of the Midwest, you see? We are great patriots out here. 'We don't burn our draft cards down on Main Street,' remember? Well, here is Main Street, all over. I was fifteen when I participated in my first anti-Vietnam march. I was scared shitless, if you'll forgive the expression, and so were the other kids. We walked down Main Street with our flags and slogans and badges, shouting, 'Bring them back alive' and 'Make love not war.'

"That was the year of the Kent State riots, when the National Guard shot those kids on the campus. So here we were walking and chanting when suddenly in front of us appeared the good American patriots." His voice was coldly ironic. "Real patriots, dyed in the wool, with their 'Stars and Stripes Forever' buttons and their bicycle chains and baseball bats. They beat us senseless, the bastards, and the police just stood there and waited for them to finish."

"You were hurt?"

Johnny bent to pick up a stone and absently tossed it into the dark. Ranger eagerly darted after it, then stopped, baffled. "I didn't mind the beating, really. But the next day the Emerald *News* had my photograph printed all over the front page, with a caption saying, 'Brett Cunningham's son active in anti-Vietnam rally.' You had to see my father. He didn't touch me, but he said to me that I had betrayed Andy. Then he stopped speaking to me. We made up only last year."

"You overdid it, don't you think?" Meredith said gently.

Johnny let out a short laugh. "The funny thing"— he stressed the wordy *funny*—"was that Andy would have approved of what I did. Before he was killed, Andy had become disgusted with Vietnam. Only my father didn't know, and nobody told him. It would have killed the old man if he had heard what the family hero had to say about that damn war."

"How do you know what he thought?" Meredith said, taken by surprise. "He wrote to you?"

"No, never. All his letters home were the same. The food is good, the weather is fine, my health in excellent, how's the farm doing. He didn't want to hurt their feelings. But what he really thought he wrote to somebody else."

Meredith thoughtfully looked at the immobile silhouette outlined against the starry sky and waited.

"Remember the girl in the photograph with Andy?" Johnny asked. "The one on the staircase?"

"The brunette?" In the picture she looked very pretty, and very much in love.

"Right. Mary. Maria da Silva. She was his sweetheart, they wanted to get married."

"Da Silva you say?"

"Yeah. Her father came from Portugal. He owns a large grocery store in town." Johnny casually leaned against the wooden fence. "Mary's married today to a lawyer, Carl Vogel."

"Andy wrote to her from Vietnam?"

"Yes. She never showed the letters to anybody, but she told me a few things about them. After I got beaten up at that rally, she suddenly calls me and she says, Andy would have been proud of you." He chuckled despite himself. "Shit, here's my father saying I am a traitor, and here's Andy's girl saying I would make him proud."

"I must meet her," Meredith said.

Maria da Silva wasn't beautiful in the real sense of the word. She was a petite woman, with small feet and hands and rather large at the hips. But her dark melancholy eyes, sunk deep in the pallor of her narrow face, conveyed a passionate, dramatic appeal. Or perhaps it was her Portuguese ancestry that gave her that dreamy, poignant look and instilled intense sadness in her large doe eyes. Meredith had seen that inner pain in the wan faces and coal-black eyes of the fado singers in Lisbon and heard it in their raucous, desperate voices as they intoned their plaintive ballads.

Maria stood very upright, elfin, narrow-waisted, her proud shoulders and high breasts spelling a mute challenge. He could imagine her seventeen years younger, disturbingly attractive, and beside her the fervent, romantic Andy Cunningham, passionately in love.

"Thank you for receiving me at such short notice," he said, shaking her small hand. She wore no rings or bracelets. Her classical white dress accentuated her dark looks.

"That's all right, Mr. Meredith." She led the way into the spacious, modern apartment. "After the kids leave for school I'm free for the rest of the morning." He had called her last night from the Cunningham farm and narrated his cover story about his research. She had asked him to hold, and he'd had a vague suspicion that she wanted to consult her husband. But finally she had agreed to meet him. He had left Karen and Johnny Cunningham, promising that his office would send over a researcher to record all the documents concerning Andy. Karen Cunningham had encouraged him to meet Maria.

"She's a good girl, Mr. Meredith, they were very much in love. Before she got engaged to Carl she came to see me. She said to me, 'I'll never love anybody as I loved Andy. I don't know if I should accept.' And I said to her, go ahead, Mary. You can't mourn him for the rest of your life, and Carl Vogel is a fine young man."

Maria gestured toward a deep armchair and perched on the corner of the sofa, facing him. The apartment was in one of the high rises in the northern suburbs of Emerald Lake, and its large windows offered a panoramic view of the endless, ripe fields.

"I told you briefly over the phone why I wanted to see you," Meredith said. "I won't ask you any questions about your personal relationship with Andy, of course. But I'm very interested in the letters he wrote you from Vietnam."

Her hands were tightly clasped in her lap. "I'd like to make something clear," she stated rather formally. Her voice was husky, hesitant, and he realized she was extremely high-strung. "I've shown those letters to nobody. Not even to Carl. And I'm not going to show them to you. Now, as far as the war is concerned . . ." She paused, apparently striving to put some order into her thoughts. "I mean, last night you told me you were interested in Andy's feelings about Vietnam. I'm ready to read to you some passages of his letters dealing with the war." She leaned toward him, watching him anxiously. "Okay?"

THE UNKNOWN SOLDIER

"That's all right, Mrs. Vogel," he said.

She seemed relieved. "Fine, I'll get the letters." She got up, tossing back her long hair in a spontaneous gesture only an attractive, confident woman could afford. He thought of Jane. She also threw her head backward that way. He had phoned her last night from the inn, but there was no answer. He had kept calling every half hour till he got fed up with the silly jingle her answering machine dutifully replayed in his ear. He spent hours turning and tossing in his bed, obsessed with the suspicion that she might have stayed with Rainey. He could have smothered her with his own hands if she had. It didn't make sense, of course, but what happened between them in her bedroom the other night didn't make sense either.

Maria was back. She returned to her seat, clasping with both hands a bunch of manuscript leaflets. "I'll spare you the pink-ribbon kitsch," she blurted with a rueful smile, then hurriedly lowered her eyes and started leafing through the letters. "His first letters were quite...normal," she said without looking up. "He described his buddies, the sights of Saigon, some local customs, the language, the landscape...but when he was sent to the battlefield—'hitting country' they called it—everything changed."

He pensively lit a cigarette and threw the match in the crystal shell-shaped ashtray on the table beside him. It happened to all of them, he thought. As long as they stayed in camp, outside the big cities, and had a night on the town once in a while, they still preserved their emotional virginity. But once out in the field, the stunning shock was bound to come.

"Here," Maria began to read from one of Andy's letters. "'I saw something today that made me ill. We entered a village that had been napalmed by our Phantoms. Burned corpses lay everywhere. I saw pigs, quite a few of them, devouring dead people. Could you imagine that? Live pork eating roast people? God, Mary, this is an upside-down world. This image shows more than anything the insane war that's being waged here. What are we doing here, for Chrissake?'"

She raised her eyes and stared at him, then went on reading. "Listen to this. 'We call the VC gooks. They're gooks, not people. Their life has no value. We rarely take prisoners. We shoot at everything that moves. Only a few guys care if they've killed a civilian. As one officer put it—if he's Vietnamese and he's dead, he is VC. That's not the fault of our boys, believe me. Most of them are decent guys. But they come over to serve their country, and here they are taught that the most sublime goal in life are large, juicy body counts. So we supply the bodies.'"

He frowned. "Did all his letters pass the military censorship?"

"I don't know," she said. "I know that Andy found ways to send me letters with friends who were returning to the States and posted them after they were in the country." She paused. "Would you like to hear some more?"

He nodded.

She resumed her reading. "Here's another one. 'Something terrible happened to us today. We had been patrolling those damn jungles for weeks without seeing the enemy. This morning we finally ran into a full-scale battle with a large unit, some say a company. They were entrenched behind a village. They opened fire, and before we saw them we already had a dozen casualties. It was a battle like in the movies—with mortar, cannon, gunships circling over. Even the Air Force dropped a couple of bombs.'

"'But at a certain moment all my company went berserk, me included. I don't know what happened. Perhaps it was the sight of our buddies who were lying there in the dust with their brains all over the place and their guts spilling out. Perhaps it was the hatred for the gooks. Anyway, we suddenly became a horde of savages. We ran through the village like madmen. We burned the huts, we threw grenades into the houses. People were screaming, women, children, but we didn't care. When we were finally on the other side, and I looked back, there was nothing left of the village but fire and smoke. We destroyed about fifty huts and houses, and people were killed, innocent people.'

"'Why did we do it? I can't tell. A sergeant told me I shouldn't give a shit because the gooks are much worse. Of course they are, I've seen their acts of cruelty, they would make you faint with horror. But we are not VC. We are Americans, we are civilized, we respect human life. What's Vietnam doing to us?'"

She paused, watching him. "This letter has a sequel," she said, impatiently leafing through the handwritten pages. "Here it is. 'Remember that insane attack on the village I wrote to you about? Since that morning I can't get rid of a guilt feeling. What did those poor people do to deserve their death? You might think I'm naive, but lately I have been trying to do something for them. Whenever we go on patrol I take in my backpack a couple of extra boxes of G-rations, some chocolate, a few bottles of medicine. You should see those wretched people tearing the packages open, as if they were Christmas gifts. And the children's eyes lighting up when they see the chocolate. Good God, it takes so little to make those Vietnamese grateful!'"

She abruptly stopped and nervously turned a few pages. The silence between them had become almost unbearable. She winced, reading a page over and over again. She bit her lip and swallowed, hard.

"What . . ." he started.

"Nothing," she said. "That's personal."

He let out a deep breath. "You loved him very much," he said gently.

She looked up, her eyes suddenly blazing. "God, how I loved him!" Her lips were trembling, and he thought she would burst out crying. "I still miss him," she said. "I long for him at night. I wanted his child. How stupid I was, at the time, when we were lovers and I restrained him. I was afraid to . . . to let him go all the way. Oh God, if I had only been less reasonable, if I just had a kid to remember him by."

She was on her feet and staggered out of the room. He heard the splatter of running water, and a moment later she was back, pale but dry-eyed. She stood by the window and spoke in a quiet, subdued voice. "Carl is a fine man, you know. A good father and a devoted husband. But something died in me with Andy. I don't know if you can understand."

He was about to speak, then leaned back.

"At least both my children are girls," she said. "I'm happy with that, they'll never go to war, they'll never face those horrors. They'll never be missing, and nobody'll send them home in an aluminum coffin."

He moved uneasily on his seat. "I didn't want to cause you all this distress," he said. "If you don't want to continue . . ."

"Wait," she said, "I'm sorry, I got carried away. There's another passage I want to read to you. Just a moment." She returned to her seat and removed a few pages from the bottom of the batch, scanning them quickly. "Here it is.

"'My father is a hero. He fought for his country and was decorated for his courage. He believes he has handed the torch to a younger generation of valiant Americans who are also fighting for their country. But when I come back I'll have a few questions for him. I'll ask him, Daddy, did you also cut Krauts' ears and wear them on a string, as a necklace, for everybody to see? Did you also burn peasants' huts with your Zippo lighter? Did you also indulge in body counts? Did you buy dope from the *mamasans* and go on patrol half-stoned? Did you pose for photographs beside a pile of dead bodies, like in a safari? Did you shoot civilians because a weapon was found in their house? What did you make of me, what did all of you make of my generation? What did you make of our ideals? But you know, Maria'"—she raised her eyes, fixing them on Meredith—"'at second thought I'll never ask him. For he'll never believe me, and even if he does, what the hell can he answer?'"

On the threshold, shaking her hand, he lowered his eyes. But on the way down in the elevator, and later, driving his car back to the Town Inn, he was overwhelmed by a sensation of immense relief. Andy Cunningham had been a wonderful young American, an adolescent of noble moral convictions and a profound faith in the ideals of the American society. And even Vietnam hadn't succeeded in eroding his attachment to the humane values of his country.

He walked briskly into the small lobby of the hotel

and headed for his room, so deeply immersed in his thoughts that at first he didn't hear the clerk calling after him. But the stubborn repetition of his name caught him finally at the foot of the stairs. He turned back. "Yes?"

"There's somebody waiting for you, Mr. Meredith." The clerk's voice was strained. He followed his look to the back of the lobby and became very still. In the golden midday light, her face flushed, a tentative smile fluttering on her lips, stood Jane Wyatt.

She didn't speak until they had reached the safe intimacy of his room. "As soon as I found your note . . ." she began, but his hungry hands were all over her, collecting her against his chest, fusing her into his body, his mouth smothering hers. "I tried to figure out where you were." His fingers were impatiently unbuttoning her blouse and sliding down toward her skirt. "Wait, what are you doing, wait . . ."

But he didn't seem to listen, and she didn't want him to, docilely sucking in her breath to let him pull the zipper more easily. "Then I figured it had to do with Andy Cunningham."

Her panties slipped down and she was totally naked now, laughing loudly to conceal her embarrassment, feeling strangely insecure in the daylight, yet her hands ventured under his shirt, trembling at the contact of his skin.

"Will you listen, Walt? I had the address of Andy Cunningham, so I phoned, it was last night." Her hands moved of their own volition, slipping to his waist, his thighs, and down his belly as he discarded his last items of clothing. "And I called the Cunningham farm . . . stop it, Walt, stop it, please." They were on the bed now, his warm body surrounding her, hovering

above her, impatiently ramming her crumbling defenses, which had been deserted long ago.

"And the lady said you had just left but you had an
appointment this morning..." His mouth was on hers,
demanding, flowing into her. She tossed her head
aside. "So I took the night flight to Denver and
switched planes to Minneapolis, and this morning...
oh God, Walt, what are you doing, wait, darling,
wait."

But he had infected her already and the fire was in
her blood, in her groin, flowing through her aroused
body, and he was inside her, so close, so deep, and she
couldn't stop him and she wouldn't for anything in the
world.

"Oh Walt, kiss me, Walt, more, more, stay in me,
don't stop, I want you, more, I love you, Walt, I love
you." And then she was screaming, falling, and there
was nothing else but his hard body and his mouth and
his flesh throbbing inside hers.

Then she recovered her senses and blissfully
stretched, opening her eyes. She propped on her
elbows and, still breathing hard, still dizzy, shakily
steered her story to its happy ending. "So I flew over
this morning from Minneapolis—they have a small
company, Lakeland Air—and reached this charming
little place just in time to be raped by a dangerous sex
maniac." She sighed dreamily. "Ain't I lucky."

And when he asked the question that had been
gnawing him for the last two days: "Of course not,
stupid, I left Rainey's house immediately after we
talked. What did you think? I drove the same night
back to Miami and reached the St. Tropez Hotel at
dawn. That's why I woke up so late and missed my
morning flight."

But the subject triggered the grim recollections she had succeeded in suppressing for a brief moment, and he sensed her body become taut, and the reserve that crept in her voice, and he asked the inevitable question, and she said yes, Steve Rainey had admitted that he had ordered Andy killed and maimed.

Why, he said, why, and she feigned not hearing, hoping to delay the dreadful answer, for she knew it would hurt him more than anything else since he had embarked on his morbid voyage. But he asked again and again, his eyes, grave and apprehensive, staring steadily into hers, and his hands clutching her arms, so insistent, so inescapable that finally she had to say it out loud, and she did, her reluctance vanquished.

"He said," she murmured, the stifling of her voice her last, useless weapon, "he said he had him shot because it was either his soldiers' lives or Andy's." She drew a desperate breath. "Andy Cunningham, he said, was a fuckin' traitor."

⭐ 14 ⭐

He stared at her, stupefied, a sudden chill invading his benumbed body.

"A traitor," she repeated.

"I don't believe it," he finally said. The blissful elation that had descended upon him a few moments before was brusquely evaporating, dispelled by a swell of helpless fury.

She moved closer to him, and gently traced the outline of his mouth with her fingers. The green eyes watched him with sad fondness. "I couldn't believe it either when he told me about it."

He shook his head vigorously. "No, it can't be, it isn't true." She couldn't understand, she didn't know anything about Andy. "It can't be true."

"He said—" she began.

"Whatever he said, he lied," he cut her off furiously. The enormity of the accusation was slowly seeping into his mind. He jumped from the bed, pulled on his trousers, and stepped toward the window. On the desk stood a slim silvery flask. His hand slightly trembling, he poured some whiskey into a water glass and gulped it down. In the last couple of weeks he had started drinking during the day, too. "You want some?" he asked Jane. A distorted face scowled at him from the flask's mirrorlike surface.

She shook her head, watching him with anxious eyes.

"What did Rainey say?" he asked.

She leaned against the headboard, pulling the bedspread across her chest. "He said I was the first one ever to hear the true story."

"Is that so?" he grunted, hostile.

"He said they were on a search-and-destroy mission against Vietcong units withdrawing from Bienhoa. They..."

"Who the hell is they?"

"A patrol of eight Marines from Bravo Company, Thirty-seventh Marines. Steve led the patrol himself, their code name was the Minerva team. They were all revenge-crazy, Steve said. During the fighting in Bienhoa the Vietcong had tortured and murdered several captured Marines. They were determined to get even with the bastards, Steve said."

"What else did Steve say?" he asked. He couldn't stand her calling Rainey by his first name after all that he had done. To Andy, to Frank Wyatt, to me, he thought.

"They detected an enemy concentration at Na-san," she said. "Andy Cunningham himself had reconnoitered the area. Na-san is a small village crossed by the Be River. It's a tributary of the Dong-Nai, which flows through Bienhoa." She pronounced the names with ease.

"I know all about Na-san," she went on. "When Frankie was reported missing I wanted to know exactly when and exactly where. I studied and memorized every detail about that damn place. I talked to scores

THE UNKNOWN SOLDIER

of Marines who had been there. I collected every map, every photograph the Pentagon would let me have. For years I've been seeing Na-san in my nightmares, to the point that sometimes I couldn't distinguish between hallucinations and reality."

She had retreated into herself, and her eyes had a haunted, inverted look. "I know the bloody place, believe me. I know exactly where the jungle ends and where the clearing starts, and where the two thatched huts stood. I know the ravine where the river flows between those muddy slopes. And I know that suspended footbridge, made of ropes and rotten planks, leading to the village itself. What I didn't know"—she paused to catch her breath—"was that Andy Cunningham died there, just at the foot of the bridge."

He held his breath, nodding slowly, and she went on, her voice a shade softer. "Cunningham came back from his reconnaissance and reported that he had spotted the Vietcong. Steve therefore ordered a surprise assault. Over the bridge and into the village. At that moment Andy Cunningham cracked."

"What?" His hand jerked and the flask overturned, the liquor spilling on the desk. He absently fumbled for it, his eyes glued to her face.

"That's the word Steve used. 'Cracked,' he said. Andy refused to carry out the order. He incited his comrades to disobey."

"Why? What was wrong with the orders?" It didn't make sense.

"They tried to silence him," she continued, ignoring his questions. "The place was infested with Vietcong guerrillas. But he kept shouting, hysterically, then blocked the access to the bridge, yelling and firing in the air."

"Firing? Rainey said firing?" Meredith was stubbornly shaking his head. It couldn't be true.

"He also threatened to shoot anybody who approached the bridge. The shots alerted the VC. They opened fire on the Marines, from the jungle and from the other bank. They fired flares in the air and the entire place was suddenly illuminated as though it were full daylight. The Minerva team was cornered like rabbits caught in a searchlight. Their only way out was through the bridge and straight at the enemy positions. But there was Andy Cunningham, screaming and firing." She abruptly fell silent.

His hand was trembling as he tried to screw the cap on the whiskey flask. "So they shot him," he said.

She didn't answer, her eyes boring into his.

"They shot him," he repeated. He had to hear it from her mouth.

"Steve ordered them to shoot him," she said in a very low, barely audibly voice. "Then he ordered them to mutilate the body and burn it. Later he swore them to secrecy."

"I don't believe a word," he said quickly. "Andy would never disobey an order." He turned around, his back to her, and leaned on the windowsill. Icy shivers shot through his body. Hectic, cruel thoughts were tearing his mind to shreds. The window faced a deserted drive-in movie and the cracks and fissures on the dirty white screen turned it into a huge maze. "What happened later?" he asked. "How were the other boys killed and captured?"

"I didn't ask," she said. "It didn't matter very much at that point, did it?"

He stared at the twisted, deep cracks in the movie

screen. There seemed to be no way out of the maze. "Steve Rainey is a bloody liar," he said.

Their departure from Emerald Lake had all the characteristics of a hurried, disorderly retreat. Distraught, restless, hounded by his private ghosts, he yielded to the urge to run away from Karen Cunningham and Maria da Silva and the good people of Emerald Lake, to carry away the awesome plague Jane Wyatt had brought from Rainey's mouth lest it contaminate the houses, the fields, and the people among whom Andy Cunningham had grown up. In a few minutes he had packed his bag, paid his bill, and gunned the rental car on the lonely southbound road. Jane seemed to understand him, for she didn't object, didn't ask any questions, and followed him quietly, her light hand on his shoulder the only support he could now tolerate.

She spoke only when the last houses of Emerald Lake vanished in the early afternoon haze and they were sailing alone in the monotonous flatness on the straight narrow road. "Steve said he had the full right to do it," she said gently, looking straight ahead.

"Even if Andy had done what Rainey claims he did, he had no right to shoot. He should have arrested him and gotten him court-martialed."

"How could he?" she protested. "They were under fire, it was a question of minutes, perhaps less. He said his overall duty was to protect the lives of his soldiers. The court-martial code—"

"Oh, so your learned friend is an expert on the court-martial code, too, is he?" His hands were frozen on the steering wheel. A huge truck, coming from the opposite direction, missed them by inches, its horn screaming.

"The court-martial code explicitly says that mutiny, desertion, and insubordination under fire are punishable by death."

"In the last fifty years the Army has executed only one poor devil who deserted his unit in France. And that was after a court-martial in which he could defend himself. Rainey didn't give Andy a chance, did he? He was only too happy to press the trigger." He fell silent to light a cigarette. He offered her the open pack, but she shook her head. "Anyway," he went on, "if Rainey was so confident he had done the right thing, why did he swear the men to secrecy? Why did he mutilate the body? What was he afraid of?"

"He . . ." she started, then fell silent.

"Listen," he attacked again. "You have no idea who Andy Cunningham was. I met his family and his sweetheart. I visited his room. I saw his books, I read what the people in this place had to say about him. He was a wonderful young man. If you knew what I know, you would agree with me that all this story about treason and mutiny makes no sense."

Eager to win her to his side, he described the outstanding personality of Andy Cunningham he had discovered in his visits to the Cunningham farm and to Maria da Silva. She was listening gravely, her crossed hands clasping her shoulders, loose hair limply hanging about her face. "All that Andy ever wanted," he concluded, "was to serve his country and be worthy of his father."

For a while she held back, strangely remote. Then she leaned on his shoulder, and he felt her eyes upon him. "You're not speaking about Andy Cunningham," she said softly. "You're speaking about your own son, aren't you, Walt? You've made Andy fit the image of Benjamin the way you would have liked him to be. And you can't accept that he might have committed an act of treason."

He stiffened. "Who the hell do you think you are? Now let me tell you—"

"It's true, isn't it?" she insisted.

He felt the knot of anger twisting again in his stomach, but she was quicker. Her fingers softly moved up the nape of his neck, caressing his hair. "Don't," she said in the same mellow, conciliatory voice. "Don't get mad again. I can't watch you going to pieces before my eyes. They're both dead, Andy and Benjamin. We can't bring them back."

His knuckles had turned white from the pressure on the steering wheel. "So let's accept what Rainey said," he muttered, "and forget about the whole matter, right? He still has a lot of influence on you."

She recoiled and turned her face away. "You must be out of your mind. I broke up with Steve more than two years ago. I don't give a damn about him. The only person I care about is you, and you know it. You just walked into my life and blew to pieces all the walls and the ramparts I'd built. Nothing's going to be the same for me, ever, not even Frankie." She impulsively turned back to him. "Let's go to Washington," she said.

He stole a quick look at her. "What for?"

"You got what you wanted, didn't you? You found the name of the Unknown. You know how he died. You wanted to prevent the burial. Now you can. You've just got to pronounce the name once and the ceremony will be canceled. As to why he died"—she hesitated—"it doesn't really concern you. Let the Pentagon worry about that. Go back and report everything you've found. And if there was a crime, let them investigate it. As far as you're concerned, your mission has been accomplished."

He shook his head vigorously. "No," he said. "They might refuse to investigate. They might cover up the whole affair. They don't want any scandals today, they want Vietnam buried and forgotten. They might accept Rainey's version, and Andy Cunningham will go down in history as a traitor and a mutineer. I can't go back, don't you see? Not before I find out what happened at Na-san that night."

"All right," she suddenly said. "We'll do it your way. There's still one witness left. Let's go and ask him."

"Who?" he said.

"Lyndon Hughes, in Montana. Did you forget about him?"

"He'll refuse to talk to us."

"No," she said, "not this time. Let's call him."

They phoned from the first gas station they reached. The public phone was out of order, but the attendant agreed to let them use his private phone for the flat fee of five dollars. Meredith dialed and handed the receiver to Jane. Once again it was Hughes's wife who answered the phone. And once again she said her husband wasn't home.

"Tell him that Jane Wyatt wants to talk to him about the Minerva team," Jane said flatly.

Some minutes passed, then a very faint, wavering voice echoed in the receiver. "Lyndon Hughes speaking."

"This is Jane Wyatt," she said. "Frankie's wife."

"I know who you are," the voice said.

"I'm here with Walt Meredith, from the Pentagon. We are flying over tomorrow to see you. We want to talk to you about that night at Na-san."

"I won't talk to you." The voice was cold and inert, and she had the feeling it was replaying a much-rehearsed formula.

"Oh yes you will," she countered, and her words, independent of her will, resounded with the grim finality of a verdict. "You'll talk to us about Minerva. And about Andy Cunningham."

Her words induced no reaction, no reply, just a deep long silence. "Hello?" Jane said anxiously. "Hello?"

When Hughes's voice reached her again it had a ring of bitter resignation. "I knew this would happen," he said, "sooner or later. You know my address." He hung up.

Jane turned to Meredith. There was no triumph in her eyes, only deep concern. "We can spend the night in Minneapolis and catch the first flight west tomorrow morning."

He left five dollars on the desk and walked back to the car.

They reached the isolated cottage in the hills above Great Falls the following afternoon, shortly before nightfall. But when they saw the police cars in the yard, their revolving lights spurting soundless flashes of red and blue light, they knew they were too late.

Lyndon Hughes, the officer at the gate told them, had been found a couple of hours before in the basement, his revolver in his hand. The man had committed suicide, the officer said.

* * *

Big, broad Police Chief Winizky stepped out of the cottage and squinted malevolently as they came out of the car. He rubbed a hairy hand on his chin, then pulled a cigar from the breast pocket of his uniform, bit and spat out its tip, and struck a match. The man had seen too many television movies, Meredith decided. His wide-rimmed hat, tilted over a grizzling temple, and the beige sheepskin vest he wore over his uniform made him look like a winter version of the Marlboro man. But under the puckered brow the small pale-blue eyes had the blunt, suspicious stare of the veteran cop, and the tight mouth suggested smoldering violence.

"Yeah?" he grumbled, chewing his cigar. "What can I do for you?" His voice suited his image, harsh, aggressive, worn out by chronic fatigue and foul tobacco. He took a couple of steps toward them, sticking his thumbs in his wide belt. The officer who had summoned him returned to his place by the gate, curiously gaping at Jane.

With a man like the chief, conscious of his power and enjoying it, authority was the only name of the game, Meredith thought. He therefore stepped confidently forward, offering his hand. "Walt Meredith, Department of Defense, on official business," he lied.

The chief's handshake was wary, tentative. "Is that so?" he said, his eyes slitting as he tilted his head. "I'm Chief Winizky, Great Falls Police Department. May I see your ID?" Frowning, he studied the Pentagon pass, his mouth incessantly rolling, sucking, and chewing the fat cigar. "Bureau of MIA Affairs?" he said, and reluctantly handed the pass back to Meredith. "I thought this MIA business was over long ago." He shrugged. "And what does the Bureau of MIA affairs want with a dead Montana citizen, Mr. Meredith?"

But Meredith ignored the question, keen to assert his status. "This is Mrs. Wyatt, from Mesa, Colorado. Her husband and Mr. Hughes served in the same unit in Vietnam."

"Ma'am." Chief Winizky impassively nodded, touching the rim of his hat with two meaty fingers. A black police officer and a civilian wearing a blue raincoat came out of the house and stood beside one of the police cars talking quietly. The man in the raincoat kept glancing at Jane.

"I understand Mr. Hughes is dead," Meredith said. He caught a sidewise glimpse of Jane. She looked distressed. She hadn't said a word since the officer had broken the news about Hughes. "He committed suicide, is that correct?"

Chief Winizky stared at him vacuously. He apparently disliked Meredith's attitude. "You came all the way from Washington to see Hughes?"

"My office is trying to identify a body found at Nasan, in Vietnam," Meredith continued in the same competent, serious manner. "We are interviewing the survivors of the battle that took place over there."

"Mrs. White—"

"Wyatt," she interrupted in a low, nervous voice. "Jane Wyatt."

"Yeah. Mrs. White is with your office?"

"No. Her husband took part in that battle, together with Mr. Hughes. She is helping me with my inquiries."

"Is she?" the chief asked innocently, turning his

255

eyes on her, then back on Meredith. "How nice of her."

The conversation was taking a nasty turn. "I called Lyndon Hughes several times," Meredith said coldly, "but his wife made me understand that he didn't want to talk to me. Yesterday Mrs. Wyatt called—"

"From where?" the chief quickly asked.

"Minnesota." He paused a moment, watching Winizky closely, but the big man didn't acknowledge the answer. "Mr. Hughes agreed to talk to us, so we flew over."

"What made him agree this time?" Winizky was suspiciously watching Jane. She mutely stared back at him, her lips tightly pressed. The chief turned back to Meredith. "I understand Mrs. White is a very persuasive woman," he concluded. "What did she tell him to make him change his mind?"

Meredith sustained his glare, inwardly fuming.

"And after you landed at Great Falls, you rented a car and drove straight from the airport," Winizky offered, taking the cigar from his mouth.

"That's right."

"Well"—the chief suddenly made a large, sweeping gesture with his right hand, leaving a wavering spiral of smoke in the limpid mountain air—"why don't you come right in? We've been expecting you."

The small entrance hall led to a large living room, sparingly furnished. The bare wooden floor wasn't waxed, and its rough, discolored surface bestowed an air of neglect on the entire room. There were no pictures on the walls, no curtains at the windows. The light-gray upholstery of the sofa was stained at several places, and loose threads dangled from the frayed armrests. The vast room was cold; the cracked fireplace hadn't been in use for a long while.

"You said you were expecting us," Meredith pointed out.

"Of course," the police chief said. "Hughes's wife told us about your phone call." He eyed Jane, scowling. "What did you tell him, Mrs. White, to make him blow his brains all over the place?"

Jane shuddered and Chief Winizky let out a short, barking laugh. "You've nothing to fear, Mrs. White. We took the body away a couple of hours ago."

"He died in this room?" Meredith asked.

"Call the woman," Winizky said to the officer who had followed them inside, then turned to Meredith. "He died in the basement. He had his workshop there." The younger officer heavily thumped his way up the stairs.

"What kind of workshop?" Meredith frowned. "I'd like to see it."

Chief Winizky ignored his question and took the cigar out of his mouth again, displaying a sudden interest in its glistening tip.

"I'm talking to you, Chief," Meredith said firmly. "I want you to know that the Defense Department will appreciate your cooperation."

The chief stared back at him, taking his time, then shrugged. "Come on," he said sullenly, obviously regretting he had to divulge such valuable information to a stranger. "I'll show you."

They descended the narrow stairs to the basement, Jane reluctantly trailing behind. It was an oblong, low-ceilinged room with an uneven concrete floor. Numerous tools, a couple of dusty machines, packages and crates of various sizes were scattered all over the place in appalling disorder. A heap of wood, chopped into small, thick chunks, was piled against the far wall under several artistic wall hangings and bright-colored rugs that were fastened to the brickwork with dully gleaming brass nails.

On an oblong table, whose legs were immersed in a fluffy mass of wood shavings, stood a score of figurines amid an array of carpenter tools. Meredith picked up one of the figurines. It was nearly finished, a masterly carved chess piece representing an Indian chief. The other chessmen, in different stages of completion, were cowboys, soldiers, and Indian fighters. A matronly squaw stood beside a lean-faced Buffalo Bill. Once colored and varnished, the chessmen would form a splendid set, Meredith thought.

On another, smaller table lay several yellow-tinged bones of some large fish, two of them shaped like small elephant tusks. The masts and upper deck of a sailing ship had been exquisitely etched on one of the bones.

And between both tables, on the dirty gray floor, somebody had drawn with chalk the outline of a sprawled body, its legs unnaturally twisted.

Meredith stared at the rough contour as if mesmerized. Lyndon Hughes had escaped the inferno of Nasan to die by his own hand in that cold, damp cellar. He glanced at Jane, who stood at the foot of the stairs, strangely subdued. "What's this place?" he asked Winizky.

"That's where he worked," Winizky said, picking up the slender statuette of Buffalo Bill, then casting it indifferently back with the others. It came to rest against a chipped telephone, precariously perched at the table's edge. "Did you ever meet him?" he asked.

THE UNKNOWN SOLDIER

"No, why?"

"A weird guy." Chief Winizky shook his head. "Boy, he was weird. You had to see him. Long hair, long beard, used to run barefoot in the woods. Never went to town. It was Vietnam, his wife said. Didn't want to see people. Didn't want to work with people. Hated people."

He seemed to derive a special pleasure from stressing the world *people*. "That's why he set up this place. To be away from people."

He wiped away some tobacco shreds from his tongue, then deftly removed the moist wrapper leaf of his cigar and shook it off his fingers. "Alone, that's what he wanted to be. Was very good with his hands, see?" He pointed vaguely around. "He wove wall hangings, did scrimshaw imitations, carved wood..." He brusquely clammed up, aware he had talked too much.

"And he made a living with this handicraft?" Meredith asked wryly.

"His father helped him some, I guess," Winizky said, and suddenly veered around, advancing upon Jane. "Why did he shoot himself, Mrs. White? What did you say to him?"

"I didn't..." Jane started, disconcerted, when a movement on the stairs caught her eye. A skeletal woman, dressed in black, was soundlessly descending the obscured steps, a spectral apparition descending into the underworld. Then she emerged into the light, her long, unkempt hair falling on a prematurely wrinkled face, thin hands loosely dangling at her sides. Her old black pullover and the outmoded flared pants hung gracelessly from a bony frame.

She was quite young—still in her twenties, Meredith guessed—but the decay that was consuming her house was hungrily gaining upon her as well. Her skin was rough, sallow, the bloodless mouth bitterly drawn, the bleary eyes drooping into sagging pouches. The gauntness of her long face accentuated the thin, pointed nose. She cast a glazed look upon Jane and Meredith, then turned to Chief Winizky, her stockinged feet shuffling on the concrete. "What do you want?" she said bluntly. "Who are these people? I told you I don't wanna see nobody."

Winizky went through his routine ritual, tilting his head, sucking his cigar, narrowing his eyes. "They're the people who called Lyndon yesterday." He seemed to enjoy himself as he nodded toward Jane. "She's the one who spoke to you. Mrs. Jane White."

The young woman slowly turned around, swaying slightly, her eyes staring dully out of a listless face. And all of a sudden she sprang forward, a flash of black, and she was all over Jane, kicking, hitting, clawing, shrill screams erupting in harsh, uneven outbursts from her distorted mouth.

"You bitch," she shrieked, her nails slashing ugly red gashes on Jane's throat, "you killed him, you fuckin' bitch, I'll kill you, I'll get you, I swear!"

Meredith grabbed her from behind, but she yanked her arms free. "Let me go, you asshole, leave me alone!"

She went on screaming even after Meredith and Winizky had torn her away from Jane, desperately writhing in their arms, kicking in the air, spitting in Meredith's face: "You motherfucker, you were with her, you are the one who called, leave me alone, you fuckin' asshole."

On and on she screamed, her foul words spurting in

raw despair. "You murdered him, you motherfuckers, all he wanted was to live in peace, and you chased him all the way to his house, you couldn't rest till he was dead."

Her hoarse shouts subsided only after Winizky and the younger officer, who had darted down the steps, dragged her to the far side of the room and forced her to sit on one of the chairs. She cried bitterly now, her raucous voice plaintively whining. Meredith grabbed Jane, who stood by the stairs, stunned, blood dripping from her throat onto her torn blouse.

"Come," he said, "let's get out of here." As he dragged her up the stairs he pressed his handkerchief against her scratches but she pushed away his hand. "It's all right," she said. "I'm okay." He left her sitting in the car, her troubled eyes staring fixedly ahead, and returned to the house. Chief Winizky met him at the door and leaned against the jamb, lazily blocking his path.

"I wouldn't go inside if I were you," he said slowly. "That woman is weird, you know, she'll go berserk again if she sees you."

Meredith hesitated. "I want to talk to her. She thinks it's our fault that he killed himself."

Winizky chuckled, steering him toward the car, and leaning down to the window, for Jane to hear: "That's the weirdest part, see? She thinks it's your fault, but she doesn't think he killed himself."

"What are you talking about?" Meredith managed. Even Jane turned her head.

"How's that throat, Mrs. White?" Winizky inquired indifferently.

"What did you say?" Meredith stubbornly repeated.

Winizky slowly turned back to face him. "I talked to

her before you came. She insists that her husband wasn't the sort of man who'd commit suicide, never. She said that after Mrs. White here spoke to him, he went back to the workshop and made a long-distance call. They had dinner and went to sleep, and he seemed quite calm. She saw him this morning before leaving for the store."

"He was alive?"

"Sure thing, he was okay. She found him when she came back, a couple of hours later."

"There was no suicide note?" Meredith asked needlessly.

"I told you she's nuts," Winizky drawled, ignoring the question. "He would never kill himself, she says. So we checked. The gun's his gun all right, the fingerprints are his own. We went through the entire house, dusted half of it. No sign of any visitor, no suspicious fingerprints. But she's as hardheaded as a mule." He sadly contemplated the moist stub of his cigar, sighed, and tossed it away. "She says Lyndon Hughes was murdered."

He closed the car door behind Meredith. "Drive carefully," he said, his fingers touching his hat in mock salute. "You have a nice evening, Mrs. White."

"You believe Hughes was murdered?" Jane asked quietly, stubbing out another cigarette in the overflowing ashtray. "You believe that woman?" They had checked into the Mountain Lodge and she was sitting with her knees drawn up to her chest on the large bed, shivering under a coarse blanket. The blood on her throat had dried, but the scratches had swollen, nasty crimson welts snaking on her white skin.

"Winizky said she was weird," Meredith said.

"Do you believe her?" she insisted.

He shrugged. "I believe I lost the only chance I had to find out the truth about Andy. There are no more witnesses." He morosely leafed through a stained hotel directory and threw it back on the desk.

"Let's assume for a moment that he was murdered, okay?" She seemed very keen to prove something. "What would be the motive? I'll tell you what. Somebody, the person Hughes called long-distance, didn't want him to talk to us about Na-san." She looked at him intensely till he nodded, and then went on. "Why? Because Hughes could tell us the truth about Andy's death."

"Maybe you're right," he agreed. "But he's dead, so we'll never know the truth."

The blanket slipped off her shoulders. "Don't you see the pattern, Walt? Eddie Paris decides to tell the truth and makes a long-distance call. He dies in a hunting accident. Lyndon Hughes agrees to speak to us and makes a long-distance call. The next afternoon he's dead." He was nodding impatiently. "The person who received those long-distance calls . . ."

"Okay, you're right, so what? The bottom line is that we've run out of witnesses." He switched on the television set. A reporter and a black athlete were discussing the Russian decision not to participate in the Los Angeles Olympics. He switched the set off and turned around. "You know what? Let's go to Washington. We've nothing to do here."

But she was shaking her head, frowning in concentration. "Wait," she said, "wait." She reached for the phone and started punching the buttons.

"Who are you calling?"

She interrupted the call, then started dialing again. "I want to see if he's home," she muttered.

"Who?" he asked, although he had already guessed the answer. She didn't reply, squeezing her lips together.

"No answer," she finally announced, and glumly replaced the receiver. Suddenly her eyes lit up and she picked up the phone again. "When you went to Islamorada," she said slowly, "you met Steve at the marina, right?"

He nodded.

"You've got the number?"

He raised his eyebrows. "I guess so, why?"

"Give it to me. Please."

He leafed through his notebook. "Here. Fisherman's Haven Marina." He read the number, and she urgently punched the buttons. "Hello?" She nodded eagerly at him, holding the receiver with both hands. "Hi. I'm trying to get in touch with Steve Rainey, captain of the *Fidelis*. Could you..." Her face quickly paled. "What? I'm...his sister, I must talk to him." Another pause. "What?"

She listened for a long moment, pallid, the fingers of her left hand nervously running through her hair. "God!" she groaned. "Are you sure?"

"What happened?" he asked, but she was totally absorbed in the urgent voice that squeaked into the phone. After a few minutes she replaced the receiver with a trembling hand.

"What did they say?" he asked, sitting beside her and taking her hand. It was cold and dry.

"They said the *Fidelis* was found this morning off Shell Key. It had capsized, probably during the night. There was no trace of Steve." She closed her eyes.

"He's been reported missing. They say it was on TV already, in the early evening news."

He sat silent for a while, then let out a deep breath and got to his feet. "And you believe that? You believe he's dead?"

"And you?" she said.

⭐ 15 ⭐

Perhaps he should have perceived an ill omen in the black storm that brewed over Washington, smothering Capitol Hill with tormented masses of murky clouds, thundering ominously over the subdued city. Or in Laura Lewis's awkward silence over the phone last night before she dryly asked him to come to the MIA League office as soon as he landed in Washington.

But he didn't believe in omens, he felt no grim premonitions and only when he saw the Iron Lady, distant and formal, flanked by her two vice presidents, only when he glimpsed the morose, compassionate expression of Martin Armstrong as the big black man sadly nodded his head, did Walt Meredith understand that something was utterly wrong.

They shook hands in tense, oppressive silence, Laura's grip firm and brusque, Waldmann's hand limp, elusive, but his eyes glowing with content. Martin Armstrong crushed Meredith's palm between his calloused hands. They hadn't talked since Armstrong elucidated the strange death of Eddie Paris.

"This is Mrs. Jane Wyatt," Meredith said, turning toward Jane, who hesitated at the threshold, apparently troubled by the bleak welcome. Laura Lewis nodded awkwardly. She didn't seem to care in the least who Mrs. Jane Wyatt was. "Will you take a seat?" she asked in an icily polite voice, gesturing toward the rectangular conference table, but neither she nor her vice presidents showed any intention of sitting down. Meredith and Jane remained standing, facing a large photograph of the Vietnam Memorial that hung over Laura Lewis's desk.

"I asked to meet with you in order to report—" Meredith started, but Laura Lewis raised her hand.

"Before you report, Mr. Meredith, I'd like to read to you a statement the League released last night." She adjusted her thick glasses and picked up the single sheet that was lying on her bare desk. Meredith had the feeling that he and Jane were passive spectators at a singular ritual, prepared and rehearsed for their eyes only.

"The executive council of the League of MIA Families met this morning—that's yesterday morning," Laura remarked, glancing at Meredith, "with the President at the White House. During this meeting the President pledged to intensify the search for American MIA's in Vietnam. He informed the council that a special envoy was on his way to Saigon to discuss that matter with the government of the Democratic Republic of Vietnam. The President assured the council that the entombment of the Unknown Soldier of the Vietnam War would in no way limit the search for MIA's. On the contrary, he said, the Arlington ceremony should enhance the commitment of the United States to find and bring to honorable burial all the nation's sons lost in the war and he is determined to proceed with the search till the last missing American is brought back to his homeland."

Jane Wyatt glanced quickly at Meredith, then back at Laura Lewis, frowning in puzzlement. Waldmann kept nodding contentedly, his face aglow with pride.

"Following the President's statement"—Laura Lewis paused, her opaque eyes gazing sternly at Meredith—"the League of MIA Families decided not to oppose the burial of the Unknown Soldier anymore." Another pause. He was beginning to understand. "The League agrees with the President that the ceremony should generate an overwhelming public pressure on the Vietnamese Government to solve the MIA issue. The League was also strongly encouraged by the recent delivery of seventeen bodies of American soldiers to the U. S. Embassy in Hanoi. The League believes that this act of the Vietnamese Government constitutes proof that the search for MIA's will continue. The executive council of the League accepted the President's invitation to assist at the ceremony at Arlington National Cemetery this week." Her reading completed, Laura Lewis removed her glasses and carefully folded the press release.

And that was it. He had just lost his only ally, Meredith realized. The President was determined to bury the Unknown Soldier and had gone out of his way to reassure the League, removing the last obstacle to his initiative. It was a strange coincidence, though, that he had invited Laura Lewis to the White House barely forty-eight hours after Meredith had revealed the name of the Unknown.

Could there by any link between his findings and the President's pledge to the League? Like some insider urging the President to call Laura Lewis and promise everything she wanted?

No, that was too farfetched, nobody in Washington

knew what he had discovered. And Rainey was too far down the ladder to achieve access to the President. Besides, Rainey couldn't possibly guess that Andy Cunningham was the Unknown Soldier.

Beside him, Jane bitterly shook her head, and he saw in her gesture an echo to his secret thoughts. He felt a frustrating sensation of defeat. What could he do now? The League had obtained the guarantees that the search for bodies would go on. The League, therefore, didn't need him anymore. And the League didn't care how the Unknown had died.

"We're not a private detective agency, we're not trying to crack a murder," Laura Lewis had told him when he had set off on his quest.

He tried, nevertheless, although without much conviction. "I identified the Unknown Soldier," he said, closely watching Laura's face. "I know his name."

"We don't want to hear it," Waldmann broke in nervously. His small chin was trembling and two vivid red spots were burning on his cheeks. "Mrs. Lewis, I move to adjourn the meeting."

"Now, take it easy, Herb," Armstrong said. "Don't forget who Walt Meredith is and what he's done for the League." He deliberately sat down, clasping his hands behind his neck and stretching his legs, as if he had all the time in the world.

But Waldmann had entrenched himself in the stubbornness of the weak. "I warned you," he breathed in his high-pitched voice. "I warned you from the start to keep out of this adventure. Mrs. Lewis, I demand . . ."

He fell silent as Laura Lewis shot him a hard, angry look. But Meredith knew her too well to expect any support from her side. She turned back to him, her face inscrutable. "I'm afraid Herbert Waldmann is right, Walt. We don't want to hear the name of the Unknown. And we don't want to know how he died. As far as the League is concerned, we never officially endorsed your initiative. It was your private operation, and we had no part in it."

"But we did promise him help, didn't we, Laura?" Armstrong said conversationally.

"Yes," she said. "We did promise to assist him in his inquiries, and we did. We're picking up the tab for all your expenses, Walt. But when we agreed to help, the circumstances were different. We all feared, you as well, that the burial of the Unknown Soldier would jeopardize the search for MIA's. Now we know this isn't going to happen. We succeeded in obtaining a solemn pledge from the President of the United States that the search will go on. And once we know that, there is no point in disclosing the name of the Unknown."

Her voice grew softer. "I have to ask you, in the name of the League, to disregard the meeting at my house and shelve the results of your inquiries. We are confident that the President will proceed with the search, and that's what we all want, isn't it?"

"Do you believe him?" Meredith blurted.

"The President?" She cast him a long look and nodded. "Oh yes, my boy, we do. Don't you?"

He lowered his eyes. What could he say, he reflected, that he had to find out why Andy had died? That he couldn't condone a murder? Laura was right, that point was of no concern to the League. As a matter of fact, for nobody but him.

"What are you going to do now?" she asked. "What are your plans?"

270

He shook his head and walked out of the room, Jane following him without a word.

Margaret Bloch, the elderly secretary of the League, was waiting for him in the outer office. "Mr. Meredith, will you please phone your secretary? She called twice already. It seems it's very urgent. Would you like me to dial for you?"

Patty's voice sounded distressed over the phone. "I didn't know how to get in touch with you," she complained. "You didn't phone me for the last couple of days."

"What's so urgent?" he said, adding on a sudden hunch, "Did the Assistant Secretary call?"

"The Assistant Secretary?" She sounded puzzled. "Oh yes, he did, but that's not so important. He just wanted to know if you'd be at Arlington this afternoon, they are rehearsing the burial ceremony."

"So what's so important?" he grunted, irritated.

"You'd better stop by your apartment," she said anxiously. "It was burgled last night. The police say it's not a very pretty sight."

It was raining hard when they reached his apartment house, and a pungent odor of sulphur hung in the air. The tan Cougar held the road well, but the wipers squeaked desperately on the muddied windshield. He had rented the Cougar at the airport, assuming that Barbara had taken his car when she left. On the way from the League office Jane hardly spoke. She had grown strangely remote after the discovery of Hughes's body. Since last night she hadn't mentioned Rainey's disappearance even once, although it had become their main preoccupation. If he had indeed simulated his drowning in Florida, and murdered Hughes, disguising the assassination as a suicide, what would his next step be? Meredith suspected he was stalking them now, determined to disrupt their plans and protect the secret of Andy Cunningham's death.

But Jane seemed haunted by other ghosts. During the flight this morning, she had suddenly murmured, looking out the window, "His wife is right, you know. I am responsible for his death. If I hadn't called, Hughes wouldn't have died."

He had judged it best not to argue with her. The events of the last few days had totally shattered her neat, well-established routine and the daily ordeal of her last twelve years looked almost benign compared to the nightmare she was living now.

He slowed by the gas station facing his building, turned left, and steered the car into the underground garage. He parked the car and got out, but Jane didn't show any intention of following.

"Anything the matter?" he asked, leaning toward her. The green eyes had a forlorn, distant look.

"You go up," she said. "I'll stay in the car if you don't mind."

"You're sure?"

"Just light me a cigarette," she said. She cupped it in both hands and sucked it avidly, as she had that night in Mesa when she found out her husband was an assassin.

He saw no police officers when he stepped out of the elevator, but the door of his apartment was slightly ajar. He pushed it open and entered. All the lights were on, crudely illuminating an ugly scene of havoc. The sofa and the armchairs lay overturned on the floor, their upholstery savagely lacerated and their gray-blue filling spilling out, like intestines out of a mutilated body. The wall-to-wall carpet and the pearl-gray wallpaper had been ripped off and torn into large uneven shapes. Chairs had been piled on top of the dining table, their seats gutted.

The bookcases had been swept clean, and hundreds of books lay strewn all over the place. The covers of several tall volumes had been systematically sliced, and a multitude of disconnected pages covered whole portions of the floor, like dirty, spotted snow. All the drawers of the low chest and the desk by the window, where Barbara used to work, had been emptied on the floor. The records had been pulled out of their covers and carelessly scattered amid bits of broken china and glass. But the television, the video recorder, and the stereo hadn't been touched.

He bent down and picked up the brown covers of an old photograph album. It had been viciously stripped, and the photographs were buried in the mass of papers and rags that covered the floor. He crouched and started collecting the yellow-edged pictures of Benjamin from the pile of litter. How quickly one's most intimate possessions turned into heaps of junk, he thought. He could understand why burglary victims felt degraded and humiliated. In one of the photographs Benjamin was toothlessly grinning at the camera as he tightly held a white-furred little dog. He had gotten it for his sixth birthday, back in California, and had named it Rin Tin Tin.

A muffled sound, coming from the bedroom, made him start. "Who's there?" he called, getting to his feet. There was a short silence, then quick light steps, and in the doorway, tall and slender, appeared Barbara.

* * *

For a moment they stood speechless, facing each other across the wreckage. He had forgotten how lovely she was. She was wearing black slacks and a light-gray turtleneck sweater. Her heavy dark hair was held back with a silk scarf.

"What are you doing here?" he asked stupidly.

She couldn't suppress a wan smile. "I live here, remember?"

He stirred uneasily. "I mean, when did you come back?"

"This morning. And you?" Her eyes were watching him evenly. They were miles apart, reserved, uneasy, conversing like two strangers.

"I just arrived, a couple of hours ago." He stepped over some books and put Benjamin's pictures on the edge of the table. "Where were you? I called your office but they said you'd left, all of a sudden."

"I wanted to be alone for a while," she said. "Had to do some thinking."

"And . . . ?"

She shrugged, and by the familiar tightening of her jaw he knew she wasn't going to talk about it, not now. "I found this mess and called the police. I'm trying to tidy up the bedroom. It's worse than here."

He didn't care to go inside. "What did they take?" he asked.

She made a puzzled face. "Nothing," she said. "Absolutely nothing. That's what I don't understand. They just wrecked the apartment."

He nodded. "That figures."

"What figures?" She frowned. "You know who it was?"

"I think it was the same man who made those weird calls that night, remember? A couple of weeks ago."

"God," she said, her lips quivering. "My God, Walt, what's going on? I want to know."

"Do you really?" he asked coldly. "I didn't think you cared."

The eloquent black eyes spelled anguish and deep, poignant loneliness. But she remained silent, repressing her humiliation.

He broke the silence. "This man's name is Steve Rainey. I believe he was looking for the file of a soldier he had murdered in Vietnam fifteen years ago."

"A soldier he had . . ." she slowly echoed, then her eyes lit up in sudden realization. "The Unknown," she said quickly, her face coloring. "You discovered the Unknown's name."

"Rainey doesn't know this boy is the Unknown," he said. Barbara raised her eyebrows, intrigued, but didn't speak. He couldn't bear those stretches of tense silence. Besides, he thought, she had the right to know. In short, compact sentences he described the highlights of the search that had led him to Andy Cunningham. He carefully omitted, however, any mention of Jane Wyatt's participation in his voyage and the fact that she was down in the garage, waiting for him to come back.

She listened, nodding gravely. When he was through she let out a long deep breath. "Would you like a cup of coffee?" she said. "I think I can fix that." This was as close to a truce as she was prepared to go now, he reckoned.

He shook his head. "No, I've got to go."

She didn't ask where. "When are you coming back?"

He shrugged. "I'll let you know." He thought of Jane, alone in the cold car in the deserted garage. He should have left now, but something kept him in his place, amid the wreckage of what had been his life for the last nine years. A man's emotions worked in obscure, wondrous ways, he thought. He was still fascinated by Barbara's presence.

"Why did you come back?" he suddenly blurted.

"I don't know." She went back into the bedroom and returned with a cigarette and a tiny wooden bowl she used as an ashtray. "Actually, I don't know if I've come back," she added with forthright frankness. "Perhaps I'm here because I don't want to lose you. And perhaps because we need a candid conversation. But not now. Not before you're back to normal, Walt."

He stiffened. "Which means I'm not normal now."

She sighed. "No, you aren't. You're a man obsessed." Her stare was concerned, unwavering, but not hostile. "You must exorcise your demons, Walt. And you must do it alone, nobody can help you."

She paused, watching him. "When I was away I thought a lot. This matter is going to end soon, I guess. Perhaps they'll bury the Unknown this week, and perhaps not. But you'll have to face a new situation and learn to put up with it."

"And how shall I do that?"

"I don't know," she said. "I'm not a psychiatrist." Her tone was very gentle, very reasonable, and that's why it was so damned effective, he later thought. She didn't scream at him, didn't resort to hysterics. "I've the feeling, by what you just told me, that you've gone too far. It's not Benjamin anymore, not even that boy, Andy Cunningham. It's far beyond that."

"I don't follow you." He thought he heard stealthy

steps on the landing, then the soft whine of the elevator.

Her voice had dropped to a low, almost apologetic tone. "You're behaving as if the entire burden of guilt for Vietnam rests on your shoulders, Walt. As if you were the incarnation of America. Uncle Sam himself." Her hand holding the cigarette had frozen in the air. "You've set on a quest across the land, searching for your black grail. You're trying to find if the Unknown's death was worthwhile, if he died in a just war or a dirty war. If the son we're burying now, the one we all lost in Vietnam, was a patriot or a villain."

She stubbed out her cigarette with an unsteady hand, then stepped to the window, looking at the storm raging outside. Rolling thunder reverberated very close, and suddenly all the lights went off. In the premature darkness cast by the low, black clouds, Barbara's burning eyes stood out against her pallid face.

"In World War Two, seventy-eight thousand Americans were reported missing," she said with wonder, as if discovering this fact for the first time. "Nobody made such a tremendous effort to find the bodies and bring them back. And you know why?"

"You tell me," he said. He tried to keep his voice cool, indifferent, but an iron vice was relentlessly contracting his throat.

"Because we knew they had died for a just cause, that's why. Because we didn't have to beg their forgiveness for sending them to their deaths. In the World War we were the good guys, remember?"

"And now?" he said.

"Now we have the feeling that the boys we sent to Vietnam died for nothing. And we're desperately trying to expiate that terrible mishap by bringing them back home, all of them." Her moist lips curved, shimmering in the half darkness, and he guessed she was bitterly smiling. "As if by bringing them to a decent burial, we'll be granted absolution."

She paused. "Your quixotic quest for proof that Andy Cunningham was a martyr results from the same guilt feeling, Walt. You want him and Benjamin and all those boys to become symbols of valor and devotion, good American boys who died in a good American war."

"A fine theory, but totally wrong," he said hoarsely. She didn't answer, and the awkward silence settled between them again.

As they stood facing each other in the dusk, the lights came back, the elevator whined in its shaft, and the strange spell was gone.

"I must go," he said. "Take care." He hesitated, then picked up Benjamin's photographs from the table and stuffed them into his inner pocket.

Barbara had turned to the window, her back erect, unyielding.

He squinted in the harsh yellow lights as he came out of the elevator into the vast, cold garage. He was still under the impact of his confrontation with Barbara, her cruel words repeatedly ringing in his ears. Perhaps that was why he didn't hear the faint plops on his left, or the dull thud as a slug bored into the brick wall. But the shrill scream and the painful sting in his left forearm jerked him out of his torpor, and he instinctively veered around.

And there he saw him, like an angel of death, in a black suit and black glasses, tall and blond and ruggedly handsome, pointing a heavy handgun with a chunky barrel at him.

"Rainey!" he gasped, and stood still, knowing it was too late, there was no escape, no way out, and the next bullet was going to be the last.

But Rainey, oddly disconcerted, didn't fire again, and only then did the repeated screams register in Meredith's mind, and he recognized Jane's voice, and Jane's figure, as she darted from the parked car toward her onetime lover. "No, Steve!" she was shouting, her voice a mixture of dread and supplication, "No, Steve, don't!"

As Rainey sharply turned to her, his dark glasses slipped and shattered on the concrete floor. And for a fraction of a second Meredith read the look of immense dismay in the pale blue eyes, and intense, unfathomable despair.

For another instant Rainey hesitated, still pointing the weapon at Meredith's chest. Then he dashed toward a small blue Mazda that stood in the middle of the driveway, its engine running. He slammed the door, and in a strident screeching of tires gunned the car toward the exit.

They impulsively ran after the small car, which madly sped up the ramp and through the gray aperture. But they had made only a few steps when they heard the tremendous explosion and a blinding yellow-red glare invaded the garage.

"God, Steve!" Jane breathed, scurrying toward the exit. He followed her, his right hand pressed against his wet, sticky sleeve.

The narrow street was illuminated by huge, ghastly jets of fire, fiercely spurting from a wrecked gasoline tanker that had collapsed sideways by the entrance to the gas station. In the middle of the twisted mass of steel, engulfed by the soaring flames and almost buried under the bulk of the enormous vehicle, Steve Rainey's Mazda was already a blackened, dead carcass. A bareheaded man in blue coveralls, probably the tanker driver, was uselessly spraying the blazing pyre with a small fire extinguisher. At both corners of the street, long files of cars were already forming, the drivers in the back impatiently honking. People were running toward the wreckage, propelled by morbid curiosity.

Meredith cast a quick glance at Jane. She stood in the garage entrance, her eyes staring in horror at the infernal trap where Steve Rainey was dying. He stepped into the middle of the street. The large raindrops were cold and hard against his burning skin. The station attendant, a stooping elderly black, gaped into the blaze, shaking his head. He was in a state of shock.

"Like a bat out of hell," he was mumbling, "like a bat out of hell he came out of the garage, and smack into the tanker. Hope he died quick, God have mercy on his soul."

A bystander, soaked with rain, eyed Meredith strangely. "Hey," he said, "you've been hurt, mister. What happened?" Meredith shot him a sideways look. Between the fingers of his right hand, clasped over his wound, drops of blood were steadily crawling, swiftly diluted by the rain into rosy rivulets. He ran back and grabbed Jane's elbow with his left hand. The wound didn't hurt much, and his fingers functioned properly.

"Let's get out of here," he said urgently. She stared through him, shaking her head, but let herself be dragged back, her face stunned, her body inert, her legs stiffly trailing on the concrete, a wooden marionette clumsily responding to her puppeteer. He steered her into the front seat of the Cougar, turned the key in the ignition, and slowly drove the car toward the back exit.

Behind them the sirens of the fire engines dolefully wailed against the thundering storm.

"We'll never know how Andy Cunningham really died," he said. Jane didn't answer. Andy was of no concern to her, he thought, not now, after she had witnessed the horrible death of her ex-lover. She was sitting erect beside him, staring fixedly at the shapes moving outside, blurred by the misted windshield and the incessant rain.

He had parked the car in a lot on Twelfth Street, off Pennsylvania Avenue, about a half hour before. Following his instructions, she had bought some bandages and antibiotic ointment in a nearby drugstore and dressed his wound. It was quite superficial. The bullet had barely grazed his forearm and disrupted some blood vessels. Meredith had thrown his bloodstained clothes into the Cougar's trunk and taken a clean shirt and a blue blazer out of his bag. But as he sat now in the car, isolated from the outside world by the mist and rain and four millimeters of tin, he slowly realized he didn't know what to do next.

With Rainey gone, and Frankie Wyatt sheltered in madness again, there was nobody left to dispel the mystery of Andy Cunningham's death. That had been Rainey's plan, actually, he realized. By simulating his drowning in Islamorada, murdering Hughes, and attempting to find and destroy Andy's file, he had tried to—and almost succeeded in—obliterating any evidence that could link him with Andy's death. Having failed to get the file, he had lost his head and tried to murder Meredith. And for that clumsy attempt he had paid with his life.

There was a sort of poetic justice in the way Rainey had died. He, who had ordered Andy shot and burned, had perished in a blast of hellfire. Still, Meredith felt no satisfaction in Rainey's death, only a strange void, and some obsessing, gnawing questions. Why didn't Rainey press that trigger in spite of Jane's cries? What did that haunted, desperate look in his eyes mean as he rushed toward his car? Wasn't his ghastly end the fulfillment of a secret death wish deeply embedded in his conscience? Some more enigmas, he thought, whose solutions he would never reach.

The sudden silence that settled upon the car tore him from his bleak thoughts. The heavy drops weren't drumming on the car roof anymore. He wiped the windshield with his sleeve. The rain had stopped and people were purposefully striding about the parking lot. He started the engine and steered the car toward the exit. He had no reason to go where he was going, but some macabre fascination compelled him to head for Arlington.

The waters of the Potomac were murky and gray, whipped by the ferocious wind into small foaming waves. He parked his car in the reserved lot adjacent to the cemetery, showing his Pentagon pass to the guards on duty.

"Come," he said gently, taking Jane by the hand. She got out of the car, asking no questions. During the ride she hadn't budged, still deep in a numbing stupor. She followed him now, alarmingly docile, her hand inert in his grip, and he thought again of a disjointed puppet with no will of her own.

There were a few people in the Arlington amphitheater silently watching the large paved court. Before their eyes solemnly marched eight honor guards from the various military services. Clad in their parade uniforms, they were bearing a casket draped in the national flag. The rehearsal of the Unknown's funeral was under way.

Meredith vaguely glimpsed some Pentagon acquaintances, but didn't return their nods. Laura Lewis was standing, stiff and collected, beside one of the sturdy white pillars. But he barely looked at her. His eyes were glued, mesmerized, to the black hole, neatly cut in the polished gray flagstones, where in three days the charred remains of Andy Cunningham would be laid.

Standing on both sides of the crypt, the ramrod-straight bearers ceremoniously folded the flag as the Marine Band played "America the Beautiful." Meredith shivered and tightly clasped Jane's small, slack hand. She stood still, oblivious to the wind that fanned her golden hair. Her glazed eyes were staring beyond the crypt, where the lawn smoothly sloped between two thickets of dark-green elms.

The music abruptly stopped, and a detachment of Marines emerged on the parade court. Tall and lean they were, marching in perfect unison, their movements synchronized to the dot, stepping, saluting, breathing as if they were one. A wave of memories from his youth surfaced in Meredith's mind. He thought of all the training and application that honed the Marines into such a perfect machine, of the rigid discipline inculcated into the boys since the moment they walked through the gate of the boot camp, and of the Semper Fidelis motto, the eternal fidelity of the Marines to their flag, their corps, their commanders. Fidelis was the name Steve Rainey had chosen for his yacht, his most precious possession.

And all of a sudden he grew very still. An odd idea flashed in his mind, sending a chilling shudder along his spine. That couldn't be, he said to himself, it was unthinkable. But the crazy hunch swiftly permeated his thoughts, offering a twisted yet logical answer to all his questions, shedding an eerie light on the riddles that tormented him. The pieces of the macabre puzzle were clicking into their places, and an ugly, revolting pattern was gradually emerging. So much deceit and so many lies, so much concealment, he thought. Could that be possible? But he knew he had to explore that pattern, be what may, and he knew he wouldn't rest before he had reached the end of that dark avenue. "I have to go," he hoarsely grumbled, and was already running down the wide stairs and toward the parking lot, Jane miserably trailing behind him.

"Where are we going?" she asked, breathing heavily as she got into the car. She was surfacing from her torpor at last.

"I have to make a couple of phone calls," he said, gunning the Cougar toward the Arlington Memorial Bridge.

In the falling dusk the black mass of the Vietnam Memorial loomed ahead of them. He spotted the lone telephone booth across the street and braked sharply. He darted out of the car, searching his pockets for change. As he grabbed the receiver he was trying to remember the numbers, but his mind was blank, his memory totally muddled. He leafed with trembling fingers through his pocket diary and dialed the first number.

The receptionist at Marine Corps Archives asked him to hold. The assistant director was still there, she said. Mr. Conway had stepped out of his office for a second, but he'd be right back. He thought of Phil Conway as he had seen him a couple of weeks ago, his owlish face cracked in a sardonic smile, lurking in his dark apartment, enveloped by pestilent cigar smoke and pungent alcohol fumes. He had gone to talk to Phil abut the Na-san file. It was still classified, Phil had said, and had spun an incredible story about human error. And then he had solemnly assured him that there had been no eighth Marine on the patrol to Na-san. "No, sir," he'd said, "no eighth Marine."

Switching the receiver to his right hand, he glanced at the car and made out the profile of Jane, stiffly gazing ahead. Then the dry, rasping voice of Phil Conway echoed in the receiver. "Phil, it's me, Walt Meredith," he said urgently.

There was a short silence. "Here goes my Saturday," Conway guffawed, pausing for effect. But Meredith didn't burst out laughing, as he was supposed to, and Conway anxiously asked, "What, don't you remember the joke? It's this guy, you know, in the war—"

"Will you shut up, Phil?" Meredith almost screamed into the mouthpiece, then regained control over himself. "I'm sorry. I've no time for jokes. I just came back to Washington—"

"Where did you go?" Phil asked, intrigued.

"I have to ask you one question, Phil. It's terribly important. I must know the truth."

Another silence. "Shoot, soldier," Conway finally quipped.

"I guess you remember my phone call about the Na-san file a couple of weeks ago. I asked you why it was still classified, and you said you'd check and call me back."

"Yes," Conway rasped guardedly.

"You called me back and invited me to your apartment, and we spoke about the file. But I must know, Phil, if you did something before you called me back."

Conway fell silent again, his laborious breath grating into the receiver. "What the hell do you think I did?" he finally grunted, plunging into a fit of hoarse coughing. Meredith asked his question, and after another, much longer silence, hinting at his inner struggle, Conway spoke. He was basically a good, decent man, and Meredith knew he'd tell the truth. And he did, whispering "Yes" in a sad, sober voice.

Meredith hung up, cutting off the rest of Conway's confused answer, and dialed the operator. "I want to place a long-distance call to Chief Winizky, Great Falls Police Department, at Great Falls, Montana," he said. "I want to charge it to my home phone."

"Hold on, sir," the operator said, and a few moments later the aggressive, cracked voice of Winizky filled the receiver. For him, too, Meredith had one single question. "I guess you've traced the long-distance call Hughes made the night before he died," he said after identifying himself.

"We sure have," Winizky grunted, and Meredith could visualize him, frowning, chewing his foul cigar. "But this is police information, Mr. Meredith, and I'm not authorized to disclose it." The last words were uttered in a contented, almost triumphant voice.

"Don't disclose it," Meredith quickly said. "I'll give it to you, and you'll just tell me if I'm right, okay?"

"You can always try," Winizky chuckled.

Meredith leafed through his diary, and slowly, distinctly, read the number. He heard the gasp of surprise even before he was through. "How in fuckin' hell did you find that?" the chief hissed. "Hello? Hello, Meredith?"

He broke the connection and made his last call.

"Colonel Briggs's residence," a male voice said. He recognized Henry's drawl.

"This is Walt Meredith," he said. "May I speak to the colonel?"

"I'm sorry, Mr. Meredith, but that would be impossible. Colonel Briggs is out of the country."

"What?"

"Yes, sir. He flew to France yesterday to take part in the ceremonies celebrating the fortieth anniversary of D-Day."

"I didn't know he planned to go to Europe," Meredith said.

"Oh yes, sir, that was decided a long while ago. Colonel Briggs is with the team preparing the President's visit to Normandy. You knew that he took part in the landing in France during the war, didn't you, sir?"

"Yes, of course," Meredith said. "Thank you."

He heard light, hesitant steps behind him and sharply turned around. Jane had gotten out of the car and was watching him searchingly. "Walt?"

"Listen," he said. Fragmented ideas were rushing through his mind. It suddenly seemed to him that all the roads led to Normandy. Briggs was there. Andy Cunningham's father was there. And the blood-soaked beaches of Utah and Omaha were the symbol of self-sacrifice that had inspired Andy from his early youth.

"Listen, Jane." He paused, striving to collect his thoughts, to sort out his ideas, but finally making his decision on the spot. "I have to go to Europe."

"Europe?" She stared at him as if he had gone mad. "What for? What happened?"

He took her by the shoulders. "I believe that I'll find the answer to all my questions in France, in Normandy. I want you to come with me." She was shaking her head, her face dismayed. "Briggs is there."

"Colonel Briggs?" she asked, her bewilderment growing. "The regiment commander?"

"Yes, and—"

"What's Briggs got to do with Andy Cunningham?"

He drew a deep breath, then slowly let it out. "I believe," he articulated, "that Briggs knows more about Na-san than he's ready to admit." She shivered as a sudden gust howled on the deserted sidewalk.

"He is in Normandy," he resumed, ignoring the new question that was forming on her lips. "And Brett Cunningham is there too. I have to talk to them. We'll take the tomorrow morning flight to Paris, and we'll be in Normandy at least twenty-four hours before the burial of the Unknown. If Brett Cunningham agrees to appeal to the White House, the ceremony can be postponed. Then we can move for an inquiry into the circumstances of Andy's death. That's our last chance."

He realized he was speaking feverishly, his voice slurred with excitement, but couldn't help it. "I've got some money, I'll buy your ticket."

"Why?" she said. "Walt, why do you have to go? Why not let them bury this poor boy? So many people have died already."

"It's very important to me," he said desperately. "Please, Jane, I need you with me."

For a long moment she stood immobile, watching him. Then she stepped close and very softly, very tenderly cupped his flushed face in her hands. "I love you, Walt," she said, her eyes locked into his. "I've fallen head over heels for you. Really." Her fingers were soothingly caressing his skin, and he knew she was going to hurt him. "But I can't cope with you. In the two weeks since I met you I've seen more death and violence than in my whole life. Hughes is dead, and Steve is dead, and Frankie . . ." She looked away.

"But it's almost over," he said. "Just this trip."

"With you and me it will never be over," she said. A heavy raindrop fell on his face, and he looked up at the cottony sky. "You're bringing back all my past, Walt, you're opening wounds that I believed healed. If I stay with you, I'll be reliving those old nightmares over and over again for the rest of my life. The same is true for you, Walt."

He took her by the wrists. "I'm not going to give you up," he said. "I've gotten attached to you like nobody else in my life. I need you, Jane."

But she was shaking her head again with stubborn determination. "No, you don't, not me. You need that woman who's been trying for years to tear you away from your obsession. You need Barbara." He thought he saw a wet streak on her face, or maybe it was another of those raindrops. "As far as I'm concerned, it's over. I'm not going to be a part of that any longer." She smiled miserably. "I'd rather go back to that poor nut in Alma Viva."

"No," he said. "Please, don't." And as she kept shaking her head he hastily added, "Wait for me. Stay in Washington for a few more days, okay? I'll be back by the end of the week. Everything will be over by then. Will you wait, Jane?" He searched her eyes. "Will you? I can't bear the thought of losing you."

She didn't answer. For a second she clung to him, her soft hair blowing against his face. He raised his head and looked at the Vietnam Wall, across the square. The last pale rays of light broke against the names engraved in the polished black granite and faintly flickered like little flames, gently fading away.

✪ 16 ✪

Under the pitch-black sky, Charles de Gaulle Airport was deserted. It was past midnight, and a couple of Algerians in blue smocks were scrubbing the floor of the circular concourse with a foam-making device. They were joking in Arabic, and their loud laughter repeatedly echoed through the long, empty hallways. A bleary-eyed immigration officer stamped Meredith's yellow disembarkation form and waved him through, barely glancing at his passport. He was smoking a strong, coarse Gauloise, and his sallow forehead was mottled with tiny dark moles.

Meredith stepped on the escalator that whirred its way up to the arrivals level in a transparent plastic sleeve. His mouth was foul, sticky, and his eyes burned from lack of sleep. The flight from Washington had been exhausting. A short delay caused by a mechanical malfunction had turned into a four-hour wait inside the aircraft. When they finally took off the passengers were in an ugly mood, venting their fury upon the harried flight attendants. Too tense to sleep, he spent the long flight reading several magazines from cover to cover. But his mind was elsewhere, tormented by the turn his private life had taken, apprehensive of the showdown that awaited him in the silent battlefields of Normandy.

The sleepy clerk at the InterRent desk was leafing through a magazine on whose cover President Mitterrand flashed a dyspeptic smile at German Chancellor Helmut Kohl. He handed Meredith a sheaf of papers, a set of maps, and the keys to a Peugeot 504. Meredith found the silver-colored car at the top-floor garage, threw his bag in the back, and set on his way.

Not far to the south, the wavering glow of Paris painted the edge of the black sky a pale-gold hue. He hadn't been in Paris in years and felt a sharp pang of nostalgia as he made out the familiar shape of Sacré Coeur stop the light-studded hill of Montmartre. But his troubled mind was impervious to the pleasures Paris could offer. As he reached Porte de la Chapelle, the northern gate of Paris, he veered to the right, speeding westward on the brightly lit Boulevard Périphérique. Spring had invaded Paris, and the streetlights shimmered in the luxuriant foliage of the trees. He remembered a balmy night like this, in April 1961, when the CIA had been accused of secretly financing a right-wing coup against de Gaulle. A top-priority cable from Langley had ordered all Company personnel to leave France, and he had sneaked out of Paris in a friend's car, reaching Brussels before dawn.

The outskirts of Paris were behind him now, and he headed west on the dark country roads. He preferred their tortuous, picturesque paths to the tedious monotony of the arrow-straight throughways. The Peugeot roared through shuttered, sleeping villages, its yellow headlights revealing aged tile-roofed buildings, stone farmhouses, thick hedgerows, and looming masses of dense woods, slightly swaying in the wind. Immersed in his thoughts, he barely glanced at the Notre Dame Cathedral at Evreux, whose ancient belfry had miraculously survived the Allied bombings in 1944.

Outside Lisieux he ran into a thick wall of fog rising from the fields, clinging to the wet asphalt of the road. Isolated manors and sleek country churches surfaced and disappeared in the opaque mist like spectral visions. A lonely cyclist noiselessly sailed out of the trembling fog like a dark mirage, vanishing at once.

The horrible truth he was trying to unravel was also shrouded in thick layers of murky fog, he thought, but a certain man, not nature, had put them on his path. A quixotic quest, Barbara had called his enterprise, and she was probably right, a man obsessed, she had labeled him, and her judgment was correct again. Coming here was a mad venture, irrationally conceived at the foot of the black Vietnam Wall.

Still, he felt he had no control even over his own decisions. He had gotten so deeply involved with Andy, Benjamin, and those thousands of boys rotting in the killing grounds of Vietnam that he practically had no choice but to carry his search to its very end.

Imperceptibly the mist changed colors, turning into a pale, milky substance. The walls and houses became more sharply outlined as a timid incandescence turned them into miniature islands jutting from a restless, smoky sea. His rearview mirror suddenly exploded in dazzling light, reflecting the first rays of the rising sun. Then the wind rose from the north, sweeping away the wavering patches of fog. And out of the mist, laying before him a carpet of bluets and cowslips, blooming like an enchanted fairyland with cherry blossoms and sweet-scented lilac, emerged the lush countryside of Normandy.

* * *

In the somber, old-fashioned lobby of the Hotel Majestic in Caen, a score of American war veterans were about to board a tourist bus waiting outside. They stood in a tight group, proudly wearing their caps, ribbons, and ornaments. Their guide, an intense, dark-haired girl, was fervently lecturing her flock:

"Caen, like the phoenix emerging from its ashes, has been painstakingly rebuilt from the ruins of a two-month battle in June and July 1944 that totally destroyed its center."

A couple of elderly men nodded. Probably they'd taken part in the battle, Meredith thought. "Perhaps you don't know," the girl continued, "that it was from Caen, in the year 1066, that William the Bastard set on his trip across the Channel to accede to the throne of England and become William the Conqueror. And nine centuries later, the allied armada made the same voyage in the opposite direction to start the liberation of Europe."

While the reception clerk was filling out his check-in form, Meredith leaned on the counter watching the veterans. At first sight they looked like a random group of men in their sixties—some bald, others white-haired, slim or obese, their faces wrinkled and ravaged by age. But in each other's company they strangely straightened up, sucking in their bellies, hardening their chests, thrusting their chins forward, recovering a shadow of the martial air they had carried about them forty years before, when young, handsome, and brave, they had hit the beaches of Normandy. They had every reason to be proud, he thought. They had fought a just war, and nobody, ever, had questioned their devotion and integrity.

THE UNKNOWN SOLDIER

In his room at last, he barely spared a glance for the antique furniture and the exquisite replica of the Bayeux tapestry narrating the Norman conquest of England. He picked up the phone directory and methodically started dialing the different hotels in town. After fifteen minutes he succeeded in locating Colonel Briggs at the Grand Hotel. As the phone rang in the colonel's room he nervously lit a cigarette and ran his hand over the bristle on his chin.

"Hello?" The familiar voice was dry, reserved.

"Colonel Briggs? This is Walt Meredith speaking." There was a moment of stunned silence, followed by a sharp intake of breath.

"Meredith? Where are you?"

"I am here, in Caen, and I want to see you."

There was a long, strained pause. When Briggs spoke again his voice sounded dejected. "You came all the way here to see me," he said wearily. "I didn't expect you."

"I know you didn't," Meredith said viciously. "But Steve Rainey is dead."

There was another moment of silence. At least Briggs didn't play games, Meredith thought, and didn't ask why he wanted to see him. "Very well," Briggs said at last. "I'll meet you this afternoon, after the veterans' memorial service, at the American Cemetery at Omaha Beach."

"Why not right now?" Meredith asked promptly.

"At sundown then," Briggs said and hung up.

A long line of chartered buses and cabs, carrying hundreds of veterans, was leaving the American Cemetery as Walt Meredith parked his car on the cliff overlooking Omaha Beach. Today's memorial service had been quite special, the reception clerk at Caen had told him. It was a joint prayer by veterans who had fought on both sides, American, English, Canadian, and German. They were all guests of the French resistance networks in Normandy. Other meetings were scheduled for the following days at Utah, Juno, and Sword beaches, as veterans would keep arriving from all over the world. The events were to reach their peak in ten days, when seven heads of state, including Queen Elizabeth and President Reagan, would be the guests of President Mitterrand at a ceremony commemorating the fortieth anniversary of the landing.

The last French gendarmes and priests who had taken part in the service brushed past him as he walked into the St. Laurent cemetery. The sky was spotlessly blue and the warm rays of the setting sun cast elongated shadows on the undulating green meadow. Meredith slowly walked in the forest of thousands of white crosses and Stars of David, each adorned with tiny American and French flags. He was not completely alone, though. He could see, scattered in the cemetery, small clusters of veterans gathered around the graves of their comrades.

Briggs was waiting for him beside the Monument aux Morts. He stood erect, a tall, rugged man wearing a black turtleneck pullover, a black suit, and a veteran's cap. About a hundred yards behind him a small trim man in an old U.S. Army jacket was standing before a white cross. His balding head was bowed between his stiff, narrow shoulders.

Meredith stopped by the monument, facing Briggs. They didn't shake hands. "I came over to hear from you the truth about Andy Cunningham," he said, his voice thick with emotion. And he suddenly realized that he had reached the end of his voyage, the final confrontation. Here, today, he had to solve the enigma of the Unknown Soldier's death.

Briggs didn't answer, just watched him, granite-faced. But Meredith noticed the tension in the tightly clamped jaws and the rigid arms, woodenly crossed on Briggs's chest.

"Steve Rainey died in Washington," Meredith said. "He had an accident after he tried to shoot me. He killed Lyndon Hughes the day before, but you must know that already. You also knew about Eddie Paris, of course."

Briggs was listening patiently, his face sealed. "It took me quite a while to establish that you were the master of this bloody game," Meredith went on. "You're responsible for the deaths of Hughes and Paris, and for the attempt on my life."

Briggs shrugged coldly. "I don't follow your reasoning," he said at last. "You told me yourself Rainey was the killer."

Meredith shook his head. "Rainey did the actual killing, but you pulled the strings. You didn't plan his death, but I guess you're rather pleased by it. He won't be here to confirm my findings and accuse you of masterminding those murders."

Briggs started walking along the neat rows of graves, occasionally leaning to read the names of the fallen. Meredith fell in step with him. "What makes you think I'm responsible?" Briggs asked very calmly.

Meredith looked sideways at the colonel's chiseled profile. "Something I saw at Arlington before I flew over."

Briggs turned sharply to him, frowning. "Arlington?"

Meredith nodded. "You see, Colonel, for the last couple of weeks I've been trying, in vain, to answer one question. Why did the Marines who killed Andy Cunningham keep the secret for so many years? Why didn't they reveal it to the press, to their families, to the Army authorities? After all, they had executed a criminal order, and they knew it. So why didn't Eddie Paris come clean and tell the truth? Why did Hughes choose to hide from people, up in his mountain? For a while I suspected that Rainey had blackmailed them into silence." He shook his head. "But he couldn't, of course. He didn't have the leverage for that."

Briggs was watching him warily. Meredith took a few more steps and bent to straighten a tiny American flag. "I suddenly thought of that when I saw the Marines parading at Arlington. They were rehearsing the burial of the Unknown. It's scheduled for tomorrow, you know."

Briggs nodded. "I know. The twenty-eighth."

"You had to see those boys," Meredith pursued. "I bet nobody else but the Marines can achieve such a smooth performance. I don't have to tell you that their discipline is something unique. And so is their devotion. To the Corps, to their tradition, their commanders."

He stopped briefly. "And while I was watching them, I suddenly stumbled upon the obvious conclusion. Only an order from their leader could make those Marines keep their secret. Not an order from Steve Rainey, a young captain more or less their age. But an order from the regiment commander, that legendary hero they all revered, Colonel Briggs himself."

Briggs tilted back his head, his piercing eyes boring into Meredith's face. "How flattering," he scoffed.

"You were watching the Marines, and all of a sudden you had a divine revelation. And right away you decided to fly over, I gather."

A small group of veterans passed near them, listening to a tall Frenchman in a blue kepi and a beige raincoat adorned with medals. A big, square-headed man trailed behind, carrying a large American flag.

"No," Meredith said, "not right away. First I called Phil Conway."

"Phil Conway? Of the Marine Archives?"

"Yes. I asked him if he'd gotten in touch with you when I first spoke to him about the Na-san file."

"And . . . ?" He discerned a flicker of irony in Briggs's gray eyes.

"He said yes, he did."

Briggs shrugged with studied indifference. "So what?" he said. "Conway called me. He didn't understand why the file was classified. I told him nothing"—he made a vague gesture with his right hand—"just that it was a secret of the Marine Corps. Anything wrong with that?"

"That's what I figured," Meredith said. "Semper Fidelis is old Phil. He'll do anything to protect the Corps. But he's such a bad liar, you know. He tried to invent all kinds of reasons to explain why the file was still classified. You told him to stall me, didn't you?"

"Now, wait a moment," Briggs said, raising his hand, the caustic smile fading away. "Phil Conway didn't do anything illegal. On the contrary. And when you came to me, afterward, I gave you the addresses of those soldiers. I helped you, and don't you forget that."

Meredith smiled. "I gave that a lot of thought. You helped me because you had no choice, Colonel. I knew you had the regiment's archives. I asked you for something very specific. You couldn't refuse. Anyway, the addresses you gave me were outdated, and you knew it."

Briggs fell silent again, and Meredith continued. "Before I came over, I also called Chief Winizky, the police officer who is investigating the death of Lyndon Hughes in Montana. The night before he died, Hughes made a long-distance call. At first I assumed he had called Rainey. But after I had that hunch about you, and after I spoke to Phil Conway, I changed my mind. I spoke to Chief Winizky and he confirmed that Hughes had called your number. The poor man, he called to tell you that he was going to confess to the Na-san murder. He wanted your support."

His voice filled with contempt. "Some support! You must have alerted Rainey immediately and dispatched him to Montana to silence Hughes. I believe you gave the same order ten years before, when Eddie Paris called."

"Who?" Briggs said. He seemed strangely detached.

"Eddie Paris, the black Marine from Baltimore. He had seen Brett Cunningham on television and had decided to confess to the murder of his son. He called you, you called Rainey, and Rainey organized a hunt." He spread his hands. "You knew about Andy Cunningham's murder all along, Colonel. And you contrived the cover-up, even if it implied another murder or two."

Briggs seemed lost in thought. He was absently looking over Meredith's shoulder at the long straight lines of white tombstones. "Why is Andy Cunningham so important to you?" he asked.

"Andy Cunningham's body will be entombed tomorrow in Arlington," Meredith slowly articulated, watching Briggs's face. "He is the Unknown Soldier."

Briggs winced. The blood drained from his face and he stared fixedly at Meredith, immense stupefaction flowing into his gray eyes. "The Unknown," he repeated, in an oddly muffled voice. "You're saying that Andy Cunningham is the Unknown Soldier." For the first time he seemed genuinely shaken. "I don't believe it," he managed. "It can't be true."

"You didn't know that, did you?" Meredith muttered savagely. "He ended up as the Unknown because of your orders. Your soldiers did such a thorough job of mutilating his body that he became the only Vietnam dead we couldn't identify."

Briggs was shaking his head, as if refusing to listen. "Are you positive?" he finally asked. "Did the lab in Honolulu confirm what you're saying?"

"That's not Honolulu's job," Meredith said.

"Did you talk to them?" Briggs insisted. "Who made the identification? Dr. Natua?"

"Andy Cunningham is the Unknown Soldier," Meredith repeated.

Briggs stared back at him for a long moment, deep bitter lines emerging at the corners of his mouth. His sarcasm and easy confidence had evaporated. He slowly turned away and touched the top of a white cross with an unsteady hand.

"Brett Cunningham's son," he murmured. "Brett Cunningham's boy."

He stood like that for a long moment, looking away, and it seemed to Meredith that his shoulders sagged. Finally his back stiffened and his eyes focused on Meredith. He swallowed hard.

"You can never prove what you're saying, of course," he began, "but I don't mind telling you now. You're right. Steve Rainey killed Paris and Hughes. But I didn't ask him to kill anybody. I just kept him informed about those phone calls. He acted of his own initiative."

"What difference does it make?" Meredith replied.

But Briggs was gravely nodding. His forehead glistened with tiny beads of sweat. His skin possessed a grayish tinge. "You're right," he admitted. "It makes no difference." And after a short pause: "I guess you're entitled to the entire story. That's what you came for, isn't it?" He glanced at Meredith.

"Yes," he said. "That's what I came for."

"I was at Bienhoa when it happened," Briggs said quickly, and resumed his restless pacing along the graves of his dead comrades. "It was the night of February 11, 1969. You know about the Tet offensive and the patrols sent after the VC."

He wasn't even looking at Meredith, but spoke with his head bowed, his hands joined behind his back, as if recounting the story to himself. "Shortly before midnight Rainey established radio contact with regiment headquarters and asked to speak to me. He reported that he had been compelled to execute Cunningham when under enemy fire. He explained why he had given the order to shoot him."

"Why?" Meredith interjected. "What was his excuse?"

"Wait," Briggs said, without turning to him, "let me tell this my way." Meredith noticed that his hands, clasped behind his back, trembled. "I had to make a decision on the spot. I knew Rainey. He was a good officer. I trusted his judgment." He suddenly stopped and faced Meredith, his eyes blunt, challenging. "I decided to endorse his order. I instructed him by radio to destroy the body to prevent its identification."

"That was a criminal order!" Meredith said.

"The next morning," Briggs continued, unwavering, "I swore the survivors to secrecy, and Rainey substituted some forms in our files so that Cunningham was listed missing in the battle of Bienhoa." He grew silent.

"I still don't understand you," Meredith said. "Why did you cover up a murder? Your duty as a Marine colonel—"

"My duty as a Marine colonel was to preserve my soldiers' morale intact," Briggs flared, a dangerous fire lighting his eyes. "We were fighting a bloody war and we had to win it. Can you imagine the public scandal in America if Cunningham's execution had leaked to the media?"

"Murder," Meredith said. "Murder, not execution."

"Hell would have broken loose all over the country," Briggs was saying. "Don't you remember what was going on those days? Antiwar rallies all over the country, bonfires made of draft cards in city squares, the baby killers' posters, the My Lai controversy? Those left-wing bastards would have crucified the Marine Corps on Capitol Hill!"

"Jesus," Meredith murmured. "Don't you care about anything else but your Marine Corps?"

Briggs wasn't listening. "I had another reason," he added in a subdued, distant voice. "I knew who Brett Cunningham was. We both had served in the Rangers during the World War. He was with the Fifth Ranger Battalion, I served in the Second. I was down there, on bloody Omaha"—he pointed north, his forefinger shaking—"when we climbed the cliff at Pointe du Hoe. When they attacked they were two hundred and twenty-five. Only ninety reached the top. And Brett Cunningham was the first. He was the Rangers' hero, the symbol of American self-sacrifice in that bloody war. We all worshiped him. I couldn't let him find out that his boy was a traitor."

"Was he?" Meredith threw back, hostile.

"Yes." Briggs's voice was sharp, cutting. "I personally debriefed Rainey and the other survivors of the operation. They reported to me the exact sequence of events, minute by minute. They all confirmed that Andy Cunningham had rebelled against his commander. Under enemy fire, dammit."

"I heard that already," Meredith said impatiently, returning Briggs's angry scowl. "But I must know why he did it. I came to France to hear the truth from you, Colonel, before I decide if I should disclose the name of the Unknown Soldier to the press and have the ceremony canceled. All I need is one phone call."

Briggs held his stare. "All right," he said, letting out a deep breath. He had understood the threat.

He awkwardly stirred, then trudged away, his face cracking into a web of deep furrows. They stepped into the shade of a lone cedar tree, stretching its boughs over the long line of white crosses. Meredith suspiciously scrutinized Briggs's face, waiting. Finally the colonel started to speak. His story followed in clear, concise sentences, with the impersonal accuracy of a military report. He briefly described the search-and-destroy operation of the Minerva team in the Na-san area and Andy Cunningham's reconnaissance mission across the river.

"On his return he reported that an enemy unit was

camping east of Na-san, quite close to the village. He suggested crossing the river at a point south of Na-san, bypassing the village, and outflanking the Vietcong. Captain Rainey rejected the plan. If they undertook such a long and complicated maneuver, the Marines risked being detected and slaughtered by the enemy. Only a rapid frontal assault, across the unguarded bridge and straight through the village, had a chance of succeeding." Briggs paused. "Are you following?" he asked.

"Yes." Meredith picked up a small fallen branch and rolled the long evergreen needles between his fingers. They had a fresh, delicate scent.

"At that point Cunningham started arguing with his commander. He said such an attack would be criminal. He grabbed his weapon and—"

"Just a moment," Meredith said. "Hold it. I never heard that part before. He called the attack criminal? Why criminal?"

"Because it implied the death of noncombattants," Briggs said reluctantly, apparently hating to report an opinion he rejected. "Cunningham maintained that a frontal attack would necessarily cost the lives of innocent civilians. He said he knew well the people of Na-san. He had been there several times before, on various missions, and knew the village elders."

Meredith nodded. He could visualize Andy on his previous visits to Na-san, a blond, sunburned youth in Marine fatigues unstrapping his backpack in the dusty square and distributing chocolate bars and cans of food to a crowd of giggling children, or engaging in a solemn conversation with the village elders in that unique Vietnamese mélange of pidgin English and stilted French.

"Cunningham claimed," Briggs continued, "that those people weren't VC supporters but peaceful civilians. He said that American soldiers shouldn't kill innocent civilians."

"God," Meredith whispered, a tremendous feeling of relief pervading his body. So that was the reason Andy had revolted against the order. "He was right, wasn't he?" he threw at Briggs. "There were women and children in Na-san. And old people. He was trying to save their lives, he was damn right!"

"No, he wasn't!" Briggs retorted. "Most peasants in that region were Vietcong supporters. Rainey told Cunningham that the VC wouldn't camp behind a hostile hamlet. And besides"—he raised his hand as Meredith was about to object—"it was either our soldiers' lives or a Boy Scout attempt to spare those civilians."

"I don't believe that was such a clear-cut choice," Meredith said. He remembered the letter Andy had written to Maria da Silva disgustedly describing the needless attack of his company on a village and the death of scores of innocent people. Andy had been horrified by what American soldiers could do, therefore he had decided to prevent such a shameful killing from happening again.

"You may believe what you wish," Briggs said. "Anyway, when Rainey gave the order for the assault, Cunningham blocked the access to the bridge, first yelling his warnings and later firing in the air. His unbalanced behavior drew heavy enemy fire, turning the team into sitting ducks for any VC unit in the area. Rainey had no choice. He had to shoot him."

But Meredith, overwhelmed by a surge of triumph and boundless pride, wasn't listening anymore. "Andy

Cunningham was a hero," he whispered, and raising his voice, repeated, "The boy was a hero!"

Briggs stopped in mid-sentence, gaping at Meredith. "Don't tell me you don't understand," Meredith lashed out at him angrily. "The boy was trying to save innocent lives, for Christ's sake. He was trying to save the honor of your trigger-happy Marines. You should have pinned a medal on him for what he did, instead of butchering him over there."

"He disobeyed his commander's order," Briggs hissed. "He incited his comrades to rebellion. He endangered the safety of his unit and..." Seething with fury, he disgustedly waved his hand and walked away.

Meredith stayed in the fragrant shade of the cedar, watching Briggs angrily stride away. Only now he realized how deep was the gap between him and Briggs. The retired colonel was still living in a past age, ruled by ruthless concepts and rigid, formalistic values. He could never approve of the conduct of Andy Cunningham.

He joined him at the foot of the monument. Briggs watched him approach, his face distorted by a hostile scowl, the pugnacious jaw sticking out. "You know that if I make Andy Cunningham's story public," Meredith said confidently, "he'll be posthumously decorated."

Briggs nodded. "Today, yes. After all that those bastards wrote and did about My Lai, they would turn him into a hero indeed. But back there in 1969 any court-martial would have condemned him. He was a traitor then, and for me he remains a traitor today. The trouble with American society is that nothing is sacred anymore. America had betrayed her ideals and her faith, and we are all going to pay dearly for that."

"What betrayal are you talking about?"

"I'll tell you," Briggs said heatedly. "We don't believe anymore that we are fighting for a just cause. We're guilt-ridden about anything we're doing, in Asia, in South America, in our confrontation with the Russians. During the war, when our boys were dying in Vietnam, we concocted a myth about the good VC and the bad American. We had to apologize for any bullet we fired, while the Vietnamese could massacre everybody they wished. And there always was some American smart-ass willing to explain how right they were. We dragged Lieutenant Calley to trial because he massacred the inhabitants of My Lai, and that was the right thing to do. But our righteous press didn't even mention the massacres the Vietnamese perpetrated, which were ten times worse. What do you know about the Hue massacre, Mr. Meredith?"

Meredith shrugged. "I'm not sure—"

"Let me refresh your memory. During the Tet offensive of 1968, the VC captured the citadel of Hue and held it for three weeks. When we finally dislodged them, we found that they had massacred, systematically, more than three thousand people. Their special squads roamed the city, carrying detailed lists, and arrested everybody linked to the South Vietnamese regime, including most of the foreign residents. They shot them like dogs, clubbed them to death, or buried them alive. Three thousand people. I didn't hear a word of protest back home."

"You should have read Andy's letter to his girl," Meredith retorted. "He admitted that the VC were horribly cruel, but their savagery didn't justify American atrocities. He was an idealistic boy, striving to wage a clean war, like his father."

Briggs let out a bitter laugh. "What are you talking about? Do you think we were saints forty years ago? Do you think we didn't fire on civilians? We destroyed half of the cities in Normandy trying to dislodge the Germans, and knowing very well we were killing innocent, friendly Frenchmen. You know how many German civilians we killed when we crossed the border? Have you ever heard of the bombing of Dresden, where we killed one hundred and thirty-five thousand civilians, fifty thousand more than the atomic bomb killed in Hiroshima? That was a clean war? There's no clean war, Meredith, and no pure weapons. If my generation had fought like Andy Cunningham wanted us to, we would still be bleeding to death down there, at Omaha Beach."

"How can you compare the World War and Vietnam?" Meredith replied. "We shouldn't have set foot in Vietnam in the first place." He raised his hands, then let them drop in desperation. "There's no point arguing with you," he said. "Your world isn't mine, and your values make me sick. At least I'll be able to go back to Brett Cunningham and tell him what he wanted to hear all his life. Andy was a brave soldier, worthy of his father."

Briggs suddenly laughed. "Oh really? That's what you'll tell him?" His eyes glinted with secret knowledge. "Why do you think I brought you out here to the cemetery?" He half turned back, gesturing toward the old man in the Army jacket still standing beside a white cross.

"There is Brett Cunningham. We all knew since yesterday that he was going to visit the grave of his best friend, who had climbed the cliff at his side. Go and tell him his son was a hero. Tell him his boy heroically disobeyed his captain's order. Tell him he was shot because of his heroic insubordination. Tell him I approved of the execution. He will be very grateful to you."

He paused, adjusting his cap. "You might have forgotten, Meredith, that Brett is of my generation. He is my kind of man. For him duty and discipline are what they were and are to me. Tell him the truth about Andy and you'll destroy him forever."

Meredith looked at Brett Cunningham, then, oddly troubled, turned back to Briggs. "What happened to the village?" he asked. "To Na-san?"

Briggs shrugged. "Our boys couldn't attack it after the shooting. They had to stay where they were, on the other side of the river."

"So the civilians were saved," Meredith said forcefully.

Briggs nodded indifferently. "Yes. A couple of hours later, the VC finally attacked the Minerva team and most of our men were killed or captured."

"But Andy Cunningham did save those civilians," Meredith repeated. "He was a brave young man, Colonel. He acted as an American and a Marine should."

"Did he?" Briggs's face was barely inches from his own. His eyes had vanished in the shade of the bushy eyebrows. "Why don't you tell his father?" he said hoarsely. "Go ahead, tell him!"

Meredith slowly turned, following Briggs's stare. Brett Cunningham stood immobile by his comrade's grave, his face solemn, collected. He felt Briggs's persistent gaze and looked up, smiling uncertainly. Then he awkwardly waved at them and turned to go, walking toward the cemetery gate. As he passed by the

Monument aux Morts, he stiffened, lifting his head proudly, and smartly saluted.

Meredith, nailed to his place by a strange force, watched him go.

The north wind, rising from the sea, moaned between the white tombstones.

Darkness was falling on Omaha Beach.

⭐ EPILOGUE ⭐

At noon the gray-metal coffin, draped in the national flag, was loaded on a caisson drawn by six gray horses. The coffin had lain in state in the Capitol Rotunda atop the same catafalque used in President Lincoln's funeral almost 120 years before. During the last three days tens of thousands of Americans had silently filed by the bier. Thus they had paid their last respects to the Unknown Soldier of the Vietnam War.

Now, as twenty-one-gun salutes were fired from Fort Myer and Fort McNair, one round a minute, the procession made its way down Constitution Avenue. It was a dark, windy day in Washington; the leaden sky hung low over the city. The funeral cortege, formed by several military bands and representative detachments of the various military services, slowly marched down the avenue between two lines of solemn onlookers. There were no big crowds in the streets and no displays of emotion, just subdued Americans awkwardly staring at the cortege that rolled through the grayness.

At the Vietnam Memorial, fifty-five veterans bearing flags from each state and territory saluted the casket of their nameless comrade. Some three hundred other veterans, dressed in camouflage fatigues and floppy bush caps, and festooned with badges and medals, spontaneously formed into a compact bloc that brought up the rear of the procession. Harried Pentagon officials had tried to prevent the ragtag crowd from joining the cortege, turning to the police for help. But after a brief confrontation with the grim legion, they had hastily retreated. A tall, bearded man marching in the front line of veterans softly played "Amazing Grace" on his bagpipes.

In the flag-draped marble amphitheater at Arlington National Cemetery, four thousand guests watched President Reagan place the Medal of Honor in front of the coffin. The President was dressed in black. His face was distraught, oddly sallow. He climbed the steps to the podium, his shoulders slightly stooped. "We know why he died," he said, his voice breaking. A gust of wind plaintively moaned in the microphones. "He saw the horrors of war but bravely faced them, certain that his own cause and his country's cause was a noble one, that he was fighting for human dignity for free men everywhere."

Hundreds of veterans, some of them in wheelchairs, saluted the Unknown comrade. Many were weeping openly. The honor guards, a team of stern-faced soldiers, lifted the flag from the casket. Four military chaplains—Eastern Orthodox, Jewish, Roman Catholic, and Protestant—proceeded with prayers of committal. After the short service President Reagan stepped down and placed his wreath beside the grave. Another twenty-one-gun salute thundered in the distance. It was followed by three rifle volleys, the poignant call of a solitary bugle, and the Marine Band struck the chords of "America the Beautiful."

The Unknown American Soldier who had fallen in Vietnam was thus interred. He was laid to rest beside the graves of three other Unknown Soldiers, who had perished in the two world wars and in Korea. His tomb would soon become a place of pilgrimage for thousands of families whose sons and fathers had never returned from the gruesome battlefields of South Vietnam.

Meredith stood behind the Assistant Secretary, his throat choked with emotion but his face blank, unyielding.

He watched the grim ceremony. As the Marines deftly gathered the flag draping the coffin, he visualized the humble figure of Brett Cunningham accepting the folded Stars and Stripes from their hands. Then Andy's young, earnest face flashed in his mind, metamorphosing into Benjamin's grave, sad-eyed visage. Meredith winced, striving to chase the haunting image from his mind, but his son's face would not fade away. His father, Meredith remembered, had often read to him the verses from the Book of Samuel in the Old Testament describing Kind David's lament for his beloved son. "O Absalom, my son!" David wept, covering his face with his hands. "O Absalom, my son, my son . . ."

Oh Benjamin, Benjamin. It was for your sake, he thought, that I set out on my quest for the Unknown. It was my guilt toward you that I tried to expiate by my voyage into the past. It was your pure, innocent image that I discovered in Andy Cunningham. And I am burying you today, my son, my Unknown Soldier, together with Brett Cunningham's fair-haired boy.

The bitter wind whipped his burning face, chilling the sweat covering his brow. He still firmly believed Andy was a hero. And yet, Briggs's angry outburst at Omaha had carried the ring of a dark, cruel truth that made him hesitate when he was face-to-face with Brett Cunningham. That terrible moment at the St. Laurent cemetery had made Andy Cunningham the Unknown Soldier once again, not because of his mutilated body, but as a result of the conflicting interpretations of his act. A hero or a traitor? He had to live with that maddening question and face it all alone, day after day. He was the only one in the thousands assembled in the immaculate amphitheater to have discovered the identity of the Unknown and the tragedy surrounding his death. And there he stood, witnessing his awesome secret being buried forever, together with the sealed wooden casket, in the hallowed ground of Arlington.

After the President's departure the crowd slowly dispersed, but he kept standing, immobile, in his place. A few officials he knew looked at him curiously as they passed by, and the Assistant Secretary raised an eyebrow in puzzlement. He probably offered a sorry sight, Meredith thought, with his forty-eight-hour bristle, red-rimmed eyes, and crumpled, soiled clothes. After the interview with Briggs in Normandy he had driven back to Paris and caught the first available flight to Washington. He had taken a cab from the airport straight to Arlington and reached his place only a few minutes before the Unknown's coffin was unloaded from the sturdy artillery caisson.

His eyes vaguely swept across the crowd moving toward the exits. He realized that against all logic he was looking for Jane. Had she gone back to Colorado or stayed in Washington? Even if she had stayed, she couldn't be here, of course. Was he going to see her again? The answers to those questions escaped him, and his mind, too befuddled with the strange events of the last few days, seemed unable to deal with the shambles of his private life. He needed a long sleep, a couple of days of total detachment from the world to make up his mind, to put some order in his conflicting emotions. He thought of taking a room in some anonymous motel before calling anybody.

But first he had something to do, and he had to do it now, without delay. The letter of resignation was in his pocket, written and signed during the flight. It had to be delivered today. The Assistant Secretary might not get it before tomorrow, but he felt he had to sever his last link with the MIA's this very day, as soon as Andy Cunningham was finally laid to rest, as soon as he had buried Benjamin's memory, if not his body.

He waited a few more minutes for his friends and acquaintances to leave; he abhorred the thought of getting a ride in somebody's car and having to endure his stupid attempts at small talk. He was the last to come out of the deserted amphitheater, and he hailed a cab that was slowly cruising by the main entrance. Ten minutes later, he walked into his office.

Patty was out, probably at lunch, but on his desk lay a stack of telephone messages that had accumulated during the last couple of days. He neatly placed his letter of resignation in the empty outgoing tray, then leafed through the phone-message pink slips. Most were from other services in the Pentagon, one from the Assistant Secretary, one from Martin Armstrong. Jane had called twice, but had left no message.

At the very bottom of the stack three consecutive slips carried the same name: John Natua. He hesitated, then glanced at his watch. It was early morning in Hawaii and John wasn't due at the laboratory for a couple of hours. What the hell, Meredith thought, if I can go without sleep, so can John. He knew Natua's home number by heart, and repeated it mentally while picking up the phone.

It took half a dozen rings before John Natua groaned raspingly into the receiver. After a long succession of growls, sighs, and moans, the director of the Central Identification Laboratory finally surfaced from what seemed to have been a profound sleep. "Walt?" he finally managed, his voice still slurred. "What happened? What's going on?"

"That's what I wanted to ask you," Meredith said, slightly disconcerted. "I found all those messages and—"

"Jesus, man," Natua grunted, "did I leave you a message to call me in the middle of the night?"

"I thought it was urgent," Meredith protested. "Never mind, I'll call you later."

"Wait," Natua said. "Wait. Don't hang up." There was a long silence, interspersed with more sighs and grunts.

"So what was all this about?" Meredith insisted.

"Nothing really." Natua sounded on the defensive. "I guess I just wanted to brag about my unique talents and hear you congratulate me."

"Congratulate you? What for?"

"Oh, come on, Walt," Natua laughed nervously. "For the identifications, of course."

"What are you talking about?"

A note of irritation slipped into Natua's voice. "You're not gonna tell me you didn't get my telex."

"Your telex? Wait." Meredith switched the phone to his left hand and with his right rummaged through his overflowing incoming tray. Natua's telex was buried between several staff memos. He pulled it out, tearing its upper right edge in the process. "Wait."

"Eight out of seventeen isn't bad," Natua was saying. "And all that in two weeks."

"Seventeen?" Meredith stupidly repeated, trying to smooth the telex with his palm. It was dated May 25.

"Now, did you get the telex or not?" Natua said.

"To be honest with you, I just found it," Meredith confessed. On the sheet of paper was a list of names.

"Jesus," Natua groaned again. "And you call yourself director of MIA affairs."

"Why don't you tell me what it's all about, John?" Meredith said curtly.

"Okay. Do you remember those seventeen bodies we got two weeks ago from Vietnam? I spoke to Patty about them."

"Of course." Patty had first told him about the return of seventeen bodies by the Vietnamese Government while he was still in Mesa. Laura Lewis had mentioned them, too, when he had seen her a few days ago. "That's the proof that the search will continue," she had said.

"Well, we got them in Honolulu on May 11, and by May 25 we succeeded in identifying eight of them. Now isn't that something?"

"It sure it," Meredith agreed, and squeezed the receiver between his jaw and shoulder while reaching for a cigarette.

"So I called a couple of times to hear you singing my praise," Natua was merrily tattling, his good mood restored.

He struck a match and its wavering flame faintly hissed, casting a bright illumination over the list of names: "SCND LTNT MICHAEL S. PALEWSKI, SRGNT RAMON L. SANCHEZ, SRGNT RAOUL S. MENDOZA, CRPRL FRED G. WILLIAMS, CRPRL THOMAS S. GROSE,

319

PFC ANDREW B. CUNNINGHAM, PFC VICTOR J. KAR-
LIN . . ."

He gasped, dumbstruck, his eyes glued to the
printed characters, his mind refusing to digest the
amazing revelation. It wasn't possible, it couldn't be.
But there it was, on the crumpled piece of paper, in
black and white, formally stated. Pfc. Andrew B. Cunningham. Officially identified last week. The burning
match fell from his frozen fingers onto the desk and
slowly consumed itself in the middle of an ugly black
stain spreading on the polished wood. A spasm of
panic squeezed his stomach and his eyes frantically
scanned the telex looking for a clue, a formula that
would explain that all this was an error, an absurd
error. But there was none. "WISH TO INFORM YOU,"
the telex started, "THAT AT THIS STAGE EIGHT OUT OF
THE SEVENTEEN BODIES HAVE BEEN POSITIVELY IDEN-
TIFIED AS FOLLOWS: SCND LTNT MICHAEL S. PA-
LEWSKI . . ." and so on. And the sixth name, between
Corporal Thomas S. Grose and Private First Class
Victor J. Karlin, was Andrew B. Cunningham.

This can't be true, he wanted to scream into the
phone, this is a monstrous mistake, Andy Cunningham
is the Unknown Soldier. I know it, I just saw him buried in Arlington. But he kept silent, his teeth clenched,
his mouth dry, cold sweat breaking out on his brow.

"Walt? Are you there? Walt?" Natua's voice
brought him back to reality.

"Yes," he managed, "I'm here." God Almighty, he
thought, could he have made such a tremendous mistake? Had he been too eager to jump to conclusions
back in Mesa? Had his entire quest been for nothing?

"What the hell is going on?" Natua pressed.

"I'll call you back in a moment," Meredith blurted

and hung up before Natua could reply. His mind was in turmoil, and he knew he had to calm down and think. He leaned forward on his desk, cupping his face in his unsteady hands. Strange suspicions were snaking into his chest like icy, tortuous rivulets. This couldn't be true, for Christ's sake, it was too much of a coincidence. They hadn't found a trace of Andy Cunningham for fifteen years, and just now, two weeks before the Unknown Soldier's funeral, his remains suddenly turn up among seventeen bodies unexpectedly brought back from Vietnam. Right on cue, Meredith thought.

His eyes briefly rested on the top line of the telex. It was dated May 25. It occurred to him that he would have found the telex on his desk three days ago had he dropped by before he flew to France. If he had, he wouldn't have made that trip, of course, wouldn't have confronted Briggs, and would not have told him ...

Another strange thought flashed through his mind. Perhaps he was supposed to find that telex on May 25, and abandon his quest then and there. Perhaps by suddenly appearing at Omaha Beach he had disrupted something far darker than Briggs's mood. Some of the questions Briggs had hurled at him at St. Laurent cemetery abruptly surfaced in his memory. "Are you positive that Andy Cunningham is the Unknown?" Briggs had asked so insistently. "Did the lab guys in Honolulu confirm that? Did you talk to Dr. Natua?"

Natua. The lab guys. Perhaps Briggs knew that Natua and his assistants couldn't have confirmed Meredith's findings. Meredith's thoughts were madly rushing forward, fusing into new, devious patterns. What if ... what if Briggs had guessed after they first met that Andy was the Unknown Soldier and had conceived a clever cover-up scheme? Maybe after he learned from Meredith that a corpse had been found in Na-san, the colonel had phoned Laura Lewis. Briggs knew her well; after all, he used to call her the Iron Lady. She might have revealed to him that Meredith was actually on the trail of the Unknown Soldier. She had always relied on Briggs's support when she dealt with the military or the politicians; she might have thought he'd help her again.

But Briggs, determined to prevent Meredith from learning that Andy Cunningham was the Unknown Soldier, had started pulling strings. A couple of discreet calls to some senior officials at the Pentagon. Perhaps a cautious conversation with the Assistant Secretary or some other top official.

"This man of yours, Meredith, what is he up to? Did you order him to identify the Unknown? You didn't. Of course, that's what I thought. Now, now, let's not get excited. No, don't recall him, he might blow the damn story all over the papers and we'll have a nasty scandal on our hands."

And the Assistant Secretary, faced with the appalling perspective of a shameful incident at Arlington, might have agreed to cooperate. Did Colonal Briggs have any idea what to do? Yes, he did, actually.

What kind of idea Meredith could only guess. Pay a price to the Hanoi Government—like a discreet promise to let them open their much-coveted Trade Mission in New York—and get in exchange a shipment of bodies those sly bastards kept handy as a bargaining asset. Then pin on one of them Andy Cunningham's name . . .

But how could Briggs make John Natua identify one of the bodies as Andy Cunningham? John was the straightest guy on earth, he would never get mixed up in an unlawful plot. Meredith reached for the phone and punched Natua's number again. His friend picked it up at the first ring. "Yes."

"John..." Meredith said, his voice uncertain. "I want to ask you about that list you telexed. Are you absolutely sure? I mean is the identification a hundred percent foolproof?"

Dr. Natua's voice resounded after a short pause, carrying an undertone of anger. "What kind of question is that? What do you think we're doing here, playing games?"

"I meant no offense," he apologized. "I just wondered about one of the names."

"What name?"

"Cunningham," he said, striving to sound casual.

"Cunningham," Natua echoed. "Why do you ask?"

He hesitated. "I know his father," he finally said. "He's a war hero."

"I didn't know that. What war?"

"World War Two. He landed at Normandy. Brett Cunningham."

"Never heard of him," Natua said. "Anyway, it's funny you're asking about his son."

"What's so funny?" Meredith wiped his forehead with the back of his hand. He was still holding his unlit cigarette.

"I thought we'd never get a positive ID on that one. It was nothing but a heap of bones, see, and the skull was totally shattered."

"And..."

"We were lucky. We found a couple of teeth, molars, that hadn't been destroyed. They had been treated a few months before his death. Some very extensive dental work, you know. We succeeded in matching them with his dental chart and afterward it was a piece of cake. Body measurements, skull shape, everything matched. We couldn't rebuild the face, though."

Meredith shivered, imagining Andy's face surfacing on the television screen of Natua's hellish device. Pacman, his Polish assistant had called it.

"Yes," he said, surrendering to the facts. "It sounds like a positive ID all right."

And all of a sudden the realization hit him, stunning him like a physical blow. Two molars? What was that nonsense about two molars? He vigorously shook his head at the mute receiver. That wasn't true. He knew Andy's file by heart. There had been no dental chart in the file, which meant that the boy had never been subjected to dental treatment. There had been no mention of dental work on two molars.

Now he understood how it had been done. Childish simplicity. The bodies had arrived at Natua's lab, he had examined them and reported his initial findings to Washington. Then somebody in Washington—Briggs and his accomplices probably—had picked out Natua's report about a badly injured body roughly fitting Andy Cunningham's measurements and faked a dental chart to suit Natua's description. The phony chart had been slipped into Andy's file, to be triumphantly discovered by some ecstatic clerk within twenty-four hours. The rest was easy.

Yes, Briggs could have done that with the secret cooperation of a handful of people—the Assistant Secretary or some other Pentagon official, perhaps Phil Conway, too, and a couple of others.

He could have done it, Meredith thought, but had

he really? Meredith hadn't a shadow of a proof to support his theory, only a couple of nebulous conjectures. He could never prove that there was a cover-up plan and that Briggs conceived it. He couldn't prove the dental chart in Andy's file was a fake. The fact that there was no such chart in the copy of the file he'd gotten from Patty didn't prove anything. The copy of the dental chart might have been misplaced.

Therefore he couldn't prove, ever, that the body in the Unknown Soldier's grave belonged to Andy Cunningham.

A strident signal tore through his confused thoughts. Meredith looked with bafflement at the receiver he was still clutching in his hand and he slowly lifted it to hs ear.

"Walt?" Natua was calling, still on the line. "Walt, do you hear me? Hello, Walt?"

"Yes, I hear you, John," he slowly said. "I'm sorry, something went wrong with the connection."

"Well, you can tell your friend, Cunningham, that soon he'll bury his son. It's so important for them, you know."

You bet, Meredith thought, closing his eyes and leaning back. You have no idea how important it really is. And he remembered Brett Cunningham, his gentle Karen, Johnny, and Maria da Silva. And his own quest, and Steve Rainey's tormented eyes when he faced him, a smoking gun in his hand. Meredith's hand slid on the desk and touched the crumpled edge of Natua's telex, which had turned everything upside down.

No, he couldn't believe it. He was living a horrible dream from which he was surfacing into an impossible nightmare. Officially, Andy Cunningham couldn't be the Unknown Soldier. Officially, he had never been the Unknown Soldier. In a couple of weeks he would be officially buried in his hometown, and nobody would ever know. But Jane would know that Andy was the Unknown. And so would Briggs, and Barbara, and himself, and they'd carry their forbidden secret in their hearts till their dying day.

He replaced the phone in its cradle and grew utterly still. An eerie question slowly emerged. If he assumed, just for one moment, that Andy Cunningham's body had indeed been identified, if it had been brought back from Vietnam two weeks ago, if his wasn't the fourth body that Meredith had seen lying on its slab in Natua's alcove, then who was the Unknown Soldier?

He leaned back in his chair, in the bleak twilight filtering through the bare windows. The realization slowly dawned on him that no one, ever, would restore a name, a face, a life story to the body entombed in Arlington Cemetery. The legend of the Unknown Soldier had remained intact. He had been naive, at the outset of his quest, to think he could overcome a legend. People, he wearily conceded, need myths and legends. That's why they always prevailed in the end.

EXTRACT FROM THE UNIFIED CODE OF MILITARY JUSTICE (1985)

§ 899. ART. 99. MISBEHAVIOR BEFORE THE ENEMY

Any member of the armed forces who before or in the presence of the enemy—

(1) runs away;

(2) shamefully abandons, surrenders, or delivers up any command, unit, place, or military property which it is his duty to defend;

(3) through disobedience, neglect, or intentional misconduct endangers the safety of any such command, unit, place, or military property;

(4) casts away his arms or ammunition;

(5) is guilty of cowardly conduct;

(6) quits his place of duty to plunder or pillage;

(7) causes false alarms in any command, unit, or place under control of the armed forces;

(8) willfully fails to do his utmost to encounter, engage, capture, or destroy any enemy troops, combatants, vessels, aircraft, or any other thing, which it is his duty to encounter, engage, capture, or destroy; or

(9) does not afford all practicable relief and assistance to any troops, combatants, vessels, or aircraft of the armed forces belonging to the United States or their allies when engaged in battle—

shall be punished by death or such other punishment as a court-martial may direct.

(Aug. 10, 1956, ch. 1041, 70A Stat. 69)

ABOUT THE AUTHOR

MICHAEL HASTINGS is the pseudonym of the author of several works of both fiction and nonfiction, including the recent novel A SPY IN WINTER.